Hail to the Chiefs

HAIL
TO THE
CHIEFS

Stephen James Poppoon

iUniverse, Inc.
Bloomington

Hail to the Chiefs

iUniverse books may be ordered through booksellers or by contacting:

iUniverse
1663 Liberty Drive
Bloomington, IN 47403
www.iuniverse.com
1-800-Authors (1-800-288-4677)

ISBN: 978-1-4759-2876-1 (sc)
ISBN: 978-1-4759-2878-5 (hc)
ISBN: 978-1-4759-2877-8 (e)

Printed in the United States of America

iUniverse rev. date: 08/16/2012

Acknowledgements

◉ ◉ ◉ ◉

Many thanks to:

James Sanford Gamble of the University of Arkansas, for his sage advice and editing.

Dr. Joe Trevino, MD, for his technical assistance.

Dedicated to my wife Nancy.

And dedicated to Patty Vangellow Leidy, for the wonderful life you led, and the tremendous battle you fought.

Prologue

◎ ◎ ◎ ◎

Although played here for decades, soccer in the United States in 1969 was, in many ways, in its infancy. The vast majority of the highly skilled high school and college players were of European origin or descent. Only one US-born player was active in the entire North American Soccer League, and most of the foreign competitors on those rosters were long past their primes.

Adidas and Puma were the prominent shoe (or boot, as they are referred to in other countries) maker, and there were few domestic manufacturers. And in the case of our high school, if you didn't buy your own shoes, which most didn't, the ones provided by the athletic department were literally boots—cut above the ankle and poor fitting. They had flat insoles and were square-toed like those of a football placekicker's, requiring two pairs of socks to prevent blisters.

The ball was also different. Heavy, with leather panels, it absorbed moisture and didn't fly like those of today. Particularly in the northern states, it was not unusual to see teams practice, and even play, using balls made of red rubber when the weather was wet and the field muddy. If the modern waterproof leather ball skips and skids when wet, imagine a rubber ball with a shiny, slick cover.

Back then, the field, or pitch, might have been a converted pasture and most likely received far less grooming than those used for football and baseball. The practice and game fields were usually one and the same, so the turf took constant pounding, and the goal areas quickly turned to quagmires in the rain. Therefore, trapping and passing were often adventures, and the quality of the play suffered accordingly.

Many youngsters had no skilled coaching and grew up kicking with their toes instead of insteps. Passing, trapping, and heading, if taught at all, were usually taught by people with little personal playing experience.

Football players who were too small or slow to play at the college level but wanted to participate in a team sport often found their way to soccer. Thus the disparity in ability among colleges of different divisions, and even within conferences, could vary greatly with the addition of one or two experienced players. This was the case of Bainbridge University in the fall of 1969, when five freshmen from a high school with a long history of winning decided to go where football and basketball were dominant and soccer had just become a varsity sport.

August 24, 1969

◉ ◎ ◎ ◎

Andrew Paxton stood in front of Roberts Hall with his parents, Louis and Marian, as they tried to say good-bye. They had dreamed about this day since their son's birth. He—the baby of the family—was the first to go away to college. His brother and sister lived two miles from the house where they grew up, and here was Andrew, five hundred miles away. Louis, a hardworking product of the Great Depression, had once shoveled snow to feed his family. For the past forty years, he was a parts manager for a Chevrolet dealership, while Marian was a bookkeeper and secretary. They saved all their lives for their son, the future doctor, to go to college—a son who had come along by accident. His father was already forty when he was born, his mother thirty-seven.

Now the years of sparse vacations and frugal living meant they had saved enough not to have to borrow for Andrew's education. He looked at many local colleges and even won a Regents' Scholarship to any school in New York State. But he and his roommate, Brian Barrett, visited the Bainbridge University campus in the fall of 1968, and something drew them back.

Bainbridge, over one hundred years old, was steeped in tradition, both academically and athletically. The picturesque grounds and older buildings had an Ivy League flavor, with huge columns and ornate stone exteriors. In recent times, however, architectural beauty had given way to modern practicality. The new dorms and classrooms looked more like office buildings, with flat roofs, large rectangular double-paned windows, and ordinary brick facades.

Built in the 1800s, Roberts Hall was the first structure on Bainbridge's campus. The six-story brown brick edifice stood on the highest point on campus and made an impressive photo for recruiting brochures. Originally filled with administrative offices and classrooms, now it was a dorm with twelve-foot ceilings, poor insulation, huge windows, cold linoleum floors, rickety fire escapes at each end, and no elevators. In 1969, little provision was made for the handicapped or disabled, and college boys were deemed perfectly capable of lugging furniture and suitcases up and down several flights of stairs.

The bathrooms were antiseptic affairs at the end of each hall—porcelain and cold, even in the summer. Brave was the first man each morning who turned on the showers to spread heat to the rest of the room. The student lounge on the third floor held the only television, a black-and-white Zenith. There were three stations, none with particularly good reception.

Each floor had a resident advisor, or RA—typically an unfortunate student who needed the free room and board in return for riding herd on, and taking abuse from, twenty-six oversexed, frequently drunk freshman males. The variety of personalities among the RAs was so great that it was hard to tell how the university chose these leaders of men. Some tried reason and understanding to keep their charges in line; some were big enough to rule by intimidation. Most just hid out in their rooms and hoped the semester went quickly.

The upheaval and social change of the Vietnam War swept across America, and it touched the lives of all students at Bainbridge. Virtually everyone on campus had a friend, brother, sister, or cousin in the service. College draft deferment was still available, and avoiding military service was great motivation for going to, and staying in, school.

Barrett and Paxton starred at a high school where soccer was everything, and they were attending a university that had won three football conference championships in the past ten years. Bainbridge was an intercollegiate Division III college and couldn't offer athletic scholarships, but treated its football players with a reverence normally reserved for major college programs. Many were gifted athletes, too small to play at the major college Division I level, who came to Bainbridge knowing they would receive the same type of training and prestige as at the bigger schools. The football Titans developed a great tradition by stressing speed, strength, discipline, and a conditioning regimen to rival any major college. The typical lineman stood just over six feet tall and weighed a comparatively meager 220 pounds. To the average person, they were huge. To the Purdue Boilermakers, they were mere water boys.

By contrast, soccer was a stepchild. Promoted from club to varsity sport the previous year, its meager facilities and budget attracted little attention from the students, administration, and alumni. There was no money for additional staff, so the lack of success was perpetuated by the junior varsity basketball coach being assigned to head the varsity soccer program, whether or not he knew anything whatsoever about the sport.

Close friends and classmates for many years, Paxton and Barrett were recruited by other programs but knew they could play varsity soccer for four years at Bain. And Tim Millwood, Jim McIlroy, and Don Penny, teammates on the powerful Amsterdam High School Chiefs, were also headed to Bainbridge.

Tim Millwood, five feet ten and 160 pounds, was a talented lineman and goalie in high school. Longtime friend of Andrew Paxton's, he had high regard for the man he nicknamed "Pappy." Millwood was a realist who saw through the baloney in life and often bluntly but intelligently spoke his mind, particularly to Paxton, whom all knew to be far too hard on himself. Tim seldom took part in the head-banging, physical play practiced by his teammates, but had good fundamentals, and Paxton knew he could be counted on when the game was on the line.

Jim McIlroy was a solid player who also saw limited game time at Amsterdam, but he'd always loved the sport. Tough, steady, determined, deceptively strong, and well liked, he'd been friends with the others since childhood. Defense was his forte, and he was fearless.

Don Penny was a rock, working out regularly with weights, which was unusual for a soccer player in 1969. At center forward, his strength and aggression allowed him to excel at a position where players normally relied on skill and finesse.

The quintessential natural athlete, Brian Barrett was tall, muscular, handsome, charming, and intelligent. Brash and confident, with lightning reflexes, he took naturally to any sport. Despite never lifting weights, his body was virtually perfect. He enjoyed soccer and excelled at the sport, but lacked Andrew Paxton's passion and dedication. He could kick a ball seventy yards or send an opposing forward face-first into the dirt, and had the rare ability, when the game was on the line, to relax and be totally secure in his skill. Allowed to roam the middle of the field, Barrett was quick to exploit an opponent's mistakes. And when tempers flared on the field, his teammates knew there was no one better in a fight. His quick fists had knocked the wind out of the sails of more than one loudmouth. No one at Amsterdam would challenge him, and even the hoods held him in high regard. More than once, he'd come to their aid in a fight between rival high schools.

His roots were set in a good family background. His self-confidence, however, often clashed with authority, and he continually tested teachers and coaches.

The envy of his high school classmates, he drove a candy apple–red Camaro convertible, and his curly brown hair, flat stomach, stunning physique, and chiseled features made him a magnet for every girl. And he was at ease with their attention. An above average student, Brian could charm any teacher with a smile, but his appealing personality was genuine.

Barrett's choice of Bainbridge had its emotional baggage. He broke up with his girlfriend, Beth Littlefield, before graduation. Theirs had been an idyllic romance. She was the beautiful, blonde, popular, and rich captain of the cheerleading squad and homecoming queen; and he was the big man on campus. They were the couple everyone wanted at their parties. He was the rake who flirted with all the girls, but Beth never minded. She had the man of her dreams, and he never strayed in earnest.

After junior year, however, things began to change. When classes ended in late May, Barrett went on a road trip out west with two other

Amsterdam students. Driving across country in his father's station wagon, it was his first adventure away from home. California was a revelation, radically different from Barrett's small-town conservative upbringing. New ideas, and unexpected experiences, were everywhere. It was the height of the Vietnam War protests. Rebellious music and outlandish dress were displayed on every street corner. The campuses were alive with activity, and it was like being on another planet.

When Barrett returned, he felt that the little town of Amsterdam was smaller and out of step with the new world he'd discovered. He daydreamed constantly about what they had seen: the massive mountains, the pristine beaches, the endless highways, the beautiful girls, and the flowing river of energy. Restless for change, he talked at length with his friends about his experiences, often to the point of boredom.

Things began to change between him and Littlefield, but she chose to ignore it. She believed—she wanted to believe—that they would go to college, get their degrees, marry, and have children. She told herself and others that all this talk about California was testosterone on overload. But she was too smart not to see the change in the boy she had loved for so long.

As the school year progressed, Barrett's unrest grew. In the spring, he quit varsity baseball halfway through the season, when he'd never quit anything in his life. He spent less time with Littlefield and seldom went over to her house. He didn't date anyone else, nor did he totally abandon their relationship. He was just in a different place in his life.

They went to the senior ball together but weren't voted king and queen as expected. It was as if their classmates, seeing the great changes looming ahead in their own lives, had decided to move on in this regard as well. Brian and Beth were no longer the couple everyone idolized, much to his relief. It seemed everyone at Amsterdam could see it but Beth.

The break finally came as a result of a large gathering in a muddy pasture in Sullivan County, New York. The same friends from the California trip talked Barrett into a weekend jaunt to something called the Woodstock Music and Art Fair. For three days, the site became home to 450,000 people. Total strangers treated them like brothers. They slept in cars and in four-man tents with six other people. They watched bands that they had never heard of before; stared at women and men dancing naked to the beat of the music; and went skinny-dipping in the stream, with two hundred other people, in the pouring rain. When it was over, they headed home, and there was no turning back. Amsterdam was in the past; the future was this glowing light on the horizon; and Beth Littlefield wasn't a part of Barrett's new world.

They had become so disconnected that Barrett was surprised at how hard she took the breakup. Beth's planning their future together had so consumed her young life that it was as if she had lost a lifelong companion in an accident. Unable to face the truth, she rationalized that Brian was scared about going off to college and growing up. Once settled into life away from home, he would come back. That was all she had, so she followed him to Bainbridge.

Paradoxically, Barrett's best friend, and now college roommate, had silently and agonizingly carried a torch for Beth Littlefield since the seventh grade.

"Pappy," Andrew Paxton's nickname, was a term of endearment, respect, and a result of his often acting more like a parent than a peer. His parents and siblings were much older, resulting in his being harassed about his conservative manner and dress. Growing up, there was no money for the latest fashion trends, so while the "in" crowd wore penny loafers and square-cut pants, Pappy had dress shoes with laces as well as slacks with cuffs to be let out as he grew.

His intelligence (people made fun of him because he read encyclopedias as a child) reflected in his nerdy conduct. However, it also translated into emotional strength. He took care of his friends when they got drunk, listened when they had problems, offered girls dumped by their boyfriends a shoulder to cry on, and generally acted far older than his years.

A true romantic, he used to give his lunch money to the brunette who sat two rows behind him in the first grade. She was twice his size and ignored him, but no matter.

The painful shyness continued throughout his school years. Tongue-tied in Littlefield's presence, he went out of his way to avoid her. She assumed he disapproved of her dating his best friend, but Barrett told her Andrew acted that way around all girls.

His level head, maturity, and intelligence led Andrew to be a leader of the Amsterdam Chiefs. His athleticism was a blend of some talent, but mostly hard work. As a child, he was round and soft—"stocky" or "husky." But he spent hours by himself pounding the ball off the high school kickboard. He then grew five inches and lost twenty pounds, and at five feet ten and 150 pounds, he was the prototype fullback: solid, smart, and dependable.

Deliberate to the point of mechanical, he became an accurate passer and shooter. Plagued with average speed and relatively slow reflexes, he could nonetheless thread passes through defenders, heave the ball fifty yards on a throw-in, and kick and shoot equally well with both feet. He could play all positions but preferred center halfback, where he could press the attack. Deceptively strong, he once scored from midfield on a free kick. And while his intent was to avoid conflict, it wasn't unusual to see him tackling the biggest player on the other side once a skirmish broke out. The Amsterdam Chiefs played soccer as a full-contact sport.

The first to forgive others, he heaped criticism on himself for every mistake or imperfection. Barrett passed off his own gaffes as part of the game and couldn't understand his friend's self-abuse. But he knew much of the Chiefs' success was due to Andrew Paxton's personality.

So five of the mighty Chiefs went off to play for the Bainbridge Titans, which generally fielded a collection of average high school players and converted football jocks.

It was now noon on Sunday, and Andrew's parents had an eight-hour drive back to Buffalo, so it was time to say good-bye. Other than one week at soccer camp and a visit to college campuses, he'd never been away from home for more than a night or two in his eighteen years. He'd worked in his uncle's business from the time he was fourteen, earning most of his own money, but every night he went home to the same house where he was born.

Suddenly, his parents looked much older. The years of toil were etched in the sadness in their faces, and the tears welled up in their eyes. His mother hugged him and said a simple good-bye. Twice a survivor of breast cancer, she was always more in control of her emotions. His father couldn't speak. His son, of whom he was so proud, was moving on, and he could no longer fight back the tears.

Andrew choked out a hushed good-bye as they embraced, and then he turned and strode quickly away, not looking back for fear they would see him crying. Once inside Roberts Hall, he ran to the bathroom, finding the first sink and repeatedly splashing water onto his face. Fortunately, the other students were at the student union having lunch or saying their own farewells. It was fifteen minutes before he could compose himself, and he used yards of toilet paper to blow his nose.

When he came out, his father's red station wagon was gone. He covered his face with his hands and, breathing out a deep, hot sigh, turned to go back to the solitude of the dorm.

"Hey, Pappy! Have you met the soccer coach?"

Millwood and Barrett were coming up the walk. "Word is that he never played soccer in his life and knows nothing about the game," said Tim. "We're headed to the field house to check out—"

They stopped when they saw their friend's swollen eyes.

"We can catch up with you later," said Tim, looking away.

Pappy shook his head. "No. I'm okay. Let's go," he said, clearing his throat. "I came here to play soccer."

They walked up the hill toward the field house.

"Where are McIlroy and Penny?" asked Paxton.

"Saying good-bye to their parents," said Millwood. "There were a couple of Silos [Psi Lambda Omega, one of eight fraternities on the Bainbridge campus] talking to them. They have a bunch of guys on the soccer team. It looks like the TDTs [Theta Delta Tau], Silos, and Lambda Kappas are the soccer players. Most of the football players are Tau Beta Taus. They're the animals on campus."

"Yeah," said Brian with a laugh. "I heard a guy once took a double-barrel shotgun with blanks and turned it on their housemother and fired both barrels … She isn't there anymore."

The field house, built before World War II, was a massive dark brown brick structure trapped in time. Its halls were dimly lit and musty, with shabby brown tile walls lined with faded photos of past football and basketball teams. Dust covered the numerous trophy cases—jammed with statues, medals, and ribbons—and the hallways echoed with every voice and footstep. The main feature was the gym, comprised of a basketball court, with retractable bleachers on both sides. At one end was a stage, providing more seats during home games.

The three Chiefs caught up with Don Penny and Jim McIlroy, and they pointed out the soccer coach, who was chatting with a couple of boys who towered heads above him.

"Here's the scoop," said Penny, taking a deep breath. "The junior varsity basketball coach here is the varsity soccer coach. It must be like punishment or some sort of initiation. No one else would do it. Football here is everything. And basketball. Even the girl's field hockey coach wouldn't take the job. At least he has a winning program.

"The soccer team hasn't won more than two games a year since it started," he continued. "Most of the guys are ex–football players and wrestlers, but a handful played in high school. The schedule is murder. Stratton State has two all-Americans, both from Europe. Supposedly, they were working in a steel mill in Cleveland when they were recruited. They don't even really attend classes, and one of them is twenty-eight and has two kids. A lot of the other teams have players from Nigeria and the Caribbean. We're going to get waxed."

Andrew sighed. "Let's go look at the field."

McIlroy smirked. "You got a car?"

"Why?" asked Brian, not wanting to hear the answer.

"Because the field ain't here. It's not on campus. It's in some park two miles from here."

"What! You're baggin' me," said Barrett.

"No, I'm not," Penny continued. "They don't have room on campus, so it's in a city park two miles away."

"How do we get there, by bus?"

"No," said Penny, "we walk … or run, depending on your mood. By the way, that's also where we practice every day."

They stood looking at each other. "Whose idea was it to come to this dump?" asked Brian. "We are stuck in hell … up to our asses."

"Well, maybe it's a good field, like a stadium," said Andrew hopefully.

"There aren't even any bleachers, and there's a big frickin' tree that hangs over the field!" he exclaimed.

"A tree?" asked Millwood. "How do you play with a frickin' tree?"

"When the ball goes up into the branches, you wait until it falls back down and play on. Simple as that," said Penny, holding up his hands for emphasis.

"Up to our necks in hell," repeated Brian.

"Wait till you see the locker room," continued Penny. "It's a dungeon. And you have to walk through the football players to get to the showers. These guys are monsters, and they eat their young."

"You are so full of crap," said Brian. "They're just like any dumb jock on the face of the earth."

There was a collective sigh.

"Let's go down to the Union. It's way past lunchtime," said Millwood.

The Bainbridge student union was the social and recreational center of campus, and it was located on the top floor with the dining hall. There were eight fraternities and eight sororities, with about fifty upperclassmen members each, most of whom took room and board at the houses. A lot of juniors and seniors were "independents" (didn't belong to a fraternity or sorority), living in houses and apartments off campus, so those dining at the Union were mainly freshmen. Service was cafeteria-style, and you could have all the food you wanted—a great drawing card for the boys from Amsterdam High. Being able to pork out any time was a high priority for eighteen-year-old boys. Food and women.

Most of the girls came from middle- to upper-class families from the East and Midwest. Dress was conservative (no hippies), and they spared no expense on their looks. The student council conveniently published a "baby book" of high school yearbook pictures, with name, and campus residence. Some photos were misleading, but most were accurate. Boys' hair varied from brush cut to shoulder length, with the "collegiate," or

"Prince Valiant," look also popular. In 1969, facial hair wasn't allowed in high schools, so college was the first chance away to experiment. Most efforts were thin and unkempt collections of strands, which resulted in more pimples.

The Union basement held a bowling alley and pool hall. Smoking was permitted, as was drinking beer in the bar, The Cellar. Ventilation was marginal, and smoke hung like a constant fog at face level. Those under twenty-one could only buy 3.2 beer, a watered-down version brewed by regional bottlers.

The main floor had several lounges, meeting rooms, a snack bar, and the bookstore. For the six days preceding the start of classes, it was a madhouse. Lines of students piled high with textbooks, Magic Markers, pens, pencils, slide rules, rulers, erasers, legal pads, notebooks, three-ring binders, paper clips, report covers, and dividers snaked through the Union. Thereafter it was abandoned, except for school memorabilia bought during homecoming or parents' weekend and the purchase of Cliffs Notes when a book report or test was imminent.

Pappy led the way up the stairs and through the double doors of the half-filled dining hall. Brian nodded to a couple of girls and then peeled off when they beckoned.

"That guy is amazing," said Penny. "Look at that blonde." Brian was now talking to two girls, one blonde and one brunette, both with shoulder-length hair and stunning figures.

"That's Cassi Hinton," said Tim Millwood, picking up a tray. "The brunette is Cindy Parker. Cheerleader types. They live in Norbert Hall."

"How do you know so much?" asked Andrew Paxton.

"Didn't you look at your "baby book?" asked Penny. "Hinton is even better looking than her picture."

"What did you do, memorize the thing in one day?" asked Paxton, filling his tray with food.

"No," said Millwood, "he spent the entire morning reading it on the john."

Barrett was rambling on and smiling, the two girls hanging on every word. Soon they were joined by two more.

"I don't remember anything like that back at Amsterdam," said Penny.

"I do," said McIlroy. "Lynn Castle. She had the greatest body I've ever seen."

"What do you mean, 'seen'?" asked Penny. "She dated that big senior. Nobody else got near her, for fear of getting killed."

"That's what you think," said Paxton.

"He's right," chimed in Millwood. "She and Alice Taggart came over to Pappy's pool one night. We were playing keep-away with a beach ball, and her bikini top 'accidentally' came partially off. She made like she was embarrassed, but she loved every minute of it. Pappy was red-faced for a week."

Barrett joined the Chiefs in the serving line.

"Gee, Brian, thanks for introducing us," said Millwood.

"Hey, you guys could've come over any time," he said, taking a tray and stealing a plate of vegetables from Penny. "Besides, they all have boyfriends at home. Frickin' football players. And they'll be dating upperclassmen in a week, just like all the other freshmen girls, so there'll be cold showers for us for a semester."

"Yeah, right," said Paxton. "You always have trouble finding women."

Just then, two boys in Bainbridge University letterman jackets with soccer ball emblems spotted the five from Amsterdam.

"Penny, how's it going?" asked the shorter of the two.

"Hi, Johnson," said Don Penny, shaking his hand. "Hi, Malloy. You guys slumming it at the Union or checking out the freshmen talent?"

"Definitely a talent check," said Glenn Johnson. A gregarious, likeable sophomore with a round face and short, curly brown hair, he was one of the "soccer converts," a high school football player with worlds of heart stuck in a five-ten frame and slow feet. No way he could compete with Bain's football talent, so he took up soccer. The change was a struggle, and two minutes into his first college contest, he was ejected for throwing a block into the opposing goalie. The boy had three broken ribs and had to be carried off. The ensuing fight lasted five minutes.

Alex "Goose" Malloy was another football orphan. Hailing from a small western Pennsylvania town, he had at least seen soccer matches at his high school, and his younger brother was on the varsity.

"I love this time of year," said Johnson. "All these little freshmen girls running around. I swear the "baby book" gets better and better each class. I'd show up for freshman orientation even if I didn't play soccer." He turned to Penny. "Are these the rest of the 'Fab Five' from Amsterdam High?"

"Yeah," said Penny. "This is Tim Millwood, Jim McIlroy, Brian Barrett, and Andrew Paxton." They all shook hands.

"Well, get ready, 'cause we really need you guys," said Johnson, taking three pieces of chocolate cake for dessert.

"So we heard," said Andrew. The group went over and sat down.

"Is it true the field is two miles from here?" asked McIlroy. "And that it has a tree on it?"

"Well, the tree isn't *on* the field," said Johnson, his mouth full of salad. "It just hangs over one side at midfield. It's not so bad."

"Right," continued Paxton, "and I suppose the field house swimming pool has rocks in it."

"Crap," said Tim Millwood, shaking his head. "And a coach who's never played the game." He gazed around the room. "Let's talk about women instead."

"Hey, there's a party down at our house this Saturday night," said Goose. "Silo house, nine o'clock. Be there. We invited every girl we could find—and just a handful of guys. We're gonna have a couple of kegs and mix up some Silo jungle juice."

"What's that?" asked Millwood.

"Must be Everclear," interrupted Paxton. "Just like we used to make at my cousin's farm. Great stuff to fry your mind."

"That's right," said Johnson. "A gallon of Everclear—almost pure alcohol—in a trash can full of cherry Kool-Aid. Makes you a zombie in five minutes. Last year two freshmen girls fell off the front balcony and broke their arms. Three others passed out naked in our showers … Nothing happened, though," he added, disappointed.

"I take it that's the only way Silos can get women," teased Millwood.

Johnson and Goose stood up to leave. "Well, you little twerps better go to your dorms and get settled in. There's usually a floor meeting the first night to warn you about the evils of smoking dope and drinking beer. There's no point in telling you about women and sex, because you won't be gettin' any here for a year. See you at practice tomorrow, three thirty sharp … Don't get lost on your way down to the field … and don't get jumped by any townies or pervs."

They sat silently. "Well," said Barrett. "Looks like we might have a chance to start on this team." He stood up. "All right, time to head on out. Hey, it's only three o'clock. Let's go up to the football field and kick the ball around for a while."

"Good idea," said Millwood. "Be there at four and we'll play a little one-touch. After the dorm meeting, we can go eat."

"I'll catch up with Johnson," said Penny, "and see if they can get a bunch of guys to join us." McIlroy went with him.

The August afternoon was still warm, but the heavily wooded campus would soon be awash with fall's brilliance. Andrew thought again of his parents leaving. High school seemed years ago, and he had a cold, empty feeling. His senior year he couldn't wait to go to college. Yet whenever alumni came home for vacations, they would all say, "Hey, don't knock high school, man. Those were the good times." Now he understood what they meant.

The three headed to Roberts Hall when they heard Don Penny calling.

"Hey, wait up," he said, on a dead run. "I talked to Goose, and he said to stay away from the football field. They don't allow anyone there except for games."

"Piss on 'em," said Brian. "We paid our money to go to this school. Let's see them throw us off."

"There's a football practice field next to the field house," said Pappy. "It's Sunday, so there won't be anyone around."

"You don't understand," continued Penny. "Johnson said all football facilities are out of bounds, even the practice field."

"Penny," said Barrett in disgust. "You are such a woman."

"And an ugly woman at that," said Millwood.

"I don't give a crap," said Barrett. "We aren't going to use the whole field. Those football wusses can bitch all they want. And like Pappy said, there ain't anybody around."

They looked at each other for a moment. "All right," said Millwood, splitting off to go to the dorm. "See you boys in a while."

The first floor of Roberts Hall was quiet. Barrett and Paxton fumbled around in their pockets for a room key.

"We've got to figure out where to hide a key," said Barrett, opening the door. "I'm gonna come home wasted one night and won't be able to get in."

"Not a problem," said a voice to their left. A blond-headed guy was coming toward them with a coat hanger. "Hi, I'm Fred Corey. I'm a sophomore." They introduced themselves.

"What's that for?" asked Andrew. Corey nudged them out of the way and closed the door again.

"Watch this," he said, sliding the curved end of the coat hanger down the wide space between the door and the jamb. Slipping it around the tongue of the lock, he pulled as he shook the handle, and the door popped open.

"Oh, man," said Brian. "That's slick."

"No sweat," he said. "Just remember, anyone can do this. Hide any money you've got real good ... and beware of water balloons."

"Water balloons?"

"Yeah," said Fred, "this campus is known for its water fights, and it's pretty clear you're not safe hiding in your room. Two years ago, they had a fight here on campus that lasted three days. It made the cover of *Look* magazine."

"Cool," said Pappy. "Anything else we should know?"

"Yeah," said Fred. "Watch out for townies when you go into the city. They hate college kids. I know a couple of guys who got jumped. One took a two iron through his jaw. Busted out all his teeth on one side. The dirt bag who did it is still in jail.

"There are three bars where everyone hangs out: the Golden Condor—

we call it 'The Bird'—and O'Reilly's and Fitzgerald's. You don't need a car to get to the first two, and it beats hanging around the Union to get drunk. If you want to wander farther, there's Fitzgerald's."

"What about the frat parties?" asked Brian. "There's one at the Silo house next Saturday."

"Oh, yeah," said Fred, his tone saddened. "They have a lot of parties." He looked away for a moment. "I was going to pledge Silo … but I didn't have the money." Pappy figured he'd probably been rejected for membership, the ultimate insult on a campus where fraternities and sororities made up most of the social life. "They're still my friends," he said. "I'm just too busy most of the time. Well, let me know if you need to borrow a coat hanger."

The dorm room was like the hallways: wide, high ceilings and cold linoleum floors. The windows were tall and dirty inside and out, and only plastic blinds, covered with dust, stood between the residents and the sunshine streaming through. On the right were wooden frame bunk beds with well-worn mattresses atop metal springs. To the left were two desks, two closets, and two dressers with mirrors on top, all built into the wall. Paxton's parents had helped him unpack, so his clothes hung neatly, and his socks, underwear, and shirts were in drawers. Pappy guessed Barrett would empty his large metal steamer trunk, which held all his clothes and possessions, sometime around Christmas.

"All right," said Paxton, "get dressed. I'm gonna toast your drawers, Bud. It's time we showed these Hoosiers how to play soccer." They put on their Adidas spikes, the preferred brand.

As they were walking down the hall, Paxton bouncing his soccer ball, Fred Corey appeared again. "Oh, soccer players," he said. "You're going all the way down to the field at this time of day? We have a mandatory dorm meeting at six."

"We're just going up to the football practice field," said Brian, flipping the ball up and keeping it aloft with his head.

Corey's face took on a scowl. "I wouldn't do that if I were you."

"Why?" said Pappy. "They aren't using it now. We were up at the field house a little while ago, and nobody was there."

"Don't do it, man," said Fred. "They'll throw you off there. Nobody uses their facilities."

Brian headed for the door. "We'll be back for the meeting," he said. Fred shook his head.

Once outside, they met McIlroy, Millwood, and Penny coming up the hill.

"Hey, maybe we shouldn't do this," said Don. "I couldn't get anyone else to come. They kept telling me we were nuts, and they'll kick our butts if we go on their precious field."

"Well, I don't give a friggin' fat one," said Brian. "Tomorrow's the first day of practice; I haven't touched a ball in a couple of weeks; and we're going to have to win spots from upperclassmen. I didn't come here to sit on the bench."

The football practice fields were between the field house and the stadium. Holding around seven thousand people, the stadium was often packed for some of the great conference games played there every year. Though Bainbridge was a Division III college for sports and couldn't give scholarships, each season it scheduled a Division II school to test its mettle and draw more fans. Although they seldom won that game, it was always a good contest, and the opposition came away with an appreciation for head coach Sam Bolger's teams.

A legend at the school, and known nationally for Bain's program, Bolger was too small to be a starter in college. He studied the tactics of major college coaches, and only two years after graduation, his hard work and dedication led to his being hired as an assistant and offensive coordinator at the largest high school in Indianapolis. At thirty, he moved on to head coach at Parker Stanley High near Brady, and after going undefeated in only his third season with the Fighting Falcons, he was approached to head up the Bainbridge Titans.

Bolger was cast in the mold of the great Division I coaches of the era. Football ticket sales generated the most revenue for the athletic department, and it garnered the greatest financial support from fanatical alumni. Basketball was also a premier program at Bainbridge, the result of the success of its coach, Alan Amory, who was as tough and competent as Bolger. Since the seasons barely overlapped, and neither program stole players from the other, both flourished.

Now in his late fifties and white-haired, Bolger had turned over the day-to-day tasks to his assistants—Jason Jugovic and Bill Borders were offensive and defensive coordinators, respectively. Both were intelligent, personable, and would eventually head their own programs.

And then there was Mel Delfino. Six feet, thinning black hair, with a bad toupee and a growing paunch, his domain was special teams, which fit his kamikaze personality. He was also the gofer, the hit man, the bad cop of the coaching staff. And he was Bolger's nephew.

Delfino made fun of players of lesser talents, particularly when injured. He derided members of the minor sports and encouraged the football players to do the same. Coach Bolger didn't condone this behavior, and most of the squad ignored this part of Delfino's personality. His small cadre of followers sometimes physically hazed and abused other athletes, necessitating the intervention of other coaches. After one particularly ugly incident, Bolger, in a rare display of temper, cursed and belittled Delfino, to the point of tears. The incidents stopped, but Delfino continued to instruct his players that they were the chosen ones, above ridicule or rules.

Paxton and company went out the side door of the field house to the practice field. They tossed the soccer ball aside and took a lap. Then Paxton led them in exercises and stretching. Retrieving the soccer ball, they made a circle and began passing to each other: first left foot, then right, diagonally, and then around the perimeter. They were one-touch passes, meaning they didn't stop, or "trap," the ball but struck it as it came to them. The shots were crisp and hugged the ground with topspin. The adrenaline was flowing as they talked about last season's triumph and about their old teammates.

"Wouldn't it have been great," said Andrew, "if the whole team could have gone to the same school? I would have put our guys against any small college in the state." (Eventually eight of the eleven starting players, and four of the reserves, from that 1969 state championship team would go on to play college soccer.)

They had drilled for about ten minutes when suddenly Andrew

pivoted, took two steps, and launched a shot dead center through the football uprights thirty yards away, clearing the crossbar by five feet. The ball caromed off the chain-link fence surrounding the field, and Pappy quickly retrieved it. They took off their shirts, placing them a yard apart at one end of an imaginary field for a goal, and played three on two, offense against defense, with Barrett and Pappy on defense.

"What are you soccer assholes doing on this field?" They turned to see a man in a T-shirt and coach's shorts jogging toward them. "This is a football practice field. Get the hell off here. Now!" The man ran up and stood toe-to-toe with Andrew Paxton, face crimson.

"Are you deaf? Get your goddamn asses off this field!" he screamed. Paxton held his ground, and Penny and Barrett stopped on either side of their teammate. The man was surprised when the boys didn't retreat.

"There wasn't anyone out—" Andrew began.

"Shut up," he said, raising his voice even higher. "I don't give a damn who was where." He grabbed Paxton by the arm. Barrett immediately stepped forward. There was no mistaking what was about to happen.

"I'd appreciate it if you'd tone down your language, Coach." Walking toward them was a short dark-haired man in his late twenties, with a stern face and rapid gait. Even at five-seven, he looked tough as nails—and in no mood for debate.

The man released Paxton's arm and stepped back, startled by the arrival of the other coach. "Coach Hancock ...," he began, stammering like a kid caught letting the air out of someone's tires. "I told these players they're not allowed on the practice field."

"No, you didn't, Coach," said Todd Hancock calmly, in a low but firm voice. "You came out here screaming and cursing at them to get off the field, and then grabbed this man. I am sure that if they had known they were not allowed out here, they wouldn't be here. I apologize for them, and they will also apologize. Gentlemen, please apologize to Coach Delfino."

Andrew was amazed by the steely demeanor of the shorter man, who had clearly intimidated his much larger associate.

"Gentlemen," repeated Hancock, in an expectant tone.

"Yeah, we're sorry, Coach," said Andrew. "We just wanted to kick the ball around before practice started tomorrow." All chimed in with an apology—with the exception of Barrett, who stood with clenched fists, still glaring at his adversary. Andrew moved between Brian and the football coach.

"Well, all right," said Delfino, still chafing but holding his temper. "No more on this field. If you want to play soccer, go down to the park—to your own field."

"Sorry again," said Hancock. "I'll take it from here."

Delfino turned and walked back to the field house.

Todd Hancock faced his new players. "All right, guys, cut the crap. You knew exactly what you were doing. Which one of you guys is Paxton?"

"I am," said Andrew, looking down on the man in front of him.

"Well, I'm Todd Hancock," he said, and they shook hands. "I'm told you're the leader of this bunch, so I'm making you responsible."

"It was all our idea," chimed in Barrett. "Who the hell does that dirt bag think he is …?"

"Wait a minute," said Hancock, going around Paxton and glaring up at Barrett. "You're going to do this my way, and you're going to treat the other coaches with respect in public, regardless of what you think of them, or don't bother showing up tomorrow. Is that clear?" he asked, now really upset. No response. "I said, is that clear?"

"Yes, sir," said Brian, but his tone was clearly patronizing.

"Good," said Hancock. "Now get off the field, and I'll see you at practice."

He walked back toward the field house. Andrew Paxton rolled the soccer ball a couple of yards ahead, ran forward, and crushed a shot from forty yards that again sailed through the middle of the crossbars. He retrieved the ball and jogged off toward the dorm with his teammates.

Coach Sam Bolger had seen the entire episode from a second-story window at the field house. He would have a word with his assistant. He would also find out about the young kicker from Amsterdam High.

The dorm meeting was a mind-numbing experience. The first-floor RA, resident advisor, was Richard Berber, a diminutive psychology major.

For an hour, he droned on against the evils of alcohol and drugs. By the end of his speech about laundry pickup, visitors in the room, and how to handle disputes over TV channels in the lounge, the boys were talking too loudly among themselves to hear anything.

Everyone went back to his room, and the stereos started blaring. Across the campus, others joined in the revelry. Andrew Paxton looked at his watch, and it struck him: there was no one to tell him when to go to bed ... no one to tell him where to go or what to wear. It was a feeling of exhilaration—and apprehension and loneliness. Suddenly, he was glad Barrett was his roommate, and that the other Chiefs had come to Bainbridge.

Pappy and Barrett, still sweaty and smelly from practice, padded down to the showers in towels and rubber sandals. No girls were allowed in the men's dorms, and vice versa, so there was no dress code and little modesty. The linens, courtesy of the laundry service, consisted of two sheets, one towel, one washcloth, and one pillowcase, and the items were dispersed every Tuesday. The towels were undersized and cheap, and they had been washed to the point of almost being transparent. For some of the larger boys, they were the size of a diaper. And all had the gentle feel of burlap.

They dressed quickly, and on their way out, they stopped by a card game of acey-deucy, with five guys playing and another dozen looking on. The pot had grown to a staggering thirty-two dollars. Dave Carr, a tall, lanky kid from Pennsylvania, was showing a king and a three, and the crowd screamed for him to match the pot. He gave in to the pressure, only to watch the dealer throw a two of spades. The mob let out a whoop that could be heard across campus, and Carr was out a month's spending money.

Monday, August 25

◉ ◉ ◉ ◉

I t was nine in the morning, the beginning of freshman orientation week. No need for an alarm clock. Barrett and Paxton awoke to dozens of shoes thundering down the six flights of metal and cement stairs and out the back door, which slammed repeatedly with a conclusive bang. They were also directly across from the vending machines, the laundry, and the mail room.

The seven hundred students divided into groups, and professors in history, political science, sociology, religion, psychology, economics, art, business, and science conducted lectures and discussions on the social problems of the day, and how their courses addressed society's issues.

Although Bainbridge was a bachelor of liberal arts college, numerous science majors like Paxton and Barrett were premed. Millwood and Penny elected business courses. McIlroy chose sociology.

At lunch, Johnson and Paul Sheffe introduced the Chiefs to John Harbaugh and Randy Williams. Harbaugh, a sophomore, was a Long Island preppy. Almost as tall as Barrett, but broader, his expensive clothes and groomed hair hid a tough, hard-nosed competitor. Randy Williams had endured three tough years as the Titan's goalie. Tall, quick, skilled, and fearless, he was a leader, good enough to have started on any other team in the conference.

The Chiefs' reputation was now all over campus. Though the upperclassmen made noises about hazing the freshmen at practice, they were thankful for anyone who would help them win more than two games a year.

"I guess you guys know about the new coach," said Williams.

"Yeah," said Penny. "We met him up at the field house, along with that dickhead football coach. It was cool the way he put that guy in his place, though."

"I'm not surprised," continued Williams. "Hancock played basketball here seven years ago and was all-conference, and he's one tough S.O.B. I don't think he really wanted the soccer job, but the JV basketball coach has no choice."

"What about the rest of the team?" asked Andrew.

"Well, each year we get some guys who've played," said Williams, "and then some football dorks like Johnson here. We have nine seniors. Some are okay. Caldwell and Bill Roush played for schools outside Syracuse and are above average. I can't say that other than Caldwell, Al Landon, and me, there's much hustle or desire among the seniors. We know we're going to beat a couple of teams each year and the rest are out of our league, so these guys do just enough to get by. Since the coach is really a basketball coach, nobody's trying to improve the program. I was surprised when we went from a club to varsity sport last year."

The Chiefs' faces were glum. None had ever played on a losing team. *Ever.* To make things worse, other Amsterdam graduates were now at schools in Bainbridge's conference, with better programs. If the Titans were really this bad, the humiliation would be unbearable.

Pappy's appetite was replaced by the apprehension and nausea he experienced before every game. The others also stopped eating. Except Barrett, one of the best knife and fork men on the planet.

The afternoon was taken up by professors pitching their departments to students uncertain about their majors. The Chiefs went to the lectures, but by two o'clock, they snuck back to their dorms one by one to drop off books and papers and pick up their soccer shoes. They needed to get to the field house early anyway to get locker assignments and pick up practice jerseys and other equipment. Luckily, there was no need for the dreaded turn to the left and cough. All entering freshmen had to have physical examinations prior to orientation.

The locker room was large, cold, and damp, with high ceilings crisscrossed with exposed beams and pipes. The fluorescent lights, yellow with age, provided less illumination than the windows, which were covered with wire grating. The Chiefs stood in line in front of a large cage like structure, housing three students tending to a steady stream of boys grabbing towels, jocks, and jerseys. The soccer players weren't getting much attention, while football players pushed to the front demanding service, sneering at those waiting.

Two equipment managers were nerdy caricatures—the last ones chosen when sides were picked. They pandered to the football squad, both from intimidation and reverence, and parroted the derisive comments toward the soccer team.

The third, Kenny Hodges, had played high school soccer, but bone spurs on his heels ended his career. He envied the Chiefs, wishing he were on the other side of the wire cage.

The majority of the football squad were normal, intelligent students who put on the intimidating air only when with their teammates. One or two were genuine jerks, but they were second or third string, and their value to the team was in their own minds.

The Chiefs' prospective teammates looked soft and marginally athletic. All were freshmen, with the same duck-out-of-water looks on their faces. One, however, stood out. Powerfully built, five feet eight, with short coarse black hair, and Asian eyes. A Hawaiian. In Spencer, Indiana.

"Hi … Brian Barrett," said Barrett, extending his hand.

The young man lowered his head slightly in a shy manner. "David Nakano," he replied.

"Man, are you by any chance, like, from Hawaii?" asked Brian.

Nakano smiled. "Yes."

"Oh, wow, are you lost," Barrett exclaimed, and they all laughed. "There ain't a beach or palm tree for a thousand miles," he continued, "and you won't see a girl in a bikini until next July."

Nakano blushed through his amber skin. He nodded without saying anything.

"A man of many words," said Barrett.

Most of the football players had gone out the double doors at the east end of the locker room, and the equipment managers started pulling the soccer gear. The Chiefs each received a towel; a red-and-blue reversible cotton pullover practice jersey, faded, with no numbers or lettering; a pair of faded red (almost pink) nylon shorts, frayed at the bottom seam; and a Master padlock with black dial, the combination scribbled on a piece of paper pierced by the lock.

"Just like high school," Pappy mused, looking down at the sad collection of equipment. College was supposed to be classy.

"You guys'll get your uniforms on game day," said Hodges. "You can turn your towel and practice jersey in for a clean one every night. Don't keep anything of value here. One whack from a hammer will open that lock like a tin can. And," continued Hodges, leaning forward and looking left and then right, "if the football team is still here when you get back from practice, don't use the showers. It's bad enough that you're soccer players, but you're also freshmen … Well, you can see that the only ones on your team getting lockers are underclassmen. The other guys change at the dorms." More happy news.

The Chiefs found lockers together at the end of the first of ten rows. A small group of football players returned, their metal spikes chattering across the cement floors, and they banged on the metal locker doors and hollered in fits of testosterone.

Then the clicking stopped two rows over.

"Holy crap, a soccer player!" someone exclaimed in a less-than-friendly voice. "And this one looks like a nip … or a Chink." There was some commotion, and a locker slammed shut.

"What the hell is a soccer wimp doing in here?" the voice continued.

"Hey, knock it off, Rattigan," said Kenny Hodges.

"Shut up, equipment wimp," said another loud voice. "The weenie soccer team must be desperate, recruiting pineapple heads."

Paxton and Barrett walked over two rows. There was David Nakano standing three feet from two football players in full uniforms, helmets under their arms. One was about Pappy's height but taller in spikes. He also outweighed Andrew by thirty pounds and had no neck. Ben Rattigan, or "Big Ben," was a sophomore offensive lineman who saw little action but used his size and bluster to harass those he deemed inferior. The second, Ned Burler, recruited as a basketball player, towered over all at six feet five. In helmet and spikes, he was nearly six-eight. Although thin for a football player, he was muscular and had hands the size of a person's head. In shoulder pads, Burler looked like a giant tack. Lacking speed and coordination, he was there to show size to opposing teams. Neither would have been at Bainbridge without sports.

They backed Nakano, who was of Samoan descent, against the row of lockers and slammed his closed. David stood staring, unflinching, into Rattigan's face. Despite his otherwise quiet demeanor, he feared no one, not even the two looming before him.

Paxton started forward, but Barrett went past and stood in front of Big Ben. Brian was looking for—hoping for—trouble.

"What's the problem, douche bag?" taunted Barrett. Big Ben was confronted with someone taller, and he saw the veins popping out of Brian's muscular arms and shoulders.

"What is this, another pimp soccer player?" asked Burler.

"You mean another dickhead football player," answered Barrett, ignoring Rattigan as he spoke past him. "Good thing I got here before this guy kicked your asses."

Faces on both sides were beet red, fists clenched. Millwood, McIlroy, and Penny showed up just as—

"Hey!" said Coach Todd Hancock, striding over to the group. "You guys have a two-mile run to practice. Get at it." Barrett tried to step forward, but Paxton pushed him backward. They turned and headed to their lockers.

Hancock stared at Rattigan and Burler. His eyes were about level with Burler's chest, but the football players knew not to mess with him.

"And I'm sure Coach Bolger has something planned for you guys as well." He stood there with fists on his hips, and the two men walked away.

"Paxton," Hancock called, and Andrew appeared from around the corner.

"Yes, Coach?"

"This is David Nakano."

"Yes, Coach, we met," said Andrew.

"You guys take him with you to the field," said Hancock, turning to leave.

"Yes, Coach."

Hancock turned back at the door. "And I don't want any more trouble with the football players. Is that clear?"

"Hey, those assholes started it," chimed in Barrett, coming forward. Pappy stepped in front of him.

"We'll try to stay out of their way, Coach," said Andrew. Hancock left.

"Exactly how are we going to avoid these dickweeds?" asked Barrett while tying his shoes.

"Let's dress in the dorm," said Millwood. "We don't even practice here. We've got our scrimmage jerseys. That way, we can wash our stuff once in a while. My locker at Amsterdam stunk so bad that I had to throw my socks and jock away after the season. Now we can smell nice while we're are getting our asses kicked."

"I don't plan on getting my ass kicked, by Clarkson or anyone else," said Penny, taking his clothes.

Johnson and Sheffe were coming into the field house as the Chiefs were leaving.

"We came to show you guys the way …," said Johnson. Both he and Sheffe looked at Nakano quizzically.

"This is David Nakano … Kono," said Millwood. Kono was the name of the tough Hawaiian sidekick of Jack Lord on the TV show Hawaii Five-O. The handle was an instant fit.

On the way over, they told Johnson and Sheffe about the encounter with the football team.

"Yeah, Rattigan and Burler are a couple of Delfino's boys. Both are scholarship players, which means they have so-called jobs on campus. Rattigan has turned being a janitor into a business enterprise. He has keys to all the classrooms and offices. Come semester finals, he will be cruising the filing cabinets, selling copies of the tests to his closest friends and anyone else with twenty bucks to spare."

They left their clothes in Paxton's room, and Johnson and Sheffe led them south down the hill and across Limestone Street, the western boundary of campus. They crossed the bridge above Sandy Creek, turning right into Darby Park. It was an easy jog, and they talked as they went. Barrett, still pumped from the encounter with the football players, ran out front with Penny.

The two-lane asphalt road wound through Darby Park, following the creek and the Baltimore and Ohio Railroad tracks. It was a beautiful late summer day. Children played on the slides and swings. Several people were fishing or feeding the ducks in the shallow pond.

After ten minutes, there still was no soccer field in sight. *Where the heck is this place?* Pappy wondered. Amsterdam had four soccer fields at the high school alone; there were two at the junior high and at least one at each elementary school. It wasn't unusual for several hundred townspeople, many of whom had played at Amsterdam years before, to turn out for a game on a weekday afternoon. Each season, over a hundred boys, about one-fifth of the entire school, tried out for varsity.

"It's just around the next bend," said Johnson, the same assurance he'd given five minutes before. They passed a playground and some tennis courts and cut left behind a small building, and there was the field. Freshly mowed and marked, there were boys at each end fastening the nets to the white wooden goalposts with athletic tape. And a huge maple tree, eighty feet tall, stood at midfield. Although the trunk was fifteen feet off the sideline, one set of branches about twenty feet up extended at least five yards over the pitch.

There were already about twenty guys kicking balls around. Johnson spotted Coach Hancock under the branches of the maple, and all ran over.

"Glad to see you boys are right on time," said Todd Hancock, with his same steely glare. "Go warm up."

The Chiefs formed their own group, making quick passes and traps while stretching. Andrew Paxton stopped to study the other players. Soon all the Chiefs were watching. It wasn't a pretty sight. Players kicked the ball all over the place. For some, just hitting it in the general direction of another individual was a major task. They had to stop a rolling ball or risk missing it entirely. Heading was another adventure. Those wearing glasses jumped at the ball with stiff necks and closed eyes, striking it with the tops of their heads. Some worked hard on their form but lacked the years of practice necessary to control the ball.

Mercifully, there were exceptions. Scott Driver hailed from Ohio, a growing hotbed of soccer. He played for two years in high school, and he could trap and pass; he understood the game. David Nakano was talented and experienced, and his compact athletic body was well suited for the game. The seniors showed some proficiency, but some seemed more interested in talking than practicing.

"Come on in!" yelled Hancock. Everyone gathered around the coach, by far the smallest individual there. He was in excellent physical condition, and he paced back and forth as he talked, his blue eyes surveying the group of eager faces.

"For those who haven't met me before, I am Coach Todd Hancock. I'm the varsity soccer coach, and junior varsity basketball coach. Some administrative things before we start. The schedule is posted on the bulletin board next to the coaches' offices on the second floor of the field house. First scrimmage is this Saturday against Brackettville. I understand they're big, tough, and very physical. They don't have a football team, so anyone there who wanted to play a fall sport is probably on the squad. If you haven't already, please pick up one of the reversible practice jerseys in the equipment room. Don't lose it. It's the only one you'll get.

"It's not hard to guess that since our field is in a public park two miles from campus that our budget is limited. We'll travel to our games in cars and vans.

"I graduated from Bainbridge seven years ago and played basketball while I was here. I've never played soccer before, and it wasn't even a club sport when I was in school. I've studied the rules and strategies over the summer, but I'm going to rely on you to teach me how the game is played. We've several seniors as well as others from successful high school programs.

"Regardless of the game, and regardless of my lack of soccer experience, certain things are fundamental to all sports. First and foremost is conditioning. We don't have enough talent to win without it. Like basketball, soccer is a constant motion sport, whether guarding your opponent or getting open for a pass or shot. You have to go one hundred and ten percent from beginning to end. Your opponents will, particularly the successful ones. If you're not in shape, you can't get into position to make the plays. Period.

"Second is hustle. This goes hand in hand with conditioning. Regardless of skill level, you can always hustle. You have to believe that every ball is yours. Soccer is a low-scoring sport. Every uncontested chance you give the other guy could mean the game.

"I have one saying that sums up my feeling: *I don't mind getting beat.*" He paused for emphasis. "*But I hate to lose.*" He repeated it, louder still.

"If we try our hardest and go after every ball, then at the end of the day, we left it all on the field. If we've lost, it was because the other guy was better—or just plain lucky.

"All right, let's form one big circle. State your name, your high school, how many years you've played soccer, and what position you want to play."

Forty guys is a big circle. Most were from Indiana, New Jersey, or New York. David Nakano won the prize for farthest to travel. The majority had played some high school soccer, but it was evident that few had made an impact at the varsity level.

Hancock passed out athletic tape to number the jerseys. The seniors led calisthenics and stretching; then they broke into groups for heading, trapping, and passing. Next was pass and shoot. It was hard to decide what was more disastrous, the passes that went everywhere or the wild shots. The field was rough, but a third missed the ball entirely. After ten minutes, Hancock blew his whistle.

"Let's scrimmage," he said. "Williams and Landon, pick up sides." The Chiefs were the first five chosen. Williams's squad, in red, included Paxton, Barrett, and McIlroy.

They lined up, and blue kicked off. Play was erratic, and Hancock was trying to referee, watch the players on the field, and make substitutions.

At first, he shouted instructions: "Don't bunch up ... Move to the open space." But after a while, he just let them go. It was clear who was in shape. The Chiefs, after playing all summer, raced up and down the field. Johnson, Sheffe, Randy Williams, Landon, and a few others were in the flow. The energy was generated by the underclassmen. The remaining seniors, some with developing beer guts, only ran when the ball was in their vicinity and played no defense.

Barrett and Paxton roamed all over the field, constantly stealing the ball from the gasping upperclassmen.

"Take it easy," said Roush to Paxton, when play stopped for an injury. "You guys are making us look bad. You're hustling for nothing. We've been here for three years. We get to play first." Paxton ignored him.

After Barrett stole the ball from him for about the fourth time in a row, Roush's anger flashed, and he tried to trip him from behind, but he ran out of gas before he got close enough.

After forty minutes, the score was four to zero, in favor of Williams's team, but it had little relevance. Twice, defending fullbacks deflected the ball into their own goal. Paxton scored on a free kick from twenty yards, hooking the ball around a wall of players and into the upper right-hand corner. The last was on a great header by Dave Caldwell from a Paxton corner kick.

Hancock blew his whistle, and everyone went to the public fountain for a drink. Many were doubled over, breathing heavily. Some stretched out cramps, and others just collapsed on the grass.

Hancock looked over the squad as he talked with Randy Williams. He then divided them into offense and defense, with three defenders and a goalie against five offensive players, and announced that he wanted to call set plays like in basketball. They all greeted this with skepticism. Several simple setups were tried, but the offense, even Paxton, Penny, Millwood, Dave Caldwell, and Bill Roush together, couldn't control the ball beyond two or three passes. The coach's frustration grew with every failed attempt. Finally, he'd seen enough.

"That wasn't bad for a first day," he said. "There were some good things happening out there. However, many of you are out of shape. This is a running game. There are no timeouts. We can substitute, but if someone comes in and does a better job while you're out, your time on the bench could be longer than you wanted. Jog back, eat right, get a good night's rest. Anyone needing to see the trainer should do so tonight. Don't wait to ice down bruises. Also, if you have a schedule conflict or you're going to be late, tell me before practice. Gather up all the balls and put them in the bags."

He stopped. "Oh, and one more thing … You're now in training in a college varsity sport. You represent this university. There's no drinking or smoking … at any time … in any place. Period. If you're caught, you'll be suspended for a week. Second time, you're gone. There are no excuses. I need to know you're committed to playing this sport, not wasting my time or yours. You are men. You'll be held accountable for your actions …" He turned away again. "See you tomorrow."

The Chiefs jogged toward campus with the group, but five seniors lagged behind, continually looking back at the field.

"Paxton, slow up," yelled Bill Roush. Pappy peeled off from the group and jogged back with Penny.

"You guys need to take it easy out there," he said as they ran. "You can see this team's going nowhere. Hustle or not, we win two games every year. Most of the other schools recruit foreign players and have eighty guys try out. We don't even have twenty uniforms that match."

Pappy said nothing, and Roush grabbed his arm and pulled him to a stop.

"Hey. You're just a freshman. You'll learn." Roush kept looking around. "By the way, seniors get to play first. We've paid our dues, taking a beating for the last three years, and are entitled." Paxton and Penny stood staring, arms crossed.

Roush saw Hancock's green Ford Fairlane coming up from behind and started to jog again. Paxton and Penny accelerated, embarrassed that the coach had seen them standing.

"Slow it down," said Roush, and all waved as the coach passed. Once Hancock was out of sight, Roush and his group were walking again.

"Wait a minute," Roush said to Paxton and Penny, but they sped up. "Okay, asshole!" shouted Roush. "We'll see you out here tomorrow."

Great first day, thought Paxton. The run-in with Rattigan and Burler, the marginal talent at practice, the seniors telling everyone to loaf, and the coach catching *me* walking.

It got worse. Two cars came up behind Roush and slowed. One was an old blue Ford Falcon with much of the paint peeling off, and the other was a newer four-door Chevy Bel Air. His group got into the two cars, driven by young girls. They then pulled up alongside the others.

"Hop in," said Roush, trying to make amends, but Paxton and the rest weren't buying. "C'mon, it's too damn hot to run."

"Roush, why don't you take a hike," said Dave Caldwell. "I'm tired of your lazy ass."

Roush's face reddened, and he moved to get out of the car, but he knew he didn't stand a chance against Caldwell, and a dozen other players glared at him.

The girl driving smiled, clearly self-conscious, and accelerated, followed by the other car.

"Usually they don't start this crap until late in the season," said Caldwell. "You know, that guy hustled in high school and scored a bunch of goals his freshman and sophomore years here, but last season he started drinking and smoking … and just gave up. They'll never be ready by Saturday. I hope this coach doesn't play guys just 'cause it's their last year."

"This is the last guy on earth who'll play someone just because he's a senior," said Paxton.

Todd Hancock sat in his car on a side street, watching his players jog past and looking at his clipboard. The first practice was painful. The structure of basketball, with set plays and ball control, was totally absent. Soccer was improvising and creating on the run. It was played with the feet, not hands, on an imperfect and unpredictable surface, and his players were likewise imperfect and unpredictable. There were no time-outs and no way to stop and regroup during the game.

The Chiefs were a bonanza. Solid, experienced, enthusiastic, and mature beyond their years (except Barrett), they gave hope for the future. Winning was in their blood. They had known nothing else. As for Brian, all coaches wanted the magnificent athlete who had no fear of failure.

Hancock watched the two cars carrying Roush and company pass by. He'd hoped the seniors would provide a leadership core, but the team seldom won, and the athletic department treated them like second-class citizens. Now they were looking ahead to life after college. He sighed and started his engine.

Paxton was surprised to see the green Ford Fairlane appear ahead. Barrett's face flushed. He and several others had considered getting into one of the cars. It *was* hot, and he *was* tired. It was clear from the coach's expression that he'd seen it all. A few yards ahead, he picked up two freshmen who were limping and then continued on his way.

It was already after six, so nobody showered. The Chiefs met at the Union and sat together. This time, Barrett didn't wander off, even though three different groups of girls came by. They talked about everything that had happened that day and decided not to tell Roush that Hancock had seen them get into the cars. It was up to the coach to deal with the situation. When things were going wrong back at Amsterdam, the seniors would call a private team meeting, without the coach, and adjust some attitudes, as the senior classes had done before them.

Tuesday, August 26

⦿ ⦿ ⦿ ⦿

P hysicals were required but had been postponed, as the doctor was
out of town. Bainbridge had a full-service medical facility, with a
permanent staff of a doctor and two nurses. Everything was free, and
many prescription drugs were provided through samples furnished by
drug manufacturers.

At lunch, the Amsterdam five shoveled down hamburgers and french
fries. In the 1960s, there wasn't a lot of research and information on
sports nutrition. For example, coaches told players not to drink water
during games because they would become waterlogged and sluggish. At
the same time, trainers passed out salt pills, theoretically to replenish what
had been sweated away. High blood pressure and kidney health weren't
considered.

The Chiefs left for practice at three and caught up with some freshmen
who were walking. There were aching muscles and plenty of bruises and
strains, but mostly the guys were out of shape and tired. The Chiefs, on
the other hand, had played all summer, and the run to the field was more
boring than taxing.

Randy Williams gathered everyone at midfield for calisthenics and
stretching. The seniors were there, but no mention was made of the
previous day.

After half an hour of passing and trapping, Hancock called everyone
to midfield.

"Anyone with an injury, say so. I don't want anyone to tear a muscle ... No takers? Okay, in the red jerseys ..."

All the Chiefs were on one team, together with Scott Driver, Dave Caldwell, Sheffe, Landon, Harbaugh, and Randy Williams. The remaining seniors were the opposition in blue. Hancock placed a ball at midfield.

"Red kickoff. Red goalie ready? Blue goalie ready?" He pointed down at the ball and blew the whistle.

Penny tapped the ball to Pappy, who chipped it over the defenders to the right wing, where Caldwell was streaking down the sidelines. The ball took a bad bounce and went out of bounds. Blue throw-in. For several minutes, the play was irregular. Players went one way while the pass went another. They bunched up or two teammates would go for the ball and then both back off. Neither side threatened for the first ten minutes, and then Barrett stole the ball from Roush and blasted it forty yards into the blue defensive end. Penny switched with Caldwell and took the ball deep into the right corner, but he crossed it too close to the goal. The keeper punted it upfield, but Roush and Dick Stewart were walking back holding their sides. Paxton picked up the ball uncontested and passed to Millwood on left wing. Tim hit a beautiful cross to Penny, who rocketed the ball ten feet over the top of the goal. Two opportunities in sixty seconds. The Chiefs and their teammates were pumped.

The blue goal kick fell short of the midline. Barrett bumped Roush out of the way, stealing the ball. From forty yards, he touched off a shot that went wide.

Roush said something to Barrett as they passed, but Paxton picked off the goal kick. Now the game was being played in the blue end, and the Chiefs were on every loose ball. A shot from twenty-five yards hit Mercer in the chest and rebounded forward three yards to a waiting Penny, who drilled it into the lower left-hand corner with the outside of his left foot. It was one to zero.

Blue kickoff. Penny quickly tackled the ball from Stewart, and the red team was on the attack. With no one hustling, blue was falling farther back on defense. Paxton or McIlroy quickly picked up every ball they cleared. Even when a red player missed a trap, the blue linemen were too far back, and too tired and too slow, to take advantage. A blue fullback handball resulted in a penalty kick, which Paxton put into the upper left-hand corner. Two to zero.

The swarming hustle of the Chiefs, which fired up their teammates, was relentless. On the other squad, Roush, Stewart, and the other seniors were tired and frustrated. And pissed off. Barrett didn't attempt to hide his glee at overwhelming the opposition. It was like being back at Amsterdam, when he could roam the field knowing his teammates would cover any counterattack.

Most substitutions were on the red team, Hancock making a point about conditioning to the seniors. He was thrilled that the young players were inspired by the Chiefs' all-out hustling style. But he'd hoped this showdown would make the older players want to fight back. No such luck.

At the end, the red team had taken over twenty shots and scored four times. Hancock blew his whistle, and all assembled at midfield, most walking, hands on their hips.

"That's it for today." He paused. "Get some water before you start back." He walked around among the players as they stood breathing heavily. "Some of you guys who smoke or drink too much beer are feeling it. I told you yesterday, there's no substitute for hustle … Okay, everybody gather up the equipment. Freshmen, bring the bags over to my car."

The Chiefs led the way back to campus. They had played well and their teammates fed off the intensity. They quickly caught up with Roush's group, which was walking. The seniors began a slow trot, knowing Hancock wouldn't be far behind.

Barrett couldn't resist. "Hey, Roush, why don't you suck on a few more cigarettes?"

Roush had a flash of anger but was too tired, and Barrett towered six inches over him.

"Cool it, Barrett," said Randy Williams. No matter. The point was made.

Hancock's car went past, and the Chiefs pulled away. Right on cue, the two cars appeared. By the time Paxton's group arrived at campus, most had slowed to a walk. They would sleep well tonight.

Wednesday, August 27

◉ ◉ ◉ ◉

Orientation continued, with registration punch cards and forms to fill out and more books to be bought. The freshmen were beginning to relax. They still didn't know what to expect from classes and professors, but dorm living was becoming more routine. They still stayed up too late, listening to music and playing poker, but that was part of their new independence.

For a small middle-class school in Indiana, the population was geographically diverse. Foreign students, although few in number, came from many parts of the globe: Mexico, Japan, Western Europe, and the Mediterranean.

It was clear that guys were guys everywhere. All liked loud music— rock, folk, and even soul. *Playboy* centerfolds went up on the walls as soon as the parents left. All were sports fanatics, and many wore high school letterman jackets. Pictures of hometown sweethearts were on desktops and inside textbook covers.

Most had telephones in their rooms, and they burned up the wires calling home, friends at other schools, and the girls they'd left behind.

Bainbridge freshmen males, for the most part, grew up in small towns, with the same females. Familiarity had bred indifference, or at least ambivalence. All the disappointing, awkward adolescent romances, bad prom dates, and other misadventures were behind them. Now, at the peak of their sex drive, there were hundreds of potential new encounters.

Strange women. Exotic women. Women of all shapes and sizes. The lure of the unknown—the fantasy. Barrett had a marked head start, but the other Chiefs had met several girls at the student union. Dates with total strangers would be a new and exciting experience.

It was still summer, and the afternoon air was hot and muggy. The Chiefs dressed at Roberts Hall and jogged down to the field. They were tired, and bruises and scrapes had multiplied. Their practice jerseys were filthy, the bacteria thriving in the heat. Players were already loosening up when they arrived. Even though it was only late August, the first hint of color was coming into the trees. The tops of the tallest swayed unevenly with the gusts, and the rustling dry leaves sounded the imminent arrival of fall. The days would grow shorter and the nights colder.

Pappy had played since he was eight, and his excitement and love of the game made each season special. Unlike Indiana, summer often came to an early end in Upstate New York. One year at soccer camp in late August on a mountaintop near Jamestown, it was so cold at night that Andrew kept a hot water bottle in the bottom of his sleeping bag. Frost formed every morning on the grass, and the boys piled on every piece of clothing they had. Goalies were lucky. They had brought gloves.

Day three of practice, and the stress of two sessions of all-out scrimmages and late night card games left even the Chiefs dazed and confused. Their feet were like lead, and everyone moved in slow motion. Passing drills were an embarrassment. Shots went in all directions. The scrimmage was no better. An hour of sloppy play and bad attitudes was all Hancock could tolerate.

"Get over here. Now! Everyone, on the double!" he screamed, throwing his clipboard to the ground. He paced back and forth, saying nothing.

"We've a scrimmage in three days, and you guys want to screw around. We don't have time to screw around! I have twenty game uniforms, and that's all I'm going to dress. There are thirty-six of you out here, so some are going to be disappointed. I don't care how good you are—or how good you *think* you are. You get here late for practice after only two days, huffing and puffing, and then wonder why you can't make a pass. Well, since you didn't come here in shape, we'll get in shape. Seven of you walked over here, so you can all take seven laps around the field, and the last five guys to finish will do five more. Now get going."

All groaned and took off jogging, splitting into small groups. Several tried to get everyone to run together, but Roush's senior cronies scoffed, and others couldn't keep up even a slow pace. Johnson and Sheffe were with the Chiefs and ten others in the first group. Penny and Caldwell finished the final lap with a sprint. The stragglers were a full field length behind the pack.

Hancock calmed down, recognizing that his anger came from the continued apathy of the five seniors. Too bad, because had they shown effort, all other things equal, he would have played them first, particularly those who had paid their dues over four years. Now they were a growing liability. To do nothing would mean hustling didn't matter.

Hancock called off practice early but had the Chiefs stay after, together with the goalies and Dave Caldwell. They practiced penalty and corner kicks. Caldwell, Millwood, and Paxton were all equally skilled at corners, but when it came to the penalty line, although Penny and Caldwell took their turns, all deferred to Paxton. He was deadly accurate with the instep or outside of either foot. Sometimes he struck the ball with such force that the goalie barely had time to flinch. Often he spun or hooked the shot, so even if the goalie got a hand on it, it would twist away.

After watching for a while, Hancock decided he was going to challenge all to a penalty kick contest. He placed the ball on the line, took three steps back, and ran forward, striking out with what looked like a size six sneaker. He stretched too far, the resulting kick little more than a tap. Several chuckled and looked away, embarrassed, but he was determined to succeed and unaffected by his misses. He'd studied the others, noting how they approached the ball, where they placed their feet, and how the goalie reacted. His shot improved each time. The players saw their coach strive for perfection in a sport he had never played, and their admiration for him grew. He had none of their fear of embarrassment. They began giving him tips and cheering his successes. He even broke a smile on several occasions, which made him even more human.

Pappy showed him how to "shoot the panels," which is a way of kicking a specific point on the ball to make it go in a certain direction. If someone struck the ball lower left, it would go in the upper right corner of the goal, and vice versa. When he came in at an angle, swung his leg, and leaned back, the ball would spin and hook. Coming straight on and snapping with his knee over the ball at impact, the ball appeared to leap off his foot. After a dozen shots, the coach was pumped. He'd now beaten the goalies three straight times and was conferring with Paxton on every shot. Finally, by the time practice had officially ended an hour earlier, the sun was low in the sky, and everyone headed for home.

Thursday, August 28

⊙ ⊙ ⊙ ⊙

Thursday, first day of registration for freshmen. The manual process required standing in long lines, often to find the class was full. The later in the day, the longer the wait and the fewer options left. Fortunately, athletes got preferential treatment. For science courses, however, athlete or not, that often meant eight o'clock morning classes. Ugh. Dawn patrol.

They all met for lunch, but Barrett tended to wander off during each meal to visit with a growing number of freshman women. Penny, Millwood, and McIlroy would pass by, hoping to be introduced, and Barrett was happy to oblige. Paxton, however, usually kept his distance. The girls knew him as "Barrett's roommate," said hi, and called him Pappy when they saw him on campus. He assumed they were being friendly to improve their chances with Brian.

Back at the dorm, Andrew wrote letters to his parents and friends at other schools. He scribbled several lines on each, knowing the more he sent, the more he'd receive. It felt as if he'd aged a year in four days of college. Amsterdam was now distant, yet his thoughts were flooded with memories.

Hometown sweethearts or not, the two main topics of conversation at Roberts Hall were college football and women. The "baby book" was studied like a scientific treatise, and notes on each girl were exchanged. Every known scandal or indiscretion, whether real or imagined, was discussed and embellished upon with hormonal relish. Girls' reputations were made and trashed in an instant, and rumors could spread throughout the entire male population in an evening.

Three o'clock came quickly, and the guys took off jogging down the now-familiar park road. Two days until they would play a real game. It seemed a lifetime since the state championship a year ago.

A small group of freshmen eager beavers had arrived first. Hancock appreciated their enthusiasm, but team spirit would count for little. Their skill level left little hope they'd see much playing time.

Roush and Stewart showed up shortly thereafter, but the other three seniors of their group were absent. After warm-ups and calisthenics, Hancock called them over.

"You can see we are missing some faces. Eight players turned their practice jerseys in today. I'm sorry to say three were seniors who played the last three years, but they're thinking about graduation, getting jobs, and moving on.

"For the scrimmage Saturday, we'll meet at the field house at eight forty-five. The vans will leave promptly at nine. If you're not there, we have many eager to take your place. Brackettville is a big team, and they play physically. I've heard a lot of talk that since you've beaten them every year, this is a guaranteed win. If that's your attitude, then you may as well stay home, because you'll get your collective butts kicked. We're not good enough to take anyone for granted. If you don't hustle, I promise you they will. I haven't seen anyone out here who doesn't have room for vast improvement.

"This afternoon we'll scrimmage for ninety minutes. Tomorrow we'll keep contact to a minimum. I want everyone healthy and fresh Saturday morning. Okay, same teams as Tuesday. Williams, you and Caldwell are captains of the red team. Set your starting lineup. I'll send in the substitutions. Landon, you're captain of the blue team. We're only going to be out here for ninety minutes more, and everyone is going to get playing time, so make the most of the opportunity."

Blue kicked off. Roush passed to Knight on left wing, but Barrett cut it off and bombed the ball deep into the blue end. The red team didn't have time to get down the field, and Hancock immediately blew his whistle.

"Who was that pass to?" he screamed at Barrett. "What have we been saying the past three days? Make every pass count. Control the ball. It doesn't do any good to kick it all over the place."

"Don't get all excited," said Barrett offhandedly. "I wanted to clear the ball down in their end."

Hancock clearly hadn't expected a response and didn't want one. "I'll get excited, Mr. Barrett," said Hancock, now headed in his direction. Pappy started to go between them.

"Stay where you are, Paxton," said the coach. "You made a great play, Roush made a lousy decision, and then you blew it by handing it to the other team. This is the third time this week we've talked about this, and I don't want to have this conversation again." Hancock turned back to the middle of the field.

"We scored twice on Tuesday from fast breaks," replied Barrett, still defiant.

Hancock turned back yet again, now furious. "We scored two goals on ourselves, not another team who is probably better than us. This isn't Amsterdam, and we are going to play this game my way."

"And what way is that?" asked Barrett.

All four of the other Chiefs groaned in unison, along with several other players.

"Barrett, get off the field! Now!" said Hancock.

Brian stormed over to the sidelines and ripped off his practice jersey. Nakano moved to fullback. At first, the red team was tentative, embarrassed by Barrett's outburst and fearing Hancock's reaction to their mistakes. Although not brash and confident like Barrett, Nakano had excellent balance, good skills, and banged into the other players like a small tank. Then the red team began to bear down on offense. Nakano replaced Barrett as Bill Roush's worst nightmare, repeatedly beating him to the ball. Hancock substituted freely but left Barrett on the sidelines.

After half an hour, Paxton began to limp, and he went over to the sidelines where Barrett stood, arms folded defiantly. "Cut the crap," said Paxton in a hush as he rubbed liniment on his right calf. "We need you on the field."

"Yeah, well, that guy doesn't think so," replied Barrett, loud enough for others to hear.

"This ain't Amsterdam, and that's not Coach Stanley. He's gonna coach the way he thinks best, and believe me, he'll do it with or without you."

"I can't take this bull, man," said Barrett more quietly. "That guy doesn't know what he's doing."

"You're right," said Pappy out of the side of his mouth, "and he knows it. But he's the only voice out there. It's his team, not ours."

Barrett walked away and paced back and forth on the sideline. Talking to Pappy was like talking to his father, and the last thing he wanted right now was a parent for a teammate, particularly when he knew the teammate was right. Paxton went back in the game.

Roush and the blue put up little struggle. The red team's banging was taking its toll. Hancock was worried. Lack of hustle by the blue meant he had few good substitutes. It was clear that the red squad would see the most action on Saturday.

After practice, Hancock left quickly. He knew most were tired, and he didn't want them to have to run back to campus. The Chiefs joined up with Barrett and others on the way, but he said little. He knew he'd get little sympathy from Pappy, and the other guys were trying to stay out of it.

They dressed and went down to dinner. The usual parade of females came by, but Barrett wasn't in the mood. Afterward, they went back to the room, and Brian put on his Beach Boys album.

"I don't know about all this," said Barrett, sitting on his bed and staring at the wall. "Sometimes I feel like hopping a bus and heading back out West. I'm tired of going to school … This team's going to suck … I could be on the road right now."

Paxton put down his book. "We've been here five days. Classes haven't even started. You have every broad on campus after you …" Something struck the window, and a dirt clod was stuck to the middle of the glass. He looked out to see three girls twenty feet away, waving from the parking lot behind the dorm.

"Pappy, where's Barrett?" called one of them.

Paxton sighed. "Your fans are here. Would you like me to leave?"

Barrett hopped out of bed and tried to open the window, but the layers of paint over the years wouldn't yield. He then waved to them. "Come on," he said to Pappy. "Let's go downtown."

"It's eight o'clock. The girls have curfew."

"So?" he said, changing shirts. "They can walk back by themselves. We can stay."

"Hancock said no drinking during the season," said Paxton.

"What are you, like, ninety years old?" asked Barrett, disgusted. "One beer isn't gonna hurt, and he can't tell us what to do after hours."

"He can kick us off the team," said Paxton.

"Well, the season doesn't start until Saturday, and school does not officially start until Monday, and I am officially going to have a beer. Are you coming?"

Everything in Pappy told him not to go. While he drank in high school like everyone else, there was nothing he wanted more than to play college soccer. But he didn't want Barrett thrown off either. So maybe he should go along and make sure nobody got into trouble. Watching Barrett dazzle women was better than the nightly card game down the hall.

Barrett called the other Chiefs, but Millwood and McIlroy couldn't be found, so it was the two of them and Penny. They walked down Freemont Avenue, toward downtown, the three girls in front with Barrett, and Penny and Paxton behind.

Fitzgerald's had been a Bainbridge haunt for years. Townies seldom came in, but on weekends it was a good idea to travel in groups, in case locals drove by looking for trouble. The small bar was poorly lit and old. The ceiling was low, and the floor was black-and-white linoleum. There were no waitresses. Imitation leather booths with Formica tables surrounded the modest dance floor. The jukebox was always blaring, playing the latest tunes, and on weekends the place was packed with drunken college students. Tonight it was half-full, with only a few women. The group sat in the oversized corner booth, and Pappy pulled up a chair. They ordered two pitchers of 3.2 beer. Rolling Rock was on tap, along with Budweiser, Strohs, and Schlitz, "the beer that made Milwaukee famous."

Free bowls of Spanish peanuts and cheese doodles were management's way of selling more drinks. Everyone poured a glass except Pappy, who kept glancing at the door as if Eliot Ness were going to raid the place at any minute. He was chided by all as "not having a hair on his ass," a colloquial term for coward.

The talk and laughter got louder as the alcohol took effect. Credence Clearwater Revival's "Rollin' on the River" rocked, but the dance floor was empty. Even though Andrew was surrounded by friends from home, this wasn't the Village Tavern, where he would have known half the people in the place.

One of the girls was engaged in an animated conversation with Penny, abandoning competing for Barrett's attention. Brian tried to bring Pappy in on the discussion, but his mind was on Saturday.

He mentally played every game in advance. In New York, he knew many of his opponents by name, particularly the stars. Amsterdam's coach Fred Stanley always had the inside scoop on the other team. Here it was the unknown.

Andrew decided to call it a night. He stood up and turned toward the door, and then sat back down. Coming in were Beth Littlefield and two other girls from her floor. Pappy checked his watch. It was after ten o'clock. What was she doing out this late? And here was Barrett, being pawed by two girls.

Pappy shifted uncomfortably in his seat. He couldn't see what was going on behind him, but he could tell that Barrett had seen Littlefield. Their group went over and sat in a booth on the other side of the dance floor.

Andrew didn't need to look at her again. The image was already burned in his head—what she was wearing … how her golden hair was combed. He worried he was a pervert for being able to recall her appearance with such detail. After five minutes of staring at the table, he decided to leave.

"I'm heading out," he said, getting to his feet. "See you guys in the a.m."

"Where you goin'?" said Barrett in a loud voice. "Sit down. Relax. The night is just getting started. We don't have anything tomorrow. I'm not getting up until noon."

"Nah, I'm beat," said Pappy, stretching and faking a yawn.

"C'mon, everyone wants you to stay. Right?" said Barrett, throwing his arms around and hugging two girls to him. "Don't be such a weenie." Pappy stared at him, and Barrett knew he'd stepped across the line.

"Adios. Nice meeting you," he said to the girls. He turned … and ran right into Beth Littlefield, carrying three mugs and a pitcher. She gasped and jumped back as the beer splashed on the floor.

"Oh my God, I'm sorry," said Andrew, looking helpless. "Jesus." He shook his head.

"Calm down. It's okay, Pappy," said Littlefield, smiling. "Relax. No harm done."

"I'll get a rag … towel … uh," said Andrew, and he lunged past her toward the bar, knocking into her again. She set the pitcher and glasses on the bar next to him.

"I can—" But before she could say anything more, Andrew was wiping up the floor. He came back and handed the towel to the bartender. Littlefield watched this normally calm, intelligent boy go berserk over spilled beer in a bar.

"Sorry again," he said, turning and walking out.

Only a few ounces had been lost, but the bartender filled it again, and she went back to join her friends.

As soon as he was outside, Pappy looked back and breathed a sigh of relief. And then, as usual, got mad at himself.

Why do I act this way? he wondered. *Why does Barrett treat her like dirt? He doesn't give a damn about her. I should just say something.* Pappy was so hyped up that he began to jog and then run. When he reached campus, he was sprinting, and he passed a group of upperclassmen in front of the Union. They stared at the freshman racing down the street for no apparent reason, and Pappy slowed to a walk, embarrassed. He hiked up the hill to Roberts Hall, where the first-floor poker games had grown smaller. Three more days of freedom and revelry before classes started, and for the card players, homesickness was being replaced by gambler's remorse.

Andrew climbed up on his top bunk, still grinding on himself for spilling the beer, also not happy about Barrett's heartless treatment of Littlefield.

It was a good night, reflected Beth Littlefield as she turned the key to her room at Weatherly Hall, sneaking in just before midnight. Seeing Barrett at Fitzgerald's had been tough, as it had been every time since the breakup, but the alcohol had numbed her senses without causing an emotional collapse. She made it back to the dorm without bursting into tears—yet. Now in the darkness, she could let go. She lived alone. Her assigned roommate decided at the last minute to go to another school, and the registrar at Bain had given Littlefield the choice of paying 50 percent more and living by herself. Money was no object, but Beth's parents were concerned about her isolation.

Smart, rich, and beautiful, her blonde hair and cheerleader looks, together with stellar grades, made her the envy of most. However, these blessings made it difficult to have many friends. No girls wanted to go to parties with her. To do so was to invite immediate comparison by every boy in the room. To the few who really knew her well, she was a true friend, without motive or pretense—too honest and genuine to hang with the popular crowd. So she spent most of her high school days with Barrett, content to allow him to revel in his own popularity.

But now she was alone at college. No old friends. No confidants. Just acquaintances. As it had been all her life, the girls in the dorm were intimidated by her stunning beauty and obvious wealth. And her seclusion only reinforced the assumption that she was cold and aloof.

Now the shroud of depression enveloped her in a kind of darkness that churned her stomach, making her body feel like lead. She wrapped her arms around the pillow, unable to feel whether the room was hot or cold. It was past the time she could console herself with dreams of Barrett coming back to her. Now she was faced with the reality that his feelings for her were gone.

Friday, August 29

⊚ ⊚ ⊚ ⊚

L ast day of orientation before real college classes on Monday, and little
was scheduled. Barrett stumbled in after midnight, but was up and
out the door by nine to go beg his way into another course that was full
when he registered. Waiting to take the class second semester would put
him behind almost a year, as the biology premed program had to be taken
in sequence. But Bainbridge would find room for him. Premed students
led to wealthy doctors and then wealthy alumni and wealthy donors.

Pappy woke late, stomach growling. His first college game tomorrow.
Classes Monday. The butterflies and frequent trips to the bathroom were
constants.

That morning, there were a few lectures, and some of the social clubs
and political groups set up informational booths at the Union. At noon,
there was a picnic in Commencement Hollow, a large depression at the
base of the main hill on campus. A live band played their renditions of
popular sixties tunes, and barbecued chicken and ribs were served. Barrett
was nowhere to be found, so Pappy met up with Millwood and McIlroy.

The three Chiefs sat and watched the girls go by. It was a sunny day,
almost seventy degrees, and the coeds were wearing as little as possible.
McIlroy and Millwood exchanged names and comments about several
they had seen in the baby book or had met through Barrett. None of them
could ever remember an adult's name when introduced by their parents, but
members of the opposite sex were etched in hormones on their brains.

They hung around for a while, and then Andrew went back up the hill to Roberts Hall to wait for the mail. His dad sent him some news clippings about the Amsterdam Volunteer Fire Company, and two girls who were friends sent letters containing long diatribes about the shortcomings of their boyfriends.

The first floor was empty, save Richard Berber, who seemed to do his laundry every day. Pappy dressed early for practice and lay on the bed, stomach turning over. Barrett came in around two thirty, making a ruckus coming through the door and leaping up on Andrew's upper bunk.

"Hi, roomie," he said, being intentionally obnoxious. Andrew smelled beer on his breath. Great. Hancock was mad enough at Barrett's recent outbursts. Now he was going to practice the day before their first game drunk. That torqued the knot in Paxton's stomach a few more notches.

Brian could see by the look on his roommate's face that he was going to get lecture number eleven. But Andrew was too wound up for confrontation.

"Do me a favor and drink some mouthwash before you go to practice," Pappy said in disgust.

Everyone was at the field early. They were down to thirty players. Hancock knew he'd have to let all dress in the future, at least for home games, or more would lose interest and drop off. They needed at least twenty-two to have eleven on a side for full scrimmages at practice.

After ninety minutes of passing and shooting drills, Hancock called them to midfield.

"Get some rest. It's Friday night. Don't do anything stupid. No beer. No cigarettes. Write a letter to your parents. Your girlfriend. Go bowling at the Union." He gave them one more glare. "Get going."

For the first time, the run back started out as a walk for the Chiefs. Hancock left quickly, so they knew he wouldn't be lurking down the road. They'd put in a good week's work and were developing into the nucleus of the team. The older guys were recounting past games against Brackettville. A small church school, the team was big and physical but not skilled. For some unknown reason, no matter what the outcome, each contest had ended in a fight. Not a full-blown bench-clearing exchange, but punches were thrown, with neither side remembering who started it.

The sky was overcast and the temperature dropping. A west wind was at their backs and picking up steam, so they began to trot. They scattered as they reached the middle of campus, making plans to meet at the Union for dinner.

Friday night and it was party time again. Upperclassmen, particularly the fraternities and sororities, were rolling into town, and it was time to kick back. The game the next morning be damned—there was just too much beer and too many women for the Chiefs (except Pappy, of course), and most of the other soccer players, to resist. Every frat house had a keg (or two) already flowing on the front porch by the time dinner was over. Some had started at noon.

Even Pappy wanted to be a part of the revelry, so long as it didn't get out of hand. But he wouldn't drink. And despite his puppy love for Littlefield, he wasn't opposed to looking at the female upperclassmen, all of whom dressed to the nines and carried an air of sophistication and worldliness that added excitement and mystery.

The other Chiefs were obvious in their intentions, but they didn't have to be suave. Or even civil. After all, they had Barrett with them, the unfailing stallion of the herd. Just watching him operate was enough to bolster their nerve.

And to their surprise, it wasn't as difficult as it had been at Amsterdam High. There were no histories of adolescent humiliations and burned relationships. The slate was wiped clean. Everyone was in the same primordial soup, their behavior prompted by loneliness, driven by hormones and the need for acceptance. Even if just for an evening.

The beer brought out the braggadocio, and often *gaping*, behavior of the boys not yet turned men. *Gaping* was a derivative of the verb *to gape*, a synonym for *flamer*—an accurate description of the conduct of an insecure nineteen-year-old male after several beers, when encountering an attractive but as yet unfamiliar female.

And by eight o'clock, the boys' libidos were in full swing. First stop was the TDT house at the north end of the campus, home to Randy Williams and Al Landon. Although they had football and basketball players among their members, they also had golfers, pool players, swimmers, wrestlers, and track stars. Their house grade point average was far above the campus norm, and many of their number were involved in student government. The only two soccer players in the house, and both about to graduate, Williams and Landon would campaign hard to get as many of the Chiefs as possible.

Not that the TDTs were nerds. Two kegs were opened and flowing, and some of the older female students were already there. Williams, who called over several brothers to put on the full-scale rush, greeted the Chiefs. Pappy and Barrett stayed to visit for a while, but Millwood, Penny, and McIlroy left after an hour, heading toward Lambda Kappa Lambda. A huge ancient boardinghouse, it had all the size but none of the impressive external features of the Silo's quarters. The wide porch looked like a row house in Philadelphia or New York City.

Most of their members congregated out front, and by eight o'clock, one of the kegs was already dry. Unlike the TDTs, who made it a point to conduct introductions, the Lambda Kappas greeted everyone who approached with, "Hi, have a damn beer." There were more girls here, and they were younger and dressed more casually than those at the TDT house. Located closer to campus, their blaring stereo could be heard all the way to the girls' dorms.

Domicile of Glenn Johnson, John Harbaugh, and a couple of other soccer players, it was decidedly more informal. The furniture looked as if it had been soaked in some form of alcohol at one time or another. The guys were as interested in the girls as they were in rush prospects, which made the Chiefs more at ease. They didn't feel they were being examined and could do their own leering at females.

Barrett soon walked off with two sophomore women, leaving Pappy at the TDT house. It was almost ten o'clock. The party was still rocking, and he could hear music all over the campus, but starting to think about the game the next day, he headed for Roberts Hall.

The dorm was deserted, although every light in the building was on. He walked down the barren corridor and into his room. Maybe he would write a few letters … There were some voices coming down the hall—female voices. He looked out to see three girls, all blondes, sticking their heads into each door. They saw Pappy.

"Say, do you know which room is Brian's?" they asked, smiling broadly from the effects of too much alcohol. Pappy said nothing at first.

One girl turned to another. "What's Brian's last name?"

"Barrett," said Pappy, trying to look at ease in front of three women he knew were looking for something, or someone, better.

They rushed over. "Are you his roommate?" the tallest asked. "Are you Pappy?" Her tone was definitely friendly, which took Andrew by surprise.

"You're the great soccer player they're all talking about," she gushed, all three pinning him in against the wall. Paxton had the deer in the headlights look and couldn't utter a word.

"Brian says you're a great guy … Brian is a great guy," she continued, with 80-proof breath. "Do you know when he will be back? He's supposed to meet us here." Pappy was still looking for a syllable, anything.

"I don't know where he went," said Andrew. "I think he might be at the Lambda Kappa house." They stood for a moment, hoping for an invitation to wait until he returned. Pappy offered none.

"Okay, well, we'll head down there. Want to come along?"

"Well, no, I was going to write some letters, and we've a game tomorrow." The girls were surprised.

"Isn't Brian playing in the same game?" asked one, but the other two were already well down the hall.

"Yeah," said Andrew, "you might remind him when you see him." They were now at the door, but one of them, the shortest, looked back and smiled before they left.

Barrett met up with the other Chiefs at the Lambda Kappa house, and they drank a while longer, but it was now eleven, and a week of practice and two quarts of beer were taking their toll. When Penny, McIlroy, and Millwood left, Barrett chastised them for wimping out and turned his attentions to the steady stream of blondes and brunettes who appeared to be on a circuit of the houses.

Things were starting to get fuzzy, but he remembered telling some sophomores to meet him at his room at eleven … or was it twelve? What were their names again? He was trying to recall their faces to determine whether he should give up this prime spot for screening talent and settle for the three ...

"Game tomorrow, Barrett," said Johnson, appearing in the doorway without a beer or a girl. "Time to hit the rack. We're counting on you Amsterdam guys. It's going to be a rough one." Suddenly, the beer and jovial talk turned serious, as things sometimes do after too much alcohol.

"Last year really sucked," said Johnson. "Playing is fun, and we've had a good bunch of guys, but it's hard to show your face on campus or tell anyone about the team when you only win two or three games the whole season." His voice became much lower and quieter.

"We all believe that with you and Don and Pappy and Tim and Jim, we can win." Embarrassed by his emotions, Johnson stepped back. "I'm takin' it to the barn. See you in the morning."

Barrett was beginning to sober up, and Johnson's words sunk in. He'd never thought about losing ... or about winning only two or three games. The concept was unimaginable. But this wasn't Amsterdam, and there were only five Chiefs.

He stepped off the porch, emptied his beer in the bushes, and walked back to Roberts Hall.

Saturday, August 30

⊙ ⊙ ⊙ ⊙

Saturday morning. The brilliant sun rose above the maple trees, and the air was clear and cool. Those still hungover squinted and shaded their eyes while heading toward breakfast. Pappy had set the alarm for seven, but he woke every hour so they wouldn't oversleep. Barrett never heard a thing from the time he crashed.

The Chiefs, last to arrive, wolfed down their food in nervous excitement. The upperclassmen were more interested in discussing the freshman coeds from last night's parties. The fact that most had girlfriends or fiancées didn't dampen their enthusiasm.

Pappy was, as usual, a nervous wreck. Perfect fodder for Barrett, who had sought for years, in vain, to find a way to ease his teammate's pregame anxiety.

"How many trips to the john so far, roomie?" asked Barrett. Paxton stood up from his tray, took a deep breath, and walked away. *Well,* thought Barrett, *I was a jerk, but now he's pissed at me and not thinking about the game.*

Three Ford Fairlane sedans and a large van were waiting in front of the field house, engines running. Hancock's familiar green buggy was there as well. Water vapor condensed out of the exhaust in the cold morning air. As would happen all season, the soccer team was on the road when there was a home football game. They'd finish in Brackettville by two o'clock and arrive back at campus just in time to miss most of the game.

They loaded up, seniors behind the wheel. Randy Williams and Al Landon took one sedan and made sure Barrett and Paxton rode with them. Never pass up an opportunity to do a little fraternity rushing. Sheffe, Johnson, and Harbaugh protested, so they got Penny, Millwood, and McIlroy in the van. Brackettville was ninety miles away, mostly on country roads, and after some brief directions from Hancock, and admonitions to stick together, they took off. Morning traffic was light, and they were out of town in just a few minutes. They separated once, when a traffic light cycled too quickly, but Hancock was leading the pack and driving the speed limit, so the rest caught up.

Conversation shifted from music to girls to the game. The Brackettville coach was like Hancock—what soccer he knew came from a book. Run and kick was the plan, as his players had little talent to do more.

The town of Brackettville, population three thousand, was four corners, with a gas station and combination town hall, volunteer fire department, and public library. Railroad tracks ran alongside the major north-south highway, and grain elevators were visible a quarter mile to the north. This was Indiana farm country. Corn, sorghum, and other grains blanketed the landscape, and farm stands selling produce were an important part of local commerce. Everyone had chickens and dairy cows to go along with the odd assortment of pigs, goats, ducks, and even some horses. Summer was waning, and fresh vegetables were dwindling. Soon it would be apples and apple cider, gourds, pumpkins, hay, straw, cabbages, and cauliflower. Stands of evergreens that would be people's Christmas trees in a few short months dotted the hillsides. Pappy looked out the window and thought back on his days of hunting and fishing in Upstate New York with his dad and brother.

The game was now less than an hour away, and he was short of breath thinking about it. Many of his Amsterdam teammates would sit the bench the first year, but today he, Penny, Barrett, and Millwood would start, and McIlroy would see plenty of playing time.

They turned off the main road through an open stone gate with an old wrought iron arch that said simply Brackettville. There was the field. Flat, wide open, well-marked, No spectators. Just the other team, all dressed in blue, and the coach and trainer.

The Brackettville "Little Giants" are pretty damn big, thought Andrew Paxton as he climbed out of the car. It always seemed the other team was larger. Two or three looked like football linemen, with blond locks, big biceps, and no necks. The Giants' short hair was in stark contrast to the Titans', who had all manner of styles and lengths.

As seniors led them on a lap around the field, they watched their opponents intently. Booming kicks were punctuated by errant passes. Head balls bounded off the tops of skulls, and some kicked using their toes. The goalie, in stark contrast to the other players, was five-seven and 110 pounds. He popped back and forth in the goal as balls rained in from all angles, most of them high or wide.

The Titans circled up for some quick calisthenics and then split into groups for pass and trap. Paxton and Caldwell took corner kicks, and Andrew, half a dozen penalties.

In a few minutes, the Chiefs were at midfield. Landon, Caldwell, and Driver joined them, becoming part of the Chiefs' tradition. But there was little to see. Skills were sparse. Sometimes the Little Giants would swing and totally miss the ball.

The referee called the captains to midfield, and the Titans won the coin toss.

"This is the first game of the season," said Hancock, "and whether it counts for anything or not, it will set the tone." He spoke in a low voice. "They're big and strong. The seniors have told you that this will be a cakewalk. Well, if you hustle and play the way I believe you can, it may well be. But if you don't, and you let them beat you, you'll have to go back and tell everyone at the dorm or frat house how you lost to the Little Giants." Several snickered but stopped when they saw Hancock's glare. He turned to the Chiefs, standing together. "I understand that you guys are not used to losing. High school is history. This is a new year, a new school, and a new team. You make your mark here, today." He then put his hand in the middle of the circle. All others put theirs on top. "One, two, three ... Titans."

The starters trotted out. It was before noon. There were small groups of four or five students, probably girlfriends of the Brackettville players, and a handful of adults. No cheerleaders. No bleachers packed with classmates and parents. It was a nonevent. *Probably just like Bainbridge,* thought Andrew. How many people would go all the way to Darby Park for a soccer game, particularly if the football team was playing?

The Titans were in a four-two-four formation, suggested by the Chiefs the second day of practice: four linemen, two halfbacks or midfielders, and four fullbacks. Hancock knew no better, so he agreed. Andrew Paxton was at left halfback and Driver at right. Penny was inside right forward; Roush was the other inside; Millwood at left wing; and Caldwell outside right. Landon, Barrett, Harbaugh, and Sheffe were fullbacks, with Williams in the goal. Pappy couldn't tell what formation Brackettville was using. There were players bunched in the middle of the field, and the rest were scattered.

The referee, in his fifties, short with balding brown hair and progressing waistline, signaled the two linesmen, checked ready with the two goalies, and blew his whistle. Penny passed to Roush, who bumped it back to Paxton. Andrew raced forward and swung his right foot toward Millwood on left wing just as the ball hit a rock and popped up. It glanced off the outside of his foot and shot straight at Caldwell on right wing, a perfect pass, which went under his foot and out of bounds. Confusion reigned the first few minutes. After numerous horrific plays and four throw-ins by each side, Barrett stole the ball from the Brackettville forward, who must have been six feet four and weighed 240 pounds, and boomed it into the offensive end. Penny arrived at the ball the same time as one of the fullbacks. The *whap* of flesh-on-flesh put both players on their backsides. Caldwell and Millwood, becoming frustrated, started angling toward the middle. Hancock reached for a whistle to call time-out. Wrong sport. No way to stop and regroup, so he substituted Nakano and McIlroy for Roush and Driver. The transformation was immediate. The four Chiefs now looked for Paxton to control the game. With four fullbacks and McIlroy next to him, Pappy was free to sweep behind the line, pushing the offense. Barrett moved up as well, pounding every loose ball toward the goal.

The first score came at the twenty-minute mark—for Brackettville. Their left inside forward tried to head a high cross from the wing, but it went off the side of his head (his eyes were closed) and straight to the center forward, who took a mighty swipe and missed it entirely. Paul Sheffe, running full tilt toward the net, never expected the ball, which became tangled in his legs, and he and the ball ran into the goal. One to nothing, Brackettville.

Hancock shook his head in disbelief. In basketball, if a player tipped a rebound into the opponent's basket, it was two points. Soccer goals were so few that this was like a player scoring twenty points at once for the other team.

The Chiefs were surprisingly unaffected. Millwood, Penny, and Paxton raced back to the center for the kickoff. The pass went from Penny to Pappy and back to Barrett. They all took off for the goal as Brian pounded the ball high in the air toward the end line. The goalie raced out to intercept, but the ball came down with topspin and, with the wind behind it, took a huge bounce four feet over the goalie's head. Penny tapped it into the empty net. Tie game in twenty seconds.

Now the Chiefs were pumped. Brackettville kicked off, but Penny stole the ball and passed quickly to Caldwell, who took it deep in the corner before the fullback kicked it out of bounds. Paxton took the throw-in, and the Brackettville defenders closed within twenty yards, ignoring Penny standing just outside the goalie box. The goalie also moved almost to the edge of the penalty area. Andrew took three steps and heaved the ball fifty yards into the goalmouth. None of the Little Giants had ever seen a throw-in that looked like a corner kick. Penny chest-trapped to his right foot and volleyed it in. Two to one.

All five Chiefs were now stealing passes and charging the goal at every opportunity. After three missed shots, Pappy intercepted the ball thirty yards out, pivoted, and hooked the ball inside the right bar. The goalie never moved. Three to one.

At halftime, guys were slapping backs and talking about the great season they were going to have, making Hancock uncomfortable. When Brackettville scored first, he'd feared the Titans would get down. Now overconfidence was the enemy. They would face opponents far more skilled and experienced. And there were only five Chiefs—all freshmen.

"All right," said Hancock as the players gathered around. "We did some good things against a pretty poor team. This isn't what we'll face at other schools. This half I want us to control the ball more, not just blast it from one end to the other. Keep the pressure on. Keep talking. Play your men tight. Paxton and Barrett shouldn't be the only ones contesting loose balls. Everyone has to push the ball up the field."

The second half began another ten minutes of players booting the ball all over the field. Then play got rough. The Brackettville players' frustrations, coupled with their lack of talent, resulted in them banging into everyone. The referee, seeing Titans were controlling the game, kept his foul calls to a minimum. At the twenty-minute mark, Penny shot from twenty yards, which hit the crossbar and bounced straight back at him. A Brackettville fullback, all six feet three and 220 pounds of muscle of him, flattened Don just as he shot, the ball sailing over the net. The referee ignored the blatant foul and signaled goal kick. Penny popped up screaming and shoved the fullback. Then the referee blew his whistle and reached for his book, a note pad where referees keep track of player warnings and ejections … but too late. Players from both sides were running toward the scuffle. Penny and the Brackettville fullback both missed with wild punches. Pappy raced in, knocked Penny aside, wrapped the much larger player in a bear hug, lifted, turned, and slammed him to the ground. Pappy went down with him, holding on for dear life, so his much bigger opponent couldn't extend his arms and pummel him. Now players from both sides, thinking the real battle was on the ground, turned their attention to pulling them apart.

"Take it easy, take it easy, take it easy!" shouted Andrew.

"Okay, okay, okay! I'm okay," said the fullback.

The referee waved his arms and blew his whistle. It had been mostly pushing and shoving. No blows were landed. Pappy's scuffle became the focus of both teams, and Penny, who'd started it all, now stood by uninvolved.

Andrew let go, stood up, and extended a hand to the now-pacified Giant.

"Sorry," said Andrew.

"Me too," said the fullback, now towering over his opponent.

"Dumb," said Pappy.

"Yeah," he said, and walked away.

Andrew turned and almost knocked over Hancock, who was standing next to him and staring. The coach was against fighting but impressed that the freshman had raced to his teammate's aid. Fortunately, he didn't realize that Paxton's main motivation for the death grip on the fullback was a cowardly act of self-preservation.

"All right, everyone off the field!" screamed Hancock, faking rage. He knew the referee's lack of control caused the breakdown, but the time would come when tempers flare in an important game, and he couldn't afford anyone, especially the Chiefs, to be baited into an ejection.

They waited while Hancock and the Brackettville coach talked. Penny and Barrett slapped Pappy on the back for vanquishing the hulk, and others praised the gutsy freshman, who was secretly glad to be in one piece.

Penny and the Brackettville player were ejected, but neither side would have to play short. Hancock agreed that Paxton and Barrett were also through for the day, as were two other Brackettville players. That was fine with Hancock, who was going to substitute freely at this point. He had lots of players to see and not much time.

Play resumed, and Bainbridge quickly scored on a breakaway by Caldwell off a pass from Millwood. Five minutes later, a Brackettville player stuck out his hand to stop a ball from going into the goal, and Pappy was allowed to reenter for the penalty, which he blasted into the upper left-hand corner. The ball was struck so hard that the goalie never flinched.

"Man, a three-beer screamer!" exclaimed McIlroy.

"A what?" asked David Nakano.

"You know, a three-beer screamer. A rocket. A frozen rope. That goalie'll need a change of underwear."

By the final whistle, everyone had played, and the team began to take shape. The talent on the Titan's bench dropped off after the first three or four substitutes, but David Nakano showed himself to be a gritty defender, constantly knocking the much larger Brackettville players off the ball and running tirelessly up and down the field. Alex Malloy and Barry

Sampson, both wrestlers, used conditioning to make up for their lack of experience. However, the value of the rest would be to have two full teams to scrimmage at practice. And it was clear what the team would look like if the Chiefs hadn't come to Bain.

They'd played their first college varsity soccer game and won. Andrew would make an excited phone call to his dad that night. Barrett was miffed that he only played a few minutes in the second half and more than once was the subject of Hancock's criticism. But the coach was right. The unskilled Brackettville forwards were easy prey for Barrett's speed and anticipation, but instead of directing the attack, he chose to bomb the ball. They would soon face much stronger, more skilled, attackers; and if Brian played the same style against Southwestern, Carthage, or other conference foes, there would be long, unpleasant afternoons ahead.

Hancock struggled with what he would say. Paxton's actions actually stopped the conflict. And he was impressed that Andrew charged in to defend his teammate against a much larger opponent.

"A pretty good effort hustle-wise. A pretty poor effort execution-wise. See you at practice Monday." He turned away and then turned back. "Team rules. No smoking or drinking. Be careful this weekend."

Back at school, they missed the football game. Stereos blared all across campus. A home game meant a party on the lawn and better-than-normal food. Pappy and Barrett showered quickly, the dirt pouring off them in brown rivers. Pappy had yet another brush burn, from numerous sliding tackles, on the top of his left calf. He couldn't count the number of times over the years the skin had been torn away stealing the ball. He'd even scored two goals that way in high school, deflecting low shots away from the oncoming goalie. He had gauze and tape in his room (they had become his trademarks), although bandaging created an infection, and the dressing would heal into the wound, requiring that it be ripped off when changed. Leaving it uncovered would cause it to ooze through his jeans—not exactly socially acceptable, but it would heal quicker. Pappy opted for the pad tonight. Tomorrow was Sunday, and he could wear shorts, leave the pad off, and let it air-dry. But no matter. There would be more the next game or in practice.

After a couple of letters to home and friends, and a few hands of acey-deucy, they headed for the Union. At eight o'clock, the sun was almost down, and there were four hundred people on the lawn. A group of ten girls, mostly upperclassmen, hailed Barrett, and he strode over with his usual confidence. Andrew ducked away as if being fired upon and found probably the only Titan more bashful than he, David Nakano.

Pappy was shy to a fault. Only moderately comfortable with girls he knew well, strangers left him speechless. He'd dated a couple of girls briefly at Amsterdam, both with mildly disastrous results. His pining for Littlefield made him a social recluse.

Pappy waved to the rest of the Chiefs coming down the hill from the chapel. With them were Beth Littlefield and a couple of other girls from her dorm. Paxton froze. *Remain calm,* he counseled himself. *No need to bolt.* God, she was beautiful.

"Hi, Pappy," said Littlefield.

"Hey," said Paxton, with his usual eloquence.

"Great job today, Pappy," said Millwood.

Littlefield was trying not to look at Barrett, and Paxton was trying to look everywhere except at Littlefield. Millwood had known of Pappy's lusting after Beth for years.

"Hey, let's get going," said Penny. "The Silo house has free beer."

"Okay, you guys go on your manly drinking ritual," said Littlefield, heading up the steps of the union.

Millwood leaned over. "You can breathe now, Pappy."

They started down the street, and Barrett quickly caught up. The Silo house was at the south edge of campus, about three hundred yards from Roberts Hall. Penny had arrived early and had a beer at The Cellar, so he belched repeatedly as they walked. Millwood had overdone the Brut aftershave and was made to walk two steps behind.

An impressive structure for a fraternity, the Silo house was a huge old three-story boardinghouse with brick exterior and long white wooden porch, which wrapped around the front and one side of the building. About fifteen guys stretched along the railing of the balcony, and there was a keg of beer in a tub of ice.

"Howdy, boys," said Paul Sheffe, handing each a beer. "Welcome to the Silo house. Let me show you around." They went inside to a large room full of well-worn armchairs and sofas. The unwaxed, scuffed, and faded wooden floors were evidence that this was once a grand house. Cigarette smoke dirtied the air, and the lamps in the room gave a faded brown glow to the faces. Andrew could see that there were about forty guys … and a total of twelve girls.

"What the hell kind of a party is this, Sheffe?" asked Barrett in mock disgust. "Where are the women?"

"Oh yeah," said Paul. "We left one of the brothers in charge of getting out the word, but he was drunk by noon and passed out. A couple of guys are at the dorms now, rounding up suspects. Relax and have a goddamn beer."

"Oh, great," exclaimed Penny, downing half a glass. "I came here to stare at your ugly face?"

"Don't worry," said Sheffe, putting Penny in a headlock. "We'll hang around here until eleven—" he raked his knuckles across the top of Penny's head "—and then go over to Norbert Hall for a panty raid."

"A what?" asked Andrew.

"That's right," laughed Brian. "Pappy doesn't know about panty raids. He may not let us go."

"Are you kidding?" said Millwood. "He'll be climbing the sides of the dorm."

Pappy sipped his beer nervously, ready to toss the cup if Hancock showed up. They talked for a while about the game. It was obvious this would not be another disastrous season on the magnitude of those before. The more they drank, the more grandiose their dreams of victory. Maybe even a few fans, besides girlfriends, would attend the games.

Barrett grabbed Paxton by the arm and nodded at two girls in the next room. "Come on," he said, "I see a couple of familiar faces. We don't have to wait for the fun to begin." They walked over to two girls sitting on a sofa, talking with a guy too drunk to sit upright.

"Hey, Jan," said Brian. "How's it goin'?"

"Barrett!" exclaimed the first girl, jumping to her feet and throwing her arms around Brian's neck. "How are you, baby?" she purred, stroking his chest with her right hand. Jan Murtaugh was five feet six, with brown shoulder-length hair and brown eyes. Her tan pullover sweater and brown skirt were both too small for her slightly stocky figure, and her large round breasts stood out as if artificially suspended. Her reputation as a nymphomaniac was already established—information he didn't share with Pappy, fearing he would run from the room.

Barrett decided it was time for his friend to loosen up, and this girl was a *loostener*. He'd met Murtaugh Friday at the Union. She eyed him going through the lunch line, and sat down at his table. After minimal small talk, her conversation became so laced with sexual suggestion that even he was embarrassed by her boldness. She wanted to "get together," but he was busy with other things, so they promised to meet at the Silo party. Now she draped herself on his arm, pressing her chest against him.

"This is my roommate, Pappy," he said, pulling the reluctant Paxton forward.

"Hi, Pappy," she said, releasing Barrett and wrapping her arms around Paxton's neck, plastering herself to him. She grabbed the back of his hair and smashed her lips down upon Andrew's, her mouth so wide open that he thought she was going to stick her tongue up his nose. He tried to pull away, breaking a panic sweat, but she was now grinding her chest and hips into his. Finally, she eased her grip but still kept her arms around him, and he gasped for air.

Barrett chuckled and turned to the other girl.

"Hi, I'm Brian," he said, shaking her hand.

"This is Marty Willman," said Murtaugh, still clutching Andrew Paxton. "She lives on our floor."

"Hi," said Marty. "I've heard a lot about you … and Pappy." This girl had brown hair too, but she wore a nylon pullover and skintight jeans, covering a nearly perfect figure.

"How come you two are out so late?" teased Brian, sitting down next to Marty. "You little freshman girls are supposed to be in bed by now."

"That's not fair," said Jan. "Just because guys don't have hours. Besides, I don't own a watch." She showed Barrett her bare wrist while ignoring Andrew's efforts to break free. "I guess we can't go back to the dorm until it opens in the morning," she sighed, slipping her right hand inside the back of Andrew's pants. Her breath was hot, as was her body, and he was increasingly uncomfortable. He sat down in an overstuffed armchair, hoping to break free, but it failed to dislodge her or her hand. She dropped into his lap and proceeded to wiggle, reveling in his discomfort. He was now sweating profusely, sure everyone in the room could hear his heart pounding. She pressed her huge breasts into his chest and wrapped her left arm around his neck, again smashing her open lips down onto his mouth, shoving her tongue between his teeth.

He tried to recoil, but the back of the chair prevented his escape.

"Pappy!" screamed Penny, grabbing Andrew from behind by the shoulders. Paxton jumped, almost throwing Murtaugh onto the floor. "Pappy, Pappy, Pappy!" he repeated, and then he laughed, pushing him back down. Already smashed, Penny sat down on the right arm of the chair, preventing the girl from resuming her death grip on Andrew. Paxton had red blotches on his neck, and his shirt was stuck to the chair.

"I thought we were going to the panty raid …," said Penny.

"Right," exclaimed Andrew, standing and tossing Jan to the side. He turned quickly, slightly stooped over, hands in his pockets, and strode across the room and out the front door.

"Barrett, I'm going to get another beer, and then we're out of here," said Penny.

Jan Murtaugh looked up at him. "Awww, you don't want to leave too, do you?" she purred, sliding her hand up Penny's thigh. "Why don't you stay for a while? We can find someplace—"

"Sorry," he said, motioning back toward the keg of beer, "I promised I'd go with these guys. But there's still time for you good little girls to go back to the dorm before they lock the doors."

Penny turned to Brian. "Hey, let's—" But his friend was sprawled on the sofa, with Marty Willman on top of him.

"C'mon, Penny, put it back in your pants and let's go," said Millwood. "Brian, you worthless toad, leave that woman alone and come on."

Without breaking the embrace, Barrett waved them to go on and continued to grope the freshman. By this time, Jan Murtaugh was on the floor next to them, trying to get in on the skirmish.

"He's worthless," said Penny, now having trouble standing upright.

"Yeah," said Millwood. "I should be so worthless."

"All right," said Penny. "Let's get the hell out of here."

Pappy returned and stood next to Paul Sheffe. Through the thickening smoky haze, they could see Jan Murtaugh on the lap of another guy.

"Gee, I really made a lasting impression on her," said Andrew.

"You'd better bunk with us tonight," said Millwood to Paxton. "Brian's going to get skanked. Besides, it looks like Penny is going to wretch his guts out later, and I could use the help."

"Do you know those girls?" asked Paxton. "I thought I was going to get raped."

"Yeah," said Tim, "Goose told me about them. They both went to his high school. A couple of nymphos. Screwed half the football team. Murtaugh once got caught naked in the boys' shower with three guys."

They walked on toward Norbert Hall, one of five women's dorms at Bainbridge. Two stories, flat roofs, antiseptic design, built in the early 1960s, it looked like an elementary school. There was a central corridor on each floor and dorm rooms down both sides. The reception area/lounge on the east end was as far as boys were permitted to go. Every woman's dorm had a supervisor and an RA on each floor. The staircases at each end of the building had doors that were locked from eleven at night until six in the morning. Freshmen girls' curfew Sunday through Thursday was eleven at night, and it was midnight on weekends, which infuriated the women's rights advocates. Hours were seldom enforced, and it was rumored that they would be repealed at the end of the semester.

There were no curfews for men, whose residences were open twenty-four hours a day. And if a woman was caught there after hours, or anytime, unless there was a formal open house, it was she who was punished.

The Chiefs heard the shouting as they reached Norbert Hall. A crowd of about seventy young men had gathered, yelling nothing in particular and clapping their hands, not sure what to do next. Twenty or thirty girls were hanging out the windows, calling to the guys, while others milled around behind them, giggling nervously. A stereo blasted the Doors' "Hello, I Love You" across campus.

A group of about twenty football players appeared from behind the chapel and walked down the hill chanting, "Pants, pants, give us your pants!" The freshmen picked up the chorus, and soon girls were squealing and cheering. Some threw panties and bras down onto the crowd. Most checked first to make sure they had removed the nametags that had been painstakingly sewn in by their mothers so they wouldn't get lost in the laundry. Several didn't bother, as they wanted to make sure the boy they targeted knew who had tossed them. Penny ended up with two pair of panties. McIlroy had one. Pappy stayed well back from the crowd.

The uproar continued for another hour, until the resident advisors came by and closed the girls' windows. Penny, McIlroy, and Millwood found Andrew Paxton standing outside the Union.

"This sucks," said Millwood. "I hope they get rid of freshmen women's curfew soon." They sat around for a few minutes. Nobody wanted to go all the way down to Fitzgerald's, and fatigue from the game was setting in.

The card game on Paxton's floor was the only remaining entertainment, so they returned to Roberts Hall. There were half a dozen stereos blaring and groups of guys hanging out on the fire escape, smoking cigarettes, drinking, and talking.

The card game had already broken up, so Penny, McIlroy, and Millwood headed toward Hartenstine Hall. Andrew walked down to his room and was raising his key to the door when he saw the *X* drawn on the steel doorknob with a black marker. It was their signal in case one of them "got lucky." Actually, it was Brian's idea, as it was doubtful Pappy would ever need it. He heard the familiar *Santana* album his roommate played constantly after his return from Woodstock, and the glow of the black light mounted over the desks was visible under the door.

Andrew envied his roommate. It would have been nice to have girls fall all over you and always know the right thing to say. No matter. The person on his mind was Beth Littlefield.

Pappy ran down the hall and out the door, spotting his teammates in the dim light of the streetlamps.

"Hey, wait up," he yelled as he jogged down the hill, and they turned back and stopped. "I think Barrett brought something home with him," said Andrew.

"Yeah, *two* somethings," said Millwood.

"You're kidding," said Pappy.

"One of the guys on your floor saw them go in. They must be the two that were at the Silo house," said Tim, shaking his head. "I'd be more worried about disease if I weren't so jealous. How the hell does he do it?"

"I guess I need a floor to sleep on," said Andrew.

Sunday, August 31

⊚ ⊚ ⊚ ⊚

Luckily, Pappy found an empty bed in the room next to McIlroy's, belonging to an upperclassman who wasn't due to arrive until that morning, so at least he got a few hours of sleep. He returned to his room at eight thirty. The place was wrecked and reeked of sweat and sour vomit. Barrett lay naked facedown, butt sticking up, on Pappy's mattress, which was next to his own on the floor.

Pappy kicked Barrett on the bottom of his foot. The corpse rose up on its elbows, head still bowed and eyes shut. Then sank back down. Paxton wanted to go back to bed, but the hallway was filled with doors slamming, clock radios blaring five different stations, and traffic to and from the bathroom, all magnified by the bare walls and linoleum floors. Barrett's head rose again.

"What have I done?" he asked, more to himself than anyone else. Then, propped up on his elbows, he looked for something to cover his naked frame. Nothing was within reach, and he crawled up onto his own bed. Paxton tossed a lump of bed sheet onto Brian's back and then lifted his own mattress and the bedding back onto the top bunk, jumped up, and lay back, staring at the ceiling.

What a day, mused Pappy. His first college soccer game. What a night. A frat beer bash, nymphomaniacs, a panty raid, and his roommate beds two women and trashes the place.

Barrett lay motionless. The commotion in the hall died down. Pappy closed his eyes and began replaying the game, in usual Pappy fashion. All the missed opportunities, the mental mistakes … At least when they won, he wasn't as hard on himself.

"Hey, ugly," said Barrett, now upright, fully dressed, and staring at Paxton and poking him in the forehead. "Get your butt up; it's almost noon."

"Crap," said Andrew in a dazed panic, jumping down. He'd fallen back asleep. "I was going to take a shower and get some breakfast," he said, dragging a comb across his head.

"Well, now it's Sunday brunch," said Barrett, opening the door. "So let's go."

As they walked, Pappy glanced at Barrett to see if he had any physical souvenirs of the previous evening. Brian looked as he usually did after ten or fifteen beers—puffy, bloodshot eyes, dark circles, unshaven face, and wrinkled shirt. But he seemed even more subdued than a hangover would cause him to be, as if he were lost somewhere in thought and it wasn't wistful remembrances of the past evening's orgy. The expected grin was nowhere to be found.

Nor was there any boastful banter. Maybe he was waiting until all the Chiefs were together to recount stories that legends were made of.

In fact, Barrett was recalling the past evening, but what he'd hoped would be the *Playboy* magazine fantasy of the decade involved more chemistry than anatomy.

He and the two girls left the Silo house after downing way too many beers, and while Barrett was able to walk upright, the girls needed a great deal of help, failing to mention that they had swilled a couple of bottles of Ripple wine before going to the party. Now the combination of cheap grape syrup and carbonated hops was taking its toll. They tried to sneak in the back door of Roberts Hall. Once inside, Barrett turned on the record player to cover the girls' giggles and chatter. The lights went off, except the black light, and Barrett pulled both mattresses onto the floor. Marty Willman turned toward him, smiled, and promptly barfed all down the front of his shirt, pants, and all over the floor. He stood stunned as she collapsed to her knees, still heaving. Brian scrambled to find a towel or something to contain the mess. He pulled the sheet off his bed, trying to mop up the ever-growing chaos, and finally shoved a wastebasket under her slumping head. Jan Murtaugh, apparently feeling left out, grabbed a shirt off Pappy's dresser, and puked into it. She apologized repeatedly, as she gasped for air between waves of nausea. Barrett was sobering up quickly. Marty was now unconscious, her arms wrapped around the partially filled receptacle. The fantasy had been replaced by the reality of the comatose drunk.

Jan's convulsions subsided as Barrett continued to mop up, and now, in her semilucid state, she apparently wanted to make amends by resuming the evening's planned activities. She fell upon Barrett, who was on his knees checking to see if Marty was still breathing, and pushed him back onto the mattress. Straddling him, she bent forward to kiss. Brian struggled to pull his face away, her breath smelling like sour milk and vinegar.

Her arms then dropped to the side, the room now spinning uncontrollably. Barrett peeled the sheet off Pappy's mattress and put it next to her head as she turned to retch but brought up nothing. Unlike Marty, however, Jan didn't lose consciousness, and after a few minutes, she was sitting up, disorientated.

Marty was a dead weight. He leaned Jan against Pappy's closet door, praying she didn't further decorate his roommate's wardrobe. They lifted Marty to her feet, slapped her a couple of times, and then half dragged her out the back door. It was now two thirty, and the campus was quiet. Brian didn't bother checking for the security police, or anyone else who might be watching, and deposited both at the rear entrance to Norbert Hall.

Returning to his room, Barrett scooped up the foul linens and shirt and dumped them in the downstairs washing machine. He added his jeans, which were also soaked in beer and vomit, and walked naked back to his room, collapsing on the mattress. So ended his first romantic encounter as a college freshman. Mental note: never date a girl who has to take her makeup off with a belt sander.

Monday, September 1

⊙   ⊙   ⊙   ⊙

Labor Day. In Buffalo, there would be no school. Actually, Amsterdam never started classes until mid-September—to coincide with harvest on the family farm.

But Bainbridge wanted to hold finals before Christmas so students wouldn't have to study over the holidays, and in Indiana, it was more important to accommodate the football schedule, which seemed longer every year.

So a national holiday was the first day of classes. Andrew was chemistry premed, and Brian was bio, but both had Chem 101 at eight o'clock. Pappy had slept little the night before. Though an honors graduate in high school and the first in his family to attend college, he feared the unknown.

Barrett was his usual unflappable self. The bathroom was a crush of activity, and students cascaded down the stairs from seven o'clock on. *Maniacs going to breakfast,* thought Brian. No way he was going to arise one minute before absolutely necessary.

Both were dressed and out the door with time to spare. The chemistry building was less than one hundred yards away and of the same era as Roberts Hall. Ivy covered, it had a stately exterior, but inside was cold and impersonal. The classroom was large, the floor terraced, and the front wall covered with blackboards. It looked full, with about one hundred students of all sizes, shapes, colors, and sexes. Most of the girls wore some sort of headgear—scarves, hats—to avoid the full hair and makeup routine at that hour.

76

The lecturer was Eldon Biederman, a bright, if not strange, assistant professor. His PhD was pending, but everyone called him Doctor. Tall, rail thin, brush cut, white shirt, blue tie, serious horn-rimmed glasses, and yes, a plastic pocket protector jammed with pens and pencils, he was the embodiment of the nerd scientist. His head, face, glasses and haircut, led to only one description: *shrimp head*. Picture the head of a shrimp, with beady eyes, feelers, and the spine across the top; it looks like someone wearing thick glasses and a buzz cut. This guy might have been the origin of the word *geek*.

Eldon was all business. After introductions, a few pleasantries, some discussion about the course materials, and description of the lab schedule, he began lecturing. Everyone took copious notes, and Biederman kept on point. He was concise and basic in his explanations. The subject was dry, but the hour went quickly.

Class ended, and for Pappy, it was on to English. Barrett went back to bed. His next class wasn't until eleven. Being on a small campus had definite advantages.

English 100 was creative writing. But instead of the pipe-smoking, tweed-jacket-with-elbow-pads caricature of a college literary professor, Doctor Sanford Wager was himself a former high school soccer player and avid sports fan. Talented and personable, he approached the daunting task of teaching freshmen how to be creative with a basic down-to-earth tenet: "Write what you know," or better, "Write what you live."

Pappy had written several short stories at Amsterdam. Many of his most colorful tales, however, had originated, and been narrated, during extended teenage drinking sessions, earning him the nickname "Story Lady," from the *Rocky and Bullwinkle* cartoons.

Amsterdam was an excellent school, and Andrew had been in the advanced classes since the second grade, although he tried repeatedly to escape. The other students were geniuses, and he felt the only reason he was in there was to anchor the bottom of the grading curve. He used to joke that his classmates would bring him to school on the day of a test to make sure their token dummy was in attendance. He was bright enough, but often his report cards contained the comment "Andrew is a good student—if only he would apply himself." It was more fun to apply himself to baseball, soccer, or anywhere else besides the classroom.

Pappy met McIlroy and Penny for lunch. The mood on campus had changed. The upperclassmen had arrived, and the carefree tone of orientation week was gone. Now there was homework. Everyone compared notes on classes—whether the professors were interesting, the style of lecture, and most importantly, what girls attended. They had pretty much scoped out the freshman talent the previous week, but now there were older women. This created a paradox. Freshman boys would take a backseat to the upperclassmen with their first year coeds. Likewise, sophomore women, no longer the new blood on campus, would be largely ignored. This created opportunity for the few freshmen males who didn't look and behave as if they were still in middle school.

Andrew went to Spanish class at one o'clock. The language department was small, only two professors each for Spanish, German, and French. The class had about thirty students, virtually all sophomores and up. Andrew had started Spanish in the sixth grade, so he took the state exam for seniors as a sophomore. That allowed him to start with an upper level at Bain and complete his language requirement with one more semester. The teacher was an attractive young woman from Barcelona, Spain, who informed them that the class would be conducted solely in Spanish. High school was truly gone.

Pappy was back at Roberts Hall at two to dress for practice. Barrett arrived around three, and the rest of the Chiefs, plus some of the upperclassmen, joined them. Darby Park was full of people that Labor Day, and they had to dodge cars and Frisbees all the way to the field.

"You might have noticed some players are missing," started Hancock in a somber tone. "Two more seniors turned in their uniforms this morning ... I wish them the best of luck." Andrew looked around. No more Roush and Stewart.

"I think we have a good nucleus here, but we have a lot of work to do to compete with the better teams. Saturday we play one of the best: Southwestern. I understand they have exceptional exchange students. We're going to have to play tight defense and take advantage of every scoring opportunity. Ball control and pressure. The less time they have the ball, the better. Okay, let's run some shooting drills."

They divided into two lines in front of each goal. Little was said about Roush's departure, other than regrets, despite his attitude. The Chiefs couldn't comprehend quitting this sport they loved, even though they had all experienced senioritis.

The second-hour scrimmage was a pitched battle beginning to end. The freshmen were burning off the tension and anxiety of the first day of classes, and they ran full tilt until play became ragged. At that point, Hancock decided to end practice early. The jog back was also fast-paced. The departure of the seniors made Hancock's message clear. Hustle was the name of the game.

Tuesday, September 2

◎　◎　◎　◎

Second day of classes was more settling in. There were some new faces and some departures, particularly in chemistry, which wasn't for the casual student. Many people went to a liberal arts college like Bainbridge because they had no idea what they wanted to do with their lives and their parents were wealthy enough that they didn't have to grow up yet. And a substantial number of guys were taking advantage of the college exemption from the draft.

The Vietnam War had engulfed the country. Nixon was President; troop strength was at the highest; and there was no end in sight. Yet in the insulated world of Bainbridge, the students' days focused on classes, attending parties, making friends, and playing sports.

For the Chiefs, their current greatest collective concern was which fraternity to join. As homogenous as the five seemed, their individual personalities would eventually split them between two houses. But for now, there was the ego-boosting courtship and the endless string of parties.

Barrett and Pappy were establishing a routine. Both studied while listening to music. Barrett fielded at least three phone calls from girls each night. Ten o'clock meant study break at the Union, and then a quick swing through the library to see if there was any action. Letters to family and friends rounded out the day. Luckily, neither snored.

Wednesday, September 3

◎　◎　◎　◎

Only three days into classes, and Barrett was becoming restless. As far as he was concerned, their schedule was already too regimented. Four more years of college. Then four years of med school. Two years internship. One year as a resident. God, he was going to be almost thirty before he was free again. Then what? Marriage? Children?

The music he played had a West Coast theme. The Mamas & the Papas, Beach Boys, The Ventures. California meant beaches, surfing, independence. A million new places to go, new sights to see, new experiences. No schedule, no teachers, no books, no classrooms. And girls, girls, girls.

His restive feeling spilled over into soccer. A natural athlete who believed in his own style of play, he continued to clash with Hancock, the in-control tactician, every practice. But the coach's preaching hustle and determination was getting through to the players, and they admired his fiery but fair personality.

Moreover, he was the coach. The only coach.

So the cauldron between the two boiled. The foam on the fire was Pappy. He aggravated Barrett with his logic and morality. Nothing more annoying than an adult who was right. Particularly if he was your roommate.

Thursday, September 4

⊚ ⓒ ⊚ ⊚

First day of chem lab. The basement of the chemistry building resembled a remodeled dungeon. One set of double doors opened into row after row of long green laminate lab tables. Andrew, claustrophobic from birth, was now in a basement with low ceilings containing one hundred-plus other souls and only one exit. Every six feet were double spigot gas outlets for the Bunsen burners. Test tubes, crucibles, mortars and pestles, beakers, funnels, clamps, Mettler balances, tongs, and all other sorts of containers and instruments were on shelves above the countertops. Supplies such as cleansers were in cabinets underneath.

The entire first hour was safety. Cabinets with glass doors housed acids, bases, and common compounds. The professor pointed out the fire extinguishers and demonstrated operation of the two makeshift showers. The use of vent hoods was highly recommended for all chemicals giving off fumes.

In the second hour, he illustrated how to conduct experiments. Several liquids were combined to show exothermic and endothermic reactions, and he demonstrated how to test for the presence of different elements.

The bell rang. Back to Roberts Hall to change. Barrett, Millwood, and Penny were already dressed, but the first clap of thunder stopped them at the door. The sky blackened at an alarming rate, and dramatic gusts of wind bent the trees almost in half. No way could they make it to the park before it hit, and there was nowhere there to ride it out.

"Let's beat it to the field house," said Barrett, already heading for the opposite exit. The lightning and wind were increasing by the second, and debris was flying everywhere. Students scurried into buildings. Pappy and company covered the hundred yards or so just before the rain hit—and hit hard. Thunder shook the building and the windows. Two or three strikes were close and as bright as camera flashbulbs. Then the power went out, making the dark and dingy halls more eerie.

Flashes came from all sides, through windows and skylights. Rain went sideways, and people stood staring out at the incredible tempest. The bushes lurched back and forth, and a blast of cold air rushed through the edges of the closed doors. The clouds were so dark that at four in the afternoon, the streetlights came on, and then there was the sound of sirens.

"Tornado warning! Tornado warning!" they heard people shouting all over the darkened building, and people were clamoring down the stairs. "Down in the basement! Everybody down in the basement!" said a secretary, and all followed.

The hair stood up on the back of Andrew's neck. He'd been deathly afraid of thunderstorms as a child, for no apparent reason, and this was an even greater terror. There were no flashlights, but the halls were illuminated as the sky outside became an eerie green. Then the pounding and clanging of hail. There had never been a tornado in Amsterdam, and the Chiefs were visibly shaken. Everyone sat against the walls. The bombardment lasted only a few minutes. Then, as if someone had sounded an all clear, the lights came back on. There was noticeable exhaling from all in the room, and they headed back upstairs even though hail was still falling.

"No practice today, guys," said Hancock. "I'm going down to the field to check on things and make sure no one was caught down there. See you tomorrow."

Ten minutes later, the sun came out. Limbs were down all over campus, but there was no apparent serious damage. The soccer Titans went straight to the Union in their uniforms. Soon half the campus crowded into the dining room, bookstore, The Cellar, and halls. The storm was the topic of discussion. Around seven o'clock, everyone's adrenaline subsided, and they headed back to the dorms. This would provide weeks' worth of great material for letter writing.

Friday, September 5

⊙ ⊙ ⊙ ⊙

Last day of classes for the first week of college. Being on trimesters meant students took three five-hour courses a week, and it was intended that courses meet every day. But as most professors didn't enforce mandatory attendance, and they also had activities and interests outside their lectures, Friday was often the start of a three-day weekend.

There was no free day in chemistry, however. Eldon held class eight o'clock sharp every morning for the entire semester. And every lecture was important. Next week would be the first quiz in both Spanish and Chem 101, and a short story of six pages was due Tuesday in English. Pappy's parents had bought him a Singer portable electric typewriter, and next to the Coke machine, it was the most important appliance on the dorm floor. Everyone wanted to borrow it. A couple of students pounded away on manual typewriters, with keys that stuck and ink that smudged.

The weather that afternoon was beautiful. After lunch, Barrett, McIlroy, and Paxton lay out in front of the dorm for two hours people watching. Brian had bits of information on every girl they saw. Tonight he was taking a sophomore to Fitzgerald's. Pappy scowled at him.

"One of these times Hancock is going to find out, and there goes our season," said Pappy. McIlroy kept quiet. He had the same plans.

"Hancock blows," said Barrett. "He's never going to get this game, and he's always going to be ragging on me. I should have gone to Clarkson."

84

"Yeah," said Pappy. "Well, the guy is trying. He didn't ask for the job."

"He ain't making it any easier on us ... or himself," replied Barrett. "What does he care if we drink? The weekends are for fun. And soccer is for bustin' it. We can't play this half-court offense. We need to ram it down other guys' throats."

To continue was useless. Pappy went back to the room, dressed, and ran down to the field by himself. He sat under a tree and watched kids playing on the swing set on the east side of the field. He didn't like being everyone's conscience, but he never knew when to stop. His dad had always played it straight, and Pappy admired no one more.

Hancock pulled up shortly thereafter, and teammates began to trickle in. It was the usual—calisthenics, pass and trap, and then shooting drills, corner kicks, free kicks, and penalties.

Finally, Hancock summoned the squad over. "Tomorrow is Southwestern. This will be our first real test. We have to go after every ball, hustle, and keep them from making clean passes ... No questions? Okay, let's head on in. Cars leave the field house tomorrow at eight. Breakfast at the Union at seven."

Back in the dorm, Andrew was sullen. Barrett ignored him, dressing for dinner and his date, until he couldn't stand it any longer.

"Look, I know you're trying to make this team work, but I don't need another father and coach for a roommate," said Barrett. "I'm here at college on my own. I have to do what is right for me, not what is right for everyone else."

Pappy sat down on the bed. "Do you think I like chirping at you all the time? You and everyone else? Do you think I can help it? You're right—this isn't Amsterdam, and we aren't the Chiefs. We are a bunch of guys playing with ex–football players, being led by a basketball coach."

"No," said Barrett. "Your biggest problem is that if we don't win, you forgive everyone else and blame yourself. You can't carry that crap around with you all the time. Ease up on ..."

Andrew looked down.

"Oh, no," said Barrett with a sigh. "Now you're being hard on yourself for being hard on yourself!" He turned to leave. "C'mon, let's go to dinner. Then come down to Fitz's with us. Drink your sodey pop. You can make sure I behave myself. I'll see if my date has a friend."

"No," said Pappy emphatically, now standing up. "I'll go by myself so I can come back to the room when I want."

"All right, let's go. I'm starving."

Brian and Andrew ate with some guys from Roberts Hall and then picked up Barrett's date at the Alpha Gamma house. Vicki Moon was blonde, five-four, and dressed to the nines. Her tan suede coat must have cost a fortune, and she had matching boots and diamond earrings. This was just like high school, when Pappy used to tag along with guys who had girlfriends.

They met McIlroy and his date along the way and arrived at a crowded Fitzgerald's to find Millwood and Penny there stag. Most of the upper-class soccer players belonged to fraternities and owned cars, so they didn't have to frequent bars where a coach might find them breaking training.

They sat for a while, and even though they ordered a pitcher of beer, no one was really into drinking. They kept checking their watches, knowing morning would come early, until finally the girls had enough of being ignored, and they all headed back. Pappy went straight to the dorm and hit the rack. It was eleven o'clock. Barrett arrived at eleven fifteen, but his roommate was already out cold.

Saturday, September 6

◎ ◎ ◎ ◎

When you're eighteen years old, five hundred miles from home, the only good reason to be up at seven o'clock on a Saturday morning is *George of the Jungle, Bullwinkle,* or *Bugs Bunny* cartoons. And nothing is going to look good for breakfast except four more hours of sleep.

The main casualties of the previous night's activities were the five Chiefs, who stared at their plates. Hancock assumed the reason for their condition was a late night, and wasn't happy, but he let it go. Everyone else seemed fairly animated.

The coach decided to dress twenty-four players for a road game. Having enough vehicles wasn't a problem because the football team was playing at home. Once again, however, they would miss most of the game.

In the past, football and women were the topics of conversation to and from the Titans' soccer games, since no one expected to win. But this time, the focus was on the game. They talked about Southwestern and the rest of the schedule. Pappy and the Chiefs were puzzled by their expectations. Of course they were going to win. The Chiefs had never done anything else. The worst record during this group's tenure at Amsterdam was twelve to four, and they were undefeated sophomore year.

The team was coming together. Guys were hustling. They could field eleven players with high school experience.

The conversation focused on Southwestern. Williams and Landon had played them three times before. Academically on a par with some of the best schools in the country, they had an active foreign student exchange program, which bolstered an already tough team.

The Titans arrived at a beautiful facility just after ten. The field was lined with new permanent steel bleachers, and there were small locker rooms. The pitch was slightly crowned, brightly lined, with thick, freshly mown grass. There were no overlaying football stripes, or extended goalposts. This was the soccer field for the soccer team.

"Man, let's transfer," said Barrett as he helped with the equipment. "This was where I was born to play."

"Yeah, and you might be fourth string here," said Millwood. "Maybe."

Everything about the Patriots program was better—their field, uniforms, coach's attire, even the nets in the goals. They had cheerleaders! And they weren't ugly.

As usual, the opposition looked bigger, faster, and older. They went through calisthenics and then broke into groups for pass and trap. Pappy took some corner and penalty kicks, and then he went to the center circle. The Chiefs joined him, followed by several other players. The two students from Trinidad were obvious: dark black skin, short hair, over six feet tall, beanpole thin, and yes, they were good. Their passes and traps were gentle and precise. At one point, they volleyed the ball back and forth in the air for several minutes, first with their feet and then with their heads.

Andrew had played against foreign players before, but that was with ten other Chiefs at his side.

Bain lost the toss, and Southwestern kicked off. The two Trinidadians played forward, and the show was on. Number four, the taller of the two, put the ball out to the wing, who raced down the field and then passed back to him. Landon came up, but with two short, quick steps, number four was wide open at the penalty line. Harbaugh and Barrett converged, but he pulled the ball back and passed to the other, number five, who spun past Barrett and then left it for the following halfback. He punched it to four, who beat Landon, then Barrett, and shot into the lower right-hand corner. It was zero to one, and less than two minutes had gone by.

The Titans kicked off but lost the ball, and the Patriots were in control again. This time, number four cut left, easily beating Harbaugh, and passed to five. Barrett tried a slide tackle but missed, and five glided by him and passed to the wing, who was all alone just inside the penalty area. His shot banged off the near post, back into play, and four calmly pulled it back as if he were playing basketball, setting it up again. Their balance and quickness was unbelievable—far above anything the Chiefs had ever seen. They could stop and change direction in an instant, and the Titans went for every head fake and side step. Now it was a two-man dribble and passing exhibition. The four Bain fullbacks had collapsed on the two forwards, once again leaving the wings open. The left wing scored on a tap-in. Two to nothing, and not one of the Titans had even touched the ball in their end to kick it out of bounds or change the direction.

At midfield, Pappy, Penny, and Caldwell took the ball down, and Andrew shot from twenty yards out, but it was wide. The goalie punted the ball past midfield, and the Patriots picked it up. The performance was on one more time.

Pappy came back as number five beat Landon yet again. He faced up, but the forward went past him and then Barrett. Andrew pursued, but his opponent merely passed to number four, who sent it back to the halfback and then out to the wing. Now the Titans were totally disorganized and arguing with each other.

"Paxton, get back on offense!" yelled Hancock. "Paxton! Paxton! Get back up the field!"

Pappy ignored him. He had to do something. Again he faced off with number four, and once more never even got close to the ball. He chased him toward the goal and then stopped. He stopped. And the rest of the defense stopped. Number four went in all alone on Randy Williams. Three to zero. Williams looked at them in disbelief. Pappy turned and walked back toward the midline, head down, totally humiliated.

"Pappy, you're out," said David Nakano as he ran toward him. At first, Andrew was so ashamed that he couldn't move.

"Paxton, you're out," called Hancock. He was the only one being replaced. Pappy jogged over to the sidelines, but when he got close to the coach, he tried to veer away.

"Paxton, you have got to stay up," said Hancock in a stern voice, following him. "You can't come back or we have no offense. You can't do their jobs for them or—" He stopped.

"I quit on it, Coach, I quit," he said, beside himself with rage and shame. "I left our goalie all alone and I just quit." He bent over and hung his head.

Hancock paused. There was no point in lecturing. His young player was consumed with guilt.

"So?" he said. "Then don't do it again … Let me know when you're ready to go back in." And he walked away.

They kicked off, and Caldwell took the ball to the corner and made a beautiful cross to Penny, but the goalie punched it out. The play came back to midfield, but now number four and five started to play with the ball. David Nakano marked number four tighter and twice picked off errant passes. Play then went back and forth, with Barrett bombing a couple of balls deep into the Southwestern end, but no one was there. Receiving his usual "Barrett, control the damn ball" from Hancock, he responded with his defiant stare.

"Whenever you're ready, Paxton," said Hancock, and Pappy joined the fray. This time, he stayed up and marked a man. But the Patriots controlled the pace on both offense and defense, so there was little opportunity to pick up loose balls near midfield. Finally, Penny took another cross, this time from Pappy, who had switched with Millwood on the fly, and banged a shot with the outside of his right foot, just wide, as the half ended.

"Holy crap," said Barrett dejectedly as they walked off the field. "Holy crap."

Pappy ran over to Randy Williams. "I'm sorry, Randy," he said, visibly upset, "I left you."

"Forget it," said Williams, putting his hand on the freshman's shoulder. "I faced these guys last year, and the same thing happened. There's nothing you can do. They're better than Division I players. You can't stop them. We can't even guard them. We're a D-III team. Just play ball."

Andrew breathed a deep sigh. "But I quit."

"So?" said Millwood, coming up from the side. "You can't beat these guys by yourself. You can't beat any team by yourself. But if you come back and try to do everyone else's job, they'll let you."

They gathered on the sidelines. Hancock let them quiet down.

"Okay," he started softly. "These guys are better than we are. But no matter what happens, there's no reason we can't out-hustle them. And we're not doing that. You can hangdog and go through the motions, and I'll treat you to a seat on the bench. None of you can be tired after that effort. You have forty-five minutes to go out there and make this a game. I told you guys I don't mind getting beat, but I hate to lose. And they haven't *beaten* you yet. It's a long ride home. Let's go."

The same Bain players that started the game were on the field to start the second half. They hustled and tried to stay with their men, but less than five minutes in, number five for the Patriots drilled a volley kick with his left foot into the upper left-hand corner from twenty-five yards that Randy Williams barely saw. At four to zero, the Southwestern coach pulled his two stars, but it made little difference. The Patriots' reserves were equal to the best of the Chiefs, and they were out to prove themselves as well. The Titans couldn't put together enough passes to threaten, and the five shots taken by Penny, Paxton, and Caldwell were outside twenty yards. The result was five to zero, the last on a penalty kick off a handball. It was the worst beating the Chiefs had ever taken.

"Okay," said Hancock. "I hope that isn't our best effort. It's clear we've a lot more work to do individually and as a team. Losing tastes pretty lousy. I don't want to feel like this again, and you don't either.

"I know you guys want to get back to campus, so we won't stop to eat. Be careful going back. Don't do anything stupid this weekend. See you Monday."

The ride home was quiet for the first hour. Then things loosened up, for everyone except Pappy. He was engaged in mental self-abuse, but Barrett and Millwood knew there was no point in trying to console him, so they ignored him.

The Titans turned in their uniforms, showered, and headed for the Union. The football team had murdered Duncan College, a team from Long Island, and the campus was abuzz with activity. There was a band at the Union that night, so after shoveling down dinner, everyone was getting in the mood. The entire freshman student body would be there, and the Chiefs had met several girls in their classes. All except Pappy. There was still, and always would be, only one girl on his mind. Would Littlefield be there? Would she be looking for Barrett? Did he dare say anything to her? Did he dare dance with her? Horror of horrors—what if there were other guys, even upperclassmen, pursuing her?

It was better to stay in and write letters or play poker. There were too many opportunities for disaster.

Barrett was gone by the time Pappy arrived back in the room. Good, nobody here. Actually, the entire first floor was deserted. Pappy put on a stack of records, starting with The Association.

Suddenly, there was a commotion in the hall, and the door swung open. Four Chiefs, reeking of conflicting colognes, barged through the door and dragged Pappy to the ground.

"I don't like this shirt," said Barrett, pulling it over Andrew's head. "I've never liked this shirt. Somebody grab another. Yeah, the maroon one. C'mon, goddamn it, we're late. I don't want those doofus upperclassmen screwing with our women. We want 'em all!" he yelled.

Pappy struggled with his shirt as they herded him toward the Union. The music was playing as they went up the stairs. There must have been five hundred people, half of whom were dancing, and there were groups of girls all around the perimeter. And many male faces he didn't recognize. Sophomores. Juniors. Seniors. Even worse, football players. It looked like the entire team. The Chiefs had met several of them in classes and at the fraternity houses, and they were all rather normal. A few were academically challenged, but there were no belligerent jerks like Burler and Rattigan.

Beer wasn't allowed in the dining room, so The Cellar was jammed, and the line at the bar was a mile long. Barrett and company opted to stay sober for the moment and started through the crowd. Brian, of course, led the pack, and he hadn't traveled twenty feet before the first herd of females latched on. While he was the main draw, much of the campus had heard of the Amsterdam contingent, and all were considered worthy of pursuit. They stayed in a group for a while, talking about the games, first soccer and then football. The band was good, and they started to pair up and dance. Five guys … four girls. Perfect. Pappy promptly said adios and headed out the door. He hadn't seen Littlefield, but he was sure she was there or would be soon. He didn't want to watch her watch Barrett with another girl, so the faster the retreat, the better.

It was a beautiful night, and the lighting on the sidewalk to the library was a sultry amber glow. Halfway up the hill, he saw a girl coming from the other way. Blonde. Attractive. Holy crap, it was Littlefield. There was no looking down or avoiding her, and she saw Pappy and came straight over and threw her arms around him.

"Hi," she said warmly, and then she whispered, "Am I glad to see you. You have to help me. This obnoxious guy has been following me all night. He's drunk, and I'm scared of him. I told him I was meeting someone."

Andrew hugged her loosely and cleared his throat. "Sure, no problem," he said, and then he saw, over her shoulder, Ben Rattigan coming at them.

"Crap," said Rattigan. "It's one of those soccer douches. Heard you guys got your candy asses kicked today, Paxton. What happened to you hotshots from Damsterdam? Must be too much inbreeding." Andrew didn't respond.

"You're late," he said to Beth. "I thought you were meeting me in The Cellar."

"I know," she said, "but I had to find one more article for my journalism paper." And then, for no apparent reason, she kissed Andrew lightly on the lips.

She was lucky he didn't pass out on the spot. He took her hand and they walked down toward the Union. She turned right at the street and headed for Weatherly Hall. Andrew studied the face he'd worshiped for so many years. Her eyes looked tired and sad, but she seemed glad to be with him.

"I can't look—is he still there?" she asked, still facing forward.

Pappy saw Rattigan going into the Union. "No, he's gone." He let go of her hand, but she held on. "I'll walk you to your dorm, or do you want to go back to the library?"

"I don't dare," she said, standing close to him, "but I still need to get some things … Could you come with me?"

"Sure," he said. He had to be dreaming.

Beth worked as quickly as she could, while Andrew sat reading the sports section. He couldn't take his eyes off her. Finally, she was ready, and they went back toward the Union.

Now she was relaxed. It was a relief, like a breath of freedom, to be out with someone from home she could talk to. Up until this point, Littlefield had become a veritable recluse, terrified of having an emotional breakdown about Barrett in public.

The stress was beginning to take its toll physically. She had lost ten pounds from her tall and previously perfect frame, and while not gaunt, her clothes now hung on, rather than enhanced, her figure.

Walking along with Pappy felt warm and safe, and not just because he'd saved her from Rattigan. Even though Andrew was Brian's best friend, somehow he wasn't a reminder of her loss. Her fear of breaking down emotionally was gone for the moment. As she walked alongside him, she slowed down to make it last longer.

"It's only eleven," she said. "How about a beer? My treat."

"Uh, no, we—I better not," he said, realizing that Barrett might still be at the Union.

"Oh," she said, obviously disappointed.

"No, it's just that we're in training and not supposed to drink … I know the other guys do it, but I can't." He sounded almost ashamed.

"Hey, no problem," she said, thankful she had thought wrongly. "I respect that. And the other guys do too."

"Yeah, everybody's father," he sighed.

"That's okay, Dad," she said, smiling and hugging his arm, and they continued toward her dorm.

Just then, Millwood and Penny came around the corner of the Union with Pam Chestnut and Sue Geller, two girls who lived down the hall from Littlefield.

"Holy smokes, is that Pappy and Littlefield?" exclaimed Tim. "It can't be."

"Nah … yes!" said Penny.

"Is that your friend with the ice princess?" asked Pam.

"Yes, and he's been puppy dog after her since he could zip his own fly," said Millwood. "But he's so afraid of betraying Barrett that he runs away every time he sees her. At least that's the excuse he's used all these years … I gotta see this. Let's follow them and see what happens."

All four crossed the street and trailed at a distance. Too intoxicated to be stealthy, they comically ducked in and out behind bushes, giggling loudly. Finally, Pappy turned at the noise and saw who it was. He tried to pull away from Beth, but she held on.

"Hi, guys," she called to them.

They came up.

"What's going on here?" blurted Millwood, making Pappy even more red-faced.

"We've been at the library while you all have been breaking training," said Beth. "Actually, Pappy saved me from some drunken football player."

"Rattigan," said Pappy, now thankful for the excuse.

"Well, we won't keep you two," said Penny, now beginning to herd everyone back toward the Union. "Pappy, you have her in by curfew or I'm gonna get out the shotgun."

"I think she's safe," said Millwood with a chuckle, embarrassing Andrew even further.

"Don't mind them," said Littlefield. "It's good to feel safe."

Pappy was even more crestfallen. Was there anyone on the planet who didn't look at him as if he were fifty years old?

"Okay, let's keep going," said Beth, hugging his arm again. "Once more around the block?"

"It's almost curfew for you," he said, turning toward the entrance to Weatherly Hall.

She sighed. "Okay." They stopped at the door. "Thank you," she said. "Thank you for being my rescuer … and I had a really nice time. I know you did this because you're Brian's friend." Andrew's eyes opened in surprise. "But I think of you as my friend too. You make me think of home. Of growing up. Of happy thoughts." She stopped, realizing Pappy was about to dig a hole and bury himself in the concrete.

"Meet me in the library anytime," she said, and then she kissed him again. She went inside, and he watched as she went down the hall and then looked back and waved.

Andrew couldn't move. Then he turned and broke into a dead run down the dark sidewalk that went along the south side of the campus. He turned and barreled straight up the long hill, past Roberts Hall to the field house, and then down another street by the football stadium. There were three or four couples walking along, staring at this raving lunatic. Suddenly he stopped, self-conscious, and headed back to his room.

What am I getting so excited about? I just came along at the right time. She wasn't looking for me. Not only that, but Penny and Millwood saw him with his roommate's girl. Suppose Barrett intended to get back with her?

Brian wasn't in the room. Good. A quick trip to the head and Pappy was in bed. Better to be asleep when Barrett arrived in case he found out about Beth and was pissed. But how was he going to get to sleep? Her face was plastered in his brain. He could still feel her lips, and his heart was pounding.

Sunday, September 7

⊚ ⊚ ⊚ ⊚

"Hey, worthless, get up," said Barrett, shaking the bunk bed frame. "It's eleven o'clock. By the time your carcass gets ready, lunch will be over."

Andrew struggled to open his eyes. He'd slept for eleven hours straight but could hardly lift his head. Barrett was reading the latest issue of *Sports Illustrated*.

"I heard about you and your lady friend last night," he said. Pappy's mind raced.

"C'mon, come clean," he pressed. "Who was she?"

Reprieve. Absolution. And maybe a way to turn the tables.

"Who've you been talking to?" asked Andrew.

"A couple of guys on the floor said you were with some tall blonde, you hound. It's always the quiet one."

Andrew turned to him with a scowl. "Yeah, your tall blonde. It was Beth. I met her coming out of the library, and she asked me to help her get away from that schmuck Rattigan."

Barrett flared red. "That miserable bastard," he said, now standing and clenching his fists. "I am going to crush his face."

"Don't worry, I took care of it," Andrew continued. "And then I took her back to the library and walked her to her dorm when she was done."

"Well … thanks," said Barrett. "Glad you were there."

97

Just what Andrew didn't want to hear. *He still loves her, or he wouldn't have been so pissed.* He shook his head. *So much for a night to remember.*

"Let's eat."

There were many parents in the dining room, and Barrett and Pappy had to wait to sit down. He saw Littlefield by the window, but before he could look away, she smiled broadly and waved. He nodded her way and then turned back. There was no point in getting his hopes up.

After lunch, a bunch of guys went down to Darby Park to play touch football. It felt good to get away from soccer for a while.

They decided that for a change from the Union, dinner would be the short walk to the lovely Donello's Pizza and Submarine Shop. There were several fast food places close to campus, including Burger Chef, White Castle, and something called Taco Bell. The Chiefs had never heard of nor seen Mexican food, but it seemed to be popular with upperclassmen. They served these weird ground beef sandwiches, which weren't really sandwiches but were on some sort of soft flat bread, called tacos, and others that looked basically the same, called burritos. There was red sauce and a kind of green paste that they poured all over the food. Ugh. Better to suck down a greasy pepperoni pizza.

After that feast, Andrew grabbed his books and headed for the library. The dorm was quiet enough, but the events of the night before raised hopes that Beth might be there again. He went through the main door and up the stairs to the study cubicles, and there she was, talking rather seriously, it appeared, with a guy ... Barrett. He stopped before they saw him, turned, and sat down at a desk out of sight. He stared at his books. How stupid could he be? She was still Barrett's girl, and there wasn't anything he could do about it. Andrew opened his Spanish book and tried running through the vocabulary words, but it was no use. He stood up, went down the opposite stairs, and back to his room.

Barrett tried to keep his voice down, but the more he talked to Littlefield, the more outraged he became. "So the son of a bitch was drunk and wouldn't leave you alone? Did you see him after that?"

"No," said Beth, "once he saw Pappy and me walking together, he went into the Union. I don't think he'll bother me again, but he gives me the creeps."

"I should have ripped his head off the first time up at the gym when he went after Nakano." He looked at Littlefield. He hadn't really seen her or talked to her in weeks. The rumors were correct. She looked thinner, and there was no hint of her cheery smile.

He could see that his presence was starting to upset her. Too late. Her eyes had welled with tears, and she pulled tissues out of her purse. "If you have any more trouble with that slug, call me … or call Pappy. He's a good man … the best."

Barrett turned and left. Littlefield went back into her cubicle and tried to suppress her sobs, but it was too much. She made it back to her room and curled up on her bed with a box of Kleenex.

Monday, September 8

◉ ◉ ◉ ◉

Second week of classes. Paxton aced the Spanish quiz. English theme due the next day. Six pages. Pappy had to pick a topic. His "First Memorable Experience in College"? The panty raid? Tempting, but better stick to the conventional this early in his college career. Write what you live. Littlefield was too sad an issue at this point, so it was the Southwestern game. He described their talented players but left out the part where he abandoned his goalie. Thank God for correction tape—and for a prof who used to play the game.

The jog to practice was quick and quiet. It was clear that Hancock wouldn't be happy with their performance on Saturday. A good reaming, followed by punishment laps around the field, would no doubt take up the first half of practice.

As predicted, after several pointed criticisms, it was four laps around the field and then calisthenics, with plenty of push-ups and sit-ups. Then kick and chase, followed by more laps.

When they were finished, the coach said, "I want you all to meet a new player. This is Roland Santander. He's an exchange student from Barcelona, Spain. Unfortunately for him, he arrived during our soul-searching session, but if nothing else, it will get you all in better shape. Okay, let's split into teams."

Scrimmage was a strange affair. Everyone was anxious, afraid to make a mistake. All except Barrett, who continued to bomb the ball and conduct his ongoing verbal battle with Hancock. After an hour, the coach substituted Santander for Paxton at halfback. Play was still disorganized, but Roland moved well without the ball and had better basic skills than anyone else on the squad. He was tall, thin, and handsome, with thick jet-black hair. While not particularly quick, he had excellent balance. One thing he didn't exhibit was Pappy's aggression.

"C'mon, Santander," said Hancock. "Move the ball up the field. Attack! We need to put pressure on the defense." But he continued his style of play.

"Coach, that's the way many teams play in Spain," said Pappy. "It's called walking soccer, and it's a very controlled game."

Great, thought Hancock. *I have one guy who walks up the field and another who fires the ball all over the place.*

They scrimmaged until almost six. If they were going to get beat, Hancock reasoned, it wouldn't be from lack of conditioning.

"Okay, that's it. Put the balls in the car. See you tomorrow."

"That Santander guy is pretty good," said Pappy as they jogged back to campus. "Did you see him pull the ball back and change directions? His passes were pretty slick too."

"Yeah, but he's a beanpole," said Penny. "And Hancock's not going to tolerate his slow play. Neither are we. We have to hustle and play pressure defense. This guy looks like he'll be done in the first half."

"We'll see," said Pappy. "It would be nice to have one stud foreigner on the team."

Tuesday, September 9

⊚ ⊚ ⊚ ⊚

The English prof was into the soccer theme. There was an A- on Andrew's paper but lots of red marks as well. If there was one thing that Pappy had learned in four years of high school honors English, it was that no matter how well you write, you have half the battle won if the teacher is interested in the subject. And if you write about sports, always draw some philosophical parallel between the game and life.

Practice was light. Tomorrow was the Kirkwood Black Knights, and the Titans would leave at noon for the long drive. It was unusual to have a game so far away on a weekday, particularly because the days were getting shorter. Pappy would have to cut Spanish, but that was okay. The teacher realized he was well ahead of most of the class.

Santander was there, comparing moves and tricks with Andrew. Great balance and control but nothing showy. He made the right pass, at the right time, on the money. Hancock now saw the talent, but it was like a basketball player who could shoot from twenty feet but lacked aggression and defensive ability.

The Chiefs went to dinner with the rest of the crowd. Pappy looked around, but Littlefield didn't show. He stayed after Barrett and the others left and then went up to the library, but she was nowhere to be found.

Wednesday, September 10

⊚ ⊚ ⊚ ⊚

The almost three-hour ride to Kirkwood was animated. The Titans left at noon—it was kind of cool to be on the road representing your college—and the Union food service made sandwiches for everyone. Only twenty-four traveled, as the athletic department was trying to cut costs. They would have to stop for dinner on the way back, and the seventy-dollar meal allowance per game meant less than three dollars each. It would be McDonald's hamburgers, but no one cared.

"This is the one game each year I dread," said Randy Williams, looking out the window at the endless farmland. "There's no reason to go. We can't win. The referee will be that fat slob, Jay Cooper. And then there's his highness, Byron McIntyre."

"Who's he?" asked Millwood.

"This arrogant asshole who plays left wing for them," said Williams. "He spent one summer in Scotland and thinks he's the second coming. He's good, but Cooper will make him ten times better. And wait until you see the fans. They line the field, swearing and throwing stuff, trying to rip your shorts off and spitting at you. And that's the girls." They all laughed but not Randy.

"I'm serious," he continued. "These women are pigs. They're rude and filthy. I can't believe the crap they say and do."

"That's all right—wait until you see what our football team does to them," said Sheffe. "Last year it was seventy-seven zip. He won't admit it, but I think Bolger left the first string in longer after what happened at the soccer game."

"Why, what happened?" asked Paxton.

"Sheffe stole the ball from McIntyre, and he got mad and punched Paul in the face, right in front of Cooper. All that lard ass did was blow his whistle and, after thinking about it for a minute, give him a warning. A warning! He threw Johnson out of the game earlier for what he claimed was a flying tackle and gave them a penalty kick, even though it was outside of the box. I'm telling you, if he's there, and he will be, we may as well stay home."

"How come we're playing here again this year?" asked Penny. "I thought we alternated each season."

"There was a conflict with the football schedule," said Johnson, with a tone of disgust. "What else?"

Not much was said after that. They pulled into the tree-lined street past the sign that pointed to the soccer field next to the football stadium. Kirkwood had been to the playoffs several times in the past decade but wasn't of the caliber of Southwestern or Carthage.

As the vans proceeded up the drive, several of the students, including the girls, gave them the finger, and screamed, "You're gonna get killed!" and "Screw the Titans!" They pulled into the parking lot and piled out, grabbing the equipment. Andrew walked alongside Coach Hancock.

"I've heard these guys think they're tough," said Hancock.

"Did you hear about the referee?" asked Paxton.

"Yes, I know about Cooper. You guys just worry about winning. I'll take care of him." Hancock stopped and then spoke in a louder voice. "And that means keep your mouths shut."

Paxton recognized McIntyre in an instant. He had curly blond hair, a lanky body, and a look of conceit. He sauntered when he jogged after the ball, imitating the foreign players, and his footwork was skilled and passes crisp as he dribbled around showing off.

The Chiefs had seen this type of player all their lives. Most of the inner-city teams had at least one. But unlike this guy, they were not cheeky or self-impressed. Other players on the Kirkwood team had ability, so this wouldn't be a one-man show.

The Titans broke into groups for short pass and trap drills. Penny and Pappy took some corner kicks and penalties.

Suddenly, there was a disturbance on the side of the field, which seemed to grow by the second. Barrett was there, with David Nakano and Sheffe. Harbaugh and Johnson ran over, and there was finger pointing and cursing. Most of the Titans headed that way. There was a small blur as Hancock shot past them and jumped into the middle of the crowd. Barrett was toe-to-toe with two guys and a girl, and she was doing most of the screaming and swearing.

"What's going on here?" said Hancock, forcing Barrett behind him.

"That slutty pig tried to trip me when I went after the ball," said Barrett.

"Why don't you kiss off, pussy," said one guy, and Paxton had to hold Penny back just inches from him.

"You people need to go back to the sidelines," said Hancock. And turning to his team he said, "Back to warm-ups. Now!" Hancock turned to leave as the fans began to disburse.

"Screw you, Coach," said the girl.

Williams and Paxton went to the centerline to meet with the referee and captains of the Kirkwood Black Knights. Jay Cooper looked like a prick. White hair and round face, he was a fifty-five-year-old with a barrel gut and powder-pale legs, which appeared comical in black shorts and knee socks.

The obligatory handshakes were exchanged, and McIntyre made it clear he considered them underlings.

Kirkwood won the toss and elected to kick off. The field was smooth and well manicured, the lines clearly marked.

Bain started with a three-man line: Penny at center, Millwood on left, and Caldwell at right wing. Pappy was middle halfback, with Driver to his left and Nakano to his right.

Williams was in goal, with Barrett and Harbaugh as the middle fullbacks, and Landon and Sheffe were on the outside. Sheffe drew the unenviable task of covering McIntyre. He would get help from Barrett, who was spoiling for a shot to take the jerk's head off, but Andrew noticed that two other players in the middle were just as skilled. One was a small Asian-looking man, number twelve, whose shorts almost covered his kneepads; and number nine was slightly taller, with curly black hair and Mediterranean features.

The referee checked with both goalies, blew his whistle, and signaled to play. Number twelve passed left to nine, who turned and immediately chipped the ball over Nakano's head as McIntyre raced down the wing. Sheffe was slow to react. McIntyre chest-trapped to his feet and took one dribble inside Sheffe. He didn't see Barrett, who came up quickly, cut him off, and blasted the ball forty yards out of bounds.

"Hey, man!" shouted McIntyre, shoving Barrett. Brian's anger flashed, but he just smiled. The referee blew his whistle and ran over. He said nothing, pulled his book from his pocket, held it up, and pointed to Barrett. Luckily, Pappy was there and pulled Brian away before he had the chance to react.

"Hey, what the hell is going on? That pussy pushed me," yelled Barrett, but Paxton drowned him out.

"Quiet, quiet, I'll handle this." Millwood kept Barrett at bay while Paxton went to the referee.

"What's the call, ref?" asked Andrew. The referee said nothing. "Excuse me, sir, but what is the call?" Cooper blew his whistle again, reached into his shirt pocket, and lifted his book over his head, pointing to Andrew Paxton. Now Pappy was enraged.

"Sir, I am the captain. I am allowed to question calls. Sir, sir, I am allowed to question calls," Pappy repeated.

"Unsportsmanlike conduct, delay of game, number seven, white," he said.

Hancock was screaming on the sidelines. "Keep quiet and get back in the game!" he yelled. "Get back on defense."

The Kirkwood right halfback threw the ball down the sidelines to McIntyre, who took it toward the corner. Sheffe came over, and Barrett, still enraged, abandoned number nine, whom McIntyre hit with a pass. Harbaugh was slow to react, and the shorter man cut back to his left and, in one dribble, was at the penalty line. Number twelve was open six yards from the goal. The linesman signaled the obvious offside, but he tapped the ball into the open goal, and the crowd went wild. The linesman stood with the flag raised, but the referee signaled score and turned his back to run to the centerline. Hancock was furious.

"Offside, offside!" he screamed. "What kind of crap is that? How in the hell can you call that?" But Cooper kept his back to him, marking the goal on a sheet of paper. Hancock threw his clipboard to the ground and kicked it several feet away.

Down one to zero five minutes into the game. The Titans kicked off. Penny passed the ball wide to Millwood on left wing. The Kirkwood halfback intercepted and knocked the ball out of bounds. Tim took the throw-in as two girls tried first to trip him and then to grab his uniform. The next ten minutes, the play was back and forth. Kirkwood had more skill and experience playing together. The two inside forwards knew to avoid Barrett and put the ball to the wings. Although they hustled, Landon and Sheffe were no match, and the Black Knights repeatedly broke free and crossed the ball in front of the goal. Williams made some great plays intercepting passes, but he couldn't stop them all.

"Mark your men tighter," said Pappy. He drifted back to help cover, allowing Kirkwood to put more men on attack. Now the game was being played in the Bainbridge end. Barrett would clear, but with only three players at midfield, against five defensemen, it was impossible to start a drive. It was only a matter of time before someone missed an assignment, and at the thirty-minute mark, the wing stole the ball back from Johnson and went straight for the goal. Harbaugh couldn't cover, and the shot from eleven yards out went into the lower left-hand corner. Two to nothing Kirkwood. The Titans tightened up on defense, but the Black Knights' pass work always left someone open.

At the forty-minute mark, Barrett chipped the ball twenty yards past the centerline, and the Titans' front line took off. Penny passed out to Millwood, and the whole team raced forward. Pappy swung to the right ten yards behind Penny, and Millwood took the ball deep in the corner, but the fullback knocked the ball out of bounds. Pappy launched the throw-in fifty yards to the middle of the goal, catching the Kirkwood players off guard. Barrett leaped and struck a header toward the upper right corner, but it was wide. The Titans scrambled back on defense, and now Kirkwood was deep in their own territory with a goal kick. Pappy headed the ball up to Penny. Don heard Caldwell yell and without looking spun and threaded the pass between the two fullbacks. Dave was cutting toward the goal at full speed. The pass was perfect; he took one dribble and was alone twelve yards from the goal. His shot tailed wide right.

Now the Titans were pumped. They lined up for a goal kick when the referee blew the whistle, signifying the end of the first half.

Tempers were hot as they walked over to a maple tree some fifty yards off the field. Kenny Hodges passed around some water bottles and salt and dextrose pills.

"Everybody sit down and shut up!" yelled Hancock.

"How much more of this crap are we going to have to take?" asked Barrett.

"I said to sit down and shut up!" Everyone was quiet. Hancock paced back and forth, regaining his composure. He wasn't mad at Barrett, and he glared back at Jay Cooper.

"All right," he began, "there's nothing we can do about this guy. But he's not the reason we're getting beat out there. Paxton, you have got to stop coming back to help out on defense. The farther you do, the more they push their guys forward. Barrett, stay on your man. I know you want to tear that guy's head off. If you just keep out-hustling these guys, we can get back in this game."

He looked over his team. "Relax for a few minutes and then go back to warm up. Anybody hurt?"

"No," they answered collectively.

Hancock walked toward Cooper, who was over on the sidelines, talking to the Kirkwood coach and smiling. Seeing Hancock, he turned and walked toward the end of the field, making it clear he wasn't going to listen to anything from the Bainbridge coach.

Hancock's face filled with rage. He'd kept his tongue for most of the first half, but this was too much. He quickened his pace and then felt a hand on his shoulder.

"Coach, same team that started?" asked Andrew Paxton.

Hancock stopped. "Yes, same team," he said, and then he smiled to himself. This freshman was wise beyond his years. The question was real, but his intent was to make Hancock reconsider what he was about to do.

"We're on it, Coach," said Paxton, running back to the center of the field.

"All right, same team that started," said Pappy. "Look, these guys up front are quick. Stay tight with them. We need to get every loose ball."

He turned to Caldwell. "Dave, you and Don and Tim need to stay at midfield. Don't get caught off sides but we are going to start bombing when we get it. The center fullback is tough but slow, and the guy on the left keeps trying to sneak forward. Dave, we're going to you. Scott, you need to stay behind and give him an outlet."

"Got it," said Driver.

The Titans kicked off, and Penny tapped to Driver, who passed back to Paxton. Caldwell broke inside the fullback, and Pappy lofted a perfect pass over the halfback's head, hooking away from the fullback and right at Caldwell's chest. He trapped the ball and immediately passed left to Millwood, whose man pulled inside to help. Tim took the ball into the corner and hit a left foot to the middle of the penalty box. Andrew Paxton struck the ball with his forehead, and it smashed off the center post, right back to him. He chest-trapped to his feet, but the ball was too high, so he volley-kicked, and unbelievably, it banged once again into the same spot on the crossbar, straight down into the hands of the startled goalie.

The tide had turned. The Titans fought for every ball. Nakano and Sheffe were tireless, bumping their men at every turn. Harbaugh stayed back, freeing Barrett to press the attack. The Black Knights were tiring. At the twenty-minute mark, Paxton took a throw-in from the right sideline and put it right on Penny's head, who passed back to Barrett, but his shot cleared the crossbar by five feet. Everyone whooped and hollered.

The defense was doing its job, but the team was relying too much on the three guys up front, and Paxton, to score. No one else could control the ball and shoot, and they were down two to zero. And Kirkwood was too skilled. At the thirty-one-minute mark, the Kirkwood left wing passed to number nine. He shot, and Sheffe, his adrenaline pumping, stuck out his hand. Immediately, he recoiled, cursing, making it more obvious, and the referee gleefully awarded a penalty kick. McIntyre strode up, smiling at Randy Williams. He placed the ball on the penalty line, took four steps back, accelerated, and struck the ball into the upper right-hand corner. Williams had guessed wrong and dived in the opposite direction. Down three to zero.

The crowd was now really into it, mocking and swearing. Some were throwing ice cubes, dirt, and stones. Suddenly, a rock struck Paul Sheffe in the side of the left eye, and he went down on one knee. Barrett, Harbaugh, and Johnson raced over, and the Titans bench dashed across the field. The referee blew his whistle repeatedly. The linesman had seen the entire incident. A girl had thrown the rock. Barrett went at her, and she recoiled, but the boy standing next to her didn't. Brian caught him flush on the left cheek, and he went down in a heap. Other fans came forward, but Harbaugh grabbed one, lifted him over his head, and threw him to the ground. Several other spectators stepped in and pulled the others back. By this time, Jay Cooper, the Kirkwood coach, and his assistants had arrived. Barrett had another boy by the throat and was choking him to death. Paxton pulled his roommate off. The fans were cursing and spitting.

Hancock ordered his players back to the other side, and Millwood helped Sheffe off the field.

"That bitch hit him in the eye with a rock!" screamed Barrett. The linesman confirmed the story to the referee. Hancock went to the Kirkwood coach. "Either control your fans or we're walking this game right now."

"Coach, I don't have control over—"

"What?" screamed Hancock. "Don't give me that crap. You either fix it or we're out of here." He turned to Jay Cooper. "And that goes for you too."

"You'd better watch your tone, Coach," he said.

Hancock threw down his clipboard. At six feet two and 260 pounds, Cooper's fat belly loomed over the five-seven coach, but there was no fear in Hancock's eyes. He reached for the bigger man, but Barrett stepped between them. It was too late.

Cooper pulled his book. "Coach, you're gone," he said, turning toward ᵗe middle of the field. "You can go to your car, but you can't stay on the ᵗdelines."

Hancock stormed off. He handed the clipboard to Randy Williams. "Come straight to the cars when the game is over," he said, walking away.

A campus patrol car and the local police were now there, but the worst fans had left.

Millwood came over to where Paxton and Williams were standing. "We gotta make some changes," he said. "Sheffe is gone. Let's switch to a four-man line and put Kono at halfback. Alternate McIlroy and Driver, putting Santander with Don up front."

Roland Santander hadn't expected to play, and he'd been dribbling the ball by himself on the sidelines. He took the kickoff, passing to Penny, who went by his defender and passed back to Roland. Out of the corner of his eye, he saw Paxton go by Penny on the right. Although facing left, he put his right foot on the left side of the ball and pivoted, flicking it past the fullback. It was so unexpected that the Kirkwood player never moved. Paxton took one dribble and shot from twenty-five yards out. The goalie was too far out, and the ball ducked under the bar. Three to one, Kirkwood.

The Titans slapped Pappy on the back, and he pointed at Santander, signaling with a clenched fist.

The Black Knights tried to kick off before the Titans were in place, but Penny jumped across the midline and pounded the ball out of bounds. Kirkwood passed back to the right halfback and up to the right wing. Nakano stole the ball and raced up the sideline. He passed up to Millwood, who took off toward the goal and crossed to Santander. Roland turned to his right and then stepped on the ball and dragged it back as the defender overplayed. The pass went to Pappy, wide open at twenty yards, but he lofted it to Caldwell, who cut inside his man. A perfect header into the corner made it three to two, Kirkwood. But there was a whistle. Offsides. Pappy looked at the linesman, but his flag wasn't up. The Kirkwood fullback kicked the ball up the field before Pappy could protest. Not that it would have done any good.

The Black Knights put the ball out to the right wing to McInty
but he and Nakano collided, the muscular Hawaiian controlling the ball
Nakano passed across to Pappy, who pushed it forward to Santande
Suddenly, a voice yelled, "Hey!" Andrew turned to see Nakano goin
toward McIntyre, fists raised. Barrett was there in an instant, and bo
teams ran over. Nakano threw the first punch, which missed, and other
jumped in. The police came onto the field, and players were milling around
But it was a ruse. McIntyre had come up behind Nakano and punched him
in the side of the face. He then yelled to get the referee's attention so that
when he turned, he would see Nakano attacking. Cooper raised his book
and pointed to Nakano, who was being restrained by Pappy.

"That's crap, you fat bastard," said Barrett. "That asshole swung first."
The book went up again, and he pointed to Barrett. Harbaugh and Penny
were now beyond control, pushing and shoving anyone they could find.
Some of the fans were on the field, but Malloy and Sampson stood there
with the rest of the team, fists clenched. Another police car arrived, and
the referee signaled that the game was over.

Hancock was now back in the middle of the field, surrounded by the
Titans. "Let's get out of here," he said. They piled into the vans, which
were now guarded by the local police, amid the curses and threats of the
Kirkwood fans.

"Remind me to tell the football team to come back here and bury these
dirt bags," said Barrett. "Wait until we get these bush hogs on our field."

Thursday, September 11

◉ ◉ ◉ ◉

Todd Hancock was already at Sam Bolger's office the next morning when he arrived. Bolger was not only dean of the conference coaches but also head of the referee committees for soccer and basketball. Jay Cooper had called the night before to tell his side of what would no doubt be a formal protest by Hancock. He blamed most of the problems on the unruly fans and attributed this to Hancock's losing his temper. He confirmed that the Bainbridge fullback was hit in the eye with a stone, stating that it had precipitated the melee. He regretted throwing Hancock out of the game, and given the actions of the crowd, he wouldn't oppose the downgrading of all of the ejections to warnings so that no one would be suspended for a game.

Unfortunately, this wasn't the first or even the tenth complaint about Cooper. Bolger had reprimanded him more than once for lying in a game report. Twice the previous year, Bolger had gone to soccer games and observed his behavior. Cooper had two or three favorite coaches who always requested him as the referee, and his bias toward their teams was criminal.

The entire conference suffered the boorish Kirkwood fans, which included not only sporting events but concerts and lectures as well. The Titans' basketball and football teams were so far superior to the Black Knights that fan conduct short of murder didn't matter. But two years before, the soccer team, then just a club, had walked off midway through the second half of a game when a Bainbridge player was assaulted in the restroom.

Cooper whined on with his excuses, complaints, and accusations, but Bolger wasn't listening. Each game, Cooper would lord over the players and coaches and then do a penance at the next officials' meeting.

Today Cooper was conciliatory from the start. After all, Kirkwood had won, which insured that he would referee all the Black Knights' home games. He had someone to blame: the crowd. He was sure Hancock would spend much of his report on the melee that took place. Finally, even though some of his calls may have been disputed, Kirkwood still outscored the Titans, at least in his report.

Bolger ceremonially thanked him for the call. He would ask the Kirkwood coach to agree to rescind the ejections, but it wasn't required. He wanted to make the coach sweat about his conduct and the fans. Bolger could fire Cooper in a moment, and both men knew it.

Bolger had great regard for Hancock. He knew that Alan Amory, the Bainbridge varsity basketball coach, was soon destined for a bigger school. Bolger had watched Hancock lead the Titans to three Indiana conference championships as a player just a few years before, and he knew he was tough, tenacious, and a born leader. To come to Bainbridge and be saddled with the thankless job of head soccer coach, with no experience, in a program with no funds, said volumes. Further, he knew Hancock would make an impact on the team for the short time he was in charge. The Chiefs, however, were an unexpected bonus. These talented individuals had passed up many better programs. They were a bright spot for Hancock in an otherwise dead-end job.

So Bolger wasn't surprised to see the young coach waiting outside his office. He decided not to have coffee but to get the unpleasant task over with at once. At least he could lower Hancock's blood pressure.

"Come in, Todd," he said, opening the door. "But before you start, let me say that Jay Cooper called me last night. All the ejections are being changed to warnings, and your ejection is nullified."

Hancock's expression didn't change. He was going to have his say.

"Wow," began Hancock. "How generous of him to remove the ejections when they shouldn't even have been warnings in the first place." His voice rose. "Did he tell you he disallowed one of our goals because of offsides, which he called from midfield, while the linesman, who was standing right there, made no signal? Did he tell you Sheffe is out with a broken blood vessel in his eye from being struck by a rock thrown by a fan? David Nakano was punched in the face right in front of the linesman. Those things happen because their coach wants the crowd to intimidate our players, and the referee lets the Kirkwood team get away with it! Now we're down another game, and one of our men has been seriously and needlessly injured. How would you feel if it were your kid?"

Bolger sighed. "Todd, everything you say is correct. But no matter what the outcome, the score isn't going to change. At least you don't have to play them again until next year, and you won't be at their school for the next two years. I'll speak to the committee, but we've always allowed the home-field coach to choose the officials. They're presumed to be unbiased and supposed to control the game, but you played basketball at Kirkwood. Their fans consider it their right to be abusive." He walked around the desk to where Hancock was sitting. "By the way, I understand that kid Barrett took out more than one fan with a couple of right hooks. He's probably lucky the campus cops didn't throw him in jail."

"Yes, and what about the black eye to Nakano?" Hancock stood up to leave. "We have hot tempers on our squad, but they showed remarkable restraint. I'll take care of Mr. Barrett. But I don't want to see Cooper again, in Kirkwood or anywhere else."

"Well, I don't know about that," said Bolger. "Bonham is another school that uses him. You won't find the fans spitting and throwing dirt there. They're too rich to soil their hands. I told Cooper that he's on probation, which for him is a constant condition."

Friday, September 12

⊙ ⊙ ⊙ ⊙

The team met at the field house at noon and took off for Bellville, on the other side of the state. Another away game, when the football team was home, and this time they would miss Friday night's pregame parties as well.

The eight-hour round trip could be done on Saturday, but everyone wanted to play early and get back for as much of the game as possible, so they voted to go the night before. It was sunny and hot, the windows were down, and the AM radio blared. WLS in Chicago was the preferred station but usually could be found only at night, when the atmospheric conditions were right. They settled for a local station that played Beatles, Credence, Rolling Stones, and just enough Elvis.

Everyone had packed toothpaste, underwear, a clean shirt, socks, and whatever else he could think of, not knowing what to expect. Pappy brought the ever-present chemistry book.

The first three hours were interstate highways. Everyone had had lunch at the Union, but they stopped after a couple of hours for sodas and chips. The last leg was mostly two-lane rural roads. Pappy rode with Hancock, Nakano, and the equipment manager, and the team razzed them for sucking up to the coach.

Andrew read until he got a headache and then put his book away. Hancock talked about his basketball playing days at Bainbridge, and Pappy recounted every detail of every game his senior year at Amsterdam.

They discussed foreign players. One school, Stratton State, later in the schedule, was essentially a city college where professional teams parked their second-string players to keep in shape.

They arrived at the Bellville campus around five and went directly to the field house. The equipment and overnight bags were locked in a supply room, and the team walked over to the student union for supper. Many of the conference schools had the same food service, so the Titans could eat there for free on their own ticket—a blessing for the meager team budget.

Next on the tour was the library, and it was made clear that they were restricted to there or the field house. Period. Anyone found elsewhere would be benched, and no one doubted the coach's threat.

Doing homework on Friday night wasn't even considered, but fortunately, there was a TV room in the library basement, and three people were allowed to go to the bookstore to buy playing cards. That was enough to keep everyone busy, and since it was the weekend, the Titans had the whole library to themselves.

By ten, they were back at the field house. Just like Bain's, it was a big old gymnasium—cold, empty, and noisy. There were twenty-four mattresses on the wooden basketball court. Each had a sheet, pillow, blanket, towel, washcloth, and small bar of soap. Like sleeping in a cave. So much for the glamour of college sports—exotic travel, expensive meals, fancy hotels. The soccer team was relegated to cars and vans, cafeterias, and the gym floor. Showers and bathrooms were down the stairs. Most played cards or talked. Lights out was at eleven. A couple of the upperclassmen had brought transistor radios, and music played until sometime after midnight.

Saturday, September 13

⊙ ⊙ ⊙ ⊙

The sun poured in the big skylights just before seven, but sneakers began clamoring up and down the cement and steel staircases sometime earlier. Maybe traveling the day before to play early and get back for the football game wasn't such a great idea. Everyone was stiff and miserable. The mattresses must have been rejects stored in a musty closet somewhere. Some tried to pull the pillows and covers over their heads for a few more minutes of peace, but by eight, everyone was up and in uniform. All their personal gear was locked in the equipment room, and they went to the Union with the coach for breakfast, but two hours before game time, nerves killed everyone's appetite.

They retrieved their belongings, packed the cars, and drove to the athletic fields at the south end of the campus. Even though Bellville's soccer team was weak, at least its field was on campus.

The Pioneers were at the field, which was in good shape. The Titans took a lap and did their pregame routine. The Chiefs and a few others gathered at the middle of the field to check out the opposition. There were no stars. The goalie was right-handed, didn't punt well, and stood stiff when fielding a shot.

"We're going to start early," said Hancock, "so we can get back to campus. We'll go with the red team from Thursday's practice. This isn't Southwestern or Kirkwood, but you'll recall a bunch of football players at Brackettville that gave you all you could handle. I didn't see anyone

118

with great speed. Let's keep our outside fullbacks up tight on the wings. The goalie doesn't punt very well, so we should get some opportunities. Landon, you and Williams are captains. There's no wind, and I don't see much difference in either end, so let's take the ball if we win the toss … Hands in … and let's go!"

Barrett was up fullback, with Landon behind him. Sheffe and Johnson were outside. Pappy at center halfback, with McIlroy and Nakano; Penny at center forward; Caldwell and Millwood at wings. The Titans kicked off and put the ball to Caldwell. He dribbled to the corner and crossed, but the goalie cut it off. Pappy backed up quickly, and the punt was short toward his sideline. He chest-trapped to his feet, passed to Tim, and broke around his man toward the goal. Millwood bumped it back. Pappy was thirty yards out, but the keeper was near the front of the penalty box. He lifted a soft arching lob shot. The goalie pivoted and raced toward the net, but it was perfect, ducking under the bar. One to zero, Titans.

They were hot, and they were sharp. Play was in the Bellville end for the next fifteen minutes. Penny scored on a header from Millwood's corner kick. Just before the half ended, Driver passed to Paxton twenty yards out. He hooked a left-footed shot into the upper left-hand corner. The goalie never moved. Three to zero.

At halftime, the team gathered under a nearby tree. Good passes and a dozen shots had led to three goals, and everyone's blood was up. The coach stayed away and let the players burn off the excitement. Take away the Chiefs and the teams were about even. However, the skill and drive of the five made it no contest. Barrett relentlessly picked off loose balls and blasted them back to the offense. Hancock finally came over.

"Good job on all fronts. Now we need to work on ball control. There will be more teams like Southwestern." His voice became sterner.

"Don't let these guys back in the game. They scored two goals on Kirkwood. Spread the ball around and keep shooting good shots. This is a conference win for us. Don't let it get away."

They weren't listening. They were winning. Dominating. Bellville kicked off and put the ball out to the right wing, who quickly returned it to the center forward. His poor trap squibbed off the side of his foot, right to their left wing, cutting behind Harbaugh. He was off sides, but the linesman didn't call it, and punched the ball with his toe just as Barrett arrived. It dinged off the left goalpost and in. Three to one in less than a minute. Instead of shocking the Titans, it made them mad. Players began cutting in front of each other, making wild passes, and committing stupid fouls. Paxton and Millwood tried to calm things down, but players were bickering.

One thing Hancock hated about soccer: no calling time-out and giving everyone an earful. He was stuck on the sidelines, screaming and throwing his clipboard. He sent in four players, pulling Barrett.

"Control the damn ball," he said to no one in particular, but Brian took it personally.

"Why did you take us out?" he asked.

Hancock was fuming, but his words were slow and measured. "Because I am the coach," he said, walking away.

Just then, Pappy shot from eighteen yards, hitting Knight in the butt and deflecting the ball into the goal. Four to one, and everyone was laughing.

With twenty minutes left, Hancock pulled most of the starters, thinking the pace of the game would change. And it did. Roland Santander was now running the offense, and he put on a show. The Pioneers' defenders couldn't get the ball away from him without doubling-teaming. In the end, it was all Titans: Five to one.

Now almost noon, they loaded the cars, still in uniforms, and took off. There was no caravan. Everyone wanted to get back to campus.

They arrived in time for the second half, but it was already thirty-five to seven, Bainbridge, and the second string was on the field. Now the focus was the barbecue, dance, and fraternity parties. They intended to make up for missing Friday night.

Sunday, September 14

◉　◉　◉　◉

Sunday morning and no one was stirring. Barrett and Pappy rose after eleven. Not many bumps and bruises from the game, but serious lobster breath from the evening's drinking. They headed down to the Union for brunch. This was the first formal day of fraternity rush. The Chiefs sat together and talked about where to go first and where to avoid.

On a small campus, fraternity life had advantages: better food, more privacy, fewer rules, more parties, and quieter sleeping quarters.

TDT was first on the list. Randy Williams and Al Landon met them at the door, dressed in ties and sports coats. A national fraternity steeped in tradition, it also had by far the best food on campus. (Always a *major* consideration.) A parade of brothers introduced themselves. Everyone had been briefed on the Chiefs. They spent an hour there, shaking hands with at least forty men.

Next in line was Lambda Kappa. Definitely more laid-back. Everyone was friendly, and the beer was flowing.

Finally, they returned to the infamous Silo house at the far south end of campus. It was the most impressive building of the three, but in the daylight, it was easier to see the years of wear and tear inflicted by young men full of beer and testosterone. This time, they got the full tour, and the house was even bigger than it looked from the outside. They watched the Giants-Bears football game until five, when they were required to leave.

The Chiefs went to Pizza Inn to talk. This was going to be tough.

There would be more visits and then the final formal week in January, but all the fraternities had great guys and showed they really wanted all five to pledge. It would be hard breaking up the group, and they talked about blocking to one house. Growing up together, however, had taught them that they were five different personalities. In the end, each would make his own decision.

Monday, September 15

◉ ◉ ◉ ◉

Chemistry was a relentless hour-long lecture of new and complicated material every morning at eight o'clock.

In English class, Andrew pulled his pen out of his pants pocket. Holy crap! A hole in his jeans, just below the belt. There were two more! And a couple on his shirt. It was true. Even though he hadn't spilled the chemicals in lab on his clothes, just the fumes were enough to eat through cloth. Imagine what this was doing to the inside of his nose, or his eyes, or any other part of his body. Hideous things must happen to people who worked with this stuff every day. No wonder Professor Ketcham wore a smock. It was down to the bookstore after class to buy an apron. He didn't care if he looked like a dork. He'd now trashed his only pair of jeans.

Spanish was a study hall, as Pappy had long since passed this level in high school. He made a stupid mistake on this week's quiz, though, and only gotten a ninety-five. Even the upperclassmen were impressed.

Practice was tough. Though they had won, Hancock would make sure no one started winning games in his head before they were ever played. It was a solid victory, but the Titans still weren't able to control the ball consistently.

Thanks to the five Chiefs, particularly Barrett, who opposed the coach every chance he got, they played a renegade version of kick and chase. No mere coach had ever been able to tell Barrett what to do. Hancock's loose cannon was his greatest athlete ... and his greatest irritation.

Tuesday, September 16

◎ ◎ ◎ ◎

Pappy and Barrett nailed the chem quiz. Practice was drills, corners, and penalty kicks. Santander showed off some juggling tricks, so Hancock had him stay to shoot penalties with Paxton, Caldwell, and Penny. Roland placed the ball on the penalty line, stood at a forty-five-degree angle to the goal, came forward, and swept his leg to the left. Randy Williams dove to his right, and everyone watching leaned left. But he struck the ball with the outside of his right foot, and it sailed just inside the right post. Awesome! Everyone was stunned.

"I have *got* to try that," said Pappy. He drilled the same spot with the same fake, but it wasn't as deceptive as Santander. Still, pretty good. Now they were all doing it, and even Hancock took a couple, although he missed the ball entirely in his first attempt. Nobody said a word.

Add one more cool surprise to the Spaniard's bag of tricks.

Wednesday, September 17

○ ○ ○ ○

The Titans were home against Newton. Another young program with no tradition and little talent. Their coach wasn't even in the athletic department; he was an English prof who played in high school and college. The meager budget was reflected in the cheap uniforms, and they arrived in a regular yellow school bus. The Chiefs thought they were back at Amsterdam High.

The Titans kicked off, still reveling in Saturday's win, which resulted in missed traps, bad passes, and even worse shots. The ball had a will of its own, and every spin and bounce went off a foot out of bounds, or out of reach. They were a step late after every loose ball, resulting in stupid fouls.

After twenty minutes, Barrett went to head the ball in the goalie box as Williams called him off. Too late. They collided, and the ball bounced into the net. Just before the half, Newton converted a penalty kick on a Johnson handball. Down zero to two against a team that lost two to zero to Bellville.

Hancock was furious but had nowhere to point a finger. Everyone was hustling—but in the wrong direction or too late.

"All right, settle down," he said, pacing back and forth. "We're going to shake this tree a little. Paxton, you move to center forward with Penny. Santander, you're now running the offense. Caldwell and Millwood, switch sides. Nakano, drop back to fullback in the middle with Barrett. McIlroy, cover the left wing. All right, you've got forty-five minutes to bury these guys. I bet they never had a lead this big against anybody, and when we put the pressure on, they'll drop everyone back on defense. Keep shooting and make something happen."

With Santander, they were a new team. Confident and skilled, he worked the ball among all four forwards. He and Paxton played give-and-go, and Andrew switched with the wings, allowing them to go straight at the goal. The result: four goals in the first thirty minutes, two by Santander and one each from Millwood and Caldwell. Scott Driver tallied on a corner kick header, and Pappy converted a penalty kick. In the end, with the reserves on the field, the starters were milling around the sidelines high as a kite, ready to play another game. The six to two final score was a stunning offensive display. Try as he did, Hancock couldn't hold back his smile. Now that was fun.

Thursday, September 18

F or once, people on campus were talking about the soccer team. The Titans had never won two games this early in the season and, including Brackettville, had a winning record. Randy Williams continued his excellent play. Al Landon and David Nakano shared equal time with the other fullbacks, allowing all to take a breather and play all out when on the field. And things were so good that Barrett and Hancock no longer "exchanged ideas" about how to play.

Chem lab. Bunsen burners. All students were given a lump of an unknown substance, which they weighed on the Mettler balance, placed in a crucible, and heated to burn off some of the material. It was supposed to be lighter. Paxton's was heavier. Four thousand percent heavier than expected, to be exact. It was as if the thing got pregnant when exposed to heat. Not enough time to do it again. He'd have to compile his findings, turn in his report next Thursday, and face ridicule from the nerdy lab rats in class.

Friday, September 19

@ @ @ @

Another free day without classes (except chem) before an away soccer game. The weather was hot, and Pappy and Barrett took their usual places on the front lawn of Roberts Hall. They'd settled into college life. Pappy had met several cute girls in his classes and wondered if he should move on emotionally as well. He hadn't seen Littlefield in some time. Barrett never mentioned her, so he couldn't figure out whether his roommate still cared. Maybe Brian was going to play the field, knowing she was always there.

Andrew didn't know how long he could remain a monk. When he pledged the fraternity next semester, there would be parties with the sororities.

Friday night around nine, Pappy made his usual swing through the union and then the library. No Littlefield. Rumor was that she had already been back to Amsterdam to see her parents. He still relived that night she came to him to get away from Rattigan. He should have kissed her back, should have told her how he felt, should have called her the next day. He should have ... Well, some things never changed. He didn't do or say anything to her that night, because he never did anything any other time—because he might make a fool of himself for all eternity.

Saturday, September 20

◉ ◎ ◎ ◉

J unction University was similar in many ways to Bain—size and makeup of the student body, the curriculum, and even the design of the buildings. The Junction Deacons' soccer team also drew heavily from high schools in the east. But the athletic program was not a powerhouse like the Titans.

The field was on the west side of the campus, fairly well maintained and no overhanging tree. The two sides were fairly evenly matched, edge to the Titans due to Paxton and company. Junction's only star was their goalie, who had made all-conference the past two years. Hancock still wasn't crazy about Roland Santander's slow style of play, but his skills were worth sacrificing one of his defensemen. As Junction had no outstanding offensive threat, it was a logical gamble.

Most slept on the two-hour drive through the country. Pappy realized he hadn't driven a car in a month. After earning his driver's license at sixteen, he'd vanished from home, his parents catching fleeting glimpses of him at meals and bedtime.

The sun shone brightly, and there was little wind. The handful of fans at the field were probably girlfriends. Millwood, Penny and Caldwell, and Santander were on the line. Nakano went to left halfback and Harbaugh to left fullback. Driver would sub for Nakano and McIlroy. Paxton and Barrett were center halfback and fullback, respectively. Landon to right full.

Titans won the toss and kicked off. The game started slowly, both teams in a funk from getting up too early on a Saturday morning. Everyone missed passes and traps, even the reliable Andrew Paxton. At the ten-minute mark, Millwood's corner kick went completely across the goalmouth untouched. At eighteen minutes, Barrett bombed the ball seventy yards up the field. The center fullback misplayed the ball, and Penny was wide open. The left fullback slid, taking out Penny's feet. The referee signaled penalty kick.

Hancock pointed to Paxton. *Nothing fancy*, he thought. *Just hit it solid.* The whistle blew, and Paxton touched off another three-beer screamer into the upper left-hand corner. The goalie was frozen.

One to nothing, Titans. That woke up both sides. The Titans were pumped, and the Deacons were pissed. Junction kicked off, and Penny stole the ball and drove downfield. Sloppy play continued, but now both teams were attacking the loose balls at full speed. There were several collisions, and play stopped momentarily when McIlroy had the wind knocked out of him. Paxton noticed Santander hanging back, acting as an outlet, dishing passes left and right. His ball control skills were better than Andrew's, and even though he was taking his job, Pappy let him control the offense.

He switched with Santander, putting real pressure on the Junction defenders, and the outside fullbacks were cheating toward the middle. This left Millwood and Caldwell open. At the thirty-minute mark, Santander passed to Millwood on the left, all alone. He took the ball to the corner and struck a perfect cross head-high, twelve yards in front of the goal. Paxton dashed forward, his timing perfect. He leaped into the air, heading the ball sideways while going forward. He never saw the goalie, and the goalie, Ted Knowles, never saw him. Knowles, at full speed, put both fists together, and punched at the ball. But it was gone a split second before he arrived. Unfortunately, the side of Andrew's head was still there. The fists struck Paxton just below the temple, in front of the ear. He collapsed as if hit by a bus. Penny gasped. His first thought was that Pappy was dead. He lay motionless, eyes closed. The referee blew his whistle. Barrett raced forward, ready to avenge his friend, but Millwood grabbed him. It was obviously unintentional, and the keeper was now doubled over, clutching his right hand in pain. Both teams gathered around the body lying in front of the goal.

Hancock knelt next to Pappy. At first, he appeared to be only stunned. "Paxton. Paxton," he said, more loudly each time, shaking his shoulder, but no response. Kenny Hodges handed Hancock an ammonia stick out of the medical kit. The coach waved it under Paxton's nose. He tried another and then another. No reaction. For Andrew Paxton, there was nothing but distant voices and a buzzing sound in his head.

"Unh …," he groaned.

"Let's get him up," said Hancock, standing and pulling at Paxton's wrists.

"No," said Pappy. "No."

It was now clear that he was really hurt and needed medical attention. There was no stretcher and no way to stabilize his head and neck, so six players, half from Junction, crossed arms and carried him off horizontally. The goalie walked alongside, cradling his hand, which was twice its normal size and had a deep purple hue.

The Titans were stunned. Their indestructible leader was gone. After a few minutes, the teams resumed play, with Driver taking Pappy's place, but the Titans kept looking over at the sidelines.

Andrew lay on the ground, still unresponsive. The Junction trainer came over and checked his eyes.

"Coach, we're going to bring a car around. I think we should take him to the hospital right across the street and get some X-rays."

"Kenny, go with him," said Hancock. "Come back as soon as you know something."

A brown Oldsmobile station wagon pulled up, and they dropped the tailgate. Jamie Knight and Barry Sampson tried to help Andrew to his feet, but he was listless and had to be carried. They laid him down in the back of the wagon. Hodges crawled in alongside, and they pulled away.

Hancock turned his attention back to the field and resumed shouting. But the heart had been ripped out of them, and play became ragged. They pressed harder to make things happen. Meanwhile, the Deacons, their goalie gone, tightened up on defense. From that point, Bainbridge was no longer in the game. With five minutes left in the first half, the left wing beat Glenn Johnson and put one into the lower left-hand corner just under Randy Williams. Three minutes later, Harbaugh went to clear a loose ball in front of the goal but suddenly turned and tapped it back to the goalie. Randy Williams had gone to the far side to cover the other post, and the ball rolled untouched into the empty net. Two to one, Junction.

At halftime, Hancock tried to get their heads back in the game, but all they could talk about was the incredible impact between Pappy and the keeper. The second half began as the first had ended. Five minutes in, the center forward hit the lower right-hand corner from twelve yards out.

After twenty minutes, the Deacon's center forward beat Barrett, who shoved him out of frustration, inside the penalty area. Junction converted to make it four to one. With fifteen minutes left, Hancock pulled most of his starters to let others get some playing time. The end whistle was anticlimactic.

Afterward, Hancock had little to say, and as he sent the team to a local restaurant, Kenny Hodges returned. Paxton was transferred to the student health center. He had a severe concussion but no fracture, and the doctors would keep him overnight for observation.

Andrew Paxton lay in a hospital bed at the health center, still in his filthy soccer uniform. There was a buzzing in his ears, and he saw lines across his vision. When he sat up, the room spun uncontrollably, so he had to take his medicines lying down.

Hancock arrived with the Junction coach, relieved by the doctor's diagnosis but concerned with his player's total lethargy. After telling Andrew he'd be back to pick him up the following day, he joined the team at the restaurant.

Pappy slipped in and out of consciousness. The Junction goalie came by, sporting a gigantic white cast covering his shattered right hand and half his arm. He apologized, but Andrew told him he knew it was unintentional.

A visibly shaken Hancock reassured his team that there was no cause for concern, but this normally stoic coach was obviously worried about his player. He didn't feel like eating, even though it was now midafternoon and breakfast was hours ago, so they headed back to Bainbridge.

It was after nine o'clock before Andrew awoke. The night nurse appeared in the doorway and then came over to the bed. She had dark shoulder-length hair, and looked as young as Andrew. He thought it strange that instead of a uniform, she was wearing a nightgown and bathrobe. Apparently, they let the overnight staff sleep when they weren't performing their duties.

"How do you feel?" she asked. "Would you like something to eat?"

"I want to go to the bathroom," said Andrew, trying to get out of bed. He was extremely unsteady.

"No, you can't," she said, trying to restrain him. "I'll get you a bedpan."

"I don't want a bedpan. I want to use the bathroom." He tried to stand but became dizzy and almost fell over.

She slung his arm over her shoulder and helped him to the commode. "I'll be outside if you need me," she said.

After a few minutes, the nurse shuffled him back to bed. He refused a hospital gown, so she washed the dirt off his legs, arms, and face and left him in his sweaty uniform. He drank part of a glass of milk with the next round of pills, but that was all he could tolerate. She removed the tray, and Pappy was asleep before she left the room.

Sunday, September 21

⊚ ⊚ ⊚ ⊚

Andrew woke around seven the next morning to daylight blaring through the flimsy curtains. The white walls magnified the glare, and he pulled the meager pillow over his eyes, trying unsuccessfully to go back to sleep. After ten minutes, still groggy, his head pounding, he made his way to the bathroom. Now nauseated, he took it slowly, holding onto the walls and furniture. He remembered little from the night before, but he knew that he smelled bad, and his mouth tasted like sour milk.

He returned to find another nurse in the doorway. This one was much older and not as pretty.

"Well, you're up early," she said, helping him back to bed. "How do you feel? How about some breakfast?"

"Can I have some aspirin? My head is killing me."

"Sure, I'll be right back." She left, and Pappy lay back.

The smell of food woke him again around nine. Juice, a muffin, and a plate under a metal cover. The sleep had cleared his head, which made it throb even more. Orange juice washed down the two white tablets on the tray, and he lay back again.

"Eat before it gets cold," said the nurse. Andrew had a piece of bacon and some toast.

"I need to take a shower, but I don't have any clothes."

"Your coach called, and he should be here anytime now," said the nurse. "We really don't have anything to lend you except a gown. I'll clean you up a bit more." He took off his shirt, and she wiped his face, torso, and limbs with a wet towel. Not as good as a shower, but he was returning to the living. The aspirin helped, as did the food.

Hancock arrived around eleven, with clothes supplied by Barrett. Pappy was glad to see him and happier still to be going home. The doctor came in and looked in Andrew's eyes and had him touch his nose. He asked his name, where he lived, his phone number, how he got there.

"You're good to go," he said. "I called your school physician, and he'll see you when you get back to campus. Good luck. I think you came out of this better than our goalie did."

Pappy thanked everyone at the health center, and they headed back to Bain.

"Thanks for coming back, Coach," said Andrew. "Sorry to take you away from your family on Sunday, but I'm glad to get out of there."

"Well, we're all glad you're okay," said Hancock. "Their goalie is gone for the year with that broken hand. It was bad."

"Yeah, he came by to see me yesterday. I don't remember what he said, but he had a big cast on it … I guess we lost."

"Yes, we lost," said Hancock. "After you got hurt, everything went wrong. They tightened up their defense to protect their keeper, and we made too many mistakes."

They talked for a while about the game and then about Hancock's family. He'd married his high school sweetheart, and they had two children, a boy and a girl, ages three and four. After an hour, Andrew was suddenly exhausted, and he fell asleep in the middle of the conversation.

Hancock became concerned and drove faster, wanting to get to a medical facility in case this was something more than dozing off.

Fifteen miles from campus, Andrew awoke. Each time he slept, it cleared some of the cobwebs, but he still had a long way to go.

Back at the health center, Dr. Raymond Hardwell looked at Andrew's swollen head and his X-rays.

"That must've been a big-time knock on the noggin," he said. He checked Andrew's reflexes and his eyes. "We're going to put you up here tonight, and you can go back to your room tomorrow. We called your professors, and you're excused from class. I'll give you some pills, and you can have aspirin. If the pain worsens or you feel dizzy, let me know. No practice or playing until I release you. If all goes well, you should be back by the end of the week. You must have one hard, hard head," he said, smiling.

Andrew took a shower and put on a gown. He watched TV and dozed until supper. The nurse gave him a sleeping pill at nine, which made him hallucinate just before he dropped off. His last thoughts were of Beth Littlefield.

Monday, September 22

⊙ ⊙ ⊙ ⊙

D r. Raymond Hardwell sat rocking back and forth, eyes darting between his office door and the telephone. He was about to have an unpleasant experience, and it wouldn't be the first time in his medical career or during his tenure at Bain. He'd joined the army after World War I, progressing from hospital orderly to medic. After World War II, he enrolled in college under the GI Bill. At the time, veterans were given preference at any university, in any vocation, so at the age of forty, Raymond began medical school. Classes were a struggle, and he barely finished his internship at fifty. From there, he joined a physician in a small town in eastern Indiana. When his partner was killed in an automobile crash, Hardwell took over the practice. While there, he met Sam Bolger, with whom he'd served for three years in the war. Bolger was wounded twice and finally stationed in Brighton as an instructor of survival tactics for field medics. After the war, he went on to teach high school and coach football.

Bolger's tough discipline and keen football mind led to many successes, and in 1950, he was given the head coaching position at Preston College, a small private school of about a thousand students. He continued his winning ways and learned that Hardwell was in the next town over. They kept in touch and went fishing together a few times. Hardwell had a checkered career as a doctor, and his practice waned as people became more mobile and went to larger nearby towns for medical treatment.

Finally, Bolger became head coach at Bainbridge, a highly coveted spot in the conference. Learning of Hardwell's struggles, he arranged for him to get the school physician post. It was perfect. Now sixty-five years old, he could look and act like a doctor without the pressures of maintaining a practice. He didn't need a vast knowledge of ailments, and he referred almost anything to local specialists. His patients were primarily girls with menstrual cramps; students who suffered the annual flu epidemic on campus; and athletes with a variety of sprains, bruises, and bumps. Unfortunately, even those minor maladies held traps for the unskilled and marginally competent.

Hardwell heard the noise level rise outside the door. Sam Bolger knocked once and entered quickly. His face was red with stress, and he glared at Hardwell.

"Jesus Christ, Ray, what the hell is going on over here?" he asked, not wanting an answer.

"I …," Hardwell began, almost pleading.

"You have three guys from the same fraternity on the football team come in with a rash and you diagnose it as poison ivy? Poison ivy?" he demanded. "Holmes had a fever of one-oh-three after the game. Burton and Torrence were just as bad. And now their parents are considering suing the school. Chicken pox! Chicken pox, Ray! Even I recognized it when my kids got it twenty years ago. The entire football team, their fraternity, and God knows who else has been exposed.

"I understand that when boys get it late in life, it can make them sterile. Not to mention the scars these guys will have from scratching their faces.

"Holmes is gone," Bolger continued. "One of the greatest kickers in Division III college football, and he's out, maybe for the rest of the semester."

"Sam, I'm sorry," Hardwell began, keeping his voice low. "I was told they had been out pheasant hunting the previous weekend, and I thought they might have gotten it in the woods."

"Pheasant hunting? Who went pheasant hunting? Torrence is from New York City. I doubt he's ever hunted in his life. Burton is from Barksdale, Arizona. He wouldn't know a pheasant if he fell over one. It's not even pheasant season." He walked over and stood above Hardwell, who stared down at the desktop.

"Ray, this is just about it. I recommended you for this job, and this is the second serious misdiagnosis within two years. You told Dennis Croft he was okay to play the second half of the Bonham game last year. The broken wrist you said was only bruised resulted in three pins and a rod in that arm. Now I'm without a kicker; we have enraged parents; and the board of trustees of the university is wondering what kind of medical degree you have … I think it's about time you look to retirement."

"No, please, Sam," begged Hardwell. "My wife's kids are not even halfway through college, and I have the house and everything. I need the money."

"You might have thought of that before you left your first wife and married a woman twenty years younger than you—a woman with teenagers. It's like a goddamn soap opera around here." He paused. "This is it, Ray. I'll speak to the president. He'll handle things with the board. But one more problem, one more embarrassment, and I won't be able to save you."

"Thanks, Sam," said Hardwell. "I owe you everything. I'd never do anything to hurt you or the school."

"I know Ray, I know. But next time it won't be enough."

Bolger turned to leave and then stopped at the door. "By the way, what happened to that kid Paxton? I hear he got his bell rung and spent the night in the hospital in Junction."

"I took a look at him yesterday when he got back," said Hardwell. "He just has a concussion and some swelling."

"How long will he be out?" asked Bolger.

"It depends on whether he has any lasting effects. It's just like football; if he isn't dizzy and can remember his own name, he can play."

"Have you ever seen him play?"

"No, I don't care much for soccer. Sissy sport," said Hardwell.

"Not the way this kid plays it," said Bolger. "Hancock said the goalie who hit him has a broken hand. And you should see him kick. He's a cannon."

"Well, I'm keeping an eye on him, but he can probably play later in the week."

"Ray, please no more surprises," said Bolger, closing the door behind him.

Pappy was bouncing off the walls at the health center while waiting to be discharged. Hardwell didn't show up until well after ten. Once free, he raced over to the dorm and took another shower. No more hospitals or health centers. But Hardwell let him go too late for English class, so he dressed and went to lunch an hour early.

Andrew watched the dining room slowly fill with freshmen. The memory of his collision flashed through his mind at least once an hour. He shook his head, trying to drive away the sensation. But that only made him dizzy.

The food tasted especially good, and he went back for dessert.

"Pappy!" He turned as Beth Littlefield threw her arms around his neck. "Are you okay? We were so worried. Penny called to say you were in the hospital. Is it true? Are you all right? What happened? I heard the goalie broke his hand. Somebody said you had an operation."

Andrew stood there not knowing what to do with his Jell-O, but the hug felt good. Beth's hair was soft across his cheek, and she smelled of Ivory soap and bath powder. The rush of blood to his face made him dizzy, and he had to hold on to the steel serving table.

"I'm okay," he said, trying to keep his knees from buckling. "It's a concussion. I can play again by the end of the week."

"God, I was worried. I wanted to call your room, but I was afraid I'd wake you ... Omigosh, your head and cheek are swollen. Does it hurt? Do you want to sit down?"

Andrew looked at her. She appeared even thinner than before, and her makeup barely hid the darkening areas under her eyes.

"Don't worry," replied Pappy. "The doctor said it's just a bruise."

"Listen, I have to go to class." She hugged him again. "But I'm glad I saw you. Please, please take care of yourself," she said, looking back as she headed out the door.

She was there for an instant and then gone. Andrew was normally tongue-tied in Littlefield's presence, but with a concussion, it was ten times worse. She'd hugged him. Why didn't he hug her back? Did he hug her back?

"There's the wounded warrior, upright and not surrounded by nurses." It was Barrett, followed by the other Chiefs. "You don't ... Holy crap, look at the side of your face! I didn't think you could get much uglier, but I was wrong," he laughed. "You should have a woman slap you around like that. At least it'd be fun."

"Thanks a bunch. And thanks for blowing the game after I left," said Andrew.

"Well, we just can't do anything without you," replied Brian. "How long before you stop faking it and get back on the field?"

"End of the week ... maybe Wednesday."

"Hey, even Eldon Biederman talked about you in chem class today. Hancock must have given you a big buildup. You're now the famous fat-faced kid." Again they all laughed.

Suddenly, it was apparent all wasn't well. Millwood pushed Barrett aside. "Hey, you need to sit down." Pappy had turned white and was holding on to the serving table with two hands. They helped him to a chair.

"You need to go back to the health center," said Tim.

"No," replied Andrew. "I want to go to my room."

They half carried him to Roberts Hall. Barrett gave up his bottom bunk, and Andrew was out until dinner.

That night, Barrett's litany of phone calls from his female admirers actually included some who wanted to talk to Pappy. He was sure they were just sucking up to Brian's poor roommate. Unfortunately, Littlefield wasn't one of them.

Everyone at Monday's soccer practice was numb. The Titans lost the game and had lost Pappy. He'd run the offense and taken throw-ins, free kicks, corner kicks, and penalty kicks. Now Santander had to fill the void. Their emotional leader was gone.

Tuesday, September 23

⊙ ⊙ ⊙ ⊙

The clock radio went off at seven forty-five. Barrett popped out of bed and was dressed before he realized that Andrew hadn't moved. He checked to see if his roommate was still breathing. Sound asleep.

Brian returned after chem. Pappy was still out. Now he was worried. He thought he'd read somewhere that too much sleep after a concussion was dangerous.

When he returned at eleven, Andrew was just getting up. Maybe he should have stayed another day at the health center. They went to lunch together, but Pappy was still groggy, so he skipped Spanish and went back to bed.

Not even practice the day before a game could bring him out of his haze. Brian went by himself. For the second day, the team seemed to be in limbo. No Pappy and no word when he would return. The game prep was the usual drills and skills, with no scrimmage. Hancock couldn't risk another critical injury, and he had them stop for the day before five.

The Chiefs retrieved Andrew and went to dinner. The concussion lingered. Hopefully, another night's sleep would be the answer. Losing Pappy, even for one game, would be a huge step backward.

Wednesday, September 24

◉ ◎ ◉ ◎

Clarkson was coming to town. The closest college geographically in the conference to Bainbridge, and similar in size and academics, several of the Chiefs' classmates went there, and all the Chiefs, except Barrett, had considered it a finalist in their choice of schools.

An established soccer program, an experienced coach, and a strong tradition made it a tough contest. Two Amsterdam players, Mike Rooker and Will Clancy, were on the team, so it would be a grudge match.

Pappy hoped against hope he might be cleared at the last minute, and he dressed in his uniform, just in case.

The Chiefs visited with their two former teammates for a few minutes at the field house. The Clarkson players were confident, having crushed Bain every year. They knew the Titans had beat Bellville and Newton, but they considered those inferior programs and expected an easy game. Clancy told his teammates not to take the Titans lightly. The Chiefs would run and gun for ninety minutes, even without Andrew Paxton.

Clarkson piled into their bus (another indication of the team's successes). The Titans had to run to the field. After warm-ups, Pappy, Caldwell, and Santander took penalty kicks, and Millwood hit some corners.

Twenty minutes to game time. Pappy kept watching for Dr. Hardwell to show up and let him play. He noticed Coach Hancock talking to a student on the sidelines. The coach then beckoned to Andrew.

"You have to go back to the health center," said Hancock. "You can't play. The doctor wants to see you right away … I'm sorry."

"I don't understand," said Pappy. "I feel fine. I *have* to play against these guys." But it was clear that Hancock passed on the information with deep regret, and that whatever the student told him wasn't good.

Hancock turned away, and Andrew got in the student's car. On the ride back, all the driver would say was that Dr. Hardwell sent him to get Andrew immediately—and that he wasn't to play due to medical reasons.

By the time they reached campus, Pappy was furious. He slammed the car door and stormed up the steps to the health center. The girl at the desk recognized him and called the doctor.

Raymond Hardwell appeared, looking concerned. "Come back here, son. We need to talk," he said, opening the door into the first examining room.

"Let me show you something," said Hardwell, holding an X-ray up to the light. This is what's called your zygomatic arch. It goes from your eye socket to your ear. See right here," he said, pointing to a small spot. "This is a crack. It has caused the arch to weaken. You can't play soccer and risk being hit there again or it could break, and then your jaw won't work right." He paused and put the X-ray down. "You need to have it fixed. You need an operation."

Andrew was stunned. "But the Junction doctors said I was okay," he pleaded.

"Yes, and they flat out missed it, as I did. You need to have surgery as soon as possible. It's been almost a week since your accident, and if it isn't done quickly, the bone will heal wrong." Hardwell sat down across from Pappy. "It's a simple operation, so simple I'll do it myself. You go into the hospital tonight. The surgery will be tomorrow morning, and you'll be back on campus tomorrow afternoon. They'll shave a small portion of your hair right here on your temple." He pointed to a spot on the side of his own head. "I'll make a minor incision, take a little tool, and pull the bone straight. Two stitches and you'll be in the recovery room. We'll send someone over to pick you up, and you can spend the night back here for observation and to let the anesthesia wear off. Then you can go back to class and do anything you want, except wash your hair. You can't get the incision wet for a week, until I take out the stitches, so you'll have to be careful. Then you'll be on the mend. The bone will take about five or six weeks to heal, so no more soccer this year. But that's about it."

Andrew was numb. He'd heard little of what Hardwell had told him, other than 'You need an operation.'

"I have to call my parents," said Andrew.

"Sure," said Hardwell, picking up the phone. "I'll explain the procedure to them."

"My dad will want to come down."

"Well, he's welcome to do so," said the doctor, "but it's such a simple procedure and will be over so quickly that it will cost far more to fly here than the surgery itself will cost."

Andrew phoned his father, who first said he'd be on the first plane out. But after talking to Hardwell, he agreed the trip wasn't necessary. Andrew assured him he would be all right and wasn't scared, which was a big fat lie. He'd spent several nights in the hospital as a child, and he used to have nightmares about the nauseating smell of ether and alcohol as well as the mask they'd put over his face to administer the anesthesia.

Andrew said good-bye to his dad and headed to his room. Hardwell told him to bring a small bag with a shaving kit and clothes to wear back to the dorm on Friday. A security guard would give him a ride to Spencer Mercy, which was only about two blocks north of the campus.

Andrew packed and returned to the gym to wait for his ride. By this time, the game was over, and the Titans had lost two to nothing. Clarkson had dressed and gone. Several of Pappy's teammates came running over, unable to believe that he was on his way to the hospital. The Titans played poorly, and Rooker and Clancy scored for Clarkson. Barrett, who'd clashed with Rooker in high school, tripped him in front of the goal, and he converted the penalty shot. Hancock chastised Brian for the bush-league move and benched him for most of the second half. Clarkson was then content to play defense and held the Titans scoreless.

"My season is over," said Pappy. A pall fell across their faces.

Todd Hancock was coming out of the field house when he spotted Andrew. "What did the doctor say?" he asked.

"I have to have an operation," said Pappy.

Hancock's eyes widened. "When?"

"I'm waiting for my ride to the hospital. They're going to operate tomorrow morning."

"I'm sorry," he said. "Do you want me to come with you?"

"No, I'll be fine. The doc says it's a simple deal, and I'll be back tomorrow afternoon." Andrew was surprised by his own lack of emotion.

"I'll be okay, Coach," he continued. "See you tomorrow."

Hancock couldn't believe his player's calm demeanor. The car pulled up, and Andrew rode without speaking to the emergency entrance of the hospital.

"Do you want me to come in?" asked the guard.

"No, thanks anyway, unless you want to take my place," said Andrew, sighing deeply. He looked up at the plain cement building and ordinary glass doors. He really didn't want to do this, but he was being pulled along by some inexplicable feeling that this was how grown-up, independent people on their own behaved, and it was pretty clear he was on his own.

As Pappy passed through the sliding glass doors, all those unmistakable, repulsive smells flooded the air. He sat down in an ordinary old green chair in front of a desk with a small sign that read Admitting. Hardwell had called ahead, so his file was already there, and much of the information was filled out. It was a small hospital, and the people were eager to serve the needs of the university. There were questions about family histories and allergies, and Andrew had to sign some papers.

He was then directed to a small room, where a young nurse had him sit at what looked like a school desk. She rolled up his left sleeve, wrapped a long piece of surgical tubing tight around his bicep, and had him pump his fist a couple of times. Then she pulled out the biggest needle and syringe he'd ever seen. His heart pounded as she struck the vein, and when the dark red fluid appeared in the syringe, Andrew began hyperventilating. The nurse's eyes grew wide as the color drained from her patient's face and he slid down in the chair.

"Are you okay?" she asked, about to call for help.

"I ... think ... so," said Andrew, gasping after every word.

"We're done," she said suddenly, pulling the needle out and covering it with a piece of gauze and then a Band-Aid.

"There, that's it," she said, relieved. "Hold your finger here and press ... Good. Now sit there for a minute and we'll get someone to take you to your room." Pappy wasn't going anywhere. He slouched in a pool of sweat, embarrassed to have been such a wimp in front of the nurse.

A large male orderly appeared with a wheelchair. "Sorry," said Andrew to the nurse as he flopped down on the seat.

She smiled. "Don't worry—you weren't the first, and you won't be the last."

Down the hall and up the elevator to the second floor. Everything was dull brown: brown linoleum floors, light brown wall tiles, and fluorescent lights tinted yellow-brown with age, which hummed incessantly. The smell of alcohol was everywhere.

Room 212. Two beds. The one by the window was already occupied.

"This is it. Home for the night. You can put your clothes and things in the closet right there," said the orderly. "There's a gown on the bed. Bathroom is right in there." He turned and left. By the time a male nurse came through the door pushing a small cart with a washbasin and some towels, Andrew had recovered enough to stand up.

"Hi," he said, offering his hand. "Are you Andrew?"

"Yes," said Pappy.

"And you're on for surgery tomorrow—zygomatic arch?"

"That's right."

"Okay, I'm Paul, and I'm here to shave you. Go ahead and put your stuff away and then come back and sit in the chair."

"The doctor said you're only going to do this small part, like here," Andrew said, drawing a small imaginary arc on his temple and looking up at him hopefully.

"Well, I have to make it so there's no dirt or germs near the incision," he said. "Don't worry, I won't go crazy."

He first used electric clippers to clear away the long hair and then a safety razor to clean the stubble. He made small talk, asking Andrew about school and how he got hurt, but Pappy had the uneasy feeling that this guy Paul was nervous. He also seemed to be cutting in places far beyond where Hardwell had said.

"There ... done," said Paul, hastily piling his equipment on the cart and heading for the door. "Good luck tomorrow—and don't look at it until I'm gone ... Sorry."

Andrew felt the side of his head. "Holy crap!" he exclaimed, going over to the mirror above the sink. He stared in disbelief. Almost half his head was totally bald! The pale gray skin was repulsive, and his long hair on the rest of his skull made it look even more ridiculous.

He glanced at his roommate, who had been watching the drama unfold without saying a word. Pappy wanted to hide. It was like the dream where you're naked in a public place. He sat down on the bed. It was bad enough being on campus with three thousand people he didn't know, but now he would really be a freak for everyone to ogle.

"Hey, don't worry," said the guy lying on the other bed. "It'll grow back ... I'm Greg ... I can't get up, or I'd shake your hand."

Pappy came out of his fog. The man looked to be about twenty-five. He had thinning black hair, a round face and body, and was about Andrew's height. He used a steel bar hanging above the bed to pull himself up. Near his feet, the sheet was bunched so his ankle was exposed. And that ankle was handcuffed to the steel rail.

Andrew's face asked all the questions.

"Yeah, I got caught in a police raid. They got me in the gut with a shotgun," he said with little emotion. "Dumb. Shouldn't a been there. Now I can't move without this damn bar. Muscles are gone ... By the way, the food in this place sucks. My girl is coming later with some burgers and beer. Want her to bring you some?"

What next? wondered Pappy. "No, thanks," he replied, clearing his throat. "I don't think I could eat anything."

"Well, if you change your mind, let me know. There should be plenty. So you got hit in the head playing soccer?"

"Yeah," said Pappy, still trying to grasp his situation.

"You go to Bainbridge. Like it there? Know lots of girls?"

"Not really," he replied. *Not really,* he thought. He realized he'd been at Bainbridge over a month and hardly said boo to anyone other than soccer players and the guys on his floor. College so far had been a turbulent sea of emotions and incidents—this one being the most unexpected and unbelievable. He was sharing a hospital room with a man under arrest, a man who'd been shot by the police.

They talked for a while, and then supper arrived. Salisbury steak, green beans, mashed potatoes … all steamed, with no seasoning. And applesauce for dessert. Greg got Jell-O and clear broth, which he pushed aside. It was now after seven, and Pappy hadn't eaten all day. Steamed or not, he ate.

Greg's girlfriend, Sherry, arrived around nine, just as visiting hours were ending. She snuck up the exit stairs carrying two paper bags from a local fast-food place—and a six-pack of beer. Greg eagerly took it all with a great rustling of wrappers. He noisily popped the cap off one of the beers with the opener and drank half without stopping. Then he let go a great belch.

"Sure you won't have some?" he asked, wolfing down a hamburger. "How about some fries?"

"Are you sure you should be eating that stuff?" asked Pappy.

"Yeah," he replied, wiping his chin with his bedsheet. "Doctors said no, but what do they know?" Andrew kept looking at the door, sure the noise and smell, which even overwhelmed the aroma of rubbing alcohol, would bring a nurse running.

He finished quickly, and Sherry put anything left over in the bags. She was small, not as round as Greg, and looked to be about the same age. Unassuming and dutiful, she attended to him as both nurse and waitress. Pappy could tell she was worried about providing the food and drink. Andrew retold the story of his injury.

Greg seemed completely nonviolent, despite the severity and circumstances surrounding his wounds. He expressed no animosity toward the police, and Andrew didn't feel threatened by him.

At ten, the nurse came around the corner. "Do you want anything to …?" She saw Sherry. "Visiting hours are long over. You need to leave right away." Andrew could tell she smelled something besides hospital. Luckily, the odor of Salisbury steak still lingered. "This young man has surgery tomorrow at seven. You need to go." Sherry kissed Greg, said good-bye to Andrew, and left.

The nurse took the blood pressure and temperature of each of them. "Yours is a little high," she said to Andrew. "Do you want something to help you sleep?"

"No, thanks," he said.

"Well, if you do, just ring your call button. It's ten o'clock and lights out."

Raymond Hardwell entered the room. "Sorry I'm so late ... Jeepers, they really did shave you," exclaimed the doctor. He sat down on the edge of the bed.

"They'll give you a shot tomorrow around seven to make you relax, and then they'll take you to the operating room. You'll probably be asleep the whole time. The operation will take about fifteen minutes, and you'll be in recovery until you wake up. Around noon, you can get dressed, and the security guard will bring you back to the health center. Nothing to eat or drink now for the rest of the night. After surgery, you can have anything you want. You'll probably sleep all day tomorrow from the anesthesia ... Nothing to worry about. Just like getting a couple of stitches. You have had stitches before, haven't you?" Andrew nodded. "And you have had anesthesia ... Did it make you sick?"

"Yes."

"Well, we'll give you something in the recovery room to take care of it. He pressed Andrew's hand. "You'll be fine ... See you in the morning."

The doctor left, and reality set in. When he'd spent the night in the Junction health center, he'd been too groggy to notice anything. Now he was wide-awake in this cold, lonely, and impersonal white room.

"That guy seemed okay," said Greg. Andrew looked over to see his roommate lying flat, alternately rubbing his stomach and head. He was sweating. "Man, I don't think I should have had that beer." He tried to belch repeatedly but wasn't very successful.

The nurse had turned off the lights, so the only illumination was from the bathroom. Andrew thought about reading, but he was too tired. He lay back. The ordeal was catching up with him, and he started to fade …

He awoke to a blizzard of activity and every light in the room blazing. The curtain was drawn around Greg's bed, and nurses were running in and out. He heard terrible retching and moaning, and then a doctor came in.

"He's bleeding badly," exclaimed one nurse.

"Gimme his chart!" ordered the doctor. "What's his BP? Never mind—he's losing too much blood. We need to get him down to the OR right now! Get a gurney in here."

"He's handcuffed to the bed, and I don't know where they put the keys," said the nurse.

"What the—" Who's his surgeon?" asked the doctor. "All right, we'll have to wheel the whole damn bed down there, but we need to do it *now*. Somebody call the Spencer police and get someone over here with the keys—stat! What's his blood type? Get two liters of blood and have four more ready. Let's go."

The whole episode lasted less than ten minutes. Now Andrew lay there with heavy eyes, badly shaken by the events, with all the lights still on. He was the forgotten patient. He rolled over and covered his eyes with a pillow, but it was like daylight. He pressed the nurse call button and then lay there half-asleep. After a while, someone came in and turned off the lights. It seemed like morning moments later.

Thursday, September 25

⊚ ⊚ ⊚ ⊚

A nurse appeared around seven. It took a minute for Andrew to wake up, and he looked over to see the bed next to him empty. Not only empty but also made up as if no one had ever been there. Any personal effects were gone, and the bar over the bed had been removed.

"What happened to Greg, the guy who was there?" asked Andrew.

"Oh, that was sad. His stomach wounds ruptured in the middle of the night, and he died this morning." The nurse held up a needle and syringe. "Here is your happy shot. All I need is a cheek."

Dead? Really dead? The nurse came over to the side of the bed.

"Roll over, sweetie," she said. Andrew did, and he felt the cool alcohol swab … and the jab. It felt like she was driving a nail into his hip. Then she began injecting the medicine. The syringe was huge and full.

"Oh, man," he moaned, beginning to breathe heavily.

"Done," she said, withdrawing the needle. "Now you just lie back. They will be by for you in about an hour."

Andrew felt a warm sensation, and his eyelids became heavy. After a time, he heard voices in the distance, and something banged into the side of the bed.

"Here we go, Andrew," said someone standing next to him. "See if you can slide over onto the gurney." Pappy was totally disoriented but tried to move where he was being pulled. He lay back and was covered with a thin sheet. It was freezing, and he tried to say something, but couldn't

152

tell whether he was really speaking. They were moving, and the cart kept crashing into doors that swung open. Then he was in a room with a big white light overhead. Several people in masks were moving around him, and another voice asked if he could slide onto the operating table.

"Now push up."

Which way is up? He pushed with his legs.

"There, that's it. Good." Something was being placed over his face. "Now count backward from one hundred."

Andrew woke in the recovery room.

"Are you okay?" said a nurse.

"I am a little sick," he said.

"I'll get you something." The nurse injected a vial into the IV in his wrist. The nausea was gone.

He woke in his room to a nurse shaking his arm.

"Time to get up. You did great. It's eleven thirty. Get dressed. You can go back to school. Your ride will be here in half an hour."

His ride would be here. That meant campus. Home. Out of this place of foul smells, bad food, huge needles, and dead roommates. Andrew was still dizzy, but he dressed as quickly as he could manage. The nurse wheeled him down to where another Bainbridge security guard was waiting. He signed some papers, although his head was still full of fudge, and then got in the car.

Back at the health center, they put him in a room with a small bed. Someone offered a gown, but he lay back and fell asleep in his jeans and T-shirt. The nurse's aide removed his shoes and closed the door.

Friday, September 26

◎ ◎ ◎ ◎

The sight of Pappy's shaved head startled Coach Hancock, and it was evident that Andrew, even in his groggy state, was humiliated by his appearance. They talked for a few minutes, but the coach was uncomfortable in the quasi-hospital surroundings. He offered to help Andrew back to his dorm, but Pappy told him it would be a while before he was released. Hancock left, but before he went, he gave Paxton his home phone number in case he needed or wanted something over the weekend.

Hardwell came in at eleven, checked the incision, gave Andrew some new gauze pads to cover his stitches, reiterated about not getting the wound wet, and prescribed Tylenol.

Andrew had dressed and was about to leave when a nurse came in with a roll of gauze. "Here, let's try something," she said. She wrapped his head around and around until it resembled a turban. Andrew watched in the mirror and then smiled broadly. It covered the wound, but more importantly, it almost totally masked the exposed side of his head. Now he had something that would explain his appearance. He was no longer a student with a goofy half-shaved head but someone who had been wounded. Or been in a bad accident. He wanted to kiss the nurse but left after saying many thank-yous.

Back in the dorm, he called his parents. Hardwell had phoned them right after the surgery, assuring all was well. It was good to hear their

154

voices, and he could tell they were extremely relieved. Andrew's eyes welled with tears, and his voice choked. He knew they had wanted to be at the hospital, as they had when he was a child, but they now had to let him face life on his own. He said he had to go and hung up quickly so they wouldn't hear him cry.

Barrett came back after lunch, stunned by Pappy's half Mohawk. The gauze wrap made him look like a World War I doughboy fresh off the line.

They talked for a long time. Pappy relayed all he could remember about the hospital, the operation, and his deceased roommate. Brian recounted the Clarkson game and ranted on about Hancock. Soccer was no fun anymore, and he'd quit before he sat the bench. Pappy let his roommate vent, envious because he couldn't play himself and concerned that if he wasn't there to act as a buffer, Barrett would leave. Tomorrow was Bonham, and the Titans stood little chance, with or without Pappy. With Andrew gone for the season, the team's collapse, and his clashes with Hancock, Barrett felt the season was already over.

"You can't give up," said Pappy. "Santander was doing a great job running the offense. Better than me. He sure has more skills."

"Yeah, but he's not tough enough."

The phone rang. "Hey, how's it goin'?" asked Barrett. "Yeah, he had surgery … No, no, he's right here. He's okay, but they made him uglier … Here, you can talk to him yourself … Yeah, I'm fine. The soccer coach is a jerk, and we stink right now. Here, let me put him on."

Barrett handed Pappy the phone. "One of your minions wants to talk to me?" asked Andrew. "Can't she just suck up to you without involving me? Just tell her I'm too weak to come to the phone, but that she should bring over six friends to help me to dinner."

"Just take the goddamn phone," said Barrett. "You need to talk to women besides nurses."

"Wait," said Barrett, putting the phone back to his ear. "Did you ever have any more trouble with that scumbag Rattigan?"

Pappy's eyes grew wide. It was Littlefield. "Yeah? Good. Just remember to call … Here."

He handed Andrew the phone.

"Hi," he said.

"Hi. How are you?" she exclaimed. "I can't believe you had an operation ... And they said you were locked in a room with a patient who had committed murder? Is that true?"

Andrew looked at the phone in his hand. "Oh my God," he said. "No, that's not true. That's crazy. Who starts this stuff?"

Beth stammered. "I didn't ... I heard it from some girls on the floor."

"No, I'm sorry. I didn't mean you. Actually, the guy was shot by the police in a drug raid. He died that night because his girlfriend gave him some hamburgers and beer."

The line was silent. "His girlfriend poisoned him?"

"No, no," said Andrew. "He was shot in the stomach, and his stitches ruptured from the food."

"Oh," said Littlefield. "But you're okay?"

"Yeah, fine."

"Okay, well, I just wanted you to know we all hope you get well soon."

"Thanks."

"Well, see you around campus. Take care."

"Thanks. I haven't seen you in the lib—" She had hung up.

"Boy, you're a smooth Chester with the ladies," said Brian with a grin. Then his face turned more serious. "How do you think she sounded?" It took a moment for Andrew to come out of his Beth-induced fog.

"Okay ... why?" asked Andrew.

"I don't know," continued Brian. "I saw her in the dining room two nights ago, and she looked sick. She's pale and has lost a bunch of weight."

"Why don't you call her back?" asked Andrew, hoping for a negative answer. "Maybe she needs some company."

"This isn't the right time," said Barrett. "Maybe in a while."

"You know, I ..." Pappy hesitated.

"Let's go hang out at the Union," said Barrett, as if he had a specific purpose in mind.

"No, you go," replied Andrew. "I'm not ready to show my new hairstyle and headgear to the public. Dinner is soon enough."

"Okay, see you there." Barrett closed the door behind him.

During the next hour, no fewer than fifteen guys showed up at Andrew's door to see if any of the wild reports running around were true. Of interest were his new do and the dead guy. Poisoned by his girlfriend? Poisoned by the police? Poisoned by the doctors? Pappy went running from his room to supper just to get away ... only to be confronted by the rest of the Chiefs and the soccer team at the Union. Eager for every sordid detail of a tale that had taken on epic proportions, even coeds flocked in to listen, and they were actually interested in Pappy and not hovering around Barrett. Finally, the story made the rounds to all the tables. Some looked disappointed that there was no actual murder, but all in all, it was a pretty cool yarn.

Back at the room, Pappy removed his headdress for the night. His worst fear—being gawked at—was replaced by celebrity. He might survive until his hair grew back.

Saturday, September 27

◉ ◎ ◎ ◎

Bonham was an expensive elite school that also recruited heavily in Upstate New York. Two of the stars were from the Buffalo area. It was like playing the LA Dodgers: the students were politely aloof; they showed up late to the games, dressed to be seen; applauded politely; and win or lose, were long gone by the end of the contest.

Their uniforms were solid crimson, too close to the Titans' colors. No problem. They brought an entire change of wardrobe, including matching shorts and socks.

Both teams did their usual warm-ups. Roland Santander moved into Pappy's spot at center halfback. Bonham kicked off, and the Titans were dead from the start. The "Big Red" were the size of Brackettville but could handle the ball. They pounded the Titans, just as the Chiefs had done to their opponents in high school, so Penny, Millwood, and Caldwell had few opportunities. They were hustling, but this was a class A program playing a class C. Pappy was on the sidelines, giving instructions and making suggestions to the coach, until a throbbing headache forced him to sit.

Caldwell's lone shot hit the crossbar. Penny's breakaway score was disallowed on a bad offside call. Randy Williams was caught too far out on one Bonham score, and the two others were struck so hard that they left vapor trails. Barrett managed to stay in the entire game, and his exchanges with Hancock were minimal. Three to zero was the final.

Almost one hundred Bainbridge students came to see the game. Just when it looked as if the campus was finally taking an interest, they were blown out.

The beating left the Chiefs and the rest dazed and disheartened. The coach was realistic: the Titans were a season or two away from being the equal of the Big Red. Santander continued to impress, but the team hadn't adjusted to losing Paxton.

Basketball practice would start in a few weeks, and Hancock found his thoughts drifting. He wouldn't abandon the soccer Titans, but it was clear that his future as a college coach was in the sport he'd played.

Sunday, September 28

⊚　⊚　⊚　⊚

Pappy had only lost one full day of class, and Spanish and English were no sweat, but he missed two chem classes and lab. And his lab session had been a disaster. He needed help.

At eight o'clock at night, Karl Zindell was in his room across the hall, door closed. The resident science nerd, he looked more like an overweight dockworker—beer belly, dandruff, shaggy black hair, rumpled clothes, beard stubble, cigarette-stained fingers, and yellow teeth. He'd earlier finished a Donello's sub with Italian sausage and peppers, and the feast had arrived in his subbasement plumbing. The noises coming from behind the door sounded like two dogs tearing up a carpet, and the smell was seeping out into the hall.

"That guy needs to be turned inside out and scraped," said Barrett, shaking his head.

But Pappy had to turn in the worksheets by Tuesday. So he bought a Coke from the vending machine, found a pack of matches, and knocked on the door. Zindell sat at his desk in boxers and nothing else. Thank God he was sucking on an unfiltered Camel, the thick layer of smoke suppressing the other stench. The Coke would, Pappy hoped, quell the potentially lethal disturbance in Karl's nether regions.

"Ketcham doesn't care about the results," belched Karl. "As long as you followed the procedure. That crap you burned isn't pure, and everyone got different results. Mine turned green. All you have to worry about is solving your unknown, which is fifty percent of the grade."

Andrew breathed a sigh of relief, even though no one else in the class had screwed up this simple procedure so terribly. Well, it was what it was, and it was time to take his pills. He was sound asleep before ten.

Monday, September 29

◉ ◉ ◉ ◉

Andrew donned his gauze for his Monday classes. He was hoping the English prof would assign another short story. His hospital visit would provide a doozy.

The growing hairs on Pappy's gray skull itched. His scalping and the operation truly looked worse than the experience, and he was proud he'd gone it alone. The swelling was almost gone, but the two ugly black stitches bulged along the incision. He was also having flashbacks of the collision with the goalie—and of the hospital.

High school friends, even those who hadn't written before, sent letters asking about his operation, relaying the version of the story they had heard. Many were wildly exaggerated. Two girls called Barrett from other colleges to say that they'd heard Pappy had died.

Paxton's afternoons were now empty and depressing. Everyone he knew was playing a sport. Barrett arrived back at the room just after four. Hancock cut the normally brutal Monday practice short to go to a basketball meeting. There was talk among the team that the coach had given up. There was no midweek game, so there would be four more days of drills and scrimmages.

Tuesday, September 30

◉ ◎ ◉ ◎

Two more days until the stitches came out, and they were now starting to prickle. Pappy did all sorts of contortions to wash his remaining oily hair in the sink without getting them wet. He picked up more gauze from the health center, as it collected grease and dirt.

Barrett was playing music and Pappy writing letters when Karl Zindell came through the open door.

"Either of you guys got some rubbing alcohol?" he asked, pointing to his bare feet.

They looked like boots with toes. Dark colored, the area between the digits had the appearance of yellow bread dough, and the nails were raised. That's when the smell hit.

"Oh my God," said Barrett, laughing out loud. "Toe cheese! Toe cheese! That is the worst case of toe jam I've ever seen. Ugh! Get out of here … And you're walking barefoot on our floors! I'm gonna be sick."

Karl lifted and crossed his leg while standing, beginning to dig and scratch at the corruption. Skin flaked onto the floor.

"Wait, wait!" pleaded Andrew. He ran over to his dresser and tossed a bottle of rubbing alcohol, a can of Desenex, a tin of baby powder, and some Merthiolate. "There, that's all I've got. Get out before I barf."

Zindell was gone.

"Holy Christmas, he's probably got head lice, athlete's foot, ringworm, tapeworm, pinworm, hookworm, roundworm, screwworm, earthworm, toe fungus, and crabs!" said Andrew. "From now on, we gotta keep this door closed."

Wednesday, October 1

◎ ◎ ◎ ◎

Another first-floor Roberts Hall student left school. Some departed out of boredom. For others, it was family problems or money issues. Every time it seemed things had settled down, something else came up.

Professor Christopher Carlson of the religion department died the previous night of cancer. Thirty-six years old, he looked seventy when he passed. Students were reluctant to remain in his class once they knew his condition. Studying religion, of all things, with a man who was dying shook everyone's private beliefs.

No Wednesday game. Practice lacked direction. The coach and his team were in a funk, and no one had replaced Paxton as leader.

Thursday, October 2

◉ ◉ ◉ ◉

One week after surgery, Andrew Paxton approached the health center reception desk. "I need my stitches taken out," he said, pointing to his bandaged head.

"Sure," said the young woman behind the partition. "Come through the door."

Andrew went into one of the examining rooms and was immediately followed by Raymond Hardwell.

"Well, how are you feeling?" asked the doctor, removing the loosely wrapped bandage and throwing it in the trash. "Yes," he said, almost to himself, looking at Andrew's incision. "Not a bad job ... It was a simple operation. Any pain, dizziness, nausea?"

"No," said Andrew. "It just itches sometimes."

"That's normal," said Hardwell. "Your hair grows quickly around it, and the follicles pushing through the skin cause the irritation." He took a long pair of tweezers and some scissors, lifted each one of the two stitches, cut and pulled. Andrew winced, but it was over in a moment.

"You won't need any bandages now that the stitches are out, and you can wash your hair normally," said Hardwell. "As I said, no more soccer until after spring break. The bone will heal quickly, but if you were to get hit there again without protection, it could mess up your jaw, your ear, your eye socket ... so just take it easy for a while. Okay?"

"Yeah," said Andrew, disheartened. He didn't know what he'd hoped the doctor would say, but whatever it was, he didn't hear it. They shook hands, and Pappy headed back to the dorm. It seemed his hair on the bald side had stubbornly stopped growing. He took a normal shower and washed his hair twice, almost scrubbing the scalp raw. Then he rewound his turban.

Then it was off to chem lab. He wore the same pair of jeans and T-shirt each time—the ones with the holes.

Barrett didn't talk much about practice at dinner. It was clear he held out little hope of salvaging the season. Saturday was Stratton State.

Friday, October 3

◉ ◉ ◉ ◉

The ruckus on campus about Andrew's injury and operation was over, and he seldom drew a nod or second look. Even Barrett's girlfriends stopped asking about him. It was fun while it lasted. He was becoming bored with college life and had too much free time to think about home. He still received letters from his dad and others. Amsterdam continued to win soccer games, and last year's triumphs were now quickly forgotten. Those heroes had been replaced.

The hours when he would have been at practice were the worst. Midterms were coming, but chem was his only worry, and he was carrying a solid A.

Barrett was back just after four. Hancock had cut practice short again.

"Man, sorry you're going to miss the festivities tomorrow," said Barrett. "I understand most of these Stratton State guys aren't even citizens, and some have wives and kids. I think if Hancock could figure out an excuse to miss the game, he would. We should just go out and get smashed."

"I can't believe this crap," scolded Pappy. "Give up a game before you even show up? You don't know these guys. We beat lots of foreign players before. We were three-goal underdogs last year in the state championship, and we killed those wimps. You've never even seen these guys play."

"Yeah, but I've seen us play," he replied dejectedly. "And I know we're all in the dumper."

168

"Hancock's not going to abandon this team," said Pappy. "I bet he never quit anything in his life. There are still a bunch of schools you can beat."

"Well, it doesn't help when it looks like he can't wait to leave practice every day. A few more whippings like we took against Bonham and the girlfriends won't even show up … On a different subject, I don't suppose you want to go with us to Fitz's tonight? My date is bringing her roommate, and I want to pawn her off early."

"I thought you were into two at once," said Pappy. "It's more fun when you have multiple people barf on your clothes."

Barrett heaved an empty beer can at him. "C'mon, do me a favor."

"Nah, not with this thing," said Pappy, pointing at his head. "It's too repulsive. Besides, why do you risk being seen drinking at Fitz's?"

"Will you stop, please?" said Barrett, exasperated. "All of the upperclassmen will be smashed at their fraternity houses tonight. I'm not doing anything different."

Pappy sighed. "I just don't want to be around women wearing this rag."

"All right, but be ready to clear out and find another bed."

"You know, you complain that you're going to get stomped tomorrow, and then you stay out late and get smashed, so you're even more worthless. How 'bout I just lay quietly under my blanket? They won't even know I'm here."

"How about if I bring them both back and you jump her roommate? We'll have an orgy."

"That's all I need," said Pappy. "They'd take one look at me, one look at you, and throw me out the door. I'll leave if you get lucky. Wait, I have an idea … How about a movie?"

"A movie?" asked Barrett.

"Yeah," said Pappy. "No booze, no sex, and it'll be dark so her roommate won't have to look at me all night."

"Have you ever been in the dark with a woman?" asked Barrett.

"Thanks a bunch," said Pappy. "If this is the only way I can keep you from destroying yourself before every game, it's worth it."

So it was a date. The girls were cute. Andrew's was barely five feet tall and had blonde hair and freckles. They walked downtown, all the while asking Pappy about his accident. Mostly they wanted to know about the dead guy. Nothing like a dead body to keep everyone's interest.

It was after eleven by the time they returned to campus, and ignoring the girls' curfews, they went by the Union. And there was Littlefield. Brian didn't see her, but for Pappy, it was beyond sad. The boys were out on dates, having a good time, and she was alone. *It's like everyone has abandoned her,* thought Andrew. Beth smiled weakly and left.

He wanted to follow her, but his date was nice, and it wouldn't be fair to ditch her. They walked the girls back to the dorm, and when Andrew went to shake her hand, she kissed him on the lips.

"I had a great time. Call me again. Hope your head gets better." Then she smiled and went in. Barrett and his date, however, were having a more prolonged parting.

Now Pappy was standing alone next to two people who were just a few articles of clothing away from a motel room. There was no easy way to remove himself, so he turned and walked swiftly down the sidewalk.

Barrett arrived at the room twenty minutes later. "Now that was great!" he exclaimed. "I'm proud of you, my boy. See, you done real good. You played it smooth; didn't act the fifty-year-old chaperone. The movie was really cool. Great suggestion. Let's do it again."

"Well, now it's after midnight, and your dad says go to bed," said Andrew.

Barrett headed for the john. Pappy lay back. He'd had fun. But what he remembered most from the night was the sad face of Beth Littlefield.

Saturday, October 4

◉ ◎ ◎ ◎

Stratton State was more or less a four-year community college, and the majority of its students were commuters. Varsity sports were confined to soccer, basketball, and ice hockey. The local professional teams kept the programs funded, while sending their reserves there to get extra playing time. Stratton was a Division III program, so there was little NCAA scrutiny.

Due to the distance between schools, it was decided that they would meet at a neutral site, so it would be about an hour and a half drive for each. State didn't care. There were few fans or school spirit. The athletes were there to play sports.

The Titans had trouble finding Mount Vernon High School. Girlfriends were told not to bother coming, as it might not be too pretty, and the team would return directly to campus afterward.

It was a trip back in time. There was the high school, the soccer field close by, surrounded by a chain-link fence, with a cinder track around the perimeter. The small sets of metal bleachers on each side were only about five rows high—and empty.

The Titans unloaded the cars and went through the gate. There was Stratton State. It was like playing the five o'clock shadow club. These guys didn't even remotely look like college students. Penny doubted if half of them could read. They outweighed the Titans by twenty pounds per man, as many were approaching thirty.

But there was no doubt they could play the game. Their passes were strong and accurate. Their shots would dip and twist. One group kept the ball in the air for what seemed to be ten minutes with just their heads and shoulders. Their only chance, Barrett thought, might be if they had to stop every ten minutes or so for a cigarette break. But this bunch probably smoked cigars.

The Titans kicked off, and it was like two teams playing entirely different games. State had complete control of the ball, but this also caused bickering among their players, particularly among the different ethnic groups. The fullbacks were excellent tacklers and anticipated every pass. It was difficult for Caldwell, Penny, and Millwood to get off any kind of shot. The State players seemed annoyed to come out on a Saturday and play such an inferior opponent. Todd Hancock made few comments during the course of the game. Barrett was free to go wherever he wanted, but his booming kicks and wild shots had no effect. They were professionals and made few mistakes, particularly in front of the goal.

The two best players were the left wing, who played in Scotland, and the center forward, from Italy. Both in their late twenties, they were solid physically, and their games were polished.

State scored at the twenty- and thirty-three-minute marks. The first was a free kick from thirty yards that hooked around the wall into the upper right corner. Williams was screened out, but it was a perfect shot. The second was a volley kick off a corner. Sheffe expected his man to trap the ball, but it never touched the ground until it was buried in the back of the net.

The second half was more of the same, although some of the older gents (twenty-six-plus years) sat and let the youngsters finish. State scored twice more on brilliant shots by the insides, who beat their defenders one-on-one. With about eight minutes left, Roland Santander dribbled up the middle and wound up to shoot. The fullback went for the fake, not seeing Caldwell dart by. Roland's pass was perfect, and Dave punched a low shot in the right corner. That brought about a litany of carping among the Stratton squad, and Barrett told a couple of them to shut up. Four to one was the final, and the Titans were glad to leave. They'd given it a good effort. A college baseball team couldn't expect to beat the Yankees, so the Titans could go home knowing they had played hard, but that was about it. For the Chiefs, there was no such thing as a good loss.

Sunday, October 5

Another round of open houses at the fraternities and sororities, but Pappy had already decided to pledge TDT; Millwood, McIlroy, and Penny were joining Lambda Kappa Lambda. The wild card was Barrett. The Silos were really putting on the rush to keep from being shut out in the Chiefs sweepstakes. Actually, the only ones who cared were the soccer players in each house. The rest of the members had never seen the team play, and nobody wanted to make an extraordinary effort to recruit members of a losing program.

Pappy's bandage wasn't mentioned. It had been ten days, the gauze itched constantly, and the dirt and bacteria caused his forehead to break out. The problem was that the right side had been shaved while the left was tapered, so there was no way to make the hair look even.

They all had dinner at Donello's, and then went back to the dorms to write letters and call home. Pappy talked with his dad about not being able to play and thanked him for the articles about the soccer team and the fire company. Thanksgiving was still seven weeks away, and Andrew looked forward to going home.

Monday, October 6

◎ ◎ ◎ ◎

It was now going on three weeks since his accident at Junction—and two since his operation. The stitches were out, and Pappy was even more restless. Physically and mentally, he felt fine. No concussion. No aftereffects from the surgery, other than a shaved head and the ridiculous bandage.

The soccer team had lost all four games played without him, and Andrew wanted to give them a boost. Barrett and Hancock were still at odds, and the coach was close to dumping his best athlete.

It was fall, and he'd played soccer every autumn since he was eight years old. At least he could go down and kick the ball around, run some drills, and keep in shape. He decided he'd let the guys go to practice and then arrive and sort of mingle in. What could it hurt? He'd promise Hancock to be careful and not do any heading or scrimmaging. Dr. Hardwell had said his season was over, but he hadn't said he couldn't practice ... technically speaking. And Pappy wasn't going to ask for permission.

Millwood, Penny, and McIlroy met Barrett and took off for the field. Once they were out of sight, Pappy donned his sweat clothes and cleats and headed down the hill to the park road. The temperature was fifty-five degrees, so Pappy put on a stocking cap, which was a great way to replace his head wrap.

After the events of the past two weeks, running the two miles to practice was like having a new lease on life. Pappy's body was rested, and his adrenaline surged as he picked up the pace. After a mile, he slowed down, wanting to arrive after calisthenics and in the middle of drills in order to be less conspicuous.

Andrew appeared as the team was doing pass and trap. They began cheering and ran over to shake his hand. Hancock watched from a distance. After a few minutes, they went back to the drills. The team was lifted by his presence, and everyone's energy level increased. Talk among the players was louder. The passes were quicker and crisper.

They formed two lines at midfield and began two-man passing and shooting. Every time it was Pappy's turn, guys would shout encouragement.

Finally, the coach put down his clipboard and walked onto the field. His look was stern. "Paxton, come here please," he said in an unemotional tone. "Williams, you and Landon pick up sides and set up a scrimmage."

Pappy ran toward his coach, smiling. But when he reached Hancock, the coach turned toward the end of the field as if heading back to campus. Andrew came alongside, and they walked, not speaking, until they were well past the end line and out of sight of the team.

Todd stopped and turned to his player. "You have to leave and not come back. You're done for the year," he said firmly.

"But, Coach," he protested, "I feel great. The doc didn't say I couldn't practice. I'll be careful … I promise." He was pleading now. Hancock shook his head.

"Everyone was glad to see me," said Andrew. "We need to win games. I can help with Barrett—"

"That's just the point," said Hancock. "You saw how they all turned to you when you arrived. You picked everyone up … and then when it comes to a game, you'll let them down."

Andrew was confused. "I won't let them down."

"Yes, you will," interrupted the coach. "You'll be a part of the team for practice, but then at game time, when things get tough, even though they know you can't play, they'll subconsciously look to you. And you can't help. You'll be the unspoken excuse when they fail. 'If only Pappy could play … When Pappy gets back …'

"Well, you're not coming back," continued Hancock. "And you can't let them think you're back. You have to leave and let them find their way. It'll be up to them whether they fail or succeed.

"Go back to campus," said Hancock, turning toward the field. "Practice is closed to you." He walked away.

Pappy stood for a moment in shock. *What is the matter with this guy? He acted like I wanted to hurt the team.* Hancock was now gone, and Andrew felt hollow inside. He walked slowly back to Roberts Hall.

Tuesday, October 7

⊙ ⊙ ⊙ ⊙

The Spanish test was easy. Tomorrow was chem. English was another theme, and Pappy wrote about the hospital. If "write what you know" meant anything, this should be an A.

He couldn't tell Brian that Hancock had banned him from practice, for fear it might tip the scales and Barrett would quit. So he said Coach talked to the doctor, but Hardwell wouldn't clear Andrew to practice.

Back to square one. Pappy felt well enough to do anything, so he borrowed a soccer ball and went up to the top level of the field house. The largest room had two one-wall handball courts with solid cement floors and walls. It was perfect. Amsterdam High had built a kickboard the size of a soccer goal next to the main field. Players could practice for hours by themselves, shooting, passing, and trapping. The original kickboard was made of plywood and two-by-four framing, but the weather and the pounding of thousands of soccer balls each year required it to have several reconstructions. Finally, a local contractor built one of brick, which was still there today.

Pappy banged away, the impact resonating all through the field house's barren walls and floors. After a few minutes, several people, including secretaries with concerned looks on their faces, looked in to see what was going on, so Andrew switched to bumping short passes. As he did, he replayed the past games in his mind. The more he dwelled on his mistakes and the fact that he couldn't play, the madder he got and the harder he kicked. After forty-five minutes, Alan Amory, the varsity basketball coach, stuck his head in, looked around, and said, "One hell of a big handball." Pappy figured he'd worn out his welcome for the day.

It was after four, so he ran back to the dorm, grabbed his wallet, tossed his gauze wrap, donned a wool stocking cap, and took off toward the Silo house. One block short of there was a small building housing, among other things, a barbershop.

There were two chairs but only one barber, and he was just finishing with an older customer. "Be right with you," he said. The shop was rather dark, with most of the light coming through the store window. It had the usual smell of hair tonic, and clippings of three previous customers littered the black-and-white linoleum floor. The man paid and left, and Andrew stood up and pulled off his hat.

"Uh, well," said the barber. "What happened to you?"

"I had an operation. I need you to even it up," said Andrew, taking the chair.

"Hmm … okay, let's see what we can do. I'm Mack, by the way."

"Andrew," said Pappy, shaking his hand.

"The problem is that one side is all the same length. I can take it down some on the left, but it still won't balance until your next time."

"That's okay," said Andrew, taking a deep breath. "Do the best you can."

The barber labored slowly and deliberately. First the clippers. Then, with a look of disappointment, he switched to scissors. He walked back and forth and around, as if plotting the demise of each hair individually. Pappy was getting antsy. He never liked getting haircuts. The barber always fastened the apron too tight around the neck, pushed and pulled his head up and down and to the side, and scraped his scalp with the comb. Sometimes he would nick an ear with the clippers. The alcohol in the aftershave stung the skin. Finally, you were left with that naked, itchy feeling for the rest of the day.

"Here, take a look at this," said Mack, presenting Andrew with a hand mirror. From three sides, it wasn't *that* bad. In the back, though, there was no way to truly blend the divide between the halves. "That is about as good as I can do, unless you want it a lot shorter."

"No, that's short enough," said Andrew. He gave the man two dollars, plus a fifty-cent tip, and headed back to campus. It was cold. He put his hat back on and kept his head down. Maybe it would look better after he took a shower and fluffed it with a hair dryer.

"Hi, Pappy," said a familiar voice. He was in front of Weatherly Hall, and there was Beth Littlefield. Of all the times … "Gosh, I haven't seen you since your operation [Andrew knew she had but wasn't going to mention the double date]. You look totally recovered … and your bandage is gone. Did you get a haircut? Can I see?" She was now standing close in front of him.

"I just had it done," said Andrew. "I was hoping to sneak back to the dorm before I saw anyone I knew."

"Let me look … No, no, the barber did a good job," she said sincerely. "You have always had really terrific hair." Then she touched the side of his head gently. Like in a trance, he was leaning forward, and so was she. What the …? Andrew snapped out of it.

"Man, this really itches," he said, rubbing his head. "It feels like I have fleas. I need to get going before I rub anymore." Her face saddened.

"Hey, what do you hear from home?" he asked, not knowing what else to say. "The soccer team is on a roll."

"Yeah," said Beth. "My mom and dad were here last weekend, and they told me all the news. Are your parents okay?"

"Yeah … I miss the place," said Andrew wistfully.

Suddenly Beth's face reddened, and she turned toward the dorm. Pappy saw her eyes well up with tears, "Yeah, me too. Gotta go. Take care," she choked, and she was gone.

He met Millwood and McIlroy headed for supper.

"Was that Littlefield I saw you with? Hey, nice haircut. Welcome back to the living," said Tim.

"Yeah," replied Andrew.

"I heard her parents had to come last weekend because she's depressed and not eating. She's getting really skinny," said Jim.

"Why don't you ask her out?" asked Tim pointedly. "C'mon, you both could use some company. There was something going on between you two that night out in front of the Union. Don't give me that crap—there was."

"You're crazy," said Andrew. "She's still in love with Barrett."

"Well, he's not going back to her. He's had a date every weekend. She ought to get the hint," said Tim.

"Back off, man," said Andrew angrily. "She's hurting ... and she can't help it." He looked back at her dorm.

"You'd know something about that," said Tim, now more somber. "You're hurting too, pal, and we all know it. We've known it for years."

That was all Pappy could take. "Well, I gotta go wash the hair off me and change my shirt. I'll see you at dinner." Andrew continued up the walk.

"This sucks," said Tim, watching his friend. "Maybe we should have a little class reunion, like Friday or Saturday."

"That's a good idea," said Jim. "Everybody's going down to Fitz's Saturday night. I'll see if a couple of girls want to come along."

Wednesday, October 8

◎ ◎ ◎ ◎

It was an hour ride to Wolcott College Wednesday afternoon, but the team had to leave at one o'clock because of the shortening daylight. They never saw the actual campus, however, because their field was part of a farm, outside of town, donated to the school the previous year. And for once, the Titans saw a program more neglected than their own. The head coach was an Amsterdam graduate, Jim Cleary, who knew Pappy well. He was surprised and disappointed at his absence, not to mention floored by the reason. He'd seen plenty of broken legs, fractured collarbones, blown knees, and torn muscles, but he'd never seen a fractured skull in soccer.

The pitch was like a cornfield that had been cut the week before. There was little grass—just clumps of weeds scattered about. The rest was dirt, now made sloppy by rain the previous evening.

The Titans laughed and shook their heads at the terrible conditions. Passes deflected off at a forty-five-degree angle when they struck the patches of stubble. The field was severely crowned, so much that once a ball headed for the sidelines, it had to be stopped or it would keep on rolling.

The Wolcott team looked like high school kids. Small and slight, with young faces, there was no one to focus on when the Chiefs stood at midfield before the game. The Titans kicked off, and for a while, the play was erratic. Mud stuck to the bottoms and sides of everyone's shoes, and the black-and-white soccer ball was a heavy, dark mess within five minutes.

The ball spun and skidded everywhere, and Millwood had his feet go completely out from under him when taking a corner kick.

After a while, Roland Santander took control. His light touch and great balance left defenders sliding by, and he dribbled solo from near the midline to score the first goal at the twenty-minute mark. He tallied again at thirty-five and forty minutes on similar plays. The first hat trick by any Titan player. Three to zero.

Meanwhile, Barrett and Hancock were at it again. Brian had two kicks spin wildly off the side of his foot in the goal area, creating opportunities for Wolcott, which luckily, they couldn't convert. Hancock screamed at him to trap the ball, but no one was going to tell Barrett what to do.

The game was under control, and Hancock was substituting freely in the second half, including Johnson for Barrett. That was the last time Brian was on the field. It ended five to zero, with McIlroy tapping in his first score ever on a loose ball in the goalie box, and Driver on a free kick.

They packed up quickly and headed for the cars. Back on campus, Barrett bundled up his uniform and threw it at Kenny Hodges. "Here," he said disgusted. "It barely got used."

He stomped out like a petulant two-year-old, kicking the lockers and slamming doors. The Chiefs knew Pappy would get an earful this evening. Man, it was like being married and having to listen to the husband bitch after a bad day at the office.

Fortunately, they went to supper first. Barrett could eat unbelievable amounts of food and never gain a pound—a trait that women felt was disgustingly unfair. Digesting the meal took blood away from his brain and calmed him to the point that he decided just to study. They had won. At least that felt good.

Thursday, October 9

◉ ◉ ◉ ◉

L ittle did Professor Gunner Ketcham realize when he awoke that morning that he would go down in history as the man whose class almost burned eighty-year-old Knox Hall to the ground.

It was the last laboratory session on experiment procedures. The one hundred or so students gathered around as best they could while Gunner stood in front of a lighted Bunsen burner with a test tube containing an amber liquid that looked like thick tea.

"Now, you're going to boil off the water that is in the solution," he said, passing the test tube over the flame. Every time the heat was applied, the contents bubbled up toward the mouth and then subsided. "You go back and forth, back and forth. Do not—I repeat, *do not*—hold the test tube over the flame. The compound is extremely volatile. Take your time. Do this slowly. It may require several minutes for the bubbling to stop, which means the water is gone. Then set the test tube in the rack and let it cool. Everyone understand?" He looked around. "Good, now only one at a time on each Bunsen burner."

Ketcham turned and walked toward the door. The girl to the right of Andrew Paxton lit her burner, picked up her test tube with the tongs, and held it straight over the flame. There was a flash and a whoosh of what sounded like a small rocket engine, and the liquid spewed across the laboratory table. The burner immediately ignited it, and the desktop was now afire. The screams and shouts were accompanied by one hundred students trying to go through a door that was only eight feet wide, while the dazed professor, who envisioned his tenure at Bainbridge burning up with the laboratory equipment, tried to fight through the stream of fleeing salmon back into the room with a fire extinguisher. He easily doused the blaze, but by that time, half the building had been evacuated. Several people had pulled the fire alarm, and Spencer's finest were on their way to what had been variously reported as a toxic chemical spill, an incendiary device, and someone setting off a cherry bomb.

The firemen seemed genuinely disappointed when they arrived, axes and hoses in hand, to find no disaster to be reported on the six o'clock news—and no young coeds to be rescued.

Friday, October 10

◎　◎　◎　◎

Barrett returned from practice in his usual mood—ready to set fire to the school and take off for California. They went to dinner, and then some of the team came by on the way to the movies. It was better than sitting in the dorm, so Pappy and McIlroy went along. Barrett had moved to another table with a couple of sophomore girls, so they left him to his exploits.

The movie was *The Wild Bunch*, and man, was it wild. After watching Gene Autrey, Roy Rogers, and John Wayne all their lives, a film about a horde of murdering, lecherous thieves being the relative good guys was startling. Afterward, they went to Donello's for a pizza, unable to stop talking about the sheer violence.

They got back to the dorm at midnight. Everyone had a game in the morning … except Andrew. There was Magic Marker on the doorknob. Crap. He had to go bunk somewhere else while his roommate was doing all sorts of wonderful and unmentionable things with some girl. Pappy had had only one date in almost two months, and it was a platonic one. McIlroy gave him a sheet, pillow, and a bunch of sweat clothes for a bed. The linoleum floor was damn hard.

Saturday, October 11

⊚ ⊚ ⊚ ⊚

They woke at eight, and Pappy was extremely stiff. He went back to the room, but Barrett had already left. His bed was rumpled, and there was a huge stack of records on the stereo. Andrew shook his head. Enough was enough. If he couldn't play soccer and his roommate was out playing the field, maybe it was time … On the dresser, he saw a pair of earrings, and Pappy's heart went dark. Beth Littlefield's dad had brought those earrings back from Paris when she was sixteen …

Humphrey College. The last nonconference soccer game of the season. At least it was at home. Roland Santander had to go back to Barcelona on family business but would return Monday.

Like Brackettville, Humphrey had no football team, but they had extremely skilled small players. Their program had developed over many years, and the school's academic reputation created a strong foreign exchange program. No flash, just quality, and they were more than the Titans could handle. Hancock saw the team he wanted to have, and he appreciated the years of building to create a squad this good.

That didn't keep him from barking at his troops. Without Santander, the Titans were disorganized on offense. Barrett's bombs had no effect, as Humphrey made no mistakes. Their triangle offense had Bain chasing from one player to the next. The Titans were down two zip at the half, and Hancock took out most of the starters, including Barrett. The few fans who'd wandered down from the campus were now gone. The second half played more evenly, mainly because most of the Titans were back on defense.

The game ended with a score of four to zero. For all, the season had reached a new low. Pappy watched from a distance, unnoticed. He paced and fumed, frustrated he couldn't play and knowing his teammates were doing the best they could. He left before the end so nobody would see him. Moreover, he didn't want to talk to his roommate right then.

Saturday evening, Paula Cole sat at a small folding table in the student union lobby with Karen Reilly. Behind her was a white poster with black letters: "Americans for the Vietnamese People." On the table was a brief policy statement composed by some faculty and students at another university and distributed to antiwar groups. Paula wasn't a member of Americans for the Vietnamese People, whoever they were. The Bainbridge antiwar movement was small and disorganized. Most of the male students had college draft deferments—and were glad to have them.

Paula wanted to do something socially responsible at Bainbridge besides playing field hockey. She was a Spencer resident, a "townie," as Bain students called them. She was an only child, her father having left when Paula was six, and her mother, Dorothy, worked as a secretary at the college, saving up to give her daughter a better life. Things had been tough, and tuition, even with the staff discount, was beyond the reach of a secretary making eighty dollars a week. Paula had worked at Love's Department Store since she was sixteen so she could go to the beautiful school that had been a second home to her and her mother for over a decade. But even with the Spencer Rotary Club scholarship, it hadn't looked as if she would be able to live on campus and be part of the student body. Then Dr. Joe Boyer, a political science professor who had known Dorothy Cole for years, talked the Lutheran Church into funding her room and board, at least for the first year. The athletic department gave her a job at the field house, and she was in.

It was a dream come true, and she and her roommate, Brenda Sykes, were instant friends. Everything was so new and exciting. She and her mother cried when Paula moved in, even though their apartment was six blocks away and she would see Dorothy almost every day in the registrar's office.

Paula reveled in the college experience, from her classes to the field hockey team to attending football games. Her picture in the freshman baby book didn't do justice to her beautiful fragile face and long brown hair, and she received an endless stream of invitations to dates and fraternity parties. But with work, school, and field hockey, there wasn't much time for socializing. She didn't drink and wasn't that into rock music or dancing. Being around the campus for so many years, she knew enough about college boys and partying to decline most offers. She was a late-life baby, surprising her mother, at age thirty-six, in a marriage long marred by her husband's alcoholism and inability to hold a job. Like Andrew Paxton, she'd grown up in an adult environment and was mature beyond her years. Tall, thin, and as attractive as a model, she wore conservative clothes and bought her first pair of blue jeans just before entering Bainbridge.

Among her classes was Political Science 100, American history. The professor, Paul Marko, was active in the protest movement and often diverged from the course curriculum to give his opinions on the war. Paula began watching the evening news as part of her class work and to keep up with current events. Three of her high school classmates who had been drafted were about to leave for Southeast Asia.

So the "Americans for the Vietnamese People" seemed like a just cause. The stated intent was to speed American troop withdrawal by establishing guidelines for elections and government programs. The petition, which so far contained eighty-six signatures, of the three thousand students at Bainbridge, was five pages long, single-spaced, and looked extremely official. Professor Marko and members of the organization were thrilled to have Paula volunteer. Not only did she add the air of maturity and intelligence, but it never hurt to have a pretty girl promote a cause, particularly with a campus of over fifteen hundred males. And Paul Marko had an eye for attractive coeds whom he could charm and impress with his noble beliefs. For him, the protest movement had its extracurricular benefits.

Paula sat for two hours, two nights a week, talking about the petition and the war. Interest was sparse, so she kept a textbook under the table and also chatted with Karen Reilly or anyone else who shared her time slot.

She filled in on Saturday nights because there was no one else, and her mother, with whom she often spent weekends, was playing bridge with friends. She also had more free time, as she'd hurt her back playing field hockey and was out for the season. Dr. Hardwell prescribed muscle relaxers, but they'd had little effect so far. So he recommended crutches to take some of the weight off her spine when she walked. Sitting was extremely difficult, particularly on the metal chairs, so she folded her nylon jacket into a seat cushion.

Karen Reilly left after about thirty minutes, and as Paula was thinking about heading back to the dorm, she noticed four boys standing to her right, talking loudly. *Freshmen*, she thought. Jocks, all wearing high school letter jackets. No way would they sign the petition. Her only hope was that they weren't drunk and looking for an argument.

Then the tallest, with curly brown hair and angular features, came over. "Hi," he said, turning the petition so he could read it.

"Hi," said Paula, with an air of disinterest, trying to brace herself for whatever inane or derogatory remark might follow.

He turned it back to her. "I can't believe it," he said.

Paula started to get angry. This dumb clown was about to say something, and she was ready.

"Don't you think we've imposed our will on these people enough?" he asked.

"What do you mean …?" she answered, confused and off guard. "We are trying to help them establish a working government."

"Look." He pointed. "It says we require them to do this, and then this, and then this …"

"It wasn't … meant to be that way," she stammered, looking down at the words.

"Well, that's not what it says," he replied, and then he signed the petition. He handed her the pen, and smiled. It was a warm smile, friendly, with no strings attached. Paula smiled back and then looked down, embarrassed. Her whole body was flushed, and her scalp tingled. When she looked up, he was walking away with the three other boys.

Paula now read, really read, the petition. He was right. It sounded like a king giving orders to his underlings. Sighing deeply, she bent down, gathering up her belongings under the table. She would take the petition to Karen, explain what happened, and tell her she was going to find some other way to work to stop the war.

"Do you like ice cream?" asked a male voice. She looked up, and there stood the same boy, holding two vanilla ice-cream cones.

"Yes, thank you," she said, now embarrassed again. Brian Barrett came around and sat next to her. Neither said a word for a couple of minutes as they ate. Paula was totally unhinged, trying to gracefully handle the dripping mess in front of the incredibly handsome and bright stranger.

"I'm Brian," he said, smiling as he continued licking. "Sorry I ragged on your petition."

"Oh, no," she blurted. "You were absolutely right. I never read it like that before. I don't really know who wrote it … but thank you for signing it anyway. I'm Paula."

"Hi, Paula. No problem," he said, crunching away on the rest of the cone. Then he wiped his hands, which were actually clean, on his blue jeans.

"Are you a freshman?" he asked.

"Yes, I live in Weatherly," said Paula.

"Do you know Patty Van …? Wait, Paula … Paula … Cole. You're in Patty Van Duren's dorm. She's an RA. Beth Littlefield lives on your floor. I knew Vandy when we were kids; she moved away before eighth grade."

'That's right," said Paula. "Are you one of the soccer players from Amsterdam?"

"Yeah, I'm Barrett."

"And you have a roommate they call Pappy?"

"Yeah, that's right," said Barrett. "Patty is a great gal." He paused for a moment. "You're a townie."

Paula didn't know how to take the comment, but it was usually derogatory.

"Best-looking Spencer resident I've ever met," he said.

Paula's head buzzed. They talked on and on about high school, Bainbridge, and being away from home, although they laughed when Paula admitted that her mother was only a few streets away. Barrett vented about the soccer team and Pappy getting hurt, saying that the team wasn't the same without him. Paula described how her mom raised her, explaining that she hadn't seen her dad in years. She couldn't believe she was telling all this to someone she had met just minutes before. Everything was so relaxed. This young man she'd thought to be an immature jock was so genuine. He listened to her every word and lent his own insight into his family and friends. When she told him how she felt about her father's abandonment, he recounted the story of spending the night at a high school friend's house and hearing him suddenly cry out in his sleep from bad dreams about his parents' breakup.

Some of the lights abruptly went off. It was eleven o'clock. They had talked for hours as if it had been five minutes. Everything was shutting down, except The Cellar in the basement.

"Want to go down and have a beer?" asked Barrett, standing up.

"Well, I don't drink," said Paula.

Barrett hesitated. "Yeah, it's pretty noisy down there. Want to take a walk?" he asked. "Or do you need to get back?"

"No," she replied quickly. "But I have a problem. I hurt my back playing field hockey and have to use these crutches."

"That's okay," said Barrett. "Stand up." She did. "Hand me the crutches." He took them in his left hand. Then he turned his back to her, crouched down slightly, grabbed her right thigh, and hoisted her up piggyback onto him.

Paula moaned inaudibly from the pain but wrapped her arms over his powerful shoulders and her legs at his waist. He felt warm and strong yet lifted her gently, as if she were liable to break.

And off they went. He carried her up and down the campus sidewalks for half an hour, talking all the time about the stars in the sky and the old buildings they passed. All types of music blared across the campus. Barrett felt Paula's hot breath on his neck as she held on tightly, but she shifted every few minutes, and he could tell that she was in pain.

"Let's go down by the Hollow," he said.

"Okay," said Paula.

It was a short walk to the bottom of the hill to Commencement Hollow. Barrett let Paula down to her feet and then turned and kissed her on the lips. She tasted salty and sweaty, but it was the softest kiss he'd ever felt. She didn't pull away but just smiled up at him. He helped her down on her back, and then he lay next to her. For a while, they said nothing, but it was a strangely comfortable silence. Then Brian leaned over and kissed her again. Paula rolled over and rested her head on his chest. Barrett recounted the soccer game, telling her how everyone needed to pull together, saying how tough it was to be playing on a losing team. After a while, he stopped. Paula had fallen fast asleep. He picked her up gently. She half awakened, looked up, kissed him on the cheek, and then dozed off again. As he carried her back to the dorm, he had the strangest, most exhilarating feeling, as if he were a prince or a knight or something, carrying his princess back to the castle. He felt proud and protective.

Brian lay Paula down on a couch in the Weatherly lobby, setting the crutches on the floor. He couldn't carry her to her room, and it was past hours, so he called Patty Van Duren.

Patty was stunned to see Paula lying there.

"What happened?" asked Patty, casting a suspicious look at her old friend.

"We just met tonight," he said defensively. "We went walking on campus, and she fell asleep."

Patty saw something unexpected in her longtime friend. "Holy smokes, you're sober ... and sincere ... on a Saturday night? With a girl?" she asked mockingly. "By the way, it's after hours. *Long* after hours. What'd you do, pick a crippled one so she couldn't run away?"

"Hey, back off," said Brian. "We had a great time. She's ..."

"A sweet girl," said Patty, "and if you hurt her, I'll personally bury you behind the chapel in a shallow grave." Then she smiled.

"We'll get her up to her room," said Patty. "You'd better go sleep off whatever has gotten into you."

Barrett was still staring at Paula.

"Good night, Barrett," said Patty in a dismissive tone. He went to the door and then looked back. He turned again several times as he walked down the street—until the dorm was out of sight.

Sunday, October 12

◉ ◉ ◉ ◉

Pappy's eyes opened around nine thirty, and remembering that it was Sunday, he rolled over to go back to sleep. But there was a noise. It was Barrett, back from the shower, already shaved. It was *Sunday* ... wasn't it? What the ...? Normally, he had to drag Barrett out of bed to make brunch before noon.

Brian dress hurriedly.

"What's going on?" asked Pappy, blinded by the sunlight streaming into the room. "What are the blinds doing open? Are you all right?"

"Gotta go," said Barrett. "Beautiful day ... going to breakfast."

"Huh?" said Pappy, rubbing his face. "Uh ... it's Sunday."

"I know. Gotta go." Barrett smiled and went out the door.

That was the last he saw of Barrett that day.

Paula Cole was asleep when Barrett had called at eight thirty, asking if she wanted to go to breakfast. Patty Van Duren, who'd come up to check on Cole, tried kiddingly to get the phone away from her and hang up, but she saw Paula's face and heard the throb in her voice. This girl had it baaaad! And Barrett, calling early on a Sunday morning—and his gentle manner with Paula the night before—made it clear that both had fallen hard.

Cole dressed as quickly as she could. Her pain was as bad as the day she got hurt, and the medicine only helped for a short time. The health center was open on Sundays, but there was no one there to write a prescription.

195

She didn't want to use the crutches, but they provided some relief. Barrett was waiting in the lobby, and they walked over to the Union, only to find that it wasn't open yet. He was embarrassed, but Paula laughed and took his hand. So they sat on one of the hard stone benches and talked.

They were the first ones in the door when the dining room opened at eleven, and they sat back in the corner by themselves. Brian brought her doughnuts, eggs, coffee, juice, cinnamon rolls, bacon, grits, hash browns, pancakes, waffles, and muffins—until the table was covered with food—and she was mortified.

They were in their own little world. He'd never felt such a rush of adrenaline or hormones or whatever, and he was as high as a kite. She was smart, kind, gentle, courteous, thoughtful, loving, and insightful. The room filled with people, but they didn't notice. None of Barrett's harem approached the table. His eyes never wandered from Paula's face. After two hours, they decided to leave, and once outside, Barrett lifted her up on his back, and off they went around the campus.

McIlroy met Paxton for Sunday dinner. Pappy had ditched his bandage but decided to keep the stocking cap. In the era of the Beatles and long hair, only eleven-year-olds wore baseball caps.

As they sat talking about nothing in particular, Andrew noticed a boy with Asian features sitting several tables away. He was small, even frail, but no other students looked Japanese, so the odds were good that he was the one who'd posted the notice about karate lessons on the bulletin board. For years, Andrew had watched TV shows like *The Man from U.N.C.L.E.* and *I Spy*, as well as the James Bond movies, and he'd always wanted to learn martial arts. He'd bought a couple of books but couldn't learn much from the tiny pictures and vague descriptions.

"I bet that's the guy teaching karate," said Andrew to McIlroy. "Let's go talk to him."

Yoshi Ayabe sat alone, eating food that, like the English language, was still unfamiliar and difficult to enjoy. He was thousands of miles from home, attending a small school in Indiana, where anyone with other than Anglo features drew stares.

"Are you the guy teaching karate?" asked Andrew, extending his hand to Yoshi.

"Yes, karate," replied Yoshi, standing. He was even shorter up close, not quite five-five, and his bony handshake was limp.

"Hi, you guys want to take karate?" said another student, sitting at the next table. "I'm Larry Nelson ... Hey, what's with the haircut?"

Yoshi had made one friend at Bain: Larry Nelson. Unfortunately, he was overbearing and at times more boss than buddy.

"I had surgery a couple of weeks ago. I'm Andrew Paxton," said Pappy, shaking hands. "This is Jim McIlroy."

"Man, you sure you should be doing this?" asked Larry. "Yoshi here is the guy," he said, going around behind the smaller man and grabbing him in a bear hug.

Yoshi tried to ignore his attacker. He needed pupils to earn money, but more importantly, he wanted someone to share the boredom of practice. And someone to spar. Someone besides Larry Nelson.

"This man is the number one second *dan* black belt in Japan," said Larry, releasing his grip. "I've been working out with him for a couple of weeks."

Yoshi acted as if Nelson weren't there. "Lessons ... Tuesday, Thursday, Sunday. Two hours, is good, I think," said Yoshi, pausing regularly to find the words. "Um, five dollars per week. You buy ... um ... I order ... Give twelve dollar. You pay me."

"Yoshi will order your *gi* for you," said Larry. "That's the white uniform. It takes about two weeks to get here."

Pappy didn't know whether to talk to Yoshi or his translator. "Here's seventeen bucks, he said, handing him a check. "When do we start?"

"First lesson Tuesday night," said Yoshi, his brow now furrowed with worry. "You head okay?" he asked, tapping his own skull.

"Yeah, I'm okay," said Pappy.

"Maybe you wait," said Yoshi, still concerned.

"No, I'm okay. I can run and stuff," said Andrew.

"Okay ... okay," said Yoshi. "Tuesday."

Great! thought Andrew. *Learn karate. Learn to kick and punch.*

Cool. Great exercise. No more sitting on my butt. What's the worst that can happen?

Andrew Paxton lay on his bed. It was eleven o'clock, and he'd been studying chemistry for a couple of hours. He took out some paper to write home, but all he could think about was the earrings. Barrett was back with Littlefield. Would he jerk her around again? Pappy considered kicking his best friend in the … In any event, he'd had enough. There was no point in pining for Beth any more. No way she would look at anyone but Brian.

And where was his roommate?

Monday, October 13

⊚ ⊚ ⊚ ⊚

Pappy woke to see Brian heading out the door. Seven fifteen? They never crawled out of bed until seven forty-five, and then they dressed, dragged a comb through their hair, and bolted out the door to make chem by eight.

Barrett arrived at class three minutes late, sat in the back, and disappeared as soon as the hour was over.

At lunch, several people told Andrew that Hancock wanted to see him right away.

Maybe he was going to let Andrew practice. Maybe the doctor thought that enough time had passed and the bone had healed. Listening to Barrett talk about the team was driving him crazy. He prepared himself. He'd tell Hancock that he would remain in the background; he'd work with the reserves on their skills; he would do anything to be allowed to participate.

Pappy arrived at Hancock's office, and the coach smiled and shook his hand.

"How is the head?" he asked, offering Andrew a chair.

"Good, great, no problem, no pain, no nothing," said Andrew hopefully.

There was a silence. "You probably heard that three of the football players, including their placekicker, got chicken pox and are out indefinitely ..." Andrew nodded, a quizzical look on his face. "Coach Bolger has seen you play; he knows how accurate you are … He asked me to ask you if you want to try kicking—"

Andrew was stunned. "I can play football but not soccer?" he interrupted, standing. "I want to play soccer."

"You can't," continued Hancock, motioning for Pappy to sit down. "The doctor won't clear you. He says your bone has to fully heal … but you can play football with a helmet. They're going to modify one to protect your jaw without touching it. They want you only for field goals and extra points, no kickoffs. There shouldn't be any contact, no blows to the head …" Hancock stopped. Paxton was staring angrily at the wall, shaking his head in disbelief. Hancock said nothing until Paxton turned back.

"Look, it's up to you. You can't practice or play with us. So you can either sit in your room and feel sorry for yourself for the rest of the semester, or you can stay in shape, kick, and maybe help this school to a shot at the conference title."

The coach came around and sat in front of Andrew. "You can pretty much name your own schedule. You won't be involved in any of the plays, so you can work out, practice kicking, and then leave.

"I know you've had run-ins with Delfino and some others on the team. But Coach Bolger is a good guy, and I promise you, you won't have any trouble."

"I'm not afraid of them," said Andrew, gritting his teeth.

"I know you're not," said Hancock. "Most of the squad are good guys. Yes, you're mad you can't play soccer. But this is the next best thing. It's all I can offer."

Andrew stared blankly. "What are the guys on the team going to say? What is Barrett going to say?"

"It's no different than if you were on the baseball team and you hurt your arm, so you went to run track. You can stay in shape. You can participate." Hancock paused. "It kills me to say this, but it's a good deal—and the best thing that could happen to you. You may as well play for someone who wants you and be on a winning team.

"I told the coach I'd talk to you," continued Hancock. "Think it over. He's ready when you are." Andrew left, still shaking his head. Unfortunately, everything Hancock said made sense. It was better for him, and for the soccer team next year, if he exercised and stayed in shape.

Andrew had watched football all his life and played pickup games in the neighborhood when he was a kid, but he knew nothing of plays or strategy. He'd seen the Titans' grueling practices and attended some games. This was a winning team, a dominant program. They were fast, powerful, hardworking, and dedicated.

The empty afternoons were really starting to drag. It came down to this: if Coach Hancock thought it was okay, he figured he would at least see what Bolger had to say.

The football offices were on the second floor of the field house. The secretary was a pleasant middle-aged woman in a strange-looking polka-dot dress and a little too much lipstick. Because of the confrontations with Delfino, Sam Bolger had always made a point of saying hello to Andrew, and he'd briefly attended one of the soccer games.

"C'mon in, Andrew." The coach came around the desk, shook his hand, and closed the door. "How are you? How's the head? It was a terrible thing. Coach Hancock told me what a brave young man you are. A serious injury and then surgery. That would have scared me half to death."

"No, I'm fine," replied Pappy. "Coach said you wanted to see me."

"Yes. I was talking to Coach Hancock and Doc Hardwell and …" He paused and leaned forward. "Now, this is entirely up to you, but we need a placekicker. I've seen you play. I like your work ethic and hustle. Soccer-style kicking seems to be the wave of the future. Guys like Gogolak and Stenerud are changing the game. The best toe kicker converts about fifty percent of the time. I understand the sidewinders are around eighty percent. Anyway, I don't know when Holmes will be back. We have a great team. They're a good bunch of guys who want to win. Our punter is trying to make the change, but he's missing half of his extra points. We end up going for it on fourth down rather than trying a field goal, and we could use your help." He paused to judge Andrew's reaction. So far, so good.

"I know you've had problems with a couple of our players," Bolger continued. "Well, I can tell you I've discussed this with my coaches— confidentially, of course—and to a man, they're all for you giving it a try. You can make your own schedule. We recommend you lift weights on Mondays, Wednesdays, and Thursdays. The team lifts early in the morning, but if you want to work on your own, that's okay too. The trainer will take you through stretching exercises. Then you practice for as long as you feel necessary and leave when you're done. All you'll do is field goals and extra points. No kickoffs. No contact. If you do get hit in a game, we'll teach you to flop like you were shot with a gun. The other team will avoid you like the plague or they'll get a roughing penalty, and it will mean an automatic first down for us. Even then, you'll probably only be clipped in the legs. We'll teach you our fake field goal plays, but you'll have no physical involvement."

"But how can I play football with a cracked skull?" Pappy asked, pointing to his head.

"Excellent question," said Bolger. "I should have told you that first." He picked up a helmet sitting on his desk. "We are going to cut away the padding by your jaw joint so it's completely clear. Nothing will be touching your incision or cheekbone. The rest of the cushion will absorb any incidental impact. The doc assures me there's absolutely no danger, even if you get hit, as there's no way to make contact with the bone."

Andrew looked at the helmet. *I wish I could wear this and play soccer instead.* He sighed.

"When do I start?" he asked.

"Andrew, you have to want to do this," said Bolger sincerely. "I have enough to do keeping sixty-two players and eight coaches happy. But I think you enjoy sports, and competition, too much to pass up this opportunity ... Think it over."

"I have," said Pappy, standing and offering his hand. "And I'm ready."

"Good," said Bolger, smiling broadly. "If you have time right now, go down to the equipment room. Pat will fit you with all your gear and give you a locker. Your helmet will be ready when you come to practice this afternoon. What's your class schedule? Do you have any conflicts?"

"Yes, I have chemistry lab on Thursdays."

"That's okay. There won't be much of a problem until after daylight savings in November. After you get your equipment, schedule a workout with the trainer."

"I'm going to lift during the afternoon if that's okay. I have chem at eight, English at nine, and Spanish at one …"

"That's fine. I recommend you practice first and then lift. Welcome aboard. I'm sorry our kicker got sick, but I am glad we could offer you this opportunity. And thanks for your help."

"Sure," said Pappy, with no conviction in his voice. "I'll be out there at three thirty."

Sure enough, Pat was waiting in the basement, listening to the radio and talking with a janitor.

"Hey, our new placekicker," he said, shaking Pappy's hand. "This is a great team …" Pat Smith stopped, as he could see apprehension in Pappy's face.

"Sorry about your injury. You were a great loss to the team, but you'll like playing for Coach Bolger. He's a quality guy and is really glad to have you." He could see his words had little impact. "Well, let's get you fitted out."

Helmet, hip pads, thigh pads, shoulder pads, cup, jockstrap, pants, jersey. Pappy felt first like a mannequin and then a pack mule. He hated trying on clothes of any kind, and this process was gruesome. The shoes were uncomfortable and worthless for soccer-style kicking, so he kept his Adidas. He jammed everything into his locker and took the helmet back upstairs. Doc Hardwell removed some of the padding with a scalpel so the injured side of Andrew's head was untouched. He dumped it in his locker and headed to the dorm.

The news would spread quickly, and the rest of the team might bitch and moan, but they would accept his decision. Barrett was the problem. It was bad enough that the team was losing and he and Hancock were butting heads—now Andrew would be teammates with Delfino and Burler.

He waited as long as he could and then went back to the field house. The locker room, empty just an hour before, now had a hundred varsity and JV football players struggling with equipment. For Pappy, it was a process, from jockstrap to shoulder pads.

"You don't need those now," said Pat Smith, coming over to help. "As a matter of fact, I remember now Coach Bolger saying since you were only kicking, you don't need hip or thigh protection."

"Hey, Paxton," called Joe Tagliarino, a freshman offensive lineman who was already one of the best in the conference and a genuinely nice guy that Pappy had met during fraternity rush. "Are you lost, man? I heard you got hurt, but they ain't gonna let you play soccer in that gear." He laughed. "I saw Coach Hancock upstairs, and he said you were going to kick for us. That's great. You have big shoes to fill in Holmes … You'll do okay, though. C'mon, if you're ready."

They ran out, helmets in hand. Four laps around the practice field and then calisthenics and stretching. It looked like an army. There were lots of moans and groans from Saturday's game, though they'd stomped Carthage. Pappy saw curious glances, but most knew him by reputation and had heard about his fractured skull.

Coach Bolger stood behind the captains with his clipboard until they were through. "Okay, listen up," he finally said. "Most of you recognize Andrew Paxton from the soccer team. After his injury, he can't play anymore, so we've asked him to try placekicking for us. If you've seen him play, you know the soccer team's loss is our gain." Bolger's demeanor became stern. "Mr. Paxton suffered a fractured skull and an operation. He is to have absolutely *no* physical contact during drills. Is that clear?" Bolger didn't wait for a reply. "Good."

He was pacing back and forth, occasionally looking at his clipboard. "You guys did a great job against Carthage. We were quick to the ball on defense, and the two fumble recoveries put us first in the conference in takeaways. Do the small things well and the big things will fall into place. There are no more breathers on our schedule. It's time to perfect everything we do."

"All right, I'll take the offense. Coach Jugovic will work with the defense down at the other end. We're going to walk through some new offensive plays, and the defense will prepare for Carnes. No helmets. Sparks, you and Rattigan stay here. The rest, let's go." Everyone took off except the two players called.

"Andrew, Sparks is the backup quarterback, and Rattigan is a center.

I want you to go over and kick for a while off the tee to get the feel. Then when you're ready, these guys will snap and place the ball for you. There's a bag of balls over there, and I'll get one of the equipment guys to shag." He handed Pappy a two-inch tee. "This is regulation."

"Thanks," said Andrew, and ran toward the south goalposts. He turned back to see Bolger talking to Rattigan. He wasn't smiling, and the lineman was looking down at the ground.

Pappy set the tee in the middle of the conversion line without the ball. It was strange. He'd seen a film of Jan Stenerud, the great Kansas City Chiefs' soccer-style kicker, and was amazed to see him bend his leg halfway up his back and then come through with such force that even though the ball was turning end over end, he routinely kicked it fifty yards or more.

Okay, he thought. *This is just like taking a penalty kick. The target is the very middle of the horizontal bar. Find the spot on the ball. But instead of kicking away from the middle, or away from the goalie and under the bar, kick it over the top.* Man, would this ruin him for when he went back to soccer? The left foot was key. The farther forward he placed it next to the ball, the more his right knee would come over the top, creating a lower and harder shot. The farther back, the higher the trajectory, but he'd lose velocity. He also had to hit it high enough to not be blocked.

Pappy took two steps and kicked over the tee where he imagined the ball would be, following its flight between the uprights. He did this several times and then placed the ball. In soccer, Andrew took at least five or six steps on free kicks but knew by watching Lou Groza and other pros that he would have time only for two or three. He tried both but settled on three. Left, right, left, kick. Thump! The ball sailed through the middle. He did it again. And again. And again. Every kick looking like the one before. After ten kicks, he stopped and rested. He looked over to see Bolger twenty yards away, watching and smiling. *Thank God I didn't know he was there the whole time,* thought Pappy. *I probably would have blasted it through somebody's windshield.*

He then moved three yards to the left, still on the conversion line, took five kicks, and then did the same to the right. The boy shagging the balls was at first excited and impressed. That gave way to boredom and disbelief, as Paxton looked and acted like a machine, doing the same thing over and over.

"Move back, Pappy!" he yelled. "Really pound one."

But Andrew followed the same routine, and increased the distance only when he was absolutely sure he couldn't miss. If he did miss, he'd move back in. It had to be automatic, just like a penalty kick. He continued until after thirty tries he was only on the fifteen-yard line. And tiring quickly. Just as in soccer, when his leg was weary, it would swing instead of snap, and he began to hook the ball. Pappy was about to quit when he heard Bolger behind him.

"Enough for today. That was very good. I don't want you to pull a muscle. Hit the training room and have them check you out." He offered Andrew his hand. "I want to say thank you again. We're glad to have you."

Todd Hancock sat in his car by the field in Darby Park, looking at his roster and the rest of the schedule. The Humphrey defeat was the fourth since the team had lost Andrew Paxton. The man who was everywhere on the field was gone, and the other halfbacks either didn't have the skill or the will to step into his shoes. The one continuing bright spot was Roland Santander. Paxton had been right. Although his walking style was agonizingly slow for a former basketball player like Hancock, he could tolerate it because of Roland's skill level. The team had moments of brilliance, but defensive breakdowns by his ex–football players in the backfield were demoralizing. Often, the rest of the Chiefs would drop back to help out, causing the offense to collapse.

And the best athlete on the team, Barrett, was a bad case of heartburn. Hancock's pushing to get him to play up to his incredible potential had, to date, resulted in nothing but conflict.

Another coach might have coasted through the rest of the season. After all, he didn't ask for the job. But Hancock didn't get to be an all-conference basketball player at his physical stature without determination … and stubbornness.

His battle with Barrett was taking too much time and energy. It might be better to end it. He didn't know how this team would take yet another major loss, particularly when it involved someone so gifted and well liked. And it would be Hancock's decision, not an injury, that removed Brian. Well, he'd have to do it before practice.

The first group arrived at the field, with Barrett leading the way. He ran over to Hancock. The attitude and posture were gone.

"Coach, can I have a minute?"

Hancock was surprised. The only question Barrett ever asked him was "Why are we doing it this way?" And it was always more a criticism than an inquiry.

"I want to win," he blurted. Before the coach could say anything, he continued. "I'm tired of losing. We've gotta find a way to work this out. Pappy isn't coming back, but Roland can run the offense. We need to play better defense, but these guys can't do it alone. You've got to leave me in the whole game. And we've got to be more aggressive." He stopped, hanging his head. "I know we disagree about a lot of things. And I shoot off my mouth too much ... and Pappy isn't here to tell me to shut up. But I know how to play fullback. And I know how to win. This ain't basketball. We don't have the skilled guys to control the ball. We have to hustle and bang like at Amsterdam. We have to shove it down their throats and stuff them into the goal.

"We just can't beat teams like Stratton and Carthage," continued Brian. "But I don't know why we can't kick everybody else's ass." He finally took a breath.

"Anyway, I am tired of this crap. Keep Penny, Dave, and Tim up front and have them stay there. Santander, Ryder, and McIlroy at halfback. Move Nakano back to fullback with me and Landon and Harbaugh."

Hancock didn't know what to say. Barrett nodded, turned, and ran over to one of the groups. Williams and Caldwell led calisthenics. Finally, Hancock called everyone together.

"I've one announcement, if you don't already know. Andrew Paxton is going to be the placekicker on the football team." No one said a word. "The doctor won't let him play soccer, but they've designed a helmet that will protect him, and he's already at practice. I know this is upsetting, but it's better than him sitting around for the next two months. He'll be back with us next season, probably better and stronger than ever." Hancock became solemn.

"That young man gave a lot to this team in the few weeks he played with us, and we should wish him the same success he wants for us—and thank him by playing our guts out.

"Saturday's game stunk. It was a poor effort," he said. "Let's never play that way again. Now let's go."

"C'mon, you guys," said Barrett. "From now on, we knock everybody on their ass."

"Damn right," said Millwood.

"All right, let's scrimmage," said Hancock. He divided them into blue and red, moving Barrett to center up fullback and Nakano behind him. They kicked off, and everyone was keyed. Players were pushing and shoving, and twice play stopped as two players almost squared off. Hancock blew his whistle.

"All right, we don't need any stupid penalties in a game," he said. "We lose the ball and they gain momentum." That calmed everyone down, but it was now a battle of wills. Barrett was suddenly Andrew Paxton—after loose balls, pushing the play forward. Nakano was steady behind him, plugging up the middle. Barrett called out the switches. Soon everyone was talking and moving to the open spaces.

Barrett would break up the opposing attack, and then Roland would run the offense. Instinctively, he knew where everyone was on the field, and he would suddenly launch a perfect pass without looking. Barrett began playing off Santander, rather than firing the ball aimlessly, and the first team totally dominated the second.

Hancock was afraid to ask what had caused Barrett's transformation— his most gifted athlete was now the leader. *Who are you? And what have you done with Brian Barrett?*

Andrew was back in the room just after five. How things changed in a day. Saturday he'd lamented not playing soccer, today he had his first football practice, and tomorrow night would be his first karate lesson.

"Hey, Pappy," said Mike Erving. "I hear you're the new kicker on the football team. Congratulations. You might even get to play for a conference championship."

It was already all over school. "How'd you find out?" he asked.

"One of the cheerleaders; she said everyone on the team was talking about you. They're calling you a crazy sidewinder ... and a lot of other things I won't repeat."

"Swell," said Andrew.

"Does Barrett know yet?" asked Mike. "Maybe you want to sleep in another dorm tonight. Or another state."

"Thanks," Paxton replied. "Just send my body home."

Pappy had homework but was starving, and he didn't want to wait for Barrett. Why get flogged before supper? He went to the Union and sat with some of the guys on his dorm floor. This was the earliest he'd gone to dinner, as he always waited for the Chiefs. Now he didn't belong with them, but he didn't really feel part of the football team either.

He looked toward the window, and there was Beth Littlefield, sitting by herself. His heart went thump. Then he saw Barrett coming up the stairs. He stopped, clearly waiting for someone. Probably members of his harem. No, it was a girl on crutches. He had a smile plastered across his face, and he never took his eyes off her. They went to a table by themselves. She sat down, and he went through the line with two trays.

There was Littlefield by herself ... and Barrett with yet another girl. Brian saw Pappy and waved.

"Hey, c'mon over here!" he yelled. Pappy assumed Barrett had heard the news, but he doubted he would be murdered in such a public place.

"This is Paula," he said. "This is my roommate, Pappy."

She smiled, and Andrew was knocked over by the electricity between them.

"Hi, I've heard all about you," she said. "You're Barrett's best friend."

Andrew was surprised by the feeling expressed with the words. "Yeah, how desperate can you get?" replied Pappy.

"So what's this about you turning traitor and joining those dirt bag footballers?" asked Barrett, first scowling and then smiling. "Hancock told the whole team. He said we should be happy for you, and that you'd come back next year even stronger and better."

"You got that right," exclaimed Andrew with a sigh of relief, sitting down. "I still wish I were playing soccer. But Bolger is a nice guy, and I make my own schedule."

"I still don't get it," said Barrett. "How can you play football and not soccer?"

"They fitted me with a helmet that doesn't touch my jawbone, and all I do is kick field goals and extra points."

"Well, I had a talk with Hancock. You'd have been proud of me." Barrett was talking to Pappy but looking at Paula. "We're going to play Chiefs kick-ass soccer from now on. I get to wander all over the field like you, and Santander is running the offense."

Then it was as if Pappy were sitting alone. Paula and Brian were hardly eating … just staring at each other.

"See you later," said Andrew. "Nice meeting you."

"Nice meeting you," said Paula. Neither looked up.

Barrett was back at the room by eleven. Pappy was studying.

"Hey," said Barrett, flopping down on the bed.

"Hey," replied Pappy.

Barrett sighed. He sat up and then went over to his dresser mirror and examined his face and hair. Pappy was still hunkered down over his book.

"Hey, look at this," said Barrett, picking up something off his dresser. "That dumb broad that was here Friday night left her earrings. They look just like the ones Littlefield's dad gave her."

Andrew's eyes opened wide. Barrett hadn't been with Beth.

"Man, I need to do some laundry," he said, grabbing his dirty clothes and some quarters. Back in three minutes." He returned and hurled himself noisily onto the bed with another conclusive sigh.

Pappy looked down at his grinning roommate and closed his book. "Yes, she's beautiful. Yes, she's sweet. Yes, she's wonderful … Anything else I forgot? I have to study."

"Yeah," said Barrett, popping out of bed and standing next to Pappy.

"Isn't she great? I mean, truly great?" He looked down. "I can't think of anything else. I can't study. I want to quit school and take her away. I want to marry her tomorrow. I want to make her well."

"Yeah, why is she on crutches?" asked Andrew.

"She hurt her back playing field hockey. Can you leave for a minute? I want to call her."

"Haven't you been with her, like, since Saturday?"

"I know. I can't help it. I can't explain." The phone rang. Barrett lurched and caught it before the second ring. "Hey," he said softly. He looked at Pappy plaintively.

"Okay," he said. "I'll be up in the second-floor reading room. Come get me when you're done."

"Thanks, man," he said. "Oh, Paula says hi."

Great. I'm popular with yet another of Barrett's girlfriends.

Andrew came down at one thirty in the morning and opened the door quietly. He'd fallen asleep while studying and assumed Barrett would be out cold. But Brian was still on the phone.

"Hey, I'm dead, and we have chem at eight," said Pappy.

"Yeah, okay," said Barrett. "I gotta go," he said to Paula. It took him twenty more minutes to hang up.

Pappy was sound asleep. Brian lay down on his bed in his clothes and stared up at the ceiling.

Tuesday, October 14

◉ ◉ ◉ ◉

Barrett waited for Paula in front of the Union at noon, but she'd fallen asleep. Her nights were filled with pain, and she struggled to walk even with the crutches. Brian wanted to carry her from place to place, but she was too embarrassed in broad daylight. She arrived half an hour late, and they sat by themselves at a small table near a window. Paula felt strange having him wait on her, but she was overwhelmed by his attentiveness, and her pain diminished when she sat. She needed stronger medicine but didn't want to leave Barrett, so she decided to go while he was at practice.

They both cut afternoon classes and headed for the library, but they went right on past, heading down the hill to the Hollow. They lay down in the grass and watched the changing leaves rustle in the cool fall breeze. After a bit, Brian raced up to Roberts Hall and retrieved a blanket. They talked about family, friends, and their childhoods. Then they simply lay there silently for the longest time, wrapped in each other's arms, oblivious to the dozens of students passing by on their way to class.

At two forty-five, it was time for a quick trip to the Union for ice cream before practice. Paula relented and let Brian give her a piggyback ride. He dropped her at Weatherly—but not before standing for the longest time in a silent embrace. Then he sprinted to Roberts Hall, dressed, and took off for Darby Park.

Football practice the second day was still strange, but the team realized that Pappy could help them win—in a big way. They watched "the machine," with the weird side approach and swinging hip, pound one ball after another through the same spot between the goalposts.

Andrew's kicks from the five yard line now sailed twenty yards out of the end zone. His lower back and groin were sore from the day before, but he'd warmed up and stretched, and he struck the ball crisply. Fortunately, the weather was dry and calm. The fun would start when the cold rain fell in sheets and the field turned to muck.

Time to kick with a center and holder. Pappy and Rattigan exchanged stares, but Roy Sparks was a team leader, and Bolger knew there wouldn't be any problems, even though he felt his new kicker could handle any situation.

After a dozen kicks, both snapper and holder tired of their monotonous tasks, as did the boy shagging. Pappy would have taken another twenty, but he'd heard enough "Are you about done?" after every kick.

Next was his first trip ever to the weight room, located on the top floor of the field house, next to the handball courts. Pappy was deceptively strong, having spent summers throwing around truck and passenger tires, which weighed between twenty and seventy pounds each—and when mounted on steel and iron rims, they could be double that.

The room was stark and cold, with cement block walls and concrete floors. Pulleys and cables on the steel machines isolated specific muscles. Bolger had ordered a light workout, making sure Paxton didn't overdo. First free weights, bench press, curls, military press, dead lifts, and shoulder shrugs. After a half hour, Pappy was done. The trainer wasn't. Now to the machines, particularly leg extensions, hamstring curls, and toe raisers. Three sets of eight repetitions, at thirty pounds to start. His muscles burned after only four or five reps. Pappy didn't ask how much weight the football players could lift. He finished shortly after five, and with karate at seven, he had to speed through the cafeteria line and eat quickly.

Excited about the first lesson, he had no idea what to wear. He didn't have Yoshi's phone number, and he wasn't sure if he could understand him anyway, so he put on sweat clothes and sneakers and took off for the field house.

The class was on the stage at the end of the basketball court, a large area with hardwood floors. Yoshi appeared almost gray in color next to his white suit, or *gi*, and black belt. Thin to the point of looking emaciated, his hands and arms were boney. The edges of his palms were calloused, as were his knuckles.

"Shoe, sock off," said Yoshi. "Bawr foot."

There were four other students plus Larry Nelson, who already had his white *gi* and white belt. They started with sit-ups. One hundred sit-ups. Everyone but Pappy groaned and strained after about twenty. Sixty was the limit for all but Andrew. It was clear he was the only athlete in the group, but one hundred was plenty.

"Wan hunord push-up," said Yoshi, lying face down on the hardwood floor. "On knuckle."

The pain was incredible, and no one could manage more than eight or ten. At fifteen, Andrew changed to his palms. Even Yoshi quit after about twenty-five, embarrassed he couldn't endure more.

Then they formed two rows facing Yoshi. "Feet apart, shoulder width," he said, with Nelson parroting/translating every word. "Knees bent. Shoulders back. Chin up. Now learn to punch. Close fists. One arm up. Shoulder height. Two knuckles line up with wrist and arm. Other arm tucked under shoulder, with fist turned up, ready to punch." Yoshi's knuckles were white, and his fists looked hard as steel hammers.

Everyone tried to take the instructor's pose, but by the time they were in the correct position, their legs shook from the strain of standing with bent knees. Even Pappy had to repeatedly stand up straight and start over. Once the correct posture (or as close as they were going to get) was achieved, they each began to punch, almost in slow motion, while trying to maintain form. The right fist went forward, palm down, while the left fist retracted under the left shoulder, palm up. Right hip and shoulder moved to follow the punch. Then the left fist went forward and twisted palm down, with the right fist pulled back. Left, right, left, right. Everyone laughed nervously as he forgot to retract the opposite hand or turn the wrist.

Yoshi walked among them, pushing chins up, pulling legs back, and poking bodies here and there. He attempted to explain diaphragm breathing and concentrating the force of the blow. This made no sense, until Larry chimed in.

"He wants you to yell on every punch. It tightens your stomach muscles and diaphragm."

Yoshi took the position and began. "Eee!" he shouted as each fist struck an imaginary target. His body's twisting motion and bent knees added force to every blow. It was like 120 pounds on the edge of his knuckles.

The class yelled Eee! with every punch. Yoshi continued pushing, pulling, poking. When he came to Andrew, he struck him hard on the buttocks, and before Paxton could react, he slugged him in the stomach.

"Kip yowr cowin," said Yoshi, slugging him again. Andrew didn't understand, but the blows got his attention. "Kip yowr cowin."

"You're supposed to tighten up so you can keep a coin between the cheeks of your butt," said Larry in his usual know-it-all manner. "You keep your ass tight, your stomach tight, and your arms and shoulders loose so you can throw punches and block."

"You're kidding," said Andrew. "How can you keep one part tight and the other loose?"

"Punch," said Yoshi. Andrew took the position and threw a left. Yoshi hit him in the stomach. "Punch," he said again, now going behind and hitting him in the butt. "Arm straight, chin back, knuckle straight, eyes in my eyes …" He kept circling while Andrew jabbed. "Aim high. Hit face. Very dangerous here." He pointed to his sternum. "Aim here and here," he said, punching Andrew on the left and then the right side of his chest.

After another ten minutes, they took a break. Andrew was exhausted, and his thigh muscles burned. He'd no sooner taken a drink than Yoshi was back in the middle of the floor.

"Now face block," he said. He took the same stance, but this time the left arm was cocked under the shoulder, and the right hand was now in a knife-edge profile, fingers out straight, with the arm across the waist. Yoshi swept his right arm upward across his face, as if knocking aside a blow. He then did the same position and motion with the left arm. He repeated it several times and then had his students try it in unison, shouting with each block.

Once again, everyone labored to copy Yoshi's form, while recoiling the opposite fist in position to throw a punch, while keeping the chin up and looking into his opponent's eyes—knees bent, butt tight, stomach tight, shoulders loose … They continued for another five minutes.

The next block was a combination to protect the face and groin. The right arm thrust up to nose level (never any higher or it would block one's vision) and then down sharply to deflect a kick.

Andrew was the guinea pig. When he looked down to check his form, Yoshi would tap his chin upward or push his head. He then stood in front of Andrew and kicked, first left foot and then right. At this point, Pappy was no longer concerned with form. He wanted to keep from being hospitalized again, so he slapped at Yoshi's legs any way he could. Yoshi would correct his hand position or balance and then start again.

This was just the first hour. At the next break, Andrew flopped straight down on the floor. It was like playing an entire soccer game with bent knees and tight butt and stomach while someone was trying to maim him.

"Next, kick," said Yoshi, apparently fresh and ready to go. "Knees bent, left foot forward, hip down, balance, kick." Yoshi's hips came forward—front knee still bent, his right foot snapped out, about at the level of Andrew's stomach—and then back. His next kick was up in Andrew's face, about a foot higher than Yoshi's own head. The class got into the fighting stance and started. No one could stay balanced or throw a kick with their knees bent. And no one but Andrew was limber enough to kick any higher than just below the belt. Thank God for soccer, thought Pappy.

After fifteen minutes of this—first left leg and then right—a short break followed.

"Now *kumite* … ummm … fight," said Yoshi.

Andrew was sure he heard wrong. "Since all beginner, you fight me," said Yoshi. "Who has time?"

There was buzzing and nervous chuckling.

"Everyone fights him because he doesn't want anyone to get hurt," said Larry, and they all burst out laughing.

"Andrew first. Pappy first," said Yoshi, smiling. Andrew felt sick. He'd been in fights before, but usually they were a few wild swings followed quickly by throwing someone to the ground. This guy was a black belt, and he was as fast as Barrett ... or faster.

"How long?" asked Pappy.

"One minute," said Yoshi.

One minute. How bad could that be? wondered Andrew. Then he remembered ...

"Hold it. My head," said Pappy, pointing to his skull. "I had an operation. No blows here." He pointed to the right side of his jaw. "Wait ... I'll be right back," he said, running out the door.

Puzzled, Yoshi pointed at Larry. "You," he said. Nelson grimaced.

Pappy dashed down to the equipment room and grabbed two wrestling head guards. He returned to see Larry doing his best to cover as much of his head and chest as possible as Yoshi kicked him in the stomach.

"Time," said the boy with the watch.

Larry Nelson exhaled and stood up straight. They both bowed, and Larry went to the bleachers and collapsed.

"Pappy ready?" asked Yoshi.

Andrew was fiddling with the headgear, donning one and trying to fit a second on top for added protection. It worked, but one covered the ear hole of the other, making him almost deaf. Knowing what was about to happen, though, he felt hearing would be less important than being able to run away.

"Okay, ready," Andrew replied, fastening the two chin straps. "Remember, no hit this side."

Yoshi nodded, but not in a way that gave Andrew any comfort. He took his stance.

"No," said Yoshi, "bow first. Hands at side, open. Bow at waist. Eyes to my eyes."

Andrew bowed and took his position, and someone said, "Fight."

Andrew was looking around his body to see that his arms and hands were in position, butt tight, when Yoshi glided forward. Andrew arms instinctively went up to protect his head, and Yoshi snapped a right-footed side kick into Pappy's left ribs. "Uh," he groaned, and shuffled backward, terrified. The blow was so quick that Pappy didn't even flinch. The other students were cheering Andrew on, likely hoping he would break Yoshi's leg or something so they wouldn't have to undergo this ordeal.

Again Yoshi advanced, and Andrew dropped his elbow to protect his ribs, so his opponent aimed higher and landed the same kick to Andrew's left jaw. Yoshi was back in his stance before Andrew's hands came up.

"Look here, my eye," said the instructor, pointing, but this guy was so quick that it didn't matter what Andrew did. It felt as if he'd been out there ten minutes. He threw a couple of halfhearted punches and then recoiled quickly, anticipating the next onslaught. Yoshi landed a straight kick to Andrew's lower stomach and then threw another, but Andrew's fist came down hard, totally by reflex, and knocked it away. "Good, good, good," said Yoshi.

"Time!"

Andrew stood up before his knees gave out. Yoshi smiled. They bowed, and Yoshi shook his hand. "Good, good, good," he said. Andrew took off his headgear and sat down. He watched the others get pummeled, and it was clear that not everyone would be back Thursday for the next lesson. Most were already grumbling about how hard it was.

Pappy returned the headgear to the equipment room. His clothes were soaked, and he drank about a quart of water at the fountain. On the way to the dorm, he threw punches and blocks. He couldn't believe he'd survived the sparring, and marveled at Yoshi's speed and power. Suddenly, he was no longer interested in football. This was ten times the workout he'd ever had in any other sport, including soccer.

Man, wait until the next time Rattigan messes with Littlefield.

Wednesday, October 15

◎ ◎ ◎ ◎

T yler College was in town. Usually a weekend match, due to the 150-mile distance between schools, it was rescheduled because of the Yellow Jackets' homecoming that Saturday. An average squad like Bainbridge, Tyler's football and basketball teams also were dominant. However, they had one unique amenity. The football stadium was one of the few in the country, regardless of division level, with Astroturf, and the soccer team was permitted to play its games there when not in use.

Daylight was waning in mid-October, so game time was three o'clock. The long run to the field allowed everyone to warm up in the cool fall air. Barrett led the pack, going faster with every stride. Paula was coming to his game. The Chiefs kept pace, but the rest fell back.

They arrived and circled up for calisthenics. Barrett was a chatterbox, pumping everyone up, so by the time Tyler arrived, the Titans were ready. Hancock learned the reason for Barrett's sudden "spiritual" transformation, wishing he'd discovered the secret to taming his great athlete much earlier. He knew and liked Paula very much, and he hoped this hormonal imbalance resulted in his problem child replacing Andrew Paxton as the team's heart.

The Yellow Jackets won the toss and kicked off. That was the first of only four times the ball came into the Bainbridge end in the first half. Barrett was everywhere. At one point, Roland Santander, who never criticized a teammate, chided Barrett to play in control, as half his kicks went over the end line.

Three were shots on goal from forty yards. Millwood scored first, at the 25:25 mark, after six missed shots, when a bullet from Penny rebounded off the goalie's chest, and Tim tapped it in. Three minutes later, Don capped a fast break from fifteen yards with his favorite shot off the outside of his left instep. Caldwell scored on a penalty kick at thirty-four minutes, and Santander hit his first penalty kick in the United States just before the end of the half, when a frustrated Tyler player tripped him in the goalie box. Four to zero, Titans.

Pappy suffered through football practice, knowing that the soccer Titans were playing two miles away. His distraction caused him to hit the crossbar twice when he pulled the ball. But now he was on the twenty yard line, and he hadn't missed in ten kicks.

Sparks, the holder, looked up at Andrew after the last shot. "Don't you want to miss just once to make things interesting? Can you really curve a soccer ball and hit someone in the hands or the gut with the ball anytime you want?"

Pappy looked around. The coaches were concentrating on their drills. The ball was snapped, and Andrew stepped too far forward, rocketing the ball into Ben Rattigan's rear end … dead center. Sparks turned away, trying to stifle his laughter.

"Sorry," said Andrew, as deadpan as he could, but it was several moments before his holder was able to continue.

He finished and then raced to the locker room, changed, and took off for the soccer field.

The second half began as the first, and after ten minutes, the score stood at six to zero. Randy Williams was replaced in goal at the twenty-five-minute mark, and most of the subs were now in the game. With ten minutes left, it was seven to zero, and Randy Williams was put in at forward. After being caught offside three penetrations in a row, he was benched, to the jeering of his teammates.

The Titans cheered at the whistle and rushed through handshakes with a completely defeated Tyler team. Brian went over and picked up Paula, hugging her tightly.

"Barrett, get over here!" Hancock screamed. "We're a team." His scowl was useless against Brian's elation. He then ran over and hugged several players and the coach. Hancock flashed the smallest grin he could contain and then said, "Good job, men. See you tomorrow."

The team walked back to campus. No free ride, even after a win. Barrett took off and caught up with his roommate, who'd left just before it ended.

"Great game, roomie," said Pappy, happy for his best friend but sad he couldn't contribute. "How come you didn't score?"

"Come to the next game and see," said Barrett, never stopping. "Gotta go."

Paula went back to her room and lay down. The cold fall air was taking a toll on her back. She held the bottle with the Darvon. *No,* she decided, even though she hadn't taken any that day. She didn't want to pass out on Brian as she had the night they met.

Barrett went straight to his room, ripped off his uniform, and raced to the shower in his jockstrap. He showered, dressed, tossed on some aftershave, and was at Paula's dorm in fifteen minutes.

Thursday, October 16

◉ ◉ ◉ ◉

Karate and football. And a hundred sore muscles Andrew didn't know he had. Good thing Bainbridge was on trimesters, as he only had three classes each term. Now with weight training, studying, football practice, karate, and everything else, he had little spare time. However, with Barrett suddenly MIA, the room was quiet. No stereo playing all night. The hundred or so girls that called or showed up at their window had seen Barrett carrying Paula all over campus and given up the chase.

Until today, other than calisthenics, Andrew had had little contact with the rest of the football team. Saturday would be his first game, so after an hour, he joined the squad to practice extra points and field goals. Now there would be a defense trying to block the kick, or distract him into a miss. The starting quarterback, Bobby Birdwell, would be the holder. The guys on the other side of the line looked huge. And mean. They pointed fingers, shouted, ran back and forth, jumped up and down, and waved their arms. Birdwell, a junior, exuded confidence and calm far beyond his years.

"Listen for the count, watch the snap, and kick the ball. No different than a penalty kick." He smiled.

Yeah, but on a penalty kick, there weren't eleven guys in helmets looking to treat me to a dirt nap.

Fortunately, the defense jumped off sides three times in a row, allowing Andrew to get used to Birdwell's signal calling.

They lined up again. Hike, snap, ball down, step, kick. Dead center. Andrew took a breath. Birdwell slapped him on the helmet. "Again," yelled Bolger, and they did it five more times. The third snap was way high, and Birdwell didn't even try to get the ball down. The rest were perfect. They moved to the ten, fifteen, and twenty yard lines. And side to side to each hash mark. The kick from the twenty was thirty-six yards, and by that time, Andrew had had over thirty attempts, including warm-ups. He was tired and began hooking the ball.

Bolger was satisfied. His freshman hadn't missed an extra point—and only once in a dozen or so other tries. While opposing teams would try harder to block the kick, he saw that Paxton was a cool customer.

"Good work, Andrew," said Sam Bolger. "It looks like you'll be ready by Saturday."

"Yes, sir. Thanks, Coach," replied Andrew, taking off his helmet and shaking his head.

"Something wrong?" asked Bolger.

"Yeah, this helmet stretches my scar, and the weight is tough on my neck. When I take it off, I'm dizzy for a couple of minutes."

"Tell the trainer to give you some neck exercises." He turned to the team. "And get some rest."

Andrew headed back to the dorm. It would be a quick dinner before karate.

The students were warming up and stretching when Pappy arrived. Yoshi could do the splits, and Andrew wondered if he'd ever be even half that flexible. Soccer gave him a great advantage over the other students, but the stance, balance, and movements were much different for karate.

After an hour and a half of blocks and kicks, and many moans and groans, it was time for *kumite*. One minute of terror. Each person fought Yoshi (took an obligatory beating) and then watched classmates suffer the same. Pappy was sure Yoshi turned it up a notch on his favorite pupil. Some favorite! Two snap kicks to the jaw and three to the ribs, almost too fast for Pappy to see, let alone block. Yoshi told him to watch his eyes, but it was difficult when the more obvious threat was the feet.

They finished after nine. Andrew drank about a gallon of water and then went back to Roberts Hall. Again, no Barrett. He wrote a quick letter to his parents and one to his brother, and then he hit the head. The mirror showed his hair was almost back to normal. Time for another trip to the barber. He never heard Brian come in after midnight.

Friday, October 17

◉   ◉   ◉   ◉

The day before Pappy's first football game. What the heck was he doing? He'd played soccer since he was eight, and in all those years, he had probably taken ten penalty kicks in games. Each was a test of his will, one on one, against the goalie. Now he was about to play a sport for the first time, at the college level, for a championship contender, and he might be tested five times in one game. All alone, with success or failure solely on his shoulders. And eleven opposing players intent on dismemberment. Running away sure seemed like a good idea.

There was nothing to take his mind off the game. Barrett was lost in la-la land with Paula. He couldn't talk to the other Chiefs about football, and he had no real friends on the team. Most of practice was spent looking at Rattigan's ugly face and butt.

It was noon, and he was restless, so he decided to wander down to the Union to see if he could eat. He'd already been to the john three times that morning, and it wasn't even game day.

He was sitting by himself when Patty Van Duren came along.

"Holy smokes, a football player," she said, smiling. "Who would have thought it? By the way, nice hair. I never got to see or talk to you after your accident, but it looks like you're okay now. What's with you and football?"

"I don't know," said Pappy, shaking his head. "Somehow I'm too crippled to play soccer, but I can play football. They made me a special helmet ... but I wish I was with Brian and the guys."

"Well, I'm glad I ran into you," said Van Duren, sitting down. "Apparently, your roommate has fallen in love or something ... He acts like he's had a shot of Novocain in his brain." They both laughed and nodded. "Paula is a sweet girl," she continued.

"Yeah, he's a goner, I guess," said Pappy. "I've only met her once, and now he's MIA."

Van Duren became more serious. "How well do you know Beth Littlefield?" she asked.

Pappy felt a rush of adrenaline. "Why?" he blurted. "Does it have something to do with Barrett? I know she knows about Paula. It probably hit her hard. She looked tired and thin last time I saw her."

Van Duren saw that his concern was beyond casual. "I noticed the same thing," she replied. "She's gone home for the weekend again. Her parents have been here as well. You know she lives alone." Andrew nodded. "And she seldom comes out of her room, except for class and meals. She turns down dates ... I'm worried, and so is the other RA. I know her breakup with Barrett was bad. I think she followed him here thinking he would have a change of heart. It never happens. But I can't ask him to talk to her, because his showing concern might give her false hope and then crush her again ..." Now Van Duren was starting to feel awkward. "Would you consider talking to her? Or can you suggest anyone?" she added quickly. "I know this is tough. I don't even know what to tell anyone to say to her ..."

"Barrett is my roommate and my best friend ...," said Andrew.

Patty sighed. "I understand." She stood up to leave.

Andrew jumped up. "But I want to help somehow," he said quickly.

Heart on his shirtsleeve. She'd hoped for this reaction. Now she worried how hard he would fall. He appeared to be past that point anyway—but would Beth feel the same way? It wasn't fair to rescue her and destroy him.

"Thanks. I think she could use a friend. Let's see how she is when she comes back from her parents'. They usually call me once a week to get a status report. I'll let you know ... and good luck tomorrow!" She walked away.

Pappy sat back down, his heart racing. No way was he going to be able to eat anything now. What football game? He'd just been asked to rescue his true love … again. This time not from the evil Rattigan but from heartache brought on by his best friend. How could he help? She wanted Barrett, not him. No way could he ever measure up. He'd faced this same dilemma all these years. Now it would be brought out into the open so he could have his guts stomped on in public.

Saturday, October 18

⊙ ⊙ ⊙ ⊙

Barrett went to the pregame breakfast. Just as well. Paula was exhausted from their late nights and meeting him every morning before class. More and more, she was confined to her bed but sleeping less and less. The painkillers upset her stomach, making it difficult to eat, and although they made her drowsy, her rest was still fitful.

The guys were too excited to eat. Wednesday's victory was still in their blood. Rusk was a .500 ball club, and the Titans were at home.

It was a beautiful fall day, and the field was in the best shape of the season. The trees burst with color, and leaves floated everywhere in the breeze.

The Rusk Lions had pure white uniforms identical to those of the Titans—inexpensive (cheap). At least they had a bus. After warm-ups, Barrett, Penny, and Millwood stood at midfield, watching their opponents. Soon the entire starting lineup came over. David Nakano had gone from super sub to starter. Although none of the Titans possessed great speed, all were steady and united. That let Barrett be a loose cannon, but more and more, he fed Santander.

The Titans kicked off. Ten minutes into the game, Caldwell crossed a rocket that never got more than a foot off the ground. Penny struck it midair with his favorite outside of the left foot shot for Bain's first score. Rusk was now being swarmed on both offense and defense. Eight minutes later, Harbaugh missed a trap, and the Lion's center forward punched the ball low into the right-hand corner to tie. It was one to one.

Now it was a battle, with the Titans putting on unrelenting pressure. Their fullbacks were so harassed by Bainbridge's forwards that they couldn't clear the ball out of their goal area. This paid off when a kick caught Penny square in the gut, knocking the wind out of him. Santander put the loose ball to Millwood, who buried it in the back of the net. Two to one, Titans.

Then it happened. There was a Rusk handball near midfield. Barrett lifted a high arching shot toward the end line. The keeper, ten yards out, thought it was another errant blast by the big fullback. It faded under the crossbar. Three to one.

He was mobbed by his teammates. He waved at Paula, who was wrapped in a blanket and sitting with Sheffe's girlfriend, each on old plastic and aluminum patio chairs.

McIlroy shut off the Lion's right halfback, forcing play back into the middle to Barrett and Santander. Penny and Knight both picked up goals, and the final was five to two. The Titans were ready to take on all comers. Hancock knew they'd beat an inferior team, but every conference win was important, and they were relentless and confident.

The mood at the football pregame meal was raucous. Their opponent was another eastern powerhouse, the Griffin Hawks. A much larger school than Bain, its players were also bigger and received more press, even in the local paper. But games are played on the field. The Titans recruited speed and athleticism. Players could get bigger and stronger through weight training, but quickness was inbred.

Andrew sat with Bobby Birdwell and the center over by a window. Birdwell was a premed major, and his small stature and average speed meant college would be the last competitive football he would play.

Everyone on the Bainbridge staff—trainers, doctors, equipment handlers—was on call the day of a home football game. Nothing spread the name of the university, or enhanced its status among prospective students, more than sports.

They dressed an hour before the game, and after calisthenics, Andrew went to the north goalposts and kicked extra points. The stands began to fill, and today he would play before eight thousand people, many times the number that would attend all the soccer games he would play in his entire college career.

Griffin was definitely bigger. They had more than one player who was almost as tall as Burler and several wide bodies. The Titans were svelte and muscular, and their pregame drills were more disciplined and organized. Size wouldn't matter.

Bainbridge won the toss and elected to receive. The return man usually had the surest hands and was the craziest individual on the team. To catch a football with eleven equally insane opponents flying at you full speed, with mutilation in mind, required a special kind of dementia.

Claude Benson fielded the ball, one bounce, on the five yard line, gave a head fake right, and took off left up the sideline, ninety-five yards for a score. Just over ten seconds had elapsed; the Titans' bench and fans were screaming and cheering; and ten guys were yelling at Pappy to get on the field. Frantically, he looked for the tee, which Birdwell held up in front of him, and then he grinned and trotted out. The other players lined up as they had done for years. Pappy froze.

"Penalty kick," yelled Birdwell, on his knee, looking back at Andrew. He backed up three long steps and then two to the side. Unlike soccer, he didn't have to glance at one side or the other to decoy the goalie. Birdwell looked forward, barked out the signals, and the ball was snapped. It was high, and Birdwell pulled it down, but Pappy had already started forward. He hesitated. The ball was on the tee, but he was too far back. He lifted the ball fifty feet in the air, almost straight up. It fluttered in the trailing wind and dropped just beyond the goalpost. Seven to zero, Titans. It had gone over. He'd done it. The fans cheered. Two guys patted him on the helmet.

Pappy stood there. Everyone else ran off the field. Now surrounded by the Griffins' receiving team, he ran for the sideline. The wrong sideline. *What now?* His mind raced. *Fake injury? Make like I lost something?* Too late to save this one.

He jogged around the field … as slowly as possible. The Titans kicked off and stopped the Hawks on the seventeen yard line. The people in the stands were watching the action, but fifty Titan teammates were pointing at Andrew and laughing.

Bainbridge's defense was flawless from the first series. The lighter and quicker linemen were in the Griffin backfield before their running backs crossed the line of scrimmage. On third down and fourteen, the Titans blitzed, and the quarterback was chased back and tackled on the four yard line. A taste of things to come.

Griffin's punt from the end zone went out of bounds at the thirty yard line. Six plays later, Pappy again stood three yards behind and two to the left of Birdwell. Extra point good. Fourteen to nothing. The game rolled along. Players went on and off the field. Many had multiple responsibilities. Andrew had only one function, so he occupied himself by mentally going through different scenarios. Every time the offense snapped the ball in Griffin territory, he would visualize kicking a field goal from that spot—lining up the angle, judging the wind, taking his steps.

Then it was fourth and one on the Hawk's eleven yard line. Andrew ran over to the coach, but they decided to go for it. The pass to the halfback looping out of the backfield in the corner of the end zone made it twenty-one zip, Titans.

Someone was calling Andrew's name, and there was the soccer team screaming from the stands. He hoped Hancock wasn't around, because all had stopped off at one of the fraternity houses for some post-soccer/pre-football celebrating. He'd heard they'd won, but not that Barrett scored.

Twenty-eight to zero at halftime, and the next two quarters were more of the same, except that giving away thirty pounds per man on the front line was taking its toll. Bain players could no longer knock the opposing Hawks back on their heels. In the end, it was 42-0, and Andrew Paxton was officially in the record books as scoring points in a college football game. The folks back in Amsterdam would never believe it.

There were congratulations all around. Bolger made a point of coming over and thanking Andrew, asking if he felt okay. The helmet was uncomfortable, but no one came close to hitting him. He was happy to have survived. Lucky day all around.

The three football frat houses invited Andrew to parties, but he declined. The players made sure he felt part of the team, but it just wasn't comfortable yet.

A band was setting up outside the Union, and the dining room was crowded with students and parents. It was almost two months since he'd seen his mother and father, and if he'd decided not to play football, he could have gone home on weekends like Littlefield did.

Where was Littlefield? *I guess Van Duren was right. She went home.* He sat with Barrett and Paula for a while. They were going to listen to the band, and then Brian would make the rounds to the parties. She had a paper to write, and sitting through both the soccer and football games wore her out.

Pappy went down to The Cellar with a couple of guys from his floor, but he only had a coke. Before long, the cigarette smoke gave him a headache, and he headed for the dorm.

Andrew had heard his parents use the expression "green around the gills" as slang for someone with an upset stomach. But he'd never seen anyone truly turn green, nor would he have thought it possible.

The body that lay before him had a dull but distinct olive shading on each side, from the ear down along the jawbone to the chin. Jim McIlroy was faceup on his bed, where Barrett and Paxton had placed him, unconscious but still breathing. From exposure to a half quart of vodka, combined with a variety of chasers, he'd evolved from casual drunk to obnoxious clod to inanimate object. A wastepaper basket was placed at the side of the bed for the inevitable whistling beef that was to follow.

Two hours before, when the alcohol rendered McIlroy comatose, Penny, Barrett, and Millwood, only slightly less incapacitated, decided to donate Jim's body to science. They hadn't bothered to include Pappy, as they were sure he would be his stodgy, proper self and shame them into abandoning the deed. Jim's remains, stripped naked and wrapped in a sheet, were placed on the front steps to the health center with a note: *My mother doesn't want me.* Their giggles and sniggering whispers while carrying out the mission were so loud that by the time they rang the doorbell, the night nurse, who watched the entire operation, had already called campus security. The Keystone Kops, after determining that McIlroy was still breathing and not wanting him planting beets in the back of their patrol car, washed their hands of the matter. The nurse recognized Jim from his visiting Pappy when he spent the night there, and she called Pappy to report the crime.

Always one button past panic when it came to people being ill or injured, Andrew, knowing that Barrett and company were the perpetrators, and imagining the fate of the soccer team when Hancock found out, immediately ran toward the health center. On the way, he found the three surviving Chiefs lying on the grass in the dark, laughing hysterically.

Pappy apologized profusely to the greatly amused nursing staff and assured them the abandoned corpse would receive proper care. Still wrapped in the sheet, which was his only garment, McIlroy was carried back to the dorm. Slight correction. As the Chiefs' powers and faculties still remained under a cloud, the body was dragged and occasionally dropped along the way, accounting for the scrapes, grass stains, and dirt Jim found on himself the next day.

Now deposited in his bed, wastepaper basket at the ready close by, McIlroy's lips started to move; it appeared he was going to speak from beyond the grave. Suddenly, he spat a rather large brown dumbbell-shaped gob hawker up into the air. It rotated once and then fell dead center into the receptacle. Those present burst into applause.

Shortly thereafter, the growing crowd of mourners voted unanimously to move the partially deceased McIlroy, together with the totally corrupted bedsheet, into the shower, mainly because all wanted a peaceful night's sleep. They also doubted that receptacle would hold what was sure to be a long talk with Ralph on the big white telephone when Jim came to. Because no one wanted to get too close or leave fingerprints on the carcass, McIlroy was dragged on the same sheet along the linoleum to the head. Twice he rolled off with a splat of flesh and had to be pushed back on.

When last seen, he was folded over in the bottom of a shower stall. Pappy forcibly restrained several with the urge to turn on the cold water, arguing that an unconscious drunk was the best kind ... and the least bother.

Sunday, October 19

◉ ◉ ◉ ◉

On a Sunday morning, Barrett usually couldn't find his own face until around eleven. He was up at eight now, showered, shaved, and doused with cologne.

Pappy was awakened by the smell. "Holy crap," he exclaimed, bolting out of bed and rushing to the closet. "We're late for damn chem again ..." He looked at Brian, who was calmly combing his hair.

"It's Sunday ... It's Sunday," he said to Barrett, first relieved, and then with a glare. "I'm up at eight thirty on Sunday," said Pappy with disgust. "*You're* up at eight thirty on Sunday. Where in the name of Christmas are you going? Have you lost your mind? No classes today."

"We're meeting Paula's mom for lunch," said Barrett.

"What time?" asked the still-dazed Paxton. "Wait. You said lunch. Lunch, like noon lunch?"

"Uh," said Barrett. "Yeah, well, we're going to church first," he announced defiantly.

"Church ... church," said Pappy softly, flopping down on the bed. Recorded history didn't go back far enough to recall the time Barrett last went to church.

Truth be known, Paula wasn't a regular either. But they were together, and that was all that mattered. It was a beautiful clear morning. She'd slept well, a result of going home early on a Saturday night so Barrett could get into trouble with the Chiefs. Brian hadn't been able to decide whether to tell her about the McIlroy incident. What were the odds the deed was infamous enough to make it around campus? Ultimately, he determined that it was better she hear it from him first, before it became common knowledge and subject to exaggeration.

Paula was full of painkillers, so she abandoned the crutches. The service was pleasant. She had a beautiful singing voice.

It was a short walk to her mother's apartment. In her midfifties, Dorothy Cole had the appearance of a person who'd led a hard life. Shorter than Paula, and matronly in build, there was little family resemblance. She was fair-skinned with dark blonde hair, and her smile was both sincere and warm. Her embrace of her daughter was deep and emotional, and she hugged Brian as well.

"Welcome. My goodness, you're as tall and handsome and strong as Paula said." Brian blushed and gave her an aw-shucks smile, but Paula was mortified.

Why do mothers say such things? Why not just pull out all the baby pictures when I was naked in the bathtub? Show him my training bra?

As Dorothy prattled on about every personal detail of her daughter's life, a thoroughly embarrassed Paula was deciding if it was better to throw herself out a window or down a flight of stairs. What would have been a four-hour dissertation regarding every photograph on display in the house was cut short by the timer dinging on the stove. She excused herself, and Paula finally exhaled.

"Well," she started, throwing up her arms in total resignation. "If you leave now, you may be able to avoid years of therapy." Barrett pulled her to him and kissed her deeply. She hugged him tightly.

"Okay, where are your Barbie dolls and all that girl stuff?" he asked.

"You sure you want to see this?"

"Yeah, I want to know what Barbie and Ken are *really* up to when no one is around."

Since Brian wasn't allowed in her dorm room, this was his first look at her personal possessions. There were pictures galore from the time she was a baby. Every event, from field hockey to first day of school, dates, picnics, and graduation was on display. Sadly, none were of her father. How could anyone walk out on a child this cute? This loving? This sweet? It made him sick thinking of the heartache she endured. The abandonment she felt.

Paula's favorite dolls were Raggedy Ann and Andy, well-worn from years of tea parties and other activities. Posters of Judy Collins and Mary Travers hung inside her closet door. The bed was a four-poster, with dust ruffles and a white lace canopy. *Just like a princess. A real-life princess.*

Brunch was bacon, eggs, orange juice, toast, and pancakes. About thirty minutes after they finished, Mrs. Cole remembered the coffee cake warming in the oven. They talked for a while, and Dorothy asked Paula about her back. She was skeptical of Dr. Raymond Hardwell's medical competence, but he was positive that Paula was suffering from a sports injury, nothing more.

Dorothy Cole saw the deep feelings that Paula and Brian had for each other, and she so wanted her daughter to find the happiness she deserved. She'd done her best to hide her profound loneliness after Paula left for school. If she had her way, they would be married and move in with her tomorrow.

Finally, she pushed them out the door. Brian thanked her, gave her a big hug, and then waited for Paula outside.

Dorothy's eyes filled with tears as she spoke to her daughter. "What a wonderful young man," she said, half asking a question, looking at her daughter for reassurance.

"Yes, he is, Mom," said Paula. "He's wonderful. And I love him."

Her mother took a deep breath. "Then go … go be with him. Have a good time … and bring him back again."

Andrew was surprised that although all he did was kick extra points, he was sore from yesterday's game. Life alone was an adjustment, so he arranged to meet the other Chiefs for meals. When and if Barrett ever appeared again was anyone's guess.

Sunday afternoon karate practice. There were only five people at class, including one new girl and the ever-annoying Larry Nelson. They started with the usual exercises: stretching, knuckle push-ups (which were not getting any easier), and sit-ups. Then drills: punches, front kicks, blocks.

They learned new blows to the jaw and temple as well as how to stave off attacks from behind. Next was their first form, or kata, a series of blocks, kicks, and punches in a set routine.

It took half an hour to go one time through all the steps and then *kumite*. Andrew now kept his eyes fixed on Yoshi's, as they tipped off when he was about to attack. The most important thing they learned that day was how to block and punch while going forward and backward. Pappy knew the "going backward" part would come in handy. This time, he kept his distance from Yoshi most of the one minute of sparring. However, not wanting to appear a complete coward, he stood his ground at the half-minute mark and took a kick in the left ribs. When they finished, Andrew realized he'd fought without headgear. His hair was almost fully regrown, and he seldom thought of his injury. Fortunately, the coaches were gone when karate class was held. After all the safeguards created so he could play football, the furor over his engaging in hand-to-hand combat would have been monumental.

Monday, October 20

⊙ ⊙ ⊙ ⊙

Barrett carried Paula all over campus, even in daylight. This pissed off the guys whose girlfriends saw the attention and demanded the same. It only takes one to ruin it for everyone else. They spent afternoons in the library, although there was little studying. Brian wasn't allowed in her dorm, nor she in his, except on weekends, when everyone looked the other way. So there were many cold showers during the week.

The days were getting shorter and the breeze cooler. Chemistry was tough and getting tougher. English became a vehicle for Pappy to recount his experiences at Bain, although the prof could hardly believe all that had happened to this freshman.

Weight training was routine, but between it and karate, Pappy was noticeably bigger and stronger, particularly in his legs. Holding his stance and balancing on one leg while kicking came easier. Stretching was imperative, as his muscles had tightened. Jogging, which he disliked, became a necessity, as it increased his body's core temperature, and made it easier to get loose.

Andrew still practiced soccer on the handball courts before football. His shot was quicker and more powerful; and his balance improved.

He saw Littlefield that night at dinner, sitting with Patty Van Duren. The talk looked serious, so he avoided eye contact. He knew Barrett was no longer interested in her, but he didn't know what to do next. Then a guy joined them. An upperclassman. Handsome, clean-shaven, curly hair. Damn! It was Frank Tritter from the theater department. Pappy had seen him on a poster somewhere on campus. They were putting on a modern adaptation of Julius Caesar.

Certainly Beth wasn't going to join the crazies in the acting group. Rumor had it that there were a lot of drugs and radicalism among them. But Littlefield was beautiful and talented. Pappy guessed Van Duren would introduce her to as many people as possible to get her out of her funk, but he was surprised she would steer her in this direction. Well, maybe he was a nice guy. One of the normal ones … He sighed to himself. This sucks.

Tuesday, October 21

⦿ ⦿ ⦿ ⦿

Ten days since Barrett had first met Paula. It was as if he'd known her all his life. He wanted to buy her something, but they weren't really apart long enough to walk downtown to the department store. And he had no idea what to get. There was no one to ask for ideas—besides Littlefield, and that was beyond heartless. They were going to her mother's for dinner. Maybe flowers. Or some wine. Flowers for Paula and wine for Dorothy. No, it was too soon. Maybe her mother didn't drink or would be upset if he brought alcohol. He remembered her dad.

Van Duren. That was it. She liked Paula and had given him a raft of crap at the dorm that night. She owed him.

She answered, and after dishing out a suitable amount of grief, she agreed to meet him at the bowling alley in the Union. No way would Paula run into them there.

"Okay, Romeo," she began. "What are you up to? Don't tell me you've got her in trouble already."

"Back off," replied Barrett. "This is a sweet girl."

Van Duren was serious for a minute. "So is Littlefield."

"I know," he said. "I never wanted to hurt her. I never cheated … It was just time."

"Well, so what's the deal with Paula?"

"I want to buy her something, but I don't want to scare her away or get too sappy or … well … I don't know … something."

"Wow, to see you stumped when a girl is involved ... Sorry. Let me tell you, you couldn't drive this girl off with a shotgun. Okay, a gift. You have known her ... a week?"

"Ten days," he corrected her.

She smirked and then furrowed her brow thoughtfully. "Well, earrings are nice, but they're almost an article of clothing. So are bracelets. Lockets are pretty but more sentimental, and I don't know if she even wears them." Patty looked into his eyes. "Judging by the moon look on your face, you're a goner. Well, a ring, then. Simple. One stone. Not a diamond. Something like an emerald or ruby or sapphire, depending on what she has already."

It was as if a light went off in his head. "Yes! Great, perfect, thanks," said Brian, popping up to leave.

"Wait," she said as he started away. "Now I need your help."

"Okay, but I have practice in an hour."

"What can you tell me about your roommate, Pappy?" she asked.

"What do you mean? You've known him as long as I have. What's up?"

"Well, Littlefield is having a tough time adjusting to life here, mainly because you're around ..." He said nothing. "She goes home whenever she can and rarely comes out of her room. Anyway, I've talked to Andrew, and I suspect he's liked her for a long time. Did you know?"

"No ... he never said anything."

God, guys are dumb, she thought. "You know Pappy would cut his own throat rather than betray his best friend."

"Well, what do you want me to do? Talk to him? Tell him it's okay?"

"No. He has to find his own courage. He's almost as stubborn as you are. I just wanted to make sure all feelings were passed. Don't do anything to give Beth false hope or let Pappy believe you still care."

"Well, I do care. I want her to be happy. And he deserves the best. They both do."

"Okay, well, that's it. I'll let you know if I see anything happening. You do the same. Now go pick out a ring!"

"Thanks."

"Don't go overboard." But he was gone.

Van Duren smiled and looked down at the solitary opal on her finger—given to her by a TDT five days ago, just two weeks after they met.

Day Brothers Department Store was less than two miles from campus, and Barrett was there in ten minutes. The jewelry department was on the first floor, and he wasn't even breathing hard when a woman in her forties approached.

"Can I help you?" she asked.

"I'm looking for a ring. Small, simple, one stone," he replied, peering down into the glass case.

"Opal?"

"Uh, no," said Brian, baffled by the array before him. "Green, like an emerald."

"Well, here, these are all pretty, and there are several colors. This looks like an emerald but is really quartz. It's nice and about one-fifth the cost. You look like a college student."

"Yeah," he said, now focusing on the stone set upon a thin gold band. "Yeah, this is it. I'll take this one."

"Very good. Let me get you a box. Would you like it wrapped … or maybe just a gold ribbon?"

"Yeah, a ribbon would be great." He paid her the $14.99 plus tax and never stopped running until reaching the dorm, tossing the box into his top drawer. He changed and raced to practice. He was twenty minutes late, but Hancock would have to put up with it.

Pappy breezed through his kicking routine. He worked his way out to the thirty yard line, which was a stretch, and while his aim was good, he barely cleared the bar. He resisted the urge to kick harder. Accuracy first. Distance didn't matter if it didn't go between the uprights.

No lifting today but karate tonight, and he headed for the library to work on an English paper. He finished his research and went off to the field house. More blocks, kicks, punches, and kata 1. He was amazed how much he could learn in two hours of intensive drills. It was the toughest sport he'd ever done, and it was about to get tougher. On the edge of the stage were canvas mats used by the wrestling team. After the first half hour, Yoshi and Larry Nelson dragged some canvas wrestling mats to the center of the floor, and folded them over twice.

"Here, punch mat," said Yoshi, thrusting downward with his right fist onto the coarse surface. Then the left. "Come, all punch mat."

The class gathered round and began to pound away. Moans and groans. Some couldn't make a proper fist or were striking with the wrong knuckles and with partially bent wrists. The fibers tore at their skin. Both of Pappy's hands were bleeding, but he continued long after the others quit. The girl's punches were meager at best, but Yoshi let them all progress at their own speed.

Then it was time for their nightly beating. Andrew watched Yoshi hook his right foot behind the left heel of his opponent, sweeping him off his feet. This seemed like a great tactic, and he used it several times to halt Yoshi's attack. He was getting smarter, if not faster.

Back to the dorm. Tomorrow was another soccer game. Pappy figured he could do his weight training early, then his kicking routine, and sneak down to the field. He'd have to hide from Hancock, but he couldn't stay away.

Barrett showered and dressed quickly after practice. Every few minutes, he took the ribbon off the box and looked at the ring, until he'd stretched the fabric limp and had to retie the bow. But he couldn't do it right, and now it looked like dirty string, so he tossed it. The box would have to do.

He met Paula at Weatherly Hall. She wouldn't let him carry her, even though she was back on crutches, which they hid in the bushes outside her mother's apartment.

Pot roast. Barrett ate his usual gargantuan proportions, which made Mrs. Cole happy, flattered that he enjoyed it so much. Dessert was apple pie à la mode. Brian couldn't understand how Paula was so thin if she grew up eating like this, but tonight she did a great deal of pushing the food around.

Paula pulled out an old Scrabble game encased in a layer of dust. "Are you brave enough?" she asked. "Mom and I are pretty tough." So they played for an hour or so, while the two women talked about the upcoming holidays and Christmas shopping.

At nine, Dorothy Cole could see her daughter was tired, and she bid them good night. Paula didn't protest when Brian hoisted her onto his back. They passed by the entrance to Weatherly Hall.

"Where are we going?" she asked, hugging his neck and kissing his cheek.

"Just a quick detour." In a few moments, they were on the Kissing Bridge in the Hollow. He set her down.

"You sly dog," she said, closing her eyes and tilting her head upward. He pulled the box from his pocket and held it in front of her face. She opened her eyes wide.

"What is this?" she asked excitedly. "What is this?" She looked inside and burst into tears. Her hands shook as she struggled to get it on. "It's so beautiful." Those were the only words she could manage. She hugged him, covering his shirt with tears.

He hid his own emotions. He felt as tall as a mountain. He swept her up in his arms—no piggyback ride—and carried her back to Weatherly Hall.

Wednesday, October 22

◉ ◉ ◉ ◉

Todd Hancock sat at his desk, reviewing events of the past week. His team had advanced from rabble to rockers. Every coach in the building congratulated him on the two wins since Barrett's emotional conversion. And all made a point to mention Andrew Paxton's contribution to the football team.

The game of soccer still frustrated him. He wanted to teach his players to make them better. Instead, all he could do was preach hustle. Maybe that was enough. He'd lost Paxton, but Roland Santander and the four other Chiefs led by example. Coupled with Scott Driver, Al Landon, Dave Caldwell, David Nakano, and the fearless Randy Williams, he felt they could compete with the rest of the teams on the schedule.

The Brady Flyers arrived at two. It was another reunion for the Chiefs. Bill Chenowith, former Amsterdam alumnus and all-city goalie, was now a senior. He'd been part of several great teams in high school. And he knew what it meant to the Titans to have four players from Amsterdam.

This would be a dogfight, start to finish. Brady came in supremely confident, having pounded the Titans four to zero the previous season. Chenowith had warned his teammates that things would be different, but what could four freshmen do to reverse last year's drubbing? And they hadn't expected Roland Santander.

They found out quickly. The Flyers were careless and sloppy. Five minutes in, the left fullback passed the ball back to Chenowith. Caldwell picked it off, took one step past the diving goalie, and rolled it in, making it one to zero. Again, after the kickoff, the Titans pressed the attack. The Flyer fullbacks couldn't clear the ball without being harassed into mistakes. Two corner kicks later, Scott Driver tallied on a header to the short side. Two to zero.

Bickering broke out among the Brady squad. Some took out their frustrations by pushing and tripping the Titans, all in front of the referee, who was in no mood for petulant players. Soon the Flyers had three warnings, and the coach had to bench one of his best forwards.

Santander, controlling the pace, hit one accurate pass after another. Barrett and Nakano wouldn't be beaten in the middle, and in the second half, they dropped McIlroy back to outside fullback. Fully recovered from his near-death experience the Saturday before, and from most of his wounds (inflicted by being repeatedly dropped and dragged by those allegedly trying to lend aid), he shut down the slower of the two wings. Brady pulled its goalie on a goal kick with two minutes left, and Barrett tallied again from near midfield. It ended with a score of three to zero.

Andrew had finally seen his roommate score from long range. He wanted to say hi to Chenowith, but mindful of Hancock's orders, he kept his distance. The team had moved on. He'd have to wait until next year.

Thursday, October 23

◉ ◉ ◉ ◉

Chem lab was about to get serious (providing no one else tried to burn the place down). Each student was given a mystery liquid and a list of experiments to be performed that would reveal its identity. Given the 4,000 percent error in his first set of experiments, Andrew concluded that he would better serve mankind as a doctor treating patients. He was never going to save lives in a laboratory.

Pappy meticulously followed the directions for each step. This was no time to wing it. Then it happened. The last procedure of the day resulted in a milky brown mixture. He should have seen a blue ring at the bottom of the test tube or brown residue in clear liquid. Crap. What went wrong? No time to start over. He'd have to come back tomorrow and redo the last couple of steps.

On to weight training. Thursday was easy, primarily legs and stomach. He was now doing fifty to one hundred sit-ups at karate as well, and his belly was flat as it had ever been in his life. He was weighed every day and was now a strapping 172. This was cool.

Pappy took kicks with the entire offense and defense in game situations, and for the first time he participated in the fake field goal plays, which included getting the heck out of the way as fast as he could. Once the fake was on, he was like any other player. No more "hands off the kicker," and it was guaranteed that someone on the opposing team would whack him, given any opportunity. He'd watched the blocking drills for two weeks and offered to provide some protection on the back side of the play, to which the players and coaches burst out laughing. Bolger ordered that he put any such notion out of his mind. Kickers were notorious wimps. Why ruin their image? When the going gets tough, faint. Flop. That's what kickers did best.

Anyway, he finished with several kicks from the thirty and was now clearing the bar by a couple of feet, so long as the wind wasn't against him.

The karate class lost another student. But the girl remained. She wasn't willing to tear her hands up on the canvas mats, but she stuck it out for the exercise and confidence building. Pappy's blocks, punches, and kicks had more snap, and he could now do a waist-high side kick and a front kick to the jaw. He no longer had to be told to keep his chin back. Several reminders from Yoshi's feet and fists during *kumite* solved that. He was getting better at keeping his coin. They learned a second kata, more elaborate than the first, and forms now took up a third of the practice.

Since there were fewer students, *kumite* was increased by thirty seconds, and everyone's endurance improved. This was only the fifth lesson. Why lengthen the terror so soon?

It was Pappy's turn, and he used every trick—hooking the ankle, gliding backward, switching front feet—to foil Yoshi's charges and survive the ninety seconds. His reflexes improved, making it difficult for Yoshi to find a target. After one minute, Yoshi threw a front kick as Andrew was coming forward, landing square in the solar plexus.

"Uh," gasped Pappy. The blow didn't hurt, but it paralyzed his diaphragm. Everything was in slow motion. He collapsed to his knees, unable to breathe, and fell forward. Yoshi calmly came around behind the slumped figure, stuck his knee in the middle of his back, grasped both shoulders, and pulled back.

Sssss. Andrew's lungs filled, and at once he was breathing normally. No gasping, no panic. He got to his feet. The other students stood there stunned.

"Sorry," said Yoshi, shaking Pappy's hand and poking him in the gut. "Very dangerous."

Friday, October 24

⊚　⊚　⊚　⊚

Only chem on Friday. Brian let Paula sleep in, and he and Pappy went to a late breakfast/early lunch together for the first time in two weeks. They talked about everything from football to soccer to chem lab to home ... to Paula.

Andrew told him how much he missed soccer and said that no matter what, this was all the football he would play. Of all the things he'd experienced in two months of college, karate was the most exciting and rewarding (since he couldn't play soccer). He knew he was gaining speed, balance, strength, and confidence. His body had been raised to another level.

Barrett babbled on for an hour about Paula. Parts of the story were tough to recount. The father abandoning her. Her mom's struggle to support them both. He then told Pappy how she reacted to the ring, and his jaw dropped.

"You bought her a *ring*? A *ring*? Who the hell are you, and what have you done with Brian Barrett?" he demanded.

"Yeah, I know," said Barrett, shaking his head. "I really don't have a clue. Everything is so relaxed with her. Nothing phony. Just us. It's like I want to do everything for her. I want her to have everything she ever wanted." Of all his friends, he could tell these things to Pappy.

Andrew Paxton had felt that way about one person for a long time. He always wanted the best for Beth, but that had never included him.

After two hours, both were drained. They'd shared some pretty heavy crap. Many deep secrets and feelings. Except one. There didn't seem any way for Pappy to tell his friend he loved Littlefield.

"What about you?" asked Barrett unexpectedly. "What about that girl you took to the movies? She was cute, man. You know, it's time for you to start thinking about yourself. You're always concerned about everybody else. There are a lot of girls out there. Paula has some on her floor ..." He looked for a reaction but got none.

"Oh, wow," said Pappy. "It's one o'clock. I need to go rerun some of my procedures in chem lab before practice." He stood up and smiled. "Be good to that girl," he said.

"You be good to yourself," replied Barrett. "See you back at the dorm."

Saturday, October 25

◉ ◉ ◉ ◉

Travel date for both the soccer and football teams. Barrett and company left at eight for the two-hour trip to Angleton. The football team was on the road an hour later for Carthage.

Angleton was only average academically, attracting primarily in-state residents. Thus the talent pool for any sport was limited to those who walked through the door. All of their teams were mediocre and received only minor consideration in the school budget. They played their soccer games at a nearby high school. Compared to this, having a tree hanging over your field had class.

The first clap of thunder rolled across the countryside shortly after the Titans started warm-ups. The storm approached quickly from the west and the sky darkened; the lightning flashes were more frequent. Minutes later, the wind picked up, and the temperature dropped fifteen degrees in five minutes. A lightning strike less than a mile away sent everyone scurrying to the cars. They sat with the radios blaring as the rain began as huge drops and then became wind-driven sheets. The gale lifted and shook the vehicles, blowing branches and leaves off the trees. Trash cans rolled back and forth across the street, and debris was everywhere. Half an hour later, the wind dropped to a steady fifteen miles an hour, and the rain was little more than a drizzle. But the quite pleasant sixty-five degrees an hour before was now a biting forty-seven, and dropping. The wind chill was in the thirties, and the Titans had nothing but their uniforms to wear.

251

Hancock was the first to emerge, and he beckoned all to gather by his van. "Well, one of life's little surprises," he said. "This is going to be lousy … We never have weather like this in basketball," he deadpanned, and all laughed, beginning to shiver. "You won't need me to tell you to hustle today. And you know what the wet ball will do. These guys will be looking for every mistake, and we better do the same. Make the most of while you're on the field, because guys on the sidelines would rather be playing. Okay, let's get out there."

Secretly, Hancock was pleased with the deteriorating conditions. The Titans were full of themselves. A few wins under their belts and they thought teams would be dirt under their shoes. The elements would make them realize they weren't as skilled as they thought.

The Titans jogged onto the field, blowing on their knuckles and cupping their hands over their ears. The Angleton Lancers had retreated all the way back to campus and now reappeared in sweat clothes, gloves, and stocking caps. *Oh, man, way to rub it in,* thought Barrett. *We really need to destroy these guys.* Just then the Lancers' equipment manager trotted over and presented Hancock with eight plastic football rain capes with hoods. "Sorry, Coach," said the young man. "This is all we could find."

"That's great. Thank you, Coach," yelled Hancock to his counterpart, who waved back.

The wind howled across the pitch, gusting above twenty-five miles per hour. Hancock called them in. "Okay, it's going to be slip and slide out there. Keep the ball down. Good traps. Shoot any time inside thirty yards—and shoot low. Bad things are going to happen in front of the goal. Look for the junk ball. No stupid fouls …"

They ran onto the field, jumping up and down to stay warm. Angleton's line kicked off and passed back to the center half. He squibbed a pass to the left wing, and it went out of bounds. Barrett heaved the throw-in forty yards in the air down the wing, but the wind blew it right back over the sidelines, never touching anything in play. That was pretty much the first half. Shots and passes skidded and dipped. It was zero to zero. The drizzle continued, so they retreated to the cars, radios and heaters on full blast.

The second half was the same, but now Santander took over. Less than five minutes in, he drilled a spinning shot that hopped three feet in the air just as the keeper knelt to field it, caroming off his left shoulder and into the goal. One to zero, Bainbridge.

Now Caldwell, Penny, and Millwood tried to imitate the move, and at the thirty-two-minute mark, Penny caught the ball square with the outside of his right foot. The goalie dove full length. He would have stopped a dry ball, but the over spin wrenched it from his hands, and it rolled into the net. Two to zero. The Titans had won again.

The football team's two-hour bus ride to the Carthage Owls was a battle of three or four blaring transistor radios. Halfway through the trip, Pappy got word that Coach Bolger wanted to see him. He made his way to the front of the bus and saw that each coach had an empty seat next to him.

"Sit down, Andrew," said Sam Bolger. "Let me ask you something. Are you crazy? Are you out of your mind? Are you trying to drive me crazy?" Bolger's tone was more concerned than angry.

"I understand you're taking karate," he continued, "and that you're fighting the instructor. Is that true? He's punching and kicking you in the head?"

Andrew pursed his lips and bowed slightly. "Yes, it's called *kumite*," he answered.

"I don't care if it's called kittens," said Bolger. "We've gone to great lengths to keep you from injury, and you're out street fighting."

"I wear a wrestling skullcap to protect me."

"Nobody mentioned seeing you wearing headgear," said Bolger.

"Well, I forgot the other night."

"And what if you forget again?" queried the coach, "And what if he whacks you on your scar or your cheekbone? Then what? Do you want another operation? Do you have any idea the liability we have?"

"Coach, I feel fine," replied Andrew. "It's been a month. My scar has healed. I have no pain. I was tired of sitting around, and I always wanted to take karate. It's tougher than either football or soccer, and it gives me self-confidence ... I'll go back to wearing the headgear."

"You have got to stop this at once," said Bolger, his voice rising. "You're too valuable to this team, but to heck with that—I don't want you to get another concussion, or worse."

Andrew's reply was unemotional. "I don't need it, but I'll go back to wearing the headgear," he repeated.

Bolger studied the freshman sitting next to him. "You're not going to quit, are you?" he asked rhetorically.

Andrew shook his head.

Bolger sighed, sat back, and crossed his arms. "Go back to your seat … and we never had this conversation."

By one o'clock, the front made it through Carthage, and the wind whistled through the stands. The crowd was half the normal size, and conditions were getting worse. The rain lasted longer than it had in Angleton, and the turf was becoming loose and soggy. The football Titans always carried several large duffels of rain gear, and Bolger personally checked the weather forecast the night before each game. Since football uniforms cover about 90 percent of the body, and the helmets were as warm as any ski cap, the only real concerns were the hands of the quarterback, the center … and the placekick holder. Footing by kickoff time was slick. The wind gusted and swirled, blowing at a forty-five-degree angle to the field.

Andrew took several extra points. The area in front of the goalposts would be wet hamburger by the third quarter. He watched Reed Hampton practice kickoffs, and the ball wobbled and hooked. Reed was a toe kicker, so his accuracy was at the mercy of the conditions the minute it left his foot. The larger surface of the instep gave Pappy more control. He knew he wasn't going to make anything outside of thirty yards, and hopefully not be asked to try anything beyond twenty, so he shortened his approach to two steps—right, left, kick. Power wasn't the objective.

The Titans kicked off, and three missed tackles put the Owls on the Bainbridge eleven yard line. But a fumbled snap on the first play from scrimmage, then a fifteen-yard loss on a blitz, and it was third and thirty-three. An incomplete pass—a punt that was blown out of bounds at the eighteen yard line—and the Titans' offense was in business. Bolger elected to grind it out, letting his quick, powerful linemen knock the defense off the ball. Bobby Birdwell was an excellent runner, adept at executing the option. Eight plays later Andrew Paxton was on for his first extra point. The snap was high and went right through Birdwell's sure hands. Andrew slammed on the brakes, and his feet went into the air, dropping him on his backside and into the mud with a thump. He covered up, anticipating the other team's onslaught, but they were too busy chasing the ball, which took on a personality all its own. The wind blew it. The players from both teams bobbled and kicked it. It squirted out when someone tried to smother it. It finally exited the playing surface at the forty-eight yard line of the Owls. Meanwhile, Pappy was still cowering on his back on the five yard line, now all alone.

Carthage bobbled the following kickoff, and three plays later, Andrew would try again. Clean snap. Clean hold. Dead center. The rest of the half, the Owls were more concerned with not making mistakes than scoring, so their punter was overworked and the Titans were skating free.

Andrew tallied five conversions that day. The Titans only punted once. The rest of the time Bolger, opted to go for it on fourth down, content to burn the clock. Forty-one to zero. Bainbridge was tied for first place in the conference.

At seven o'clock, the team was back at campus, uniforms turned in, and they showered and dressed. Several guys said "good game" to Andrew, but most reminded him of his half gainer on the first kick. The game films had no doubt captured the graceful flop.

There was a special team meal at the Union, which all attended. Afterward, Andrew went down to the bowling alley. There were six lanes, all in professional condition. He'd bowled in Amsterdam since he was eight years old, and he hoped he'd remember to bring his ball after Christmas break.

It was ten o'clock, and it had been a long day. His clothes now reeked of tobacco and his eyes burned, so he headed up the stairs.

"Wait, c'mon back," said a male voice behind him. "C'mon. Hey, I didn't mean anything."

A girl was coming up toward him. "Leave me alone," she said.

"Hey, quit being such a bitch. You're a stuck-up ice queen."

The boy bounded up the steps toward her. She reached the top, and Andrew caught her hand and pulled her to him. It was Beth Littlefield. She saw his face and threw her arms around him.

"Hey, you, that's …" Then Rattigan saw it was Paxton. "Well, if it isn't our pussy placekicker. Butt out, pal. I know she's not your girl."

Andrew stared at him and then looked at Littlefield. She was near tears. He lifted her chin and kissed her lightly on the lips. She put her head on his shoulder.

"Back off, Rattigan," said Pappy. "Go suck on another beer."

"You don't scare me, pussy, with your TV karate crap," he said, standing eye level. "That stuff is a lot of bull." Rattigan's right fist shot toward Andrew's face. Automatically Pappy's open left hand came up, catching and stopping it cold a foot from his face. Ben's eyes opened wide. Andrew was expressionless. Rattigan pulled his hand back and then walked away.

Pappy turned back to Littlefield.

"How on earth did you do that?" she asked.

He shrugged and shook his head. "I've absolutely no idea."

"Thank God you did," she gushed, still shaken and holding onto him. "He's called me and even been around the dorm. I told him to leave me alone, but he must have followed me here to The Cellar … Thank you, thank you so very much … I just …" And then her eyes welled up with tears. The emotions of the past weeks hit her. She put her head on his shoulder and cried.

It felt great to hold her; but he felt terrible for her. He looked for a place to sit down.

"Come on, let's go," he said softly, leading her outside. They sat on a secluded bench under a tree near Norbert Hall, and she rested against him for a few minutes, until her tears subsided. He took off his coat and wrapped it around her shoulders. She lay down lengthwise, put her head on his lap, and fell asleep.

An hour later, Pappy's teeth were chattering. His wool sweater would have been enough if he were moving around, but he sat motionless, lest he wake her. Now he had to find a restroom or burst at the seams. He lifted her shoulders until she sat up.

"Oh, what time is it?" she asked. "Did I fall asleep? I am so sorry."

"No, it's okay. C'mon, you need to get back to the dorm," he said, helping her to her feet.

"No, it's so nice here," she said. "Just a little while longer."

"I can't ... I ... You have hours. You need to get back."

She looked at him apologetically. "I know. I'm sorry. You save me ... and then I fall asleep."

"No ... I like ... I ..."

She let go of his arm and started toward the dorm. He caught up and walked alongside. He opened the lobby door for her. "Why are you so good to me?" she asked. Then she took his face in her hands and kissed him full on the lips. "My knight in shining armor. The guy with the shoulder ..." She bit her lips so they wouldn't tremble. She turned and was gone.

Sunday, October 26

⦿ ⦿ ⦿ ⦿

Barrett stood in front of the mirror at the obscene hour of eight thirty. Pappy had tossed and turned half the night, remembering "the kiss" and trying to unscramble both Littlefield's life and his own.

"Give me a frickin' break," said Pappy, looking at his watch.

"Time for church," replied Barrett. "Go back to sleep."

Ugh. Finally, Barrett left. Andrew closed his eyes but could hear every door in the hall open and close, and there were the clattering footsteps up and down the metal stairs.

Now he had a headache. He was tired. And all he could think about was Beth. Somehow Barrett was to blame for all this. He was the one who'd abandoned her, who'd screwed her up.

He took a shower, shaved, and got dressed. At least he wouldn't run into Barrett at the Union.

But it was worse. There was Littlefield. And Frank Tritter. And Alicia Whitestone, the head of the theater department. Small and beautiful with long brown hair to the middle of her back, Whitestone dressed as if she slept in a trash can. Her mismatched clothes qualified as thrift store rejects and her hair appeared to have been combed with a mop.

What is this, a recruiting meeting? Well, why not? Littlefield is tall, beautiful, athletic, great singing voice. His face turned more and more red. *Go ahead, then. Forget about me. Shack up with him.*

Now Pappy was engaged in a monster-size self-pity party. *Man, I am getting so sick of this,* he fumed as he pushed his tray along the line. *Everybody thinks they have enormous problems. Everybody wants me to listen. Girls cry on my shoulder about other guys. Enough. The goddamn doormat has had enough. I can't play soccer. I'm stuck on a football team with goons like Rattigan. Then I save the girl I love from him—twice—and what does she do? Runs off with an upperclassman!*

Andrew pounded his fist on his tray. Everyone in the entire dining room turned to look, and the silverware flew into the air and onto the floor. Dead silence. He picked up the utensils, abandoned his tray, and walked out of the building.

Another childish move. He ran to the dorm, changed into his new karate *gi* that Yoshi had dropped off the day before, and headed to the field house. It was an hour before practice, so he went to the weight room and pumped iron until he was too sore to continue, and then he went to class.

All through karate, he held the same focused glare. He punched the hardest and yelled the loudest. And everyone kept his distance. He messed up several times performing kata 1 and kata 2, something he rarely did.

Finally, the end … except for *kumite.* Pappy was weary of this as well. *Bolger tells me I can't do karate. Hancock says I can't come to soccer practice. I am so, so tired of people telling me what I can and can't do … That's it, dammit! Today I finally land a punch on Yoshi.* He bowed to his opponent, squared off, and raced forward. In an instant, he was on his butt, not sure how he got there. Dazed, he realized that there was blood trickling out of his mouth and a small mouse growing above his right eye.

Yoshi smiled and offered a hand. "Kip yowr timpor," he said, checking out Andrew's wounds. "No good mad." He turned away. "Next man." There were no volunteers.

Monday, October 27

⊚ ⊚ ⊚ ⊚

Andrew was up an hour before chemistry class, and he made as much noise as possible to annoy his roommate. Barrett threw anything within reach at him and then finally relented and got up.

Someone had witnessed the encounter with Rattigan Saturday night, and the stories being passed around the shower room that morning had been exaggerated to the point where Pappy saved Littlefield from certain rape by karate-chopping Big Ben into submission.

Andrew debated whether he wanted to quell those rumors. They sounded pretty good. Back in the room, though, Barrett wanted the facts.

"Is it true?" he asked heatedly. "Did that mother lay a hand on her? Goddamn it! I'll rip his face off!"

Andrew was surprisingly calm. "I took care of it. He won't bother her anymore."

He described in detail what happened (leaving out the kiss).

"Man, I wish I had seen that," said Barrett, surprised. Pappy never shied away from a fight, but he was usually the peacemaker. Slow reflexes made it better for him just to grab hold of his opponent and wait for help.

"I gotta check this karate stuff out," he teased. "I don't want you to get so good I can't keep you in line. And I don't want you running around campus beating up bullies."

"You don't go looking for a fight," said Pappy. "It gives you the confidence to not have to fight."

A thin smile broke across Barrett's face. He would now make sure it didn't happen again.

Classes continued to drone on. On the way to weight training, he encountered Coach Bolger in the hall. Andrew realized that the lump, courtesy of Yoshi, was still protruding above his eye, and he tried to hide it—just about the same time the coach saw it. He scowled and then shook his head.

"I don't even want to know," he said, passing on by.

Football practice. Rattigan. Andrew sighed. The stories flying around campus about Saturday night made it to the football Titans. Rattigan would have to restore his tough guy reputation, and that meant a fight. Some of the players in the locker room had seen the mouse over Andrew's eye. The logical assumption was that the story of the battle was true. If so, then what did Big Ben look like? He supposedly was the vanquished.

Andrew took a deep breath and trotted out onto the field. He went through the warm-ups, but there was no Rattigan. The coaches gave their assessments of Saturday's game, and then the players split into their respective groups. Andrew walked down to the end zone with his bag of footballs and began kicking off the tee. Bolger sent over a snapper and holder, and he finished his routine. It was almost five when Andrew headed back to the locker room. Just then, Rattigan came through the door. Their eyes met, and Andrew stiffened, but the other man tried to avert his face, and he went by quickly. One glimpse told the story. Knobs on the chin and above both eyes, a swollen nose, and a small bulb on the lower lip. Now the gossip tongues would really be wagging. Pappy, the apparent master of the flying pork chop, triumphantly defended the girl's honor.

But Andrew knew differently.

Barrett was preoccupied at lunch, and his quick exit, leaving Paula to walk back to the dorm by herself, ended with him "educating" Littlefield's assailant. Since few people had seen Yoshi hit Pappy and there were no witnesses to the battle between Barrett and Rattigan, it was logical that

Big Ben would prefer that everyone assume a karate master on the football team, rather than a soccer player, beat him. Thus the legend of the Saturday night fight, which never took place, was left to be told and retold.

Pappy was torn. Evidently, Barrett didn't believe that his roommate could protect Littlefield, and he'd inserted himself back into that relationship. But there was nothing Andrew could do. Eventually, Littlefield would find out that Barrett was her champion. The only hope was that when she did, she wouldn't think he was coming back.

Tuesday, October 28

⊚ ⊚ ⊚ ⊚

The soccer Titans were counting the numbers. They had won three times more games than the previous year. Now they looked back on Kirkwood and others, wondering what could have been. Southwestern and Stratton State were just too good. Bonham would have been tough. But now they faced teams at their own level and saw the opportunity for a winning season. Hancock no longer ended practice early to rush off to basketball. Santander continued to teach by example. And Barrett was the fire.

Pappy was enjoying the benefits of karate and weight lifting. Every practice, he was striking the ball with more force and adding a yard or two to his kicks.

Barrett and Paula had become fixtures at the library—at least until they could no longer keep their hands off each other, and then it was off to the Hollow or some other secluded place. Paula's appetite improved slightly, so she felt stronger, but now there was a tingling at the ends of her toes. Hardwell warned that if the disks pinching the nerve didn't improve in a couple of months, she would have to have surgery. Such procedures had barely a 50 percent success rate at the time. The vertebrae might have to be fused. Without the operation, however, the muscles in her legs would atrophy. In any event, it was always better to wait, particularly for someone so young.

Karate always held a new experience. Tonight was no exception. Since

Yoshi hadn't yet run off the only girl, it was time to put her to use. After warm-ups, Yoshi, with the help of Larry Nelson, tried to convince her to climb up on Pappy's shoulders. Then he would go up and down the floor, knees bent, blocking and punching. At first, both were sure something was lost in the translation. But after some graphic gesturing, it was clear what Yoshi intended.

Well, yes, it made sense. And yes, it was only part of the exercise routine. And yes, it would make him dramatically stronger. There was nothing sexual about it. But it *seemed* really weird.

Despite her uneasiness, Sherry agreed. Andrew got down on one knee, put his head between her legs, and stood up. He started a little wobbly but then got his balance. After the second lap, he stopped and let her down. Amazing. He'd done it.

More and more, Andrew was standing his ground during *kumite*. Yoshi could still knock him off his feet with a sweep, and he was too quick for Pappy to block all his blows, but he was no longer running for the exits. He could also make it through all three katas without mistakes, albeit slowly, and Yoshi said he could test soon to move up in rank.

Wednesday, October 29

◉ ◉ ◉ ◉

The Lockhart Pilots came from just across the border in Ohio. A quality school with a history dating back to the late 1800s, its claim to fame was an excellent graduate program in meteorology.

The weather hadn't warmed from the weekend, and many trees surrounding the Titans' field were now barren. This had been a close game the previous two years, with the Pilots taking both contests by one goal.

The Titans kicked off, and during the first penetration, they found a glaring weakness. The Lockhart fullbacks were only marginal at trapping and heading the ball. Immediately, Caldwell and Company applied the pressure, making it impossible for the goalie to lay the ball out to the side. Therefore, he was relegated to punting, which allowed Barrett and Nakano to pick up every cleared ball. By the end of the half, the Titans were up two to nothing, and only two Lockhart players were at midfield. The rest were on defense, trying to deal with their swarming opponent.

The hundred-plus Bain fans in attendance were getting into the game. Pappy arrived for the second half and stood off in the distance. Not long after, Hancock spotted him, smiled, and nodded his head. The final score was four to zero, and it could have been much worse. Paula sat bundled up in an old sleeping bag she'd brought from home and was the envy of the other girls, who wouldn't sacrifice fashion for comfort and stood shivering most of the game.

One bit of entertainment, courtesy of the star athlete. Just before the first half, the Titans were driving when Barrett gecked a bug. Shouting out the switches, mouth wide open and breathing heavily, he sucked a gnat or some such thing right down his throat. He folded over, coughing and gagging. Driver kicked the ball out of bounds, and the Lockhart player delayed throwing for a few moments until the hilarity subsided.

Back at the dorm, Barrett and Pappy were washing up for dinner when the phone rang. Barrett answered, and it was his dad. His expression turned quickly to one of concern and then sadness. Pappy could tell someone had died, someone close. Brian started talking about airplanes and funeral arrangements, but mostly he just listened.

Barrett hung up and then pulled out his suitcase and started packing. "My uncle Earl had a heart attack," he said. "He died this afternoon. I have to go home." He was close to his father's brother, having spent time on his farm during the summers. College life was usually insulated from much of reality. This was an unwelcome call from the outside world.

"My parents booked me on a plane at eight thirty, but I have to get to the airport. Do you have any cash?" he asked Andrew. "I don't think I've enough for a cab."

"Don't call a cab," said Pappy. "You pack and call Paula. I'll be back in ten minutes." He ran out the door. Past the field house, he turned right, then left after the stadium, and in less than five minutes, he was at the TDT house. They called Randy Williams, who pulled into the parking lot shortly thereafter. Half an hour later, Barrett was on his way to the airport. Pappy said he would take care of Paula (whatever that meant), call Hancock as soon as he could find his telephone number, let his professors know he would be back Monday, and tell the soccer team to stomp whomever they were playing.

Thursday, October 30

◉ ◉ ◉ ◉

The room was sadly vacant. There had been nights when Barrett hadn't come back until dawn, but now he was gone from school—back to the town Andrew missed so much. He'd called Paula the night before to ask if she needed anything. They ended up talking for over an hour. Pappy filled her in on his own life with Brian's family. Earl was a great guy, instantly liked by everyone who met him and generous with his time and possessions. It would be a terrible funeral. A great loss to family, friends, and the community.

Pappy felt uncomfortable but offered to take Paula to lunch, dinner, or anywhere else she and Barrett went every day. She laughed when he asked if she needed a piggyback ride.

He went through his normal day, but the death of Earl Barrett made him long for the security of home, parents, and those things familiar. He stopped by Brian's classes and told the professors the reason for his absence. Todd Hancock found out from Randy Williams after he returned from the airport. Pappy told the Chiefs, and the rest of the soccer team, at lunch. They would be without their leader on Saturday.

Paxton's lab procedures went smoothly. Weight training and football practice were uneventful. There wasn't a peep out of Rattigan when Pappy decided to take an extra ten practice kicks before heading in. He almost skipped karate, but it was better than going back to an empty room. Sherry again put up with being hoisted on his shoulders.

Back in the dorm just after nine, it had been a busy and emotional day. But there was one more situation. Beth Littlefield was close with all Barrett's relatives. They loved her, and she loved them. Earl thought she was the greatest thing ever to happen to Brian, and he'd had difficulty understanding why they broke up.

It wouldn't be fair for her to find out from just anyone. Yet Pappy knew Brian wouldn't call her. He thought about Van Duren, but concluded it was up to him. Should he tell her over the phone? In person was better. It was lousy either way. Wait. Was he doing this just so he could see her? Maybe she was out with Frank Tritter. Andrew couldn't bear seeing her with him.

It was almost ten o'clock, and he was running out of time. "Goddamn it," he muttered as he picked up the phone. "Don't answer. Please don't answer," he said softly to himself.

"Hello," she answered.

"Beth …" He had to clear his throat. "Beth, this is Pappy."

"Oh, hi," she said, her voice warming. "How are you? I meant to call and thank you again for last Saturday. You were great."

"Can you meet me in your lobby right now?" asked Pappy.

"Uh … sure," she said. "Is something wrong?"

"I just wanted to see you for a minute—if that's okay," he said.

"Sure. Come on down. I'll meet you there."

He jumped up, combed his hair, and went back and forth in his mind for half a minute before deciding to put on some aftershave, just in case he smelled from karate class.

Beth was waiting in the Weatherly lobby, in a blue sweater that made her eyes almost glow. She hugged him, but his response was more reserved.

"What is it?" she asked.

"Sit down," he said, and then he took her hand. "Brian went back to Amsterdam last night." Pappy took a deep breath. "His uncle Earl died of a heart attack yesterday."

"Oh no," she said. "Oh no …" She looked away and covered her mouth. "How awful. How is that possible? He was so strong. He was so healthy …" Suddenly, she clutched her chest and began to breathe rapidly. Her throat was raspy, and she fell forward in a faint. Pappy laid her down on the floor.

"Help! Somebody help!" he called. Three girls appeared at the door. One was an RA, Kelly Holborn, a registered nurse, who rushed over, checked Littlefield for a pulse, and then looked in her eyes. "She fainted. What happened?"

"I had to tell her some bad news, and she began breathing heavy and just collapsed," said Andrew.

"Was this something about Barrett?" She turned. "Somebody get a couple of wet towels right away!" The two girls ran down the hall.

"You know what's been going on?" asked Pappy.

"Yes, Van Duren and I have had several conversations about her. She's a mess … in really bad shape." She looked at him. "You're Pappy … Andrew Paxton."

"Yeah," he said, now touching Littlefield's forehead lightly.

"Do you know if she's taking any medicines?" asked Kelly, now considering calling an ambulance.

"No," said Andrew, even more concerned. "I know she's been depressed …"

Littlefield's breathing became more normal. The color was returning to her face, and her pulse was slowing.

"I think she'll be okay," said Kelly. She continued to monitor Beth's pulse. "What happened? What did you tell her?"

"Barrett's uncle died last night," said Andrew. "She was really close to all of Brian's family but Uncle Earl in particular. He thought she was the greatest. I knew it would hit her hard."

"Why don't you tell this girl you love her?" she asked suddenly. "It would be the best thing for her … and for you too."

Pappy sat back. "What …?" That's all he could come up with.

The other girls appeared with towels. Kelly placed one behind Beth's head, and the other she used to wipe her face and brow.

"You can go," she told them. "She'll be okay." They went back down the hall.

Kelly looked up at Pappy. "Apparently this is the only person in the civilized world who doesn't know how you feel."

Andrew shook his head. "She just needs my shoulder to cry on. She's seeing that guy from the theater. Tritter."

"Frank Tritter?" said Kelly. "Ha, I've got news for you, pal. If Alicia saw him so much as look at another girl, there would be nothing left of him but his socks. He's her property. Has been for two years. She almost got fired because of it."

Littlefield's eyes fluttered. She was still pale, but she could move her head.

"You fainted, and Prince Charming here caught you," she said. Andrew recoiled from the words. Littlefield was barely conscious.

"She's going to have to lay here for a while, and you need to leave … now," said Kelly. He was still looking down at her. "Well, go ahead," she said, grabbing the back of his head and pushing him down to Littlefield's face. He kissed her forehead. "Not the forehead," she scolded, pushing their lips together. "Okay, get out. Call her tomorrow."

Friday, October 31

◉ ◎ ◉ ◎

Friday. Chem class, practice, and no roommate.

Barrett phoned about ten to make sure Hancock and everyone else knew where he was. Pappy told him about Littlefield.

"Yeah," said Barrett. "My family was asking about her. Thanks for taking care of it. I felt lousy, but I just couldn't see calling her. It would have been bad all the way around. Hope she's okay … It's pretty sad here."

"I'm sure," said Pappy. "He was a great guy. I remember all the times we went fishing."

Barrett asked about Paula, but Pappy hadn't talked to her since the day before.

"I called her last night," said Brian, "and this morning. She's tired, and I guess the numbness in her feet won't go away. She may have to have the back surgery. I heard it's awful. They use a hammer and chisel on your spine, and you have a big scar."

Andrew could hear voices in the background.

"I gotta go," said Brian. "Do me a favor: check on Beth again. Her parents called mine, and they're pretty worried. I told everyone about Paula, and they weren't happy. I know they'll like her once they meet, but they're really concerned Beth might do something … you know."

"Yeah, okay," said Andrew.

271

Beth Littlefield stared at the telephone for over an hour. She wanted to call Brian and his family to say how sorry she was about Earl Barrett. He'd always given her a big hug every time they met and considered her part of his family as well.

Last night was a fog. Her only recollection was hearing the bad news and then someone helping her to her room. She was embarrassed about fainting. It was the third time in a week. Luckily, the bruises from the falls were covered by clothing. The situation with Brian just seemed to get worse and worse. She ached seeing him with Paula all over campus—and everyone saying how cute they were together and how much in love they were.

She worried that Pappy would tire of being her emotional crutch. It would be terrible if he wouldn't see her anymore. He was the only great guy left in her life, and she felt she was driving him away. She seemed to remember that he'd kissed her the night before, but maybe not. The RA who'd helped her back to her room said something about Andrew being in love. It must be that girl she saw him with on the double date with Barrett. They were all moving on with their lives, everyone but her.

Saturday, November 1

⊚　⊚　⊚　⊚

Patty Van Duren was coming back from the shower when she thought she heard someone yelling for help. Girls came into the hall as the sound grew louder. Patty realized it was Paula's voice and knocked on the door.

"Paula, what's wrong?" shouted Patty. "Let me in."

"I can't! Help, please!"

Patty found her master key and opened the door. Paula was on the floor, a terrified look on her face.

"Help me up," she said, reaching out her arm. "I can't move my legs. They're numb." She began to sob.

Patty knelt next to her but didn't know what to do. Her legs were totally motionless. Patty touched one, but there was no reaction. Kelly Holborn pushed through the girls at the door.

"What happened?"

"She can't move her legs," said Patty.

"I'll call an ambulance," said Kelly, already out the door.

It seemed help took forever to arrive, and the attendants were uncertain as to how to proceed. Normally, paralysis meant a broken back or neck, but Paula had had no trauma. They decided to treat her as an accident victim anyway, and they strapped her to a hard stretcher before lifting her onto the gurney. Paula groaned several times in agony as they shifted her legs. Kelly had called the health center and then Dorothy Cole, who'd arrived just as

Paula was being loaded into the ambulance. She flinched and groaned at every bump and turn of the vehicle, so they went as slowly as they dared.

In the emergency room, Dr. Joe Trevino took vital signs and examined Paula briefly. Then he called in an orthopedist and neurologist. He ordered X-rays, drew blood, and gave her some mild pain medication, but her vital signs were stable, and there was no apparent injury. Given her obvious distressed condition, he knew her problems were beyond his internal medicine practice, so he waited until the specialists arrived. But he'd developed a preliminary diagnosis of her illness. And it wasn't good.

Barrett telephoned Paula's room around ten, but there was no answer. Her roommate had gone to Clarkson for the weekend, so he thought Paula might be at lunch or maybe in the shower. Pappy was on his way to the football game. Well, he'd try her later.

The soccer team arrived in Mason around ten o'clock. The Raiders were an up-and-coming ball club, with good speed and a lightning-quick goalie.

It was eerie without Barrett. There was no one barking out orders. Landon and Nakano took turns on goal kicks but had only half the power and distance of Barrett, and Driver and McIlroy were nowhere near as quick. So the Titans were forced to play an even slower game, with Santander in control. Normally, Barrett would pick up the first attacker through, and the others would fill in the gaps. Nakano was skilled and determined but lacked the self-confidence to lead the charge. Mason kept creating opportunities and scored when their center forward picked up a loose ball off a corner. One to nothing.

Millwood gathered everyone at the midline. "We've got to drop one guy back and play three up front, with Roland and Scott behind us. Keep the pressure on."

But the Raiders were in control. The field was in excellent condition, allowing clean traps and passes. The Titans were covering and switching better with the extra defender, but the Raiders' fullbacks were quick enough to play at midfield and still get back on fast breaks. At the forty-minute mark, Randy Williams made a spectacular deflection of a rocket from twenty yards at the upper right corner, but a handball resulted in a penalty kick. Two to zero, Mason.

At halftime, Hancock pretended to be angry, but he recognized that the Mason players were a step quicker than the Titans. He had no choice but to keep his fullbacks back deeper, and the Titans were not skilled at offside traps. So instead of run and gun, they directed all the passes at Santander. The idea was right, but the execution wasn't there. Roland was double-teamed when he got the ball, and with a two to nothing lead, Mason brought its players back on defense. At thirty-eight minutes, David Nakano shot from fifteen yards. The ball took one skip along the ground, and the goalie deflected it off the goalpost, but Penny was standing there. Two to one.

Now the Titans were fired up but running out of time and gas. Hancock had limited substitutions, and the Titan defenders expended a lot of energy chasing their foes. With three minutes left, the Mason center forward again beat Harbaugh and punched it low past Williams. Final score three to one. It was a tough loss. It pointed out the lack of speed and strength off the bench. Todd Hancock couldn't make them faster, and only time would make them better.

Pappy was on his way back to Junction, this time with the football team. He didn't remember much of the drive last month.

This was a fair test for the football Titans. Junction had a powerful offense but only average defense, so the potential was for a high-scoring contest. The stadium was old and small, like Bainbridge, and there would be fewer fans.

The Titans dressed and went through their pregame routine. Pappy wondered if the goalie from the soccer team was there, and if he would realize that the Bainbridge kicker was the same guy he'd put in the hospital. It was an overcast day, and the temperature was only about forty-seven degrees.

The Titans won the toss and elected to receive. The crosswind was just enough to make it difficult for the Falcons to keep the ball away from Claude Benson. He fielded it on the ten. Cutting up through a seam on the left side, he almost broke free, but a diving linebacker just got a piece of his foot on the fifty, and he fell forward to the forty-three. Again, the surging offensive line opened up quick hits. Birdwell ran the option right and kept the ball, diving to the twenty-two, for another first down. On the next handoff, the fullback bobbled the ball and dove on it back at the thirty. Three plays later, fourth down and four. Andrew Paxton was standing on the twenty yard line for his first field goal attempt. He looked at the right goalpost and picked a spot one yard inside. Three steps back. Two to the side.

Ball snapped, he came forward and then dodged to the side as Birdwell took off right and threw a pass to the corner of the end zone. That was the third, of now three, fake field goal plays they'd practiced. Andrew converted, and it was seven to zero. Everyone congratulated Pappy on a great fake, but it was Birdwell and the line feigning left that sold it.

The Titans kicked off, and the Falcons started at their own thirty-two. They drove to the thirteen, and settled for a field goal. Seven to three.

Birdwell was masterful, running traps and sweeps as well as the option. He had nerves of steel and would stretch out the defense, holding the ball to the last possible moment before shoveling it to the running back. Andrew couldn't believe how many times Birdwell got thumped every game, but he never flinched from the contact.

It was twenty-one to three when Junction's running back took it in from the twenty-two yard line. Twenty-one to ten. With fifty seconds before the half, again Benson broke free and was caught from behind at the sixteen of the Falcons. Three plays later, Andrew hit his first field goal ever, from the fifteen yard line. At the half, it twenty-four to ten, Bainbridge.

The lead was enough that in the second half, Junction would have to pass the ball. The Titans had set up two different blitzes just for this situation.

The teams went back and forth for the entire third quarter, and Bain had an uncustomary small lead going into the fourth. The first play was a halfback pass that covered sixty-eight yards for a score. Now it was thirty-one to ten, and Bolger could let Paxton try from anywhere. With no pressure, it would be a good tune-up for later games.

But the Bainbridge second string showed they could play as well, and it was soon thirty-eight to ten. With less than two minutes left, they were stopped on the twenty. This would be about a thirty-seven yard attempt, but Bolger wouldn't run up the score. They ran a play from scrimmage. The Falcons took over, and the game ended with a score of thirty-eight to ten.

Dorothy Cole stayed with Paula through all the tests and prodding and poking. Both were scared. Hardwell warned that surgery might be necessary, but they had hoped the symptoms would subside, not get dramatically worse.

Orthopedist Dr. Steve Fox arrived after lunch and went to confer with the ER doctor. They looked at the X-rays and concluded they needed a more elaborate set, including the skull, lungs, and liver. They also examined her neck, breasts, under her arms, and her stomach and groin.

"I don't understand," said Dorothy. "I thought she had a bad disk."

"Your daughter's problems appear to be neurological and centered on her back," said Dr. Fox. "We're ruling out any other possible origins. In the meantime, we've given her some morphine to ease the pain. If you can stay with her, she needs to eat as much as possible. She's very thin and hasn't many reserves. The pain has probably curbed her appetite. We'll be giving her vitamins and other dietary supplements and will help her along through her IV."

"Is she going to need an operation?" asked Dorothy.

"We don't know yet. I've called in another specialist, but he won't be here until Monday. We want to keep Paula here so we can control her fluids and manage her pain. We're not going to operate until we know the exact cause of her problems. It appears something's pressing on the sciatic nerve on her left side, so she may have ruptured her L5 disk. However, it's unusual that she has paralysis in both legs. We also need to confer with Dr. Hardwell regarding his original diagnosis and treatment regimen."

"She got injured playing field hockey," said Dorothy.

"That's what she told us, but this is pretty severe trauma for that sport," said Fox. "Maybe if she landed flat on her buttocks, it might have this result, but we would've hoped to see some reduction in inflammation by now." Dorothy bowed her head and took a deep breath.

Dr. Fox touched her on the shoulder. "Let me assure you that we're giving Paula the best care possible," he continued. "We'll transfer her to a private room and keep her comfortable until we decide which course of action to recommend. You can stay with her as long as you wish. We can even set up a cot if you'd like to be here after hours. The hospital is fairly empty, so you won't be bothered." He looked up. "The television even works. And there are magazines in the emergency room lobby." He looked down the hall. "I think our new X-rays are ready. Her tests are over for today. If you need anything, have the hospital page me."

Dr. Fox walked to the first ER room and closed the door. Dr. Joe Trevino had already put the X-rays up on the viewing screen. "Crap," said Trevino. "Crap, crap, crap. Such a beautiful girl. Such a sweet kid. This is bad."

"My exam didn't show any involvement of the lymph nodes in her neck or armpits," said Fox. "Nothing in the breasts, but possibly in the groin. We'll need biopsies tomorrow. She has been through enough today."

"Look at this," said Trevino in frustration. "Am I reading this right? She has multiple lesions along her spine and the back of her rib cage."

"Yes, that's what I see," said Fox, frowning. "It's a wonder she can move at all. The pain must be off the charts. Tell the nurses to up the morphine and watch for any reactions. We need her to eat and sleep."

"How could Hardwell have missed this?" asked Trevino.

"Well, we don't know what the pictures looked like a month ago ... or what views he took. I suspect this is growing very rapidly, so they were probably much smaller then."

"Or this could be another one of his screwups," said Trevino.

"Well, whether he screwed up or not, it wouldn't have made any difference," said Fox. "This has spread too far for me to do anything surgically ... Weege is going to have his hands full."

Back on campus, people were talking about the ambulance that took some girl from Weatherly Hall to the hospital—she was having leg pains or menstrual cramps or something. Andrew didn't think much about it until he saw Patty Van Duren in the Union at supper.

"They took Paula to the hospital this morning," she said, extremely upset. "She couldn't move her legs. They may have to operate. We haven't heard anything more."

"Has Barrett been told?" he asked.

"I don't know," she replied.

"It's probably that disk in her back," said Pappy, trying to be calm and logical. "Barrett said she might have to have surgery."

"Well, I hope they do something quickly," said Van Duren. "She was in really, really bad shape."

"I'll call Brian." Pappy got to his room just as the phone rang.

"Where the hell have you been?" screamed Barrett. "Where the hell has everyone been? Where's Paula? I've called all day. I called her mother's house. I've called everyone I could think of. What the hell is going on?"

"Calm down," said Andrew. "They took her to the hospital this morning. Her back was really bad, and she may have to have surgery. Her mom is probably with her. I doubt if they'll operate before you get here ... This will give you more excuse to carry her around campus," he said, trying to put his friend at ease.

"I gotta talk to her," said Barrett.

"It's almost eight. She's probably asleep, and they won't let you through the switchboard this late. I know from experience ... Hey, that hospital fixed my skull; they can take care of your girlfriend's back. This may be for the best. She sure wasn't getting any better."

Barrett exhaled. "Maybe ... I don't know ..."

"I'll go over tomorrow and see her myself. Then I'll call you. Don't call me. They don't let people in until one o'clock. Take it easy; she's in good hands."

"Yeah, yeah, I guess so," said Barrett. He sounded tired and defeated.

"Go get some rest ... and hug your mom for me." Pappy hung up.

Sunday, November 2

⊙ ⊙ ⊙ ⊙

The phone rang at nine. It had to be Barrett.

"Do me a favor and call me from her hospital room so I can talk to her," he said. "I'll pay whatever it costs."

"It's nine o'clock in the morning," said Andrew. "I told you I can't get in until one."

"Actually, it's eight," corrected Barrett. "Daylight savings was last night. Fall back."

"Yes, all right, yes, I will. I'll try to call you. Good-bye."

"Wait, how'd the soccer team do?" asked Brian hopefully.

"They lost three to one."

"Oh, crap," said Barrett.

Pappy flopped back in bed, but it was impossible to go back to sleep.

He had to be at the hospital by one, because karate was at two, so brunch was short. Littlefield was nowhere to be found. Hopefully, someone had put her straight about Tritter and the lady professor.

Going back to Mercy was going beyond the call of duty. He *hated* hospitals. Nothing good ever happened there. People could even die from too many beers and burgers. In addition to his own childhood experiences, he'd been there for his mom's two radical mastectomies, his father's kidney operations, and numerous relatives fighting many diseases.

He stopped cold at Paula's door. She lay sleeping, almost swallowed by the bed and looking as pale as her pillow. An IV hung next to her. A woman, presumably her mother, was lightly snoring in a large chair. The bleakness of the room was overwhelming, and he felt he might retch. He went to the nurses' station, but all they would say was that Paula Cole was undergoing some tests and being treated for a bad back. She was heavily sedated, so there was no telling when she would awaken.

There was no point in staying, so Andrew got out of there as quickly as possible. Karate would be a breeze compared to this, no matter how many times Yoshi pummeled him.

His phone call to his roommate wouldn't be pleasant.

Monday, November 3

◎ ◎ ◎ ◎

D r. Warren Edward George sat at a metal desk outside the nurses' station at Spencer Mercy Hospital, rubbing his eyes and sighing heavily. Six-year-old Amy Pallischeck's parents had brought her to the emergency room at one-thirty in the morning, vomiting uncontrollably—a frightening side effect of the treatment that was paradoxically saving her life. An IV restored vital fluids, and several layers of blankets eventually subdued her shivering.

At thirty years old, "Weege" (his nickname at Boston University Medical School) was already recognized as a leader in the fight against leukemia, a disease that, in its many forms, just two decades before had a mortality rate in excess of 90 percent but now could offer a one in two chance of surviving five years or more, with the odds improving almost every year. Warren had seen the dread on the faces of dozens of parents and their terribly ill children, who often were too young to comprehend what was happening to them. His world was consumed with the ravages of the disease, the weight loss, the bruises that came too easily and seemed to never leave, the fevers, the night sweats, and the constant fatigue. And the terrible treatments he prescribed to make them well.

Dr. George grew up outside Spencer. He was valedictorian of his high school class and a National Merit Scholar. He entered BU at seventeen years of age under a new accelerated combined undergraduate/medical school curriculum and was through his college courses in just over two years.

Even in high school, he was of a single mind and purpose toward children's medicine. At six years old, he attended his dad's company Christmas party at the home of one of the executives. Before going, his mother told him to be nice to the host's daughter because she was dying of a terrible disease. He remembered her being cute—and that she spent the entire party sitting on her father's lap, resting her head. Warren couldn't help staring, but she was too tired to notice. On the ride home, he told his father that it wasn't fair that children got sick. The little girl never hurt anyone, and when he grew up, he wanted to become a doctor so he could cure her.

Warren's father fought back his own tears, imagining if it were his child. Dads were supposed to protect their families from any harm. This girl was dying, and there was nothing the father could do.

This morning, Weege would go down the same path with Paula Cole. He reviewed the file. She had been misdiagnosed as having a pinched nerve and was now totally paralyzed from the waist down. Dr. George shook his head. Hardwell had ordered a single X-ray and prescribed ice packs and aspirin. The painkillers then progressed to Darvon, but no follow-up assessment had been ordered.

The extensive X-rays confirmed a rapidly growing nest of tumors invading her spine just above the coccyx, or tailbone. In addition, there were numerous growths along the inside of her rib cage. Now it had metastasized to close off the nerve impulses to both legs. The pain must be incredible.

Dr. George contemplated how he would tell the girl she had a disease, the mere mention of which caused many to give up all hope. The treatment protocol would be exhausting and the cure almost as bad as the disease. The chemicals he would pump into her body would include the vilest poisons known to man. Their mission: to destroy cancer cells, the fastest growing in nature. But these weapons were indiscriminate, attacking any rapidly dividing cells, particularly hair follicles and the lining of the stomach. The result: the embarrassment of hair loss, particularly to one so beautiful. The death of stomach tissue would cause the body to expel the damaged cells through repeated intense, uncontrollable vomiting. Most critical, however, and the most difficult to gauge, was the damage to the heart muscle. The severity of the regimen would threaten Paula's survival.

The good news, if any, was that Dr. George had had remarkable success treating this exact form of the disease. Paula appeared otherwise strong and healthy, a good candidate. With luck, the results could be dramatic. The alternative was certain death.

So he prepared himself mentally and emotionally for the first meeting with the patient. Tired and frightened, she was unaware of the news he brought ... or what danger lay ahead. His solace was that the advances in research offered a life managing the disease rather than a death sentence.

He was reaching for his coffee, now cold, when Steve Fox leaned his head through the open doorway. "Paula and her mom are ready," he said. "They'll be wheeling her into treatment room one."

"I'll bring her files and X-rays and meet you," said Warren.

Dr. Fox flipped on the fluorescent lights in the treatment room. "Green," he observed aloud. "Why are all hospital walls bleak, dull green or brown, and all the floors white, brown, or black linoleum?" Formerly the doctors' lounge, the large room had been converted to Dr. George's specifications (or as much as the limited hospital resources would permit). There were cabinets with glass doors and various medical supplies piled inside and on the top.

There was no bed. With all the wires, hangers, and tubes for the instruments, monitors, and IVs, it was easier for the patient to be moved from room to room in a hospital bed. The treatment room was close to the maintenance room containing the boilers and furnace, so heat and hot water were plentiful. And it had a window air-conditioning unit—unusual in Indiana in 1969, even for a hospital.

A white-haired woman entered with a nurse pushing a bed, on which lay a beautiful girl with long straight brown hair. Paula's eyes were sunken and gray, and she was almost too tired to be frightened. Dr. Fox had given her the highest dose of anti-inflammatant he felt she could tolerate, together with the continued morphine drip, which further sapped her strength. The drugs had reduced the pressure on her spine, allowing some feeling back into her legs, but she no longer made the effort to walk.

"Paula, this is Dr. Warren George," said Dr. Fox. "He's the fellow I've been telling you about, our home-grown medical genius."

"You're just a boy!" Dorothy Cole blurted, sounding disappointed. George's face blushed, and Fox chuckled involuntarily, a relief from the tension.

Warren walked over to Paula and put a comforting palm on her forehead. She closed her eyes with a sigh. He then took the mother's hand.

"I assure you, Mrs. Cole, that I have my driver's license," he said.

She put her face in her hands, overcome by the moment, gushing a flood of tears. The young doctor's intelligence and proficiency were obvious in an instant. Her daughter was in good hands.

"How are you today, Paula?" he asked.

"Better than I was," she responded weakly, "but my back hurts, and the medicine has been making me sick. And I itch."

"That's the morphine," said Dr. George. "I'll switch you to something else after treatment begins."

His smile was now gone. "I want to show you something, Paula," said George, standing before an X-ray projection box mounted on the wall.

"This is your lower back," he began. "Here is your spinal cord, your ribs, and your pelvis. And here," he said, pointing with his finger at some small shadows that looked like misshapen marbles, "these fuzzy little things … are tumors."

The word struck Mrs. Cole through her heart, and she gasped. She tried to speak but could only manage to shake her head.

Dr. George took the hand of his frightened patient. The news weakened her further, and he knew not to drag out the inevitable. The quicker the devastation, the sooner he could give them the hope they so desperately needed.

"Paula, you have leukemia. Specifically, you have something called acute lymphoblastic leukemia, or ALL. That's why you've been losing weight; the fast-growing cancer cells are robbing the rest of your body of nutrition. You're tired all the time because you're anemic. And the tumors put pressure on your spinal cord, pinching the nerves, making your legs numb, and your back hurt. And that's why I'm here. I specialize in curing young people like you."

"He's the best there is," interjected Dr. Fox, but Paula was in a trance.

She heard "leukemia" and not much more. It was as if the room were turning dark from the edges toward the middle.

And then the word "cure" burst through the haze of doom.

"The tumors," he continued, pointing once again to the screen, "are also along the lining of your chest cavity … But …" He paused for emphasis and smiled ever so slightly at her. "Your tests show you're a perfect candidate for the treatment we've developed, called chemotherapy. Actually, it's been around for many years but not as well known or understood as it is now. People have been using primitive poisons to kill cancer for a long time. We've developed new drugs and have made them more effective.

"These chemicals are going to seek out the bad cells and kill them," he continued. "Then your body will throw them out, and the tumors will shrink."

It was as if everything coming out of the doctor's mouth was now positive.

"When do you want to start?" asked Paula's mother, still trembling but now determined.

Dr. George looked at her hopeful face. "There are risks. Serious risks. And some unpleasant side effects. The medicine attacks all fast-growing cells, such as hair follicles and the stomach lining. You'll become extremely nauseated and will keep throwing up long after your stomach is empty. You'll lose all the hair on your body, but it'll grow back once the treatments are completed."

Then Dr. Warren George's expression grew more somber. "It may also damage your heart. We don't know much about this yet, but the heart muscle is always working and constantly being rebuilt with new cells. It also has huge amounts of blood in and around it, so it will be bathed in the poison.

"The doses will be measured and administered according to your body weight, but the treatment seems to work best when delivered in massive amounts. Its impact will be powerful.

"Your immune system will be weakened, as your blood cells will also fall victim to the toxin. You'll need to avoid anyone who has a cold. Do you live in the dorm?"

Paula nodded, for the moment too choked up to speak.

"Well," he continued, "it'll probably be best if you move back home for the time being. You'll no doubt be too weak to attend class for a while, which will also help you avoid every sneeze and sniffle.

"We'll try to minimize all of these things," said Warren. "But the best way to cure you—and we will cure you—involves a long, hard road."

For Paula and her mother, there was only one question.

"When do you want to start?" Dorothy repeated.

Warren George sat down and took a deep breath to relieve the stress, which was almost as great on him as on the two women.

"Today … right now … this afternoon. We already have the drugs prepared."

"How long …? I mean, how long will it take? How long will the treatments last? Does she have to do this the rest of her life?"

"There will be seven cycles in all. Young people, particularly children, seem to tolerate the regimen best, and for this particular type of leukemia, the long-term survival rate is now approaching eighty percent. The first round will last five days. Then you will be off for three weeks. Then five more days of chemotherapy and another three weeks off. We'll alternate drugs between courses, and believe it or not, your body will adjust, so with each successive course, the side effects will diminish."

During the explanation, Paula was silent. Now, as Dr. George finished, she looked over at her mother, with her graying hair and drawn face, her eyes watering. This person had cared for her all her life and brought her through all the struggles of childhood and adolescence. Paula couldn't let her down.

She embraced her mother, and Dorothy sighed several times, her breath hot with distress.

Steve Fox felt awkward, but Warren George was mentally preparing himself for the afternoon procedure.

After a couple of minutes, Paula turned to Dr. George. "I'm ready. Let's do it," she said. "I hurt too much to go back."

"Good," said Warren. "What have you had to eat today? Did they give you the orange juice and green beans?"

"Yes," answered Paula, puzzled.

"That was to give you some vitamins and iron." He looked at his watch. "It's eleven now. Go back to your room and the nurse will give you something to relax. We'll bring you back down here around two o'clock. It will take about thirty minutes to get you acclimated, and then we'll start the drip. It will last about four hours, and then you can go back to your room. I'm afraid you will be on standard hospital fare—Jell-O and warm vegetable soup—if you can tolerate food at all, and we'll give you nutritional supplements and some nourishment through your veins."

He took her hand again. "I've done this many times before. We've had wonderful successes with this treatment. It will be scary at first. The unknown always is, and I cannot prepare you for the nausea. It's a terrible consequence, but if you only understood how lucky you are—how lucky we all are—to have these drugs ..." He paused as a wave of emotion came over him as he recalled some of the battles he'd won and lost, not to mention the patients, mostly children, who put their faith in him—not to mention their lives. He stood up. "See you both in a few hours."

They smiled, but fatigue was taking over, and it was all Dorothy could do to follow Paula's bed back down the hall to her room. The anti-inflammatant and painkillers were wearing off, and her lower back stiffened and spasmed in anger. The nurse gave her another injection and left to get an ice pack, but when she returned, both mother and daughter were sound asleep.

Dorothy Cole woke to the shuffling of feet in the room. She had nodded off in one of the small upright chairs, and it felt as if her head were locked to one side. The nurse was putting a second intravenous tube in Paula's right arm. She protested little, still sedated.

The two nurses struggled to maneuver the bed through the doors. Spencer Mercy Hospital had been built some forty years before and was a poor fit for the newer equipment. The halls were deserted, as the patient's meals had been served.

Paula would be the twenty-seventh patient in the chemotherapy program now headed by young Dr. George, and the referrals were pouring in. He knew the demand for treatment would soon outstrip Mercy Hospital, but for now, it drew attention from medical facilities all over the state and country.

Mother and daughter had made the decision to go forward, but now it felt as if they were being dragged down into an abyss. The hope conveyed by Dr. George was now overshadowed by the dread of the unknown.

The nurse's aide placed a large pile of blankets on one of the cabinets in the treatment room. Dorothy pushed what looked like a secretary's chair over to the edge of the bed and took her daughter's hand.

"We've some things that we'll have to do just as a precaution," said Dr. George. "Mrs. Cole, you can stay or wait out in the lounge. This can be a difficult ordeal to watch. If you stay, you can help, and that might reduce your anxiety. I know I always prefer to know what is going on rather than be stuck in the waiting room."

"Yes, I'm staying," said Dorothy.

"Good. Now, Paula, we're going to hook you up to a heart monitor, which is just a strap around your chest, plugged into this machine. It will beep, and the little blips on the screen will let you know you have a heart." Warren smiled, but it wasn't much of a joke. The nurse wrapped the white elastic band around Paula's ribs just below her breasts. Weege turned a knob, and a green screen with horizontal lines appeared. It blipped and beeped with every heartbeat, and it was beeping rapidly.

He hung a plastic bag filled with amber liquid next to the intravenous solution going into her right arm. It had writing that Paula couldn't read, as well as the word POISON in bold letters, with a skull and crossbones. Dr. George motioned to the two nurses standing in the hall to come in. The first was carrying a large bedpan full of crushed ice. The second pushed a device that looked like a huge toaster with dials, and wires were attached to porcelain handles. She recognized it from doctor shows on television. It was a crash cart.

The first nurse handed the bedpan to Paula's mother and then tucked several of the towels around Paula's neck and shoulders.

"Mrs. Cole, I want you to remain calm. I promise you I've done this many, many times. In a moment, I'm going to start the drip. When I do, the medicine is going to hit Paula's system hard. I want you to take the ice and shove it into her nostrils, as the small capillaries and blood vessels in her nose will burst, and the ice will stop the bleeding."

Dorothy Cole gasped, but Dr. George continued. "This is a crash cart. It's here just as a precaution. It's been our experience that when the medicine reaches the heart, in about seven percent of the patients, the heart muscle will arrest … stop. But we *will* bring her back," he said with great emphasis.

Paula's head sank deeper into the pillow, and her lips began to tremble. Dorothy Cole felt overwhelming claustrophobia and wanted to run away in fear, but the process had started. Dr. George jabbed the needle from the amber bag into the IV running into Paula's arm, opened the metal clip, and the liquid moved down the tube.

Dorothy stood up as if moved by some unseen force. Paula turned her face to her mother, and she took a few pieces of ice and pushed them up into each nostril. Paula recoiled from the cold and felt the chemicals coming up her arm and then moving throughout her body. Her breathing became labored, and Dr. George listened to her heart and lungs as he watched the monitor. "More ice, please," he told Dorothy. Paula began to struggle against her, as the water was now running down the back of her throat. She gagged and choked, coughing up blood on the towels and Dorothy's arm, but her mother took no notice.

Dr. George looked at the clock on the wall. Fifteen minutes had passed, and he signaled the nurse to remove the crash cart. That danger had passed. He was so tense that when he exhaled, it made a loud whistling sound.

Barrett appeared at the door. Startled, he stepped back. There before him was Paula, a mass of tubes, with blood and water running down her face, white towels splashed with crimson blotches surrounding her. Her skin was as colorless as the bedsheets, and her long brown hair was now matted and twisted.

He staggered forward. Paula's mother turned and saw him. "Brian, you shouldn't be here," she said.

"What's going on?" he asked as he reached the side of the bed. Then Paula's eyes rolled back and her head shot forward, hurling the contents of her stomach across her mother's chest and the lower part of Barrett's pants. She tried to cover her mouth, but the tubes going into both arms were restrictive, and she retched again. She saw the fear on Barrett's face but continued to vomit. She gasped between spasms, and tears rolled down her cheeks. Dr. George said nothing but continued to monitor her heart and lungs. Paula's mother wiped up the mess as best she could and then pulled Barrett toward the door.

"You should leave. She doesn't want you to see her this way."

"What is all of this?" he asked. "Why is she here? Her RA said she was still in the hospital."

"Paula has cancer," said her mother. Dorothy realized that was the first time she had said those words to anyone. She hadn't even called the university to say where she was or why she was absent from work. "She has leukemia. She woke up Saturday morning and couldn't move. This doctor is an expert on cancer. This is a new treatment."

Barrett lost her after hearing the word cancer. He was looking at the small body lying in disheveled bedclothes and blood-strewn towels.

"Is she going to live?" he choked. Those were the only words he could think to say, and he felt terrible after asking. But he'd just come back from his uncle's funeral, and death seemed to be everywhere.

"This medicine is going to make her very sick," said Dorothy, looking back at her daughter, "but the doctor says she has an eighty percent chance." She touched him on the arm. "You go back to the dorm, and I'll call you after the treatment to tell you how she's doing."

Barrett put his hands on her shoulders and looked her in the eye. "I'm staying." He walked over to Warren George, who was standing by the bed, looking at his watch and writing in her chart.

The heaving was almost continuous. Dr. George rolled up some ice in a towel and placed it against the back of Paula's neck. She stopped convulsing and rested against the pillow.

Weege took another deep breath and stood up, straightening his back, which had been stooped for almost fifty minutes, saying, "The worst of round one is over, Paula, and you were fabulous." She looked over at him, smiled weakly, and promptly vomited again. Barrett looked down on her. She looked smaller … and extremely frail.

Paula took his hand. "You need to go," she said almost in a whisper. "I don't want you to see this." She promptly threw up on their clasped hands and then fell back and began to cry. Ignoring the mess, he took the last clean towel and gently began to wipe her mouth and eyes.

"It's been ninety minutes," said George. "The nausea will come and go. We've given her something for it, but it won't stop entirely. Let's dry her off and change the wet bedclothes and towels. She's going to begin to shiver, so pile on the blankets and crank up the heat. It's going to get hot in here. If you want to stay, you need to go over to the sink and wash your hands. Have you had a cold or any kind of illness lately?"

"No, I'm fine."

"Well, you can stay for now," said the doctor. "But later in the week, the treatments will knock back her immune system. You'll have to stay away, because you'll be carrying millions of germs you're exposed to on campus every day."

"How long does she have to do this?" asked Barrett, now at the sink.

"Five days for this first round," he said, "Then, if everything goes well, she can go home for three weeks." Paula's teeth begin to chatter. "Let's have some more blankets." The air vent rumbled, and the room warmed rapidly. Warren turned to the nurse. "Better call maintenance and tell him to close some of the vents on this floor or everyone will be complaining."

Paula was shaking more vigorously. "The shivering will last for about an hour. We're putting a large volume of liquid into her system, and it's acting like antifreeze in a car. Don't worry. She's very strong, and shivering is the body's way of exercising to keep warm."

Warren George headed for the door. He didn't want to show it, but he was totally exhausted, as happened with each new patient, and he needed to sit down. But first he had one more thing to do. He motioned for Dorothy to join him in the hallway, and she saw him manage a smile.

"She did wonderfully. Just as well as can be …" Dorothy leaned against him and began to cry from relief, joy, and just plain exhaustion.

"The nurse will stay with her, and we've made arrangements to have another at night. She will sleep, but she needs to drink water or at least chew on some ice. Tomorrow won't be as bad. Her heart took the initial shock well, so she's past that crisis. Whatever blood vessels were going to burst in her nose have done so. The nausea and shivering will subside. When she finishes this course, we need to fatten her up. She is skin and bones from the cancer. Her appetite will return after about a week. All in all, you both did very well." He wiped a tear from her cheek and looked back where Barrett sat, wiping her face every so often with a towel. Paula was dozing, despite the shivering, which was visible even from twenty feet away.

"That's quite a young man," he said, nodding at Barrett, who looked as old or older than the baby-faced doctor.

Dorothy went back to her daughter and the boy holding her hand.

Barrett left Paula drifting in and out of sleep, while the dreadful liquid continued to pour into her, and walked back to the dorm down the tree-lined sidewalk along Freemont Avenue. Dorothy Cole had cleaned him up before he departed but missed the vomit on his shoes and socks.

It was windy and cold, but he felt nothing. Away from the treatment room, where his mind was occupied taking care of Paula, the word cancer pounded away at him. Three days ago, he'd left her with a sore back and an ice-cream cone in her hand. Now his uncle was dead, and this girl, who never did anything bad to anyone in her life, was dying. His face reddened, and his pace quickened. His eyes watered, and his nose started to run. The more he struggled against them, the more the emotions flooded his body. He went off the sidewalk and collapsed under a tree, sobbing uncontrollably.

"Buddy, Buddy, come here. Leave that man alone—come here," said a woman's voice. Barrett felt something bump up against him. It was a big white dog—a puppy, really—putting his paws on him and nuzzling his right ear. As soon as the dog got a taste of his tears, he began licking in earnest.

"C'mon, come back over here," said the woman, walking toward Barrett. She stopped when she saw his face. "Oh, I'm sorry. Come on, Buddy." And the dog bounded away.

Andrew came back after supper to find Barrett asleep in his clothes, his suitcase still packed. He woke after a couple of minutes and sat up.

"Paula is sick. She has cancer," said Brian, staring at the floor.

Andrew, writing a letter, dropped his pen, which rolled off the desk. He pushed his chair over to the edge of the bed.

"It's terrible," continued Brian. "She has tubes going in and out of her. She can't stop throwing up, and she shivers and shakes, even though they covered her with blankets." Barrett's eyes watered, and he sighed deeply. "They're pumping her full of poisons … How could this happen, man? How could it happen? First my uncle and then this …"

"My mom had two radical mastectomies," said Andrew quietly. "She has survived ten years. I guess that's longer than most. But she's scarred badly. What do the doctors say?"

"This guy is supposed to be the best. He says he's going to cure her … but she looks so weak … so helpless … and there's nothing I can do …" Barrett wiped his eyes on his shirtsleeve. "The hospital room is miserable. It's old and cold and freaky. That place is like a dungeon."

"I know," said Pappy. "I've been there. I think they make hospitals like that so you don't stay too long."

"I don't know if she can make it … I don't know if she's strong enough. She has a whole week of this. And she's still in pain." Barrett, always cocky and self-assured, now looked fearful and uncertain.

"C'mon, you need something to eat," said Andrew, putting on a shirt.

"No, man, you've been there already," said Barrett, with no conviction in his voice. "I'll be okay."

Pappy was already heading out the door. "Let's go. You need sustenance—the Salisbury steak was delightfully greasy tonight, and the skin on the Jell-O was nice and leathery—and then we can walk back to the hospital."

Tuesday, November 4

◉ ◉ ◉ ◉

B arrett and Paxton were early to chem. Paula had been asleep the night before, and the doctor was restricting visitors because of risk of infection. Barrett called the nurses' station that morning just before they went to class. Paula had slept and eaten some of her breakfast. The nurse's voice was calm and reassuring, reducing Barrett's anxiety.

Pappy briefed the Chiefs at lunch before Barrett arrived. They sat in disbelief, sickened by the story. Each had had relatives with cancer, but none so young, beautiful, and full of life. Soon other soccer players showed up, and before long, the table was full, all discussing the tragedy.

Barrett went by Hancock's office. The coach expressed his condolences at Earl Barrett's passing and said he knew about Paula. They discussed her treatment in detail, and Barrett said he wanted to be at the hospital every afternoon. It was only for the week, and then she would be off for the next three. Brian promised to work out on his own, in the gym, every night.

The coach was torn. The team depended on their leader in a season that could be the keystone for the future of the program. On the other hand, faced with the same situation, he probably would want to do the same.

"What can you do for her?" asked Hancock.

"I can be there," replied Barrett.

"Are you there for her ... or for you? I ask because if she's in this condition, maybe your presence would be more stressful. She doesn't want you to worry or see her like that. Try to think about it rationally."

"I can't stay away," said Barrett. "I just can't." He looked down.

"Okay, here's a compromise," said the coach. "Come to practice at three. Stay until four. Then I'll have one of the guys take you to the hospital in my car."

Barrett smiled broadly, greatly relieved. "Thanks, Coach, thanks." He jumped up, shook Hancock's hand, and raced out of the building.

Barrett was early to practice, and he ran laps around the field until the players and coach showed up. The drills were cut short, and they started scrimmaging after only half an hour. Quieter, yet just as determined, Barrett led the attack, and everyone went all out. At the end of the hour, Hancock blew his whistle and told Glenn Johnson to take Barrett to the hospital. As if on cue, the entire team turned toward Barrett and quietly applauded. He didn't know what to do, so he waved over his shoulder as he trotted to the car.

Brian arrived at Paula's room around four thirty, but the second day of chemo was already over. She lay there covered in blankets and bathed in sweat, yet she was still shivering. She smiled at him weakly and then pulled the sheet over her head. There were no bloody white towels, but her eyes seemed more dim and hollow. Her mother, wearing a surgical mask, smiled at him and then put some petroleum jelly on Paula's dry lips. There were two bedpans, both empty.

"If you want to come in here, you have to wash your hands over there and put on a surgical mask and cap," said the nurse. "Even after you do, we recommend you keep your distance. I don't want to alarm you, but any infection is potentially deadly to her."

Barrett did as he was told but was still in his filthy uniform, so they gave him a set of surgical scrubs. As he stood at the end of the bed, he watched Paula doze on and off, most of her speech incoherent babble. At one point, she raised her left hand and showed him the ring he had given her.

"She won't take it off," said Dorothy, "even after the doctor insisted."

Barrett realized Hancock had been right. Paula was straining to respond to him, but what she really needed was undisturbed rest.

He turned toward the door. "I want to stay," he said to Dorothy, "but …"

"No," said Dorothy, "it's enough that you were here and she saw you. If you stay, she won't sleep. The vomiting and shivering take all her energy. They're feeding her intravenously. If she wakes, I'll tell her you went downstairs to get something to eat. She won't know the difference. Really, it's okay," she reassured him.

"All right," said Barrett. "I'll come back at eight in case she wakes up." As he took off his gown, he looked over at the utility cabinet.

"Your friends sent those," said Dorothy.

Millwood, McIlroy, and Penny had each chipped in two dollars and bought Paula a box of Russell Stover Candies and a plant. They'd had a formal meeting on the matter and agreed, in this instance, that it was okay to buy another guy's girlfriend flowers and candy, but they'd argued at length whether it should be flowers or just a plant. They opted for the less personal.

Brian felt bad that he hadn't brought something himself, so he headed for the grocery store and was back at eight o'clock with a huge bouquet of daisies, Paula's favorites, and a box of pinwheel chocolate-covered marshmallow cookies. He stayed in the doorway, and when she woke, she blew him kisses and mouthed the words "I love you."

"Will you still let me give you piggyback rides after you're cured?" he asked.

Wednesday, November 5

◉ ◉ ◉ ◉

Day number three of chemo was to be the worst. Paula's body was in full-scale revolt. Her bones were on fire, and she was throwing up the little food she ate. Her veins collapsed, and she groaned and gasped as the nurses tried to take blood samples. The morphine made her skin itch and crawl, but provided the greatest pain relief.

Being bedridden created pressure points and bedsores. Alone with her thoughts, the darkness of death seemed close. She would fight, if for no other reason than her mother had experienced enough heartache and loneliness in her life. But the endless pain, the paralysis, and the severity of the treatment made Paula yearn for an end.

Even Dr. George, who visited her several times a day and even at night, showed signs of strain. Paula wanted to stop, but he wouldn't let her.

"Friday we will know," he said. "Friday we will know. Two more days."

"I don't know if I can take two more days," she said.

He sat down next to her. "What about that brave young man who was here? I think if he could, he would take your place."

Paula's tears flowed freely, and she blew her nose. She smiled and nodded.

"You can decide after the first round. After Friday, we can discuss it again. But I promise you, after today it will be better."

The soccer game was at home against Dickens College. Another school without a football team but smaller than the Brackettville Little Giants. The Titans' starting eleven were reunited, and the confidence was back. Hancock felt he was just along for the ride. He didn't hesitate to chide them for lackadaisical play, but he left the playmaking to Santander and the passion to Barrett.

The wind whipped around at game time, and the temperature hovered near forty. The referee gave the option of allowing players to wear sweat pants, gloves, and wool caps, but everyone declined. The crowd was sparse. Many had never heard of the Dickens College Cyclones. Watching them warm up, though, the Chiefs saw a disturbing resemblance to Mason.

Bainbridge kicked off. The Cyclones picked off an errant pass and started to work their triangle control game—except no one was open. The Titans played tight defense, and every pass was contested. Everyone was bumping and slide tackling, and Nakano and Barrett cut off the passing lanes. On offense, Santander fed the ball to the wings, and Caldwell and Millwood were switching inside/outside with Penny. Barrett's bombs were more controlled. He ran a couple of give-and-gos with Roland, breaking free at the seventeen-minute mark. Two fullbacks converged on him, and he tapped left to Penny, who rolled it in. On the ensuing kickoff, Santander cut off a pass, and they ran the exact same play. This time, neither fullback challenged Barrett, and he left the ball for Roland, who placed it in the lower right-hand corner. At the thirty-six-minute mark, the Cyclones' right wing beat Harbaugh and put one in the nearside goalpost just under Randy Williams. At the half, two to one, Titans.

"We're not shooting enough," said Hancock. Santander continued to wait for the perfect opportunity, which was driving the coach crazy. "This goalie isn't that good. Let's keep the pressure on and make things happen."

Ten minutes into the second half, Penny shot from thirty yards. The keeper was too far out and sprinted back to the goal. The ball caromed off the crossbar, hit him in the chest, and bounced into the goal. Three to one.

The Titans dominated the rest of the game. Penny and Caldwell each hit the goalposts. Barrett was tripped just outside the penalty box, and Roland Santander hit the free kick five feet over the crossbar.

At the end, the temperature had dropped to thirty-six degrees, and most of the fans, even the girlfriends, were gone. Without hat or gloves, Pappy stood freezing in his usual hiding spot. Hancock congratulated his team and gave them the next day off. He had to go to a basketball meeting at Clarkson, and they could use a break from the grind.

He tossed the ball bag into his trunk and told Barrett to get in. They hadn't gone far before they saw the partially frozen Andrew Paxton jogging along the road.

"C'mon, before you catch pneumonia and Bolger has to find another kicker," said Hancock, pretending to scowl. Pappy needed no more encouragement. They sped back to campus, and the coach dropped them at Roberts Hall.

"You don't need to hide anymore," said Hancock. "Our team has a new leader."

"You mean I can come to practice?" asked Andrew hopefully.

"No," replied Hancock quickly. "I also know about this karate business. Coach Bolger said you won't quit. Well, I think you're crazy too, and you're not going to reinjure yourself on my watch."

After dinner, Barrett and Pappy walked over to the hospital. It was a short visit. It had been a bad session. Paula was restless afterward and had just fallen asleep. Dr. George had stopped the morphine because of the itching, but it took a while for the other painkiller to catch up. Brian noticed the bandages on her arms from the botched attempts to draw blood. They had also taken biopsies in the morning, using a local anesthetic, which had now worn off.

The boys were about to leave when Andrew said, "Wait, she has to know you were here. You need to leave something for when she wakes up. Haven't you got anything?" Barrett checked his pockets. Only the dorm room key and his wallet.

Andrew went down the hall, peering into every room. He returned with a balloon that read "Happy Birthday." Brian and Dorothy burst out laughing. "Well," said Andrew, "some guy must be stuck in the hospital on his birthday … At least it doesn't say 'Happy Hysterectomy.'"

Thursday, November 6

⊚ ⊚ ⊚ ⊚

Day four of chemo. Dr. Steve Fox was in early to check Paula's reflexes and response to stimulus in her legs. The improvement was dramatic. It was evident she had changed positions several times in the night. He felt her forehead. No fever to the touch, and none reported on her chart. Then he saw the strands of hair on the pillow. Weege's timetable was right. The drugs were exacting a price on her appearance.

He met Dr. George in the doctors' lounge at ten. Fox said nothing— just presented his narrative in her chart. Weege had no reaction. "Did you see what I wrote?" Dr. Fox asked excitedly. "After only three days?"

Warren smiled. "I told you she'd respond," he said. He then rubbed his young face. "Steve, she's still very sick. Her platelets are extremely low, lower than I wanted, and she is anemic. I almost put her on oxygen during yesterday's session. Today I'll run another EKG to compare it to her baseline and just pray there's no change. The critical test will be on Saturday."

He took a deep breath. "And there's the possibility of infection. I'm reading more and more that this is a serious problem in other hospitals. I'm going to tell the nurses no more visitors until Saturday, and we'll keep her here at least until next Wednesday. Her mother can stay so long as she doesn't go back to work on campus. That place is crawling with every bug known to man. Pretty soon we're going to have to build an isolation ward for chemo patients or we're going to lose some of them."

Paula made it to Thursday. She was able to keep some food down the night before, and she enjoyed the oatmeal and brown sugar for breakfast. She didn't notice the balloon until her mother arrived around ten, and she burst out laughing.

"I didn't know he was here," she said.

"Yes, he came with his roommate, Andrew. You were exhausted, and the nurses wouldn't let them in the room," said Dorothy. "But he wanted you to know he was here."

Paula closed her eyes and tried to think of Brian, not the ordeal to come.

The soccer team was back on track. There was talk about practicing, even though they had the day off. It was decided, however, that if they did, and someone got injured, Hancock would … Well, it was too scary to contemplate.

Pappy's weight training and karate were having dramatic results. At 176, he was now twenty pounds heavier than he'd been his senior year at Amsterdam. His improved balance, reflexes, and flexibility were most evident in *kumite*. The headgear had long since been discarded, but unless Yoshi made it a point to target his head with multiple blows, Pappy was able to block most attacks.

The young Japanese teacher was still the master. Paxton was amazed at his incredible speed and seeming immunity to pain. Blocking punches and kicks during *kumite* was bone against bone, and Pappy clenched his teeth in agony. Yoshi was expressionless.

Back at the room, Brian lay on the bed, staring at the ceiling.

"I can't get in to see her," he said. "Not even to stand in the door. They're afraid of germs. And she doesn't have a phone, so I can't talk to her. Now they're saying they'll keep her until at least next Wednesday or Thursday … I'm going to do my homework just because there's nothing else to do. Who knows—I might get an A and wreck my GPA."

Friday, November 7

◎ ◎ ◎ ◎

P aula Cole woke at eight in the morning. *Ugh, it's hot*, she thought. Her legs were sweaty and clammy, so she tossed off the covers. She moved her legs and bent her toes. Paula gasped as her right foot cramped. She could *move*! Her lips trembled as she slowly bent her knees and then put them back down, exhilarated but exhausted.

Dr. Fox entered the room. Seeing Paula's legs move, he no longer tried to conceal his emotions. A week ago, he'd thought he was witnessing the agonizing decline and death of a patient. The reversal was spectacular. He wanted to take new X-rays, but Weege calmly told him to wait until Saturday, at the earliest, to evaluate the treatment's success. It would also give them markers to follow for the second round of chemo in three weeks and afford important parameters for treating similar cases.

"It's like … what's happening?" she asked, both excited and worried. "Is it real …? Is it really working?"

Steve tried to remain calm. "After today, we'll do additional tests and take more X-rays, but yes, your improvement is beyond what we would expect."

Paula was weak, but adrenaline rushed through her. The death sentence had been lifted, or so she hoped. The pain was almost gone, and she had feeling in her legs. Suddenly, she could endure anything. She looked at her arms, black and blue from numerous punctures. *One more day of this. One more day.*

Barrett and Pappy returned from dinner around seven, and the phone rang.

"Hello," answered Pappy. "Hey, how are you?" He looked over at Barrett. "You're welcome. Well, that's great ... I don't know. He's been pretty busy. I'm taking all his calls."

Crap, thought Barrett. Another one of his admirers. "You talk to her," he mouthed to Pappy.

"Are you sure?" he asked, and then he grinned and handed Barrett the phone.

"Hey," Brian said softly when he heard Paula's voice. He collapsed in the chair, head down, rubbing his brow. Pappy grabbed his chemistry book and took off for the library.

Andrew avoided the stacks. Too many people playing kissy face and huggy bear.

"Hi, remember me?" It was Beth. "Are you the famous placekicker from Amsterdam, New York?"

"Hey," he said, smiling. Andrew must have frowned at the sight of her condition, because she became self-conscious. Thinner still than the last time he'd seen her, it looked as if she had painted Vaseline on her lips, which were chapped.

"I keep passing out on you," she said, apologetically.

"My fault. I only come around when things are bad," replied Pappy.

There was an awkward silence.

"Hey, are you coming to the football game tomorrow? I might get to play again," he joked.

"Gee, that would be ... No, gosh I ... I'm going with some people to Mellville to look at the theater. I'm designing some sets for them," she said. "Maybe we could ..."

Frank Tritter approached and put his arm around her shoulder. "Oh, hi," she said, embarrassed. "Frank, this is my friend from Amsterdam, Andrew Paxton."

"Yeah, Pappy," he said, shaking Andrew's hand and then resting it back on her shoulder. She was uneasy and kept her arms at her side. "Everyone knows about you. Soccer player turned placekicker ... and defender of my girl here."

Andrew felt as if a truck had hit him. Just like in high school, watching her with Barrett. He glanced at his watch. "Well, I gotta go," he said. "Nice meeting you." And he started to walk away.

"Nice meeting you too," said Tritter.

"Call me, Pappy," said Littlefield, but she couldn't tell if he heard.

Back at the room, Pappy threw his chemistry book on the desk. "I'm the one who needs to go to California," he said in disgust, going up to the third floor to watch television.

Saturday, November 8

⊙ ⊙ ⊙ ⊙

The nurse came in with Paula's breakfast to find her sitting up on the edge of the bed. "I have to go to the bathroom," she said.

"The doctor said you have to stay in bed," said the nurse.

"I *want* to go to the bathroom."

"Wait a minute," said the nurse, and she called for help. Untangling the bedclothes, unhooking the monitors, and protecting the IVs took about five minutes, but Paula was up for the first time in a week. She had wobbly legs, and the bottoms of her feet felt like pins and needles, but she was done with that damn chemotherapy ... at least for now. And more than anything, she wanted to go to the bathroom by herself.

Dr. George showed up around nine and restrained his elation with Paula's condition. "Let's take some new pictures," he said. "Fox has been bugging me for two days. Then we'll take some blood levels and see where we stand." He smiled broadly.

The next opponents for the soccer Titans were the Dawson Blazers. This would be a tough one. A state school of about six thousand students located near Cincinnati, it would soon move up to Division II in soccer, basketball, and baseball. Drawing from the metropolitan area, Dawson had experienced high school players whose heritage included Irish, German, Polish, and Italian immigrants.

The pitch was one of the best in the conference. They had seen this referee before and had called the game tight but fair, allowing the Titans' physical style of play.

Bain kicked off, and the Blazers went into their control game, using short one-touch passes. It was clear Dawson was superior. The harassment by the Titans didn't rattle the Blazers, but it caused them to rush some passes, resulting in mistakes. Caldwell picked off a pass from the right fullback across the front of his own goal, flipping the ball over the diving keeper and under the crossbar. One to zero, Titans.

Four minutes later, Barrett made a mistake. He turned to pass back to a trailing David Nakano. But it wasn't Nakano but the Dawson center forward, who volley-kicked it past Randy Williams. So much for that lead. One to one.

The Titans kicked off. Santander beat two defenders and then chipped the ball over the fullback's head. Penny was there, and he put it low and left. The linesman signaled offsides. Don was furious. A bad, bad call.

With less than a minute left in the half, Glenn Johnson attempted to slide tackle the Dawson center halfback just inside the penalty area. The ball was gone, and all Johnson got was an ankle and a great acting job. The penalty kick was converted. Two to one, Dawson.

At halftime, Williams and Landon had to restrain the coach from going after the officials, and his tirades continued until the second half kickoff. Play was even until the thirty-one minute mark, when Roland Santander, wide open twenty-eight yards out, saw Caldwell cut through the seam. But instead of passing, he let go with a blistering shot that took the goalie totally by surprise. Two to two. Hancock smiled and banged his clipboard. He'd finally gotten his Latin star to shoot more often. At least this time.

And that was how it ended, after ninety minutes and fifteen minutes of overtime. Both squads had had opportunities and were now exhausted. Randy Williams had his best game of the year.

For Hancock, this was a totally new and unsettling experience. There were no ties in basketball. This was a conflict without resolution.

Dr. Steve Fox and Dr. Warren George poured over Paula's films and saw 70 to 80 percent shrinkage of the tumors in her spine, back, and ribs in only five, albeit murderous, treatments. The cancer was in retreat.

"What now?" asked Steve, fearing the reply.

"I don't want to stop," said Weege. "It's clear the incredible strides she's made. I'm certain with one more week, we can reduce the tumors to negligible size so that the next round will put her in total remission." Then he looked off into the distance. "But I almost killed her Monday and Tuesday. It looks as if she's suffered about 10 percent damage to her heart. If I hit her this hard again in her weakened state, I may be trading her cancer for a different death sentence."

"And if you stop now, what is your experience with other patients?" asked Fox.

"Nothing is certain," said George.

"So the paralysis may return, and she will die a painful death," said Steve.

Weege smiled grimly. "I should have been a plumber … Let's go talk to the patient."

At ten in the morning, Beth Littlefield waited in front of Weatherly Hall for Frank Tritter. They were riding down to Mellville, about twenty miles away, to look at the theater. Littlefield was an incredibly talented artist and designer. Several prominent schools had offered her scholarships, and she could have gone to Pratt or Drexel or Yale—had it not been for Barrett. At the urging of Patty Van Duren, Alicia Whitestone had approached her about designing some production sets for plays. She was astounded at Beth's work and immediately included her on all their planned projects. Beth was reluctant at first, uncomfortable with Tritter's behavior. The story was that he and Alicia were lovers, but he was always touching and hugging and groping her when Whitestone wasn't around.

But Beth was terribly lonely, and this group embraced her—recognizing her immense talent and giving her an outlet for her true vocation.

She caught a glimpse of Pappy going into the Union for the pregame meal. She wanted to accept his invitation. She felt at ease with him. There was genuine warmth, gentleness, and affection when he hugged her, unlike the unwanted pawing of Frank Tritter. And he was a pretty good kisser.

Dr. Warren George found Paula sitting up, talking with her mom and smiling.

"Well, if you couldn't guess, your tumors have shrunk dramatically." Both women hugged each other and started to giggle and cry. "It's great news." The box of Kleenex was almost empty in moments.

Weege waited for the elation to subside. "Paula, you have done marvelously. The ability of the human body to endure this grueling regimen never ceases to amaze me. I would say overall, you're my most successful case to date. You are indeed a lucky young lady."

He then took a deep breath, exhaled, and sat down on the edge of the bed. "For all of this, you're still very sick," he said. "The cancer is still active … and dangerous. It's spreading to other parts of your body as we speak, but is too small to see. We've knocked it down, your pain has subsided, and you can walk … but if we don't continue, there are no guarantees. To wait until the next round might allow it to take hold in other organs and lymph nodes. You might lose all you've gained. I want three more days. Three more tough days."

Paula snapped back to reality. She looked down at her bruised arms, emaciated frame, and pale skin. How could she withstand the darkness again? There was supposed to be a respite.

"Before you make your decision, you should know that your blood tests and EKG revealed some minor damage to your heart. Whether we continue treatment now or wait three weeks, the danger remains the same." He looked into her eyes. "What I believe I am offering is three days of hell, with the chance to drive this thing from your body. Then your treatment course in three weeks has the real possibility of putting you in remission for a long time … maybe for good." He leaned forward for emphasis. "I'll also tell you that every one of my other patients would give everything to be in your shoes." He sat back. "I'm going to leave you to talk it over with your mom. I want to start tomorrow. Monday at the latest." He smiled. "It's a beautiful fall day. The nurses can bundle you up and wheel you outside for a few minutes if you like … and make sure you eat all your food."

Beth Littlefield walked along the road through Darby Park, looking over her shoulder every few moments to make sure she wasn't being followed. Her coat was pulled tight against the cold. It was half a mile back to campus.

Her trip to Mellville had gone as far as a side road in Darby Park. Frank Tritter pulled over, saying Alicia wouldn't be at the theater for a couple of hours so there was no reason to hurry. He immediately began to grab and grope Beth. She resisted. He tried to kiss her, and she shoved the heel of her hand under his nose, causing it to bleed. He still wouldn't stop, so she fired a chopping right to his mouth, knocking his head to the side and back and splitting his lip; then she bolted from the car and ran down a small hill until she was on the main road.

She arrived back at the dorm just as Patty Van Duren and Kelly Holborn were leaving for the football game. "Beth, are you okay? What happened? Where have you been?"

She described the incident, feeling surprisingly calm. Patty was furious and ready to report it to the campus police, but after Beth demonstrated the right cross and they saw the marks on her knuckles, it was clear there would be no more problems with Mr. Tritter.

"I should have gone home," said Littlefield, disconsolate.

"No," said Kelly, "you should go to the football game. Saturdays at college are for football and soccer games, beer, and parties. Not working in a musty old theater."

"We'll make it a point not to tell Pappy," said Kelly. Littlefield looked at her quizzically. "After what he did to Rattigan, we'd find Tritter's body lying in a ditch somewhere." She stood up. "Speaking of Pappy, let's go to the game … right now!"

"You said it," said Van Duren, grabbing Littlefield's arm. "Get your coat and c'mon. Dave is going to wonder where the heck I am."

Pappy was getting used to the attention and the novelty of being the first soccer-style kicker in Bainbridge history. He was also more accurate than Holmes, who held every school record. Now he was practicing from farther and farther out, and Bolger's confidence in the freshman was unquestioned.

The conference championship playoffs were taking shape. The Titans were solid favorites to win the South.

The Bellville Pioneers took the field. Big but slow, it seemed they were always in a rebuilding year. The number one sport on campus was baseball, and they were a national powerhouse, competitive even with Division I and II schools.

The Titans were overwhelming, and it was twenty-eight to zero at the end of the half. Pappy had four routine chip shots for conversions. At thirty-five to zero, Bolger turned loose the second team. Ever mindful of running up the score, Andrew tried only one field goal. Line of scrimmage the thirty-one yard line. Ball on the thirty-six. At forty-six yards, the goalposts looked tiny. But Andrew had taken shots in soccer games from this distance, and the football goalposts were almost as wide. Plus, there was no goalie to avoid. He aimed just inside the right post—in case he pulled the ball trying to swing his leg harder—and hit it dead center, clearing the crossbar by five feet. The crowd cheered but didn't understand what had just happened. Most college toe kickers, and many pros, would hit 30 percent or less from that distance. Some might not even attempt it. Andrew made it look easy, and they now had one more weapon.

The final was thirty-eight to zero.

Sunday, November 9

⊙ ⊙ ⊙ ⊙

Barrett didn't sleep well. He was looking forward to Paula coming back to campus, but now she faced three more days of intensive treatment. He had to be positive. She had a chance at a cure. But he could tell in her voice that she was disappointed, tired, and scared. She wanted a respite from the needles, the vomiting, the chills. And the loneliness of the fight.

He'd talked to her for almost an hour last night. He wanted her well. Cured. All he could do was hope for the best. Her treatment would start that afternoon, so Brian had to stay away. It would be over Tuesday afternoon.

Round two. The same depressing room and the same tubes, wires, monitors, and needles. At first, nothing went right. The room was hot and dry, causing discomfort and static discharge from the sheets and blankets. The bed wouldn't adjust properly, so Paula was propped up with extra pillows that afforded less support. Each puncture was torture as the nurse, acutely aware of the hurt and stress she was inflicting, tried repeatedly, and unsuccessfully, to find a receptive vein. Finally, they called in a surgical nurse, and the IV was started.

With the nausea and shaking came a splitting headache. To add embarrassment, she wet the bed. Her mother could only sit and fret. How much more of this could her daughter take? Warren George darted in

312

and out of the room like a butterfly that wouldn't light. He'd only tried this follow-up protocol a couple of times before, with varying results, so he'd called colleagues around the country to confer about blood counts, different combinations of medications, and possible unexpected results. At one point Saturday, Paula's temperature had spiked and she was sniffling, so they feared she had contracted a cold. What antibiotics were available, and in what doses, given her other medications, became urgent topics of discussion. Fortunately, the fever was gone by Sunday morning.

By five o'clock, it was over, and everyone was exhausted. The nurses spent the next hour changing bedding, cleaning, and trying to make Paula more comfortable. Dr. George checked the prescribed medicines; took Paula's blood pressure, pulse, and temperature; listened to her chest, heart, and carotid artery; and reviewed her latest EKG. A meal was brought in for both Paula and her mother, but neither was hungry. Weege phoned the director of operations for Spencer Mercy, and the maintenance man came in on a Sunday to fix the television and make sure the room thermostat was working properly. One day down, two to go.

Barrett waited by the phone all afternoon and into the evening. Finally, Dorothy Cole called at eight. She put Paula on for a moment to say hi, but she was dozing off and on. Dorothy said everything went okay. Paula had no more pain or paralysis in her back and legs, but every bone in her body ached to the core, and her nose wouldn't stop bleeding. Dorothy promised to call tomorrow afternoon, but Paula was in isolation. Only limited hospital staff members were allowed near her, and even Dorothy was thinking of staying away for fear of bringing infection.

For Brian, it was as if he were in isolation. He had terrible visions of what she must be enduring. What if she died? What if he never saw her again? But he knew how terrible it would be if he exposed her to a germ that proved fatal. It was too much. He put on his coat and headed for the field house.

Monday, November 10

⊚　⊚　⊚　⊚

D ay two. Dr. George marveled at her strength and determination, although he feared it was because she was too weak to protest. They replenished her fluids intravenously, and she had lost bladder control again. It was a game of cat and mouse as to know when enough was enough—and whether he was doing her more harm than good. When the day's course was over, he ordered another EKG, but then he canceled it. He wasn't sure what he could learn after only two days, so he would wait until after the treatment ended to evaluate the damage.

Dorothy called again at eight, sounding exhausted. Paula was resting, and shouldn't be awakened. "One more day," she said.

"I'd like to see her, even if it's just from the doorway," said Brian hopefully.

But Dorothy knew he would be appalled at the sight. "No," she said, "if she sees you, it will agitate her, and she is too weak. Wait until Thursday or Friday. Please."

She was right, and Brian reluctantly agreed. "She knows you want to be here," said Dorothy, her voice faltering. "That's more hope and joy than she's ever had in her life before. You can't do more."

Tuesday, November 11

⊙ ⊙ ⊙ ⊙

Despite his promise to stay away, Barrett raced to the hospital after practice. He approached the room quietly to find the door closed, and there was an official sign that said "No Admittance", so he peeked through the window. Mrs. Cole had gone to dinner, and Paula was sound asleep.

What he saw made him sick. Paula had lost even more weight. Warren George had contemplated steroid treatments and possibly blood transfusions, but he wanted the terrible chemicals to have their maximum impact. Unfortunately, that renewed the attack on her stomach, skin, and hair. Brian could see strands on her pillow, and her skin had gone from pink back to a gray pallor.

Barrett fled the hospital. He needed to talk. And talk to a grown-up. That meant Pappy. It was after seven, so he headed to the field house. Even outside the building, he could hear Andrew and the others yell *Eee!* and he wanted to see what had brought about the change in his friend.

He came in the back door of the stage and went up into the bleachers. The students were engaged in kicking drills, and Yoshi, seeing Barrett, headed in his direction. Pappy followed, planning to act as interpreter and hoping to persuade Yoshi to allow Brian to stay. Ayabe was still struggling with English. The other day at practice, he'd mentioned Sherry's "boots" to Pappy and Larry, but she was barefoot. He kept saying boots and giggling—to the point that all thought he had a foot fetish. They finally realized he was trying to say "boobs."

315

"You student?" Yoshi asked Brian. "You want be karate student?"

"No, thanks," said Barrett.

"Yoshi, this is my roommate, Brian Barrett," said Pappy. They shook hands. "This man is great warrior … great fighter," said Pappy, mimicking Yoshi and patting Barrett on the back.

"Great fighter," said Yoshi. "You can come fight with us … train with us."

"No, thanks," said Barrett again. "Okay if I watch?"

"Yes, you watch. Maybe you can be student," said Yoshi, going back to the drills. It was Tuesday night, so it would be a full session. After exercises and kata 1 and 2, they pounded the mats until their fists were bloody. Then Andrew put Sherry on his shoulders and went up and down the floor, blocking and punching. Barrett couldn't believe the workout. No wonder Pappy's body looked so hard and fit.

Then *kumite*, now lengthened to two minutes. Larry Nelson went first, and his strategy consisted of trying to sweep Yoshi's left leg, to knock him off balance, and then backing up rapidly when the teacher attacked.

Pappy was last. After two months, he still hadn't landed a punch or kick on Yoshi, who was just too fast and experienced. His blocks were like being hit by a steel pipe, and his kicks, when they penetrated Andrew's ever-improving defenses, whacked into his ribs and shoulders. After two minutes, they stopped and bowed, and Yoshi called everyone into a circle to end class.

"Whoa, my turn, my turn," said Barrett, bounding down out of the bleachers. He pulled off his socks and shoes, went over to Yoshi, and bowed … sort of.

"C'mon," said Barrett, assuming his best imitation of Andrew's fighting stance. "You won't hurt me." Then Barrett looked into the eyes of his opponent. "And I won't hurt you."

"Wait a minute, Barrett," said Pappy, but Yoshi already had on his fighting face.

"No hit here, here, here, and here," as he pointed to his throat, sternum, solar plexus, and groin. The other pupils booed, telling Barrett he was about to be killed. But he no longer heard them. He was looking into the eyes of Yoshi Ayabe, who bowed and then took his stance.

"Time," said someone with a watch, and Yoshi rushed forward throwing punch after punch. Barrett backpedaled rapidly, slapping the blows aside with an open hand. "Oh, crap," he said under his breath. He moved to the side as Yoshi stopped his attack, but the teacher charged again, side kicking first at Barrett's ribs, which he blocked, and then to his left cheek, which he did not, but he pulled his head back quickly so it was a glancing blow. At first, Brian seemed unsure of what to do. Then he set himself and threw two left-right combinations. Yoshi was out of reach, but Brian wanted to see how he blocked. Again the teacher threw a flurry and then a side kick that caught Barrett flat in the stomach with a *fwap*.

Brian laughed nervously as he fought off the attack. He'd often charged headlong into a fight, but he never underestimated his opponent. He'd studied Yoshi sparring with the others but was still unprepared for the quickness and force of his blows. Two more kicks and punches by Yoshi, all slapped away by Barrett, and then "time." The timekeeper was totally engrossed in the action, and the battle had lasted almost four minutes.

Yoshi bowed. Barrett returned the gesture, and both broke into broad smiles.

"Great warrior," said Yoshi enthusiastically. "Great warrior," he repeated, pumping Barrett's hand up and down.

"No, you great warrior," said Barrett. "Mighty big warrior."

"You come back," said Yoshi. "You bring him back," he said to Pappy.

Wednesday, November 12

◉ ◉ ◉ ◉

D r. George ordered Paula to sleep all day and have no visitors. Nurses could make her comfortable and clean her up but not disturb her rest. They maintained the fluids and intravenous feedings at high levels, adding more supplements. She was to eat anything she could hold down and was given small doses of painkiller—just enough to keep her relaxed. Blood pressure, pulse, and temperature checks were kept to a minimum. Dr. George came in every two hours and twice found Steve Fox sitting at the end of Paula's bed. He couldn't stay away from this girl engaged in the fight of her life.

The Newcastle College Blue Devils were running late and asked that the game be pushed back to three thirty. That would make it hard to finish in daylight with sunset earlier each day. As an added complication, that morning a cold front roared through, dumping a torrent of rain, scattering tree limbs everywhere, and dropping the temperature to forty degrees, with a crisp north wind at fifteen to twenty-five miles per hour. Hancock notified the referee of the change and then requisitioned rainproof capes from the football team, posting a sign telling all to wear gloves and wool hats. (In case they weren't bright enough to figure that out.)

Few got word of the delay, so at two o'clock the team was milling around the field house. It was a great excuse to skip afternoon classes, but they were anxious to play.

318

At three, it started to snow. Not a lot at first, and it was wet, barely sticking. Newcastle arrived at three fifteen. The teams warmed up quickly, and at three thirty, the Devils kicked off in what was an intensifying storm. At first, the snow was beautiful. Within ten minutes, the field turned sloppy. Both teams were disoriented. Any hard pass or shot skipped and skidded, resulting in the first Newcastle goal when a bouncing ball pancaked and slid under Al Landon's foot in front of the goal. One to zero, Newcastle.

After thirty minutes, the air became colder and dryer, and the flakes were larger and more numerous. By the half, the field was covered, except for some prominent muddy spots in front of each goal. New territory for Hancock. It never snowed on basketball games.

For the second half, the Bainbridge offensive line stepped up its defensive pressure. Newcastle's fullbacks had trouble handling and clearing the ball, so the task fell to the goalie, who wasn't a great punter. After misplaying several bouncing balls at midfield, Barrett and Nakano started using volley kicks or headers. The Titans now rained shots on goal, and their fullbacks came up to midfield, as Newcastle couldn't control the ball on a fast break in these conditions. Quick goals by Penny, Caldwell, and Santander, and the Titans had iced the game. Bain players took a dozen more shots, but by the end, it was snowing so hard that the forwards had difficulty seeing passes in the air, particularly from the wings. It was surprising there were no penalty kicks, as the players were sliding and colliding all over the place, but none were intentional or flagrant. At the end, it was three to one, Titans.

The snow had almost stopped, but there were some chapped faces, ears, and hands. "Guys, this was a great one," said Hancock. "You were smart, you executed well, and you used the conditions to your advantage." He then pointed to Pappy, who was jumping up and down to stay warm. "Now, get out of here before Paxton freezes to death."

The phone rang at seven. The voice on the other end was soft and sleepy, but it was all Barrett needed to make his heart pound. They talked for less than two minutes, and he could hear Paula yawning. A couple of times it sounded as if she dozed off. She said good night and abruptly hung up, almost dropping the phone.

Please, please, please, Dr. George, let this be the end of it, he pleaded.

Thursday, November 13

◎ ◎ ◎ ◎

P aula woke Thursday morning, and with no coaxing, she ate oatmeal, toast, yogurt, and orange juice and then slept until after lunch. They took her EKG, temperature, and blood pressure without her waking. She was conscious to draw blood, but Dr. George had the nurse take the absolute minimum amount necessary.

At two o'clock, she had lunch and sipped some ginger ale. The nurses gave her a sponge bath and then wheeled her down for X-rays. Steve Fox had been hanging around the doctors' lounge since one, and he and Weege reviewed the films together. The suspense was terrible.

The two doctors walked into Paula's room accompanied by the two nurses who had been most active in Paula's care. Dorothy Cole stood when they arrived. As if a ceremony, Dr. George handed the large envelope to Dr. Fox and then bowed comically.

"Ms. Cole," he began, "your tumors, for all practical purposes, have disappeared."

What? Paula didn't speak. *What? Disappeared? What?* Dorothy was almost gasping as she cried.

When is he going to tell me he wants more treatments? thought Paula.

Warren George sat on the edge of her bed. "Paula, you're still a very sick girl. You have cancer. But at this point in your life, you've beaten it."

She stared at him, and he nodded. She leaned forward—IVs, tubes,

321

and all—and threw her arms around him. Not to be left out, Dorothy Cole hugged Steve Fox.

"We are going to continue to monitor your white blood count, but your blood levels are near normal," said Dr. George, "And we are going to pump you full of antibiotics just as a precaution. But you might phone that big lug who was hanging around here before and see if he wants to take you out of here tomorrow for the weekend."

After Paula called with the report, Barrett went to the shower and threw up. He returned, swallowed some mouthwash, stood in front of his bed, and jumped up and down as high as he could to release the stress. He turned the volume on the stereo to maximum and played the Beach Boys' "God Only Knows."

Now Pappy was the one who was going to be sick. His roommate had finally snapped. And thank God it was because of good news.

Friday, November 14

◉ ◉ ◉ ◉

B rian arrived at the hospital at six thirty that evening. Negotiations were going on between mother and daughter. Dorothy wanted Paula home so she could take care of her. Paula was going back to Weatherly Hall even if she had to crawl. Finally, Mom relented. In reality, she was thankful. Her daughter had endured more hell in two weeks than most experience in a lifetime. She was now truly independent; she wanted to get on with her life and wanted to be with the boy she loved.

Paula couldn't run into Brian's arms, but they hugged until Dorothy said, "Okay, you talked me into letting you go to the dorm, so let's go."

Paula was made to promise that she would take all her medicines promptly; report immediately any fever, sniffle, or sneeze; and call if she had any shortness of breath or pressure in her chest. She wouldn't consume any alcohol, and she would be in the dorm, in bed, by ten o'clock. *No exceptions.*

Barrett wanted to carry her up the dorm steps, but she walked on her own. Brenda Sykes let out a shriek when she saw Paula, and girls came out of their rooms and cheered. There were hugs, ever so gentle, all around. Brian was then ordered to the lobby. Paula and Dorothy joined him minutes later. Both were clearly exhausted. Her mother waited outside while the two kissed and hugged. Tomorrow would be a new beginning for all.

Saturday, November 15

⊚ ⊚ ⊚ ⊚

Paula awoke for the first time in two weeks in her dorm room, but she'd slept so soundly that she had no idea where she was. Her head felt as if it weighed fifty pounds as she looked over at the clock. Twelve thirty. She had been asleep for fourteen hours. And still she could hardly move. Her legs felt heavy too—but normal. No numbness or pain in her back. She was slightly nauseated, and her mouth and eyes were dry.

There was an unfamiliar tingling on the side of her head. She scratched and, without thinking, pulled at her tangled hair. Dozens of strands filled her palm, and hundreds more lay strewn across her pillow.

Paula struggled to her feet and went over to her dresser mirror. She looked away, but it was too late. There, for everyone to see, were the ravages of the drugs. At first, she tried not to touch her hair, and then she gently pulled it aside, but every movement shed more and more. Dr. George had tried to prepare her, but there were no words to describe the shock.

There was a key in the door. Brenda Sykes had thought her roommate was asleep, and she gasped at the sight of the handfuls of hair. Paula sat down on the bed, covered her face, and cried. Brenda rushed over and put her arms around her roommate, weeping.

Brenda grabbed a box of Kleenex. "Here," she said, "I'll split it with you."

Paula smiled through her tears. They talked for a while, and then Paula turned pale and fell backward. She remained conscious, but Brenda pulled out a tin of chocolate chip cookies her mother had sent, making Paula eat two and drink a glass of water.

"You need something to eat," said Brenda. "I'm going over to the Union. How about some soup, salad, and above all, dessert? You lie back and eat cookies until I return." She raced out the door, not waiting for a reply.

Brenda was back in less than ten minutes with vegetable beef soup, crackers, an apple, a glass of ginger ale, two pieces of chocolate cake, and a bagel. Paula ate the soup and crackers, but her stomach gurgled with every swallow, and the warm food and stress from crying made her sleepy again. Brenda put the food on her desk and went to the lavatory to get a wet towel. When she returned, Paula was out again. She took the phone off the hook and went out into the hall to update the other girls. There was no point in calling Barrett. The team was probably on its way back from the game.

Paula woke again at four. It had been a deep, restful sleep, but the drugs had sapped her strength. Staggering to the dresser, she looked in the mirror. At least one third of her hair was gone, and what was left was translucent and wispy. *How can I let Brian see me like this?* she thought. Down fifteen pounds, her nose was pointy and temples almost concave.

Brenda came in with a couple of the other girls. They were stunned by Paula's appearance.

"Hey, Paula," said Susie Walker, one of only thirty black women on the Bainbridge campus. "Tim Millwood called. The boys won again. I think he said they may have an outside chance of making the conference playoffs ... You feeling okay?"

"I have a date tonight with Brian," she said, staring into the mirror. She pulled at a few strands of her hair and sighed. "What am I going to do? Anybody have some glue?"

"No glue, but I have an idea," said Sue. "Give me a hanger."

She left. There was a commotion down the hall, and she reappeared with her hands behind her back.

"Barrett told me that secretly he prefers ... blondes," she announced, producing a blonde wig. "This is just the thing."

"You have a blonde wig?" Brenda exclaimed.

"Yeah," said Sue sarcastically, hands on her hips. "All us black gals secretly wish we were blondes. I borrowed it from the ice princess," she continued, setting it on top of Paula's head. "Her rich daddy won't mind."

"I ... I don't know anything about wigs," she said. "Besides, I'd look dumb wearing it ... and she'll be mad when she finds out."

"First off, lots of people wear wigs," said Brenda, now arranging it on Paula's head. "Some girls have thin hair. I have a friend who had scarlet fever when she was little, and she has one. Some like to change their looks for their boyfriends or husbands. Plenty of actresses wear them ... and I doubt if Littlefield will even miss it. Second, she went home for the weekend, so we'll have it back before she knows."

"I wonder why she even has it," questioned Brenda.

"Probably so she doesn't have to get a perm or have it colored all the time," guessed Sue.

"God, it's gorgeous. Well, then, let's get to work," said Pam Chestnut, picking up a pair of scissors.

"What are you going to do with those?" asked Paula. Pam said nothing.

"Okay," said Paula softly, "in a couple of days it won't matter anyhow."

Pam tried to comb Paula's hair, but it was coming out in clumps. Paula stared straight ahead as Pam began cutting just above the collar. She stopped after a few minutes.

"How much do I leave?" she asked, but no one knew. "See if it fits now." They put the wig on Paula's head, turning and twisting to make it seem natural. There were strands sticking out everywhere.

"You need a skullcap," said a voice standing in the door. It was Beth Littlefield. The expression on her face was more sad than angry. "At least you could have asked ...," she said, going down the hall. The girls looked at each other, mortified.

Beth returned, this time carrying what looked like a makeup case. She walked past the girls and stood behind Paula. Pam and Sue couldn't leave the room fast enough.

"The best way for this to work is the shorter the better. The skullcap will fit more evenly, and will adhere better. She took the scissors, and in a few minutes, Paula's remaining hair was barely an inch long all around.

"You're lucky I have two skullcaps. My head is a lot bigger than yours, so we'll cut this one down." Littlefield slipped the cap on Paula's head as tightly as she could, and then pared the edges. Paula sat silently. This was Barrett's former girlfriend who still loved him …

"I'm sorry we took your wig," said Paula. "And I'm sorry about Brian. I know you must still care for him."

Littlefield stopped for a moment. She pursed her lips. "I probably would have done the same thing," said Beth, still working.

"I'll have to wear this thing forever," said Paula. "I've thrown up all over Brian. He has seen me with tubes and needles sticking out of me … and now this." Her eyes welled up again. "How much more of this will he take?"

"He's a prince," choked Beth, lips trembling and tears streaming down her face. She turned her back to Paula. After a few moments, she took a deep breath, wiped her cheeks, and resumed her task. "And I think he loves you." Strangely, Littlefield didn't falter on the words. She finished fitting the wig, which was really too full for Paula's frail face, but otherwise it looked natural.

"Comb it any way you like," said Beth, packing up the case. "I'll be back in a while to help with makeup." She smiled weakly at Paula and opened the door. Pam, Brenda, and Sue had been lurking there, picking up as much of the conversation as they could, and they scattered like birds.

Beth went to her room, closed the door, and leaned back. It was over. He was gone forever. But somehow, it seemed anticlimactic. Down deep, she had known since his return from California, but until now, she'd been too frightened to let go. It had been the fear of being alone and of risking it all by following him to Bainbridge. Now she no longer hurt.

Sue, Pam, and Brenda gathered around Paula.

"Wow," said Sue. "She did a terrific job."

"Now I really feel lousy for what I thought about her," said Pam. "I bet she'd be interested in what Millwood and the other soccer players said about Andrew Paxton."

"Apparently, everyone on campus knows but her," said Sue. "Both Kelly Holborn and Patty Van Duren told me the same thing. Let's go pay her a visit."

"I'm coming too," said Brenda. They went down the hall and knocked on Littlefield's door.

Beth took a deep breath, looked in the mirror, and opened it to find three grinning faces.

"Yes?" said Littlefield. "Did I miss something?"

"Yes, but not for long," said Brenda, and they went in and closed the door.

Both the soccer and football teams won. Newcastle College was one of two stout challengers to Bainbridge's football dominance, but the Titans emerged victorious, twenty-four to fourteen. Andrew had his first field goal blocked, a forty-yard attempt he tried to keep too low into the wind. The second he hit from forty-one in the fourth quarter, and the Titans held on.

Barrett was home by four from the victory over the Saranac Bears but agreed to wait until Paula called when she awoke. They were going out to dinner at O'Reilly's Pub and then to Fitzgerald's to meet Kelly and Patty and their boyfriends.

Paula called at six to say she would be ready by seven. Brian was standing in the lobby when a tall blonde came walking up. His mouth fell open. All the way to the restaurant, he stared while she told him the whole story. It was so great to be walking without crutches. To be pain-free. Barrett kept bugging her until she let him give her a piggyback ride.

They ordered spaghetti at O'Reilly's, and she drank milk, per doctor's orders. They took up right where they had left off, although it was difficult talking about Uncle Earl's death.

The walk to Fitzgerald's was cold, and Paula let Brian carry her to

keep warm and to get there faster. The music was blaring, and the place was packed. Many football players were breaking training, as were some of the soccer players. Paula saw Patty and Kelly sitting in a booth, their boyfriends returning with some beers. As they worked their way through the crowd, Barrett heard a voice.

"Oh, crap, look, a soccer puke and his scarecrow," said Ned Burler. He then grabbed the back of Paula's wig and gave it a playful tug. It came off and fell to the floor. Paula cringed in embarrassment. Burler stood stunned. Barrett's anger flashed. He stepped by Paula, almost knocking her down. The right cross struck Burler in the left eye, making a *pok!* sound, followed by a left crashing into his nose. Blood gushed, and the third was a murderous uppercut, catching the bigger man under the jaw and lifting him off the floor. He landed, already unconscious, on top of a girl in a booth, who screamed. It was over in five seconds. Barrett turned to a wide-eyed Rattigan, who backed away.

"Are you okay?" he asked Paula, rubbing his fists.

She was breathing heavily and felt weak. "Yes, but we better go before you get into trouble," said Paula, recovering the wig. "I think the bartender is calling the police."

They went out the front door, with Kelly, Patty, and their boyfriends in tow. Once back on campus, they split up. Brian took Paula back to Weatherly Hall, and they sat hugging in the lobby until ten. It would be all over campus by morning.

Sunday, November 16

● ● ● ●

B arrett was awake at eight in case she wanted to go to church, and then he remembered that she'd decided to sleep as long as she could. That didn't stop him from worrying, and by eleven he was about to call the police, an ambulance, and the FBI (he had been hanging around Paxton too long). But she phoned to say she'd be ready to go to brunch in fifteen minutes. She came down, still wearing the wig, with Littlefield. Paula's headgear needed some minor adjustments, and Beth obliged. She smiled at Barrett, and they walked to the Union together.

"Where's Pappy?" asked Littlefield nonchalantly, and then her face flushed.

"He should be here," said Barrett. Paula took the stairs slowly. Once inside, she had to sit down, so Brian and Beth went through the line. Pappy was sitting at a table near the windows with McIlroy, watching this strange sight.

Barrett said quietly to Beth, "My roommate is in love with you. Apparently, he has been since you two were in diapers." Littlefield froze and then looked around. Her eyes met Pappy's, and she almost dropped her tray. *Now where do I go?* she thought. She sat with Paula and Brian.

Andrew had heard nothing McIlroy said. What was going on over there? Barrett was sitting with his ex-girlfriend and his new girlfriend. And everyone was smiling. He wanted to leave, but the three were between him and the door. And his misery was about to be compounded.

"Hey, Pappy," yelled Barrett, over the din of students and parents enjoying a quiet meal. He beckoned Andrew like Captain Ahab to his doomed crew. Pappy waved back timidly but sat still.

"C'mere," he said, still audible to all. Clearly, Brian wasn't going to shut up, and everyone in the place was listening to the exchange, so Pappy rose, waiting for McIlroy to join him. No such luck. He mustered the courage and went over and sat next to Littlefield.

"Ta-da," said Barrett triumphantly, pointing to them.

Pappy knew that something was up, and it would probably result in him enduring some form of humiliation for days or weeks thereafter. "Uh, I have to go," said Andrew, rising.

"The hell you do," said Barrett. Andrew now suspected he was drunk. "It's Sunday, and you don't have a damn thing to do. Relax. Get acquainted. We were sitting here saying how handsome you look today. You might just get rid of that, though ..." He pointed.

Andrew felt his throat and removed the piece of toilet paper with dried blood from where he'd shaved earlier. Ugh. What next? Was his fly open?

"I've got an idea," said Barrett. "Let's all go down to the Hollow and have a picnic."

"That sounds great," said Paula. Littlefield and Paxton looked at each other.

"You're nuts," said Pappy. "It's freezing out there. It might even snow."

"Oh yeah," said Barrett. "Okay, how about a movie?"

"Yeah, let's go see a movie," said Paula. "C'mon you guys, I just got paroled two days ago. I need to get out ..."

"I can't," said Beth. Barrett and Paula glared at her. "Honest ... really. I promised Alicia Whitestone I would go to Mellville with her right after lunch to look at the theater down there. I'm designing some sets for the play they're putting on for Christmas. Honest. They're depending on me. We're running out of time. Thanksgiving break is coming up, so we'll lose an entire week, and then the play starts the week before Christmas."

Beth checked her watch. "I have to go. She's outside Weatherly Hall waiting for me." She looked at Pappy and saw in his eyes what she'd missed all these years. "I'm really sorry. I would love to go. Let's do it next week. For sure. Call me."

Monday, November 17

⊙ ⊙ ⊙ ⊙

Pappy was excited about going home for Thanksgiving. It had been almost three months since he'd seen his family. Fall was his favorite time of year in Upstate New York. Next week there would be roast turkey and pumpkin pie and candied sweet potatoes and stuffing and gravy and mashed potatoes and apple cider and eggnog. He'd see all his Amsterdam classmates. And best of all, he would see his mom and dad. He could hear the sadness every time they spoke on weekends. It would be an emotional homecoming.

For all the notoriety, Pappy still had no great love for football. He wanted to help the team to the championship that was within their grasp, but he knew this would be his only season, unless he managed another fractured skull. There were even rumors that Fred Holmes was ready to return. Even though Andrew was longer and more accurate, Holmes had won several games for the Titans in his four years, and Pappy felt he deserved to have his job back.

Between karate and weight lifting, Andrew was a rock. His legs had never felt stronger, and his shots on the handball court had incredible snap and velocity. Most of his clothes no longer fit, and he wore the same few things repeatedly.

He was also zeroing in on solving his unknown compound in chemistry lab. He no longer needed help from Karl Zindell, which risked catching some hideous and deforming plague involving either worms or parasites.

English and Spanish were solid As, and he had to plan his schedule for next semester. Calculus, physics, biology, and Chemistry 102. Professor Wager urged him to do more writing, but it didn't fit the rigorous premed course requirements.

Paula was back at the hospital for X-rays, blood count, and EKG. There was no point telling her now, but there had been additional damage to her heart. Time might reverse some tissue loss, but the treatments had taken their toll. On the plus side, the rest of her body was recovering rapidly. Pain and numbness were minimal. All her hair, including eyebrows, was gone, but new sprouts were appearing. The dark, sunken eyes now shined, and the smile was back for her doctors and her young man.

Dorothy Cole slept all day Saturday and most of Sunday. Then it was back to work, and she was delighted to be there.

Tuesday, November 18

◉ ◎ ◉ ◎

Todd Hancock had just spoken with the soccer commissioner for the conference, confirming what he'd already figured. The Titans had an outside chance to make the playoffs. But first they had to beat Buckingham on Wednesday. That would necessitate a makeup game Saturday between Stratton State and Clarkson for the latter to clinch the eighth position. At the same time, Bainbridge would play Kirkwood. There was no way for Clarkson to beat Stratton, so the Titans' game would decide the last spot.

Should he tell his team about their chances before the Buckingham game? If they played at their current level, it would be no contest. But knowing they could go from an epic losing season the year before to one of the elite teams in the conference might cause them to try too hard. This was as much superstition as psychology.

Pappy tested and moved up to green belt in karate. In this ranking system, there were nine positions below black belt: three white, three green, and three brown. Then there were ten levels of black, one being the lowest and ten the highest. Yoshi was a second degree, or *dan,* and one of the best in Japan. Andrew passed all three katas, and then was judged on kicks, punches, and blocks for form. In two months, he'd moved three levels. His speed and balance, while not near those of Yoshi's (or Barrett's), had increased tenfold.

335

That night, the class picked up a new student. Sporting a brown belt, Bob Moore had seen Yoshi's old notice on the Union bulletin board. Six-three and lanky, he towered above the class, particularly his instructor, so Yoshi decided to test his newest pupil with his latest promote, Pappy.

Andrew had never fought anyone but his instructor. Other than watching him kick and punch for an hour, he had no idea what to expect of his opponent—or himself. Both bowed and took their stances. Figuring the best defense was a good offense, Pappy attacked, throwing three punches, the third striking Moore's nose with a solid crunch, and the big man flew onto his backside, blood flowing. Andrew stood stunned, feeling terrible but exhilarated. Bob seemed to be a nice guy, had never done anything to deserve it, yet Andrew had punched him out. Paxton apologized profusely, but Moore waved it off. Yoshi's prize pupil had arrived.

Wednesday, November 19

⊚   ⊚   ⊚   ⊚

Hard to believe it was the last game of the year. Everyone was fired up. Word had spread around campus, so there would be more than the usual twelve spectators. It was a beautiful fall day, if not frigid. There was frost at sunrise, but game time it promised to be a balmy forty-six and sunny. Paula was bundling up, and Brenda and Beth brought extra blankets just in case.

The team gathered at Roberts Hall and ran down together. Fans and locals were honking their horns as they passed, and there were almost two hundred people there when the Buckingham Scarlet Knights arrived, with more on the way. Today Pappy would be there, as would all the football coaches and many of the players. Practice was cut short so they could watch the second half.

All eleven Titan starters stood at midfield watching the Scarlet Knights, but they had no stars. It was like looking back three months. Then this would have been an even match. Now Bain was competitive with almost any school in the conference.

Bainbridge kicked off and blitzed down the field. Driver, at left half, passed wide to Millwood, back to Driver, to Santander, who stepped over the ball, tapped one short dribble, and hooked the ball into the upper right corner from twenty yards. One to zero, Titans.

Fans were trickling in all the time, and the far side was lined almost end to end. The linesman had to keep pushing them back as they edged forward to watch the action. Barrett and Nakano controlled the middle, dishing the ball left and right. The Eagles' forwards were intimidated by Brian's booming clears and the harassing Titans' defenders.

Santander converted a penalty kick off a handball at the twenty-three-minute mark. Caldwell did the same, at thirty-nine minutes, off the same infraction. By the half, their opponents were clearly defeated. Three to zero.

Finally, Hancock called them together. "This is the last game of the season. You have come a long way as players, as individuals, and as a team. I want to thank you all. Seniors, I can't tell you how much your leadership has meant to this team. I hope you have the same success in life that you have realized here. There are only forty-five minutes left. Make the most of them. They will be gone before you know it."

The Chiefs came out breathing fire. Penny scored twice in five minutes on breakaways, and Hancock pulled all the starters who weren't seniors. Final score, 7-0.

"Great effort," said Hancock. "See you all tomorrow at practice." He turned and walked away and then came back, smiling at the quizzical looks. "Because you won today, Saturday we play Kirkwood for the final conference playoff spot." The team exploded into cheers, together with the fans that had stayed. "If we win and Stratton State beats Clarkson, we're in … Let's have a good practice tomorrow."

Thursday, November 20

◉ ◉ ◉ ◉

Thursday evening everyone was wound up about the playoff against Kirkwood. Compared to this, the undefeated football team held little excitement for Pappy, and while he felt proud for the team, he felt empty not being able to play. Louis Paxton and Otto Millwood, Tim's father, were making the long drive from Amsterdam to attend the game, and they planned to be at Bainbridge just after supper. Both had taken every opportunity to watch their sons at Amsterdam. They were not going to miss a contest that might put Bainbridge in the conference playoffs, and Pappy's dad never thought he'd see his son play football.

Barrett and the team were at the field house being briefed about Saturday's travel schedule. It was a morning game, and then the players had the option of coming back to campus or staying at Kirkwood. The football team was also playing the Black Knights, and the Titans relished the opportunity to crush their hated rivals and their vulgar fans.

Afterward, Brian wandered up to the top floor to see who was in the weight room, and he went through a few sets of bench press and curls with Joe Tagliarino. He switched to the leg machines and began to sweat after a few minutes. Finally, he realized it would be dumb to pull a muscle before the Kirkwood game, so he headed back downstairs.

He stopped by to watch the end of Pappy's karate class and stood in the doorway until Yoshi waved him over. They shook hands and tried to make small talk, but Ayabe's English limited the conversation, so they stood, arms folded, watching the students perform the katas. The doors of the big old gym were open to air out after basketball practice, and it was rapidly cooling in the crisp fall air. Barrett went down to the locker room and asked one of the equipment managers to lend him a dry shirt to wear back to the dorm. All that was available was a football practice jersey, so he promised to return it the following day and walked out the side door and across the parking lot.

"Hey, soccer player. Barrett … or whatever your name is." Brian looked to the left and saw Delfino headed toward him at a jog. His face was fixed in the same snarl as when they'd first met weeks before on the football practice field.

"Where did you get that damn jersey?" he demanded, reaching for Barrett's arm.

Pointing his thumb back at the gym, he said, "I just borrow—"

"It belongs to the football team. Take it off—now!" said Delfino, his voice rising as he tightened his grip.

Barrett's temper flashed for a moment, but the coach's face was beet red, and Barrett chuckled.

"Wipe that grin off your smart-ass face and give me the damn jersey … now!" He grabbed Barrett's right sleeve, and Brian pulled back, causing the shorter man to lose his balance and fall forward. Now angry and embarrassed, he stood up and took a wild swing at Barrett's head. Brian easily avoided the punch, but Delfino followed with a sweeping left, just grazing Barrett's shoulder. That was enough. Barrett squared, caught the shorter man with a chopping right to the left eye, a left to the right cheek, and—stepping forward—a crushing straight right to the bridge of the nose, knocking Delfino spread eagle five feet back onto the ground. His eyes watered, and blood gushed from both nostrils. He lay stunned, his aggression now turned to fear. But Barrett was done, now realizing he had slugged a coach and faculty member.

There was a shuffle of feet and a swish, and Ned Burler brought his textbook crashing down on the left side of Barrett's skull. Brian collapsed on all fours, barely remaining conscious. He struggled to get to his feet, dazed. Burler pulled him up, pinning Brian's arms behind his back.

Rattigan's fist dug into Barrett's ribcage, and he buckled, more out of reflex, as the pain felt far off in the distance. Again and again he pounded Barrett's chest and stomach.

"Yeah, yeah," chortled Burler. "Smash the son of a bitch."

Delfino was now recovering quickly, and he saw that the two were out of control. "Stop! Stop, goddamn it," he yelled.

"Smash that pretty boy's face!" urged Burler. Rattigan raised his aim.

A hand came across, stopping Rattigan's fist cold. His head turned as Pappy's knee came up and across, catching Rattigan square in the gut. The air whooshed out of his lungs, and he collapsed to his knees. Paxton's left fist pounded Rattigan's right ear, and he fell back stunned.

Burler turned and had just begun to release Barrett when a right foot knifed into the outside of the big man's left thigh, just above the knee, where the bone has little muscle for protection. He dropped as if shot by a gun, the pain firing up his spine like an electric shock. Now he and Yoshi Ayabe were eye-to-eye. Before Burler could react, the smaller man landed a left foot snap kick to the solar plexus, a jarring right to the left ear, a devastating hook to the bridge of the nose, and another right to the jaw. Yoshi's left arm swung yet again but was stopped by Andrew Paxton's hand.

"Kip yowr timpor," said Paxton. Yoshi's rage subsided.

Both looked down at Burler, who was unable to breathe. He'd pissed his pants, and he feared for his life.

"I'll get Barrett," said Pappy, lifting his friend to his feet. "Fix those two guys." Yoshi went first to Burler, jamming his knee indelicately into the middle of his back and pulling his shoulders. The big man gasped and fell backward. Yoshi did the same to Rattigan, who was now on the verge of blacking out, and then pushed him on his face on the asphalt. Paxton, Barrett's arm draped over his shoulder and moaning in pain, looked down at Delfino, who sat bleeding and looking ashamed.

Yoshi took the other arm, and they walked across the parking lot. Pappy turned first toward the health center but stopped. This was a violent attack on campus involving football players and a coach. A neutral site might be better to receive treatment. Pappy's father and Otto Millwood would be there at any time, and he wanted to them to hear what happened before the football coaches, or anyone else, could invent the "official" story.

"We better get him to the hospital," said Pappy. Yoshi wasn't sure he understood, but they were heading east down Cecil Street when a car pulled up beside them. Coach Sam Bolger rolled down the window.

"In here," he said, getting out and opening the back door. "We'll take him to the hospital." Paxton hesitated, but Brian was badly hurt, and he didn't know where else to turn for help. They laid him across the backseat. Pappy thanked Yoshi and told him to go back to the dorm and say nothing to anyone about what had just happened. He'd come back later and report on Barrett's condition. Yoshi nodded, turned, and walked toward his dorm. They sped down the street and turned left toward Spencer Mercy. Barrett was coming out of his stupor, and he groaned with every bump and turn.

"We'll be there in a couple of minutes," said Bolger. He looked over at Andrew Paxton, who was unsure of the driver's intentions.

"I saw everything," he said, bowing his head slightly. "I was in my office, but it was all over before I got down there. Don't worry. I didn't hear what started it, but I saw Delfino throw the first punch. He got what he deserved."

Nobody said anything until they pulled up to the emergency entrance at the hospital. Pappy went in to get help and came back with two nurses and a gurney. They recognized Sam Bolger and immediately called the staff physician. Barrett was wheeled off to an examining room, and there was a buzz of activity. One of the nurses spoke first to Bolger for about five minutes and then came over to Pappy. He gave them Barrett's name and contact information for his family. Paxton also briefly described the attack. She thanked him and asked that he remain. As much as he hated and feared hospitals, Pappy wasn't going anywhere.

The waiting room was small and stark, with two nondescript pictures on the wall and some inexpensive lounge furniture. The magazines were mostly old issues of *Reader's Digest* and *Life*, but Pappy could only sit with his face in his hands. His first semester in college and he'd been involved in a violent attack with students and a coach. His best friend was beaten and was in the hospital. Suspension. Expulsion. He hadn't done anything wrong, but who knew what stories were being told back on campus? In the past few weeks, he'd come to know Sam Bolger as honest and decent. But Delfino was a faculty member and coach. Would he and the university protect him?

He looked at his watch. It was well after nine. His father and Otto Millwood should be there by now, and they would be looking for him. He asked to use a phone and called Tim. He explained the situation and told him to bring their dads to the emergency room as soon as they arrived. The parents had just walked into Tim's room. "We're on our way," he said, and hung up.

Pappy started to call Paula but hesitated. He didn't want to worry her in her weakened state. He had little to tell her about Barrett's condition. On the other hand, word of the attack would be all over campus in a matter of hours. Better she heard from him, so he dialed her number.

"Beth, this is Pappy," he stumbled.

"Hi," she said.

"Something's happened, and I need a favor," he said.

"Okay, sure," she replied.

"I'm at the hospital. Barrett has been hurt. I need you to go down the hall and tell Paula that he's all right so she hears it before the story is all over campus."

Pappy kept the explanation brief. "He may have some broken ribs and a concussion. No one has said anything yet, but there are a lot of doctors and nurses running around."

"I'll get my car and bring her to the hospital," said Littlefield.

"I don't know how long we'll be here—or if she's up to it," he replied.

"I know her, and I know what I'd do," said Littlefield. "I almost came up to the hospital when you had your operation."

"Okay, see how she feels. We're in the emergency room." He told her bye and hung up.

Tim came through the sliding glass doors with Andrew's dad and Otto Millwood. A rush of emotion hit Pappy, and tears came to his eyes. They shook hands, and then Andrew hugged his dad. Right now, it would feel really good to be home.

Both men took off their topcoats and hats, laying them over a lone metal chair in the hallway. Weary from the almost eight-hour drive, both dads, in their late fifties, now looked their ages.

They were also visibly on edge, having heard just enough of the story from Tim to be fuming. Andrew recounted the attack in detail, and they were as stunned as they were angry.

As Andrew was describing how Bolger came along, Otto Millwood had heard enough. He walked past the nurses' station, pushed through the swinging doors, and saw Barrett lying back, flanked by two doctors and a nurse who were asking questions and taking down information.

Barrett smiled through partially opened eyes.

"Hi, Doc," said Brian, trying to sit up.

"Lay still, big boy," he replied, coming over and putting his hand on Barrett's arm. He turned toward the others.

"I'm Doctor Otto Millwood," he said, leaning over and lifting each of Barrett's eyelids with his right thumb. Satisfied, he stood up. "I am an orthopedic surgeon from Buffalo, New York. Brian is a friend of the family. I understand he was beaten and struck in the head."

"Yes, that's what we've been told by Coach Bolger and Brian's friend Andrew," said Dr. Joe Trevino. "I'm head of internal medicine here at Spencer Mercy, and this is our orthopedist, Dr. Steve Fox, whom I called in to consult." They shook hands. "We've done a preliminary examination. The boy is a little groggy, but his pupils are responsive, and there is no evidence of subdural hematoma or other brain injury. Reflexes are normal. We are about to run him down to X-ray to confirm—and also to check his ribs. They're severely bruised, but there doesn't appear to be a puncture to the lungs or damage to the spleen or other organs. The blood work should be ready in about an hour. You're welcome to stay with him or wait outside with the others."

"Thank you," said Otto, "I'll report to his friends. I also need to call his parents. Let me know as soon as the X-rays and lab are ready, would you, please?"

"Certainly," said Trevino.

Otto Millwood went back out to the reception area, and it was evident that his agitation had subsided, to the relief of all there.

"Ribs and a possible concussion. That's all we know for now," said the doc, addressing the group. "He's having some discomfort breathing, but his eyes are clear, and there doesn't appear to be any internal damage. We'll know more shortly."

He turned to Pappy. "So let me get this straight for when I call his parents. He was attacked by a coach and then two football players?"

"Yes, sir, that's correct," replied Pappy.

"And Brian did nothing to provoke the attack?" asked Dr. Millwood, leaning forward to make sure he got the right story. "I know he sometimes has, shall we say, trouble with authority figures."

"No, sir," replied Andrew emphatically. "We saw the whole thing. Coach Delfino was screaming at Brian to take off the football jersey. When he wouldn't, the coach tried to rip the shirt off him and then threw two punches at Brian. That's when Brian decked him. Then the football players showed up. Burler hit Brian in the head with a book, and they started to beat him, but Yoshi—my karate instructor—and I pulled them off. I thought Yoshi was going to kill the guy."

"So you knew them?"

"Yes, sir." Andrew nodded. "We had had problems with them before, even when we first arrived at school. Coach Delfino threw us off the football practice field the first day we got here for playing soccer there.

"Brian had a run-in with the bigger one, Ned Burler, down at Fitzgerald's last weekend," continued Andrew. "Brian's girlfriend, Paula, has cancer, and her hair fell out. She was wearing a wig, and Burler pulled it off. Brian went nuts and knocked him out cold."

Dr. Millwood's look of doubt was now gone.

"None of it was our fault, honest," said Andrew. "Everyone knows Delfino is a jerk. Coach Bolger apologized for what he did when we were riding over here. He saw it all."

The girls arrived. Paula was pale and walking with Littlefield's help, in obvious distress from the news. Her wig had been put on in haste and was slightly turned.

Littlefield, on the other hand, looked beautiful.

"Where is he?" asked Paula. "How is he?"

"I'm Dr. Millwood, Tim's dad," said Otto. "It looks like nothing serious, but we'll know in a while. Everyone go back to the waiting room, and I'll check on progress."

Otto went through the green doors, and the others went in and sat down. Tim was talking to Beth and Paula; Pappy sat with his dad.

"It's good to see you, boy," said Louis, putting his hand on his son's knee. "Sorry this had to happen. You've had a rough first semester. Is your head okay now?"

"Yeah, I'm fine. Here's the incision," said Andrew, turning his head and lifting his hair. "My hair's grown back, so you almost can't tell. They told me they were only going to shave a small section but then did half my head. I wore bandages for a month, until it grew back."

Louis looked at his son and smiled. He was so proud. It was just good to see him well.

They talked about everyone at home, the weather, and Andrew's classes; but every few moments, Louis noticed Beth glancing over at Andrew and then looking away as if being caught. And she was smiling.

Dr. Millwood reappeared.

"No concussion. Three bruised ribs. No internal bleeding or organ damage. They're going to keep him overnight, which is fine. I called his parents, and they're driving in on Saturday for the weekend. He's coming around, and when they told him he won't be playing Saturday, he almost leapt out of the bed. They're about to give him something to sleep and transfer him to a room, so if you want to see him, you'd better go in now."

Paula stood up, with Beth's help, and they all went through the green doors. Barrett was propped up in the bed, and the doctors were wrapping his chest in gauze and tape. He smiled at Paula and then grimaced when the bandages were pulled tight.

His eyelids were heavy from the painkillers. Paula came over and took his hand. The others waved and then withdrew back outside the door.

"Aren't you tired of this place?" She smiled and kissed him passionately. "Time for me to take care of you," she whispered while hugging him. "Want a piggyback ride?"

Back at the nurses' station, Andrew noticed that Coach Bolger was gone.

"So how are you doing?" asked Dr. Millwood. "What's this about your having a fractured jaw?" He moved closer and put both hands on each side of Andrew's face, feeling around the joint. He frowned.

"Yeah, I got hit in the zygoma," said Andrew.

"But that was back in September, wasn't it?" he asked, still examining the jaw.

"Yeah," said Andrew.

Otto put his hands down. "Hmm. I see the incision, but I don't feel any callus."

"Callus?" asked Andrew. "Like a corn?"

"No, in the case of a broken bone, callus is where the break heals. There should be a rise or lump … and you've been playing football but not soccer?" asked Otto, frowning.

"Yes."

"Well, how does that work? How bad was the break? Never mind." His brow crinkled, and he shook his head. "If it was bad enough to keep you out for the season, you shouldn't be on any athletic field, helmet or no helmet. But a greenstick fracture should be healed in four to five weeks if the joint wasn't involved. Sometimes even quicker. Who did the operation?" Again he felt Andrew's jaw.

"Doctor Hardwell," said Andrew.

"The GP at the health center?" he asked. "Did a fractured zygoma? How long were you in the hospital?"

"I went in one night and came back to campus the next day right after the operation."

"Something's wrong here," said Dr. Millwood. "Your zygomatic arch and mandibular joint seem normal." He looked away. "What is a GP doing performing surgery on a face bone?" he asked no one in particular. "Most of them shouldn't even be setting a simple fracture. And he cleared you to play football but not soccer?"

Andrew nodded.

"When you got hurt, didn't they say your X-rays were normal at the hospital?" asked Dr. Millwood.

"Yes," said Andrew, now feeling uneasy.

"I'd like to see your X-rays. I'll bet your files aren't here, though. Probably at the health center. Lou, if you and Andrew will permit me, I want to find out what's going on. Let's go see this doctor in the morning and take a look at Andrew's case."

But Andrew now had a different thought … and plan. He glanced at his watch.

"Dad, I need to go over to the dorm to change my clothes," he said, starting for the door. "Can I meet you down at the student union—and maybe we can get a pizza or something?"

"I'll come with you," said his father, starting after him.

"No, you go over and check in to your hotel and meet us at the Union in an hour." Pappy grabbed Tim Millwood by the arm, and both went out the door. Once clear of where their parents could see them, they broke into a dead run toward campus.

Ben Rattigan snuck back into his room, avoiding any inquiring eyes, although there were few visible signs of his encounter with Andrew Paxton. He sat on his bed, wondering what to do next. Would the police come for him? Would Barrett press charges? Maybe he could make up a story with Delfino and Burler. Maybe they could say that they saw Barrett attack Delfino and tried to help. Then Paxton and the Jap jumped them. But Rattigan had left Burler still on his knees, bleeding, and Delfino had walked off in the direction of the field house.

So he was alone. He went to pick up the phone, but whom could he call? How could he tell anyone a five-four Japanese guy beat up a six-five football player? He was sure Barrett had broken ribs and a concussion.

Maybe worse. He might be arrested. Or expelled. His lone protector, Delfino, might try to save himself by saying he tried to stop Rattigan and Burler from attacking Barrett.

He got up and paced back and forth. Maybe he should pack and go home. His football career was over, as was his janitor's job—and his lucrative business of using his set of keys to steal exams and sell them to students.

He lay down on the bed but sat upright every time he thought he heard people coming.

Then there was a knock on the door. Rattigan popped up but stood silently. He heard the clack of someone using a coat hanger to pick the lock. The door swung open, and there stood Tim Millwood, Don Penny, and Andrew Paxton.

Pappy pushed forward, Penny at his side, in the mood for a fight.

"Get your keys," said Paxton, now staring directly into Rattigan's face. "Get your goddamn keys!" His voice was now rising, and Rattigan was just plain scared.

"What keys …?" Rattigan started. "Where do you want to go?"

"The health center," said Pappy.

"It's still open," said Rattigan, reaching under the desk and pulling out the hidden set of keys.

"We're not going in the front door," said Paxton.

The two fathers sat in the student union lobby. It was now after eleven, and most of the building was shutting down. Food service had stopped, so they'd have to find someplace off campus to eat with the boys.

"Andrew must be exhausted," said Otto. "I hope he can sleep in tomorrow."

"I don't know his class schedule," replied Louis.

"He's a fine young man," said Otto. "He's the leader of those boys."

Suddenly, there were three heads coming up the front steps. Penny, Millwood, and Paxton came over, and Andrew handed a manila folder to Otto.

"My file," he said with an air of satisfaction.

Otto took it. "I won't ask … Let's go find somewhere else to eat, and I'll take a look at all this."

Penny left, but the other two boys got in the backseat of the rental car, and they traveled south on Freemont Avenue. Donello's was the only place open. The tiny hole-in-the-wall freestanding building with bright lights had the overwhelming aroma of pizza sauce, pepperoni, and oregano. The tables were few and Spartan, and there were two boys stacking pizza boxes for delivery.

They ordered and then sat down to watch the doc look at the file. He scowled.

"Here is the report from the hospital in Junction," he said, turning pages. "They had an orthopedic surgeon look at the films, and there was nothing there. Significant concussion … And here is the blood work and other information from Spencer Mercy … Did you have another X-ray before your surgery?"

"No. He said they had missed the fracture on the ones from Junction," said Andrew.

"Here is their set of films … Yup." He looked up and pointed to the X-ray. "This has been altered. You can see it on each view. Here, here, and here," he said, now leaning back. "I wonder what the doctors at Junction would say. This is damn serious."

He looked over at Louis Paxton, who was now extremely upset. "Lou, you and I better pay a visit …" He turned to Andrew. "Where *do* we take this? I don't know who's involved or who had knowledge."

"Coach Hancock will know what to do," said Tim, and Andrew nodded.

"I'll go see him first thing in the morning," said the doc. "Does he have an office?"

"Yeah," said Tim, "at the field house on the second floor."

"What if Delfino or Coach Bolger get to him first?" asked Tim.

"I talked briefly with Bolger at the hospital," said Otto. "He seemed genuinely shaken and upset by the attack on Brian, and he knows that we all are fully aware of what happened. He said he intended to take care of the matter and to call Barrett's parents personally. I believe he'll be well into the problem by the time we get there." Otto looked at Louis Paxton, who had a stern look on his face. "If he changes his story between now and the morning, we have this second bombshell to drop on him about your having unnecessary surgery and then being allowed to play football but not soccer. I hope it's a surprise. I hope Bolger wasn't in on this, for his sake. I've heard nothing but good things about him. We've no desire to destroy the football program here."

Andrew shook his head. It was all some bad dream.

Friday, November 21

⊚ ⊚ ⊚ ⊚

Wild rumors were racing across campus. Bolger had moved quickly, notifying the conference that he'd dismissed one of his coaches and two players. He set a meeting with the dean and the school's legal counsel for eleven in the morning. Mel Delfino had already cleaned out his desk.

Just after ten in the morning, Dr. Raymond Hardwell was deciding whether to go to the health center before noon. Friday mornings were always slow. Monday was the busy day, when everyone wanted to be excused from class or needed treatment for some mishap over the weekend. The doorbell rang. Must be a neighbor looking for his dog or something. He peered out the window, and standing on the front porch was Sam Bolger.

"Good morning, Sam," said Hardwell cheerfully, but his attitude changed quickly when his friend said nothing. They went into the kitchen. He handed Hardwell a large brown envelope with the name "Paxton" handwritten on the outside. Then he stood, arms crossed, while the doctor's mind raced.

"I, uh, don't ...," stammered Hardwell.

"Before you start," said Bolger, his voice rising, "I had a visit this morning from Andrew Paxton's father and an orthopedic surgeon. Those X-rays have been altered."

"Altered?" he asked. "That's—"

"Stop! Stop it, Ray," said the coach. "They were examined by orthopedists in Junction—and now here. There was no fracture. You performed unnecessary surgery, which I'm told you were not qualified to do." Hardwell now looked away.

Bolger continued. "This is beyond belief. To say Paxton's father is upset is a colossal understatement." Again the doctor stood silent.

Finally, Hardwell looked at him plaintively. "I wanted to help. You needed a kicker. I wanted to make it up to you. I owed you."

Bolger shook his head in disbelief. "So you cut open this kid's head for no medical reason? Ray, we are a D III school. The rules allow for Paxton to play soccer *and* kick for us."

Hardwell was stunned and sullen.

"I have to meet with the dean and the lawyers at eleven," said Bolger. "Have your resignation in his office by then. Don't go to the health center. You're done."

Raymond Hardwell's Lincoln was conspicuously absent from its parking space behind the health center. The university hastily called Dr. Joe Trevino to fill in.

Andrew Paxton woke to the phone ringing. It was his dad. "It's just after nine," said Louis. "I guess you missed your class. We met with Coach Hancock at eight—and then Bolger. Coach Delfino has been suspended, and Rattigan and Burler have been kicked off the team. The dean will probably ask them to leave the school. How long will it take you to get ready?" asked Louis. "You need to shower and shave."

"I'll be ready in half an hour," said Andrew, now gathering his razor, soap, and towel.

"We'll meet you in the Union."

Pappy hung up, and immediately the phone rang again.

"Hello," he said, thinking it was his father, that maybe he'd forgotten something.

"Pappy, it's Beth ..."

"Hi," he said. Silence on both ends.

"How are you? How's Barrett?" she asked quickly.

"They should release him this morning," said Pappy.

"I know," she replied. "Paula and I stayed there until about eleven. I thought I was going to have to carry her home." She stopped, now embarrassed. If she'd stayed after Pappy left, why was she asking about Barrett?

But Pappy passed it over. "I need to go meet with my dad. Can I call you back?" he said.

"Oh, sorry, I'll let you go," she said, and she began to hang up.

"Thanks for coming last night … for bringing Paula," he blurted. "That was really great. And thanks for lending her your wig …" He didn't know what else to say, but now he didn't want her to go.

"I wish I could do more," said Littlefield. "She's nice. I don't know what it would be like to be so sick."

Silence again.

"Well, I better go," said Pappy. "Call you later." He hung up before she could say good-bye, realizing he'd acted like a doofus *again*, and then raced down the hall to the men's room.

Andrew, his dad, and Dr. Millwood went to the hospital to spring Barrett. The doctors cleared him to be discharged, and after Otto visited briefly with the staff, they drove over to the local Howard Johnson's for lunch. Brian was still drugged and in obvious pain, and he walked slightly stooped from the bandage across the ribs. His huge appetite was absent, and his head drooped through much of the meal.

Dr. Millwood had called Brian's parents late the night before to assure them he was all right. The Barretts thanked him for being there but decided to drive to Bainbridge Friday afternoon rather than waiting—just for their own peace of mind. They also wanted to see Brian play soccer and to meet this girl who had turned their Don Juan of a son into a babbling fool.

Louis Paxton could see the troubled look on his son's face. It was a lot for a man of fifty-eight, who had never gone past high school, to accept all that had happened on a presumably safe college campus. And to be attacked by a coach and two football players was even more repulsive. Then the campus doctor had performed unnecessary surgery and falsified records. Louis's first instinct was to take his child home. He'd assumed Andrew was through playing for Bolger, but his son said although the head coach should have done something about Delfino long ago, he'd handled the matter quickly and completely. And Dr. Millwood had satisfied himself that Andrew was perfectly healthy.

They met again with Sam Bolger and Todd Hancock at two o'clock. Delfino and Hardwell were gone, as were Rattigan and Burler. Andrew and Brian wouldn't press charges as long as they and Yoshi were absolved of any liability for the fight. Bolger called the conference and cleared Andrew to play soccer, and Hancock added him to the roster. It would be bittersweet for the team to regain its original leader but lose its best—and now most inspired—athlete on the eve of its most important game.

Food, another nap, and some additional drugs, and by six o'clock, Brian Barrett was ready to wage his campaign to play the following day against Kirkwood. "No" wasn't an option.

Saturday, November 22

⊙ ⊙ ⊙ ⊙

Pappy and Barrett were at the team breakfast at seven. Andrew had already visited the head three times and, to use his own words, "was wound tighter than a banjo in an igloo."

Still taking painkillers, Brian's stomach was upset and his head groggy, but he was determined to play. Coach Hancock took one look at Barrett and shook his head.

"No way," he said, leaning over the table for emphasis. "It isn't worth it … End of story." Brian stood up defiantly but immediately collapsed, grimacing in pain.

"You gotta let him come with us," said Pappy. "Tim's dad will be there, so there'll be a doctor present. He doesn't have to play. We're going to crush these bastards anyway."

"All right," said Hancock. "But he's riding in my car. Both of you."

"And, Coach," said Andrew. "I think the guys who got you this far should play …"

"Too late," interrupted Hancock. "Nakano and five other guys came to me this morning and said you should start in their place. They didn't know about Barrett, but I told them that they were too valuable and we wouldn't have gotten this far without them. They then replied in unison that you would've been there except for the lying doctor … You'll start in Barrett's spot."

It was a two-hour drive to Kirkwood, and they had to play at eleven,

356

as the football game was at two. The cars took off in a caravan, traveling as a team.

The last half hour of the drive was in total silence. It had been a long three months, starting with the loss of the seniors, then the debacle at Kirkwood, and finally losing Pappy at Junction. Just when everyone thought the season was over, the skill and experience of Roland Santander and the fiery leadership of Barrett resurrected the team. No one could have dreamed that a first-year coach, in a sport he'd never played, could turn this collection of ex–football players and freshmen into a playoff team.

They pulled up next to the field, gathered together, and took a lap around the field. The Knights were already there, and McNair smirked as they went past.

"Hi, ladies," he called. "Glad you could make it. You're in for a long ride home."

There was no reply. The Titans warmed up, and Paxton and Santander took penalty and corner kicks. Then the referee blew his whistle. It was Jay Cooper.

Hancock looked over in disbelief. Cooper beckoned both coaches. Hancock didn't move.

"Coach, I need you and your captain over here right now for the coin toss," said Cooper.

Hancock folded his arms.

"Because of the football game, we're going to start early. Coach, send your captain over here or I'll have the coin toss without him …" McNair was there, but the Titans stood waiting for Hancock to signal.

He walked over toward the referee and the Knights' coach. "You're not the referee. Sam Bolger disqualified you, and Billy Hughes is to officiate." The coach looked away.

"I received no such notice, and Mr. Hughes isn't here, so we'll start." He turned to McNair. "Call it in the air."

"Heads." The coin landed tails up.

"Tails. Bainbridge, your choice."

"We'll take that end," said Hancock, pointing downwind to the west.

"We are officially playing this game under protest." Cooper turned and walked away, making sure Hancock could get no closer.

"Coach, set your team," he said with his back turned.

Hancock called them over. "Let's go, guys. This jackass is going to do everything he can—"

Paxton interrupted. "Coach, he can't stop us. They can't stop us."

They trotted out to midfield for the kickoff.

Cooper moved to the midline and then turned toward Andrew Paxton. "What's your name, son?" he asked in a serious tone.

"Andrew Paxton."

He was looking at some paper he had in his hand. "Mr. Paxton, I don't have you on the roster."

"I was …"

"You're not on this list." Cooper turned quickly to Hancock. "Coach, either remove this player or I'll give him, and you, an ejection, and you will play the game short."

Hancock started out on the field. "Bolger called you and the conference and added—"

"Coach, stay off the field," said Cooper. "I told you I received no such notice. This man is ineligible. Kirkwood to kick off."

Hancock waved to Pappy, who raced off, and Knight took his place. It was a good thing Barrett's ribs were so bad, for there was no doubt he would have beaten Cooper to death.

The Black Knights kicked off, and the Titans tried to reorganize without Barrett or Paxton. The defense tightened, but without Brian, the Bain fullbacks had to sag farther and farther back. Kirkwood scored after ten minutes, when McNair pushed off on Landon in the penalty area and punched the ball into the far corner. At the twenty-four-minute mark, McNair converted a penalty kick off a handball. The third goal was a good play, with the Black Knights' outside left scoring on a corner kick. Throughout the half, McNair continued mocking and taunting the Titans. At one point, Cooper chastised him so all could hear, no doubt wanting to appear unbiased. Meanwhile, Hancock and the others fumed on the sidelines. Landon received a warning for asking a question of the referee, despite being the team captain.

The Kirkwood fans were in fine form. Beth Littlefield had brought Paula Cole, Brenda Sykes, and Sue Walker to the game, and they were now enduring insults, threats, and spitting from the Knights' faithful. At one point, they almost retreated to the cars as rocks and dirt were hurled in their direction. Bainbridge's players also endured a hail of missiles.

At the forty-minute mark, the Kirkwood left wing crossed the ball to McNair, who collided with David Nakano. Indignant, McNair pushed Nakano from behind. Cooper came running over and began pulling out his book. He was about to signal a foul on Nakano, and as he pointed to the penalty line, he looked up. Standing behind the goal, arms folded, was a furious Sam Bolger, with Billy Hughes. Cooper stopped cold, and his book fell onto the ground.

"Uhh." He turned away, clearing his throat, picking up his book, and holding his book in the air. "Number twelve, Kirkwood," he announced, pointing to where the kick was to be taken. He then ran toward the center line. McNair cursed and spat in Nakano's direction. The kick went to midfield, and play continued back and forth until the whistle ended the half.

Bolger and Hughes were at midfield in an instant, along with Hancock, forming a ring around Cooper. The Kirkwood coach went with his team away from the field.

"What in the hell do you think you're doing?" said Bolger, now screaming in Cooper's face.

"Uhhhh ... I never got the message ...," stammered Cooper.

"Like hell you didn't! If you say you didn't get it, then how'd you know there was one? You lying son of a bitch. Get off the field now! Now! You're suspended pending a conference review, but I promise you your days as a referee are done."

Cooper began to say something but turned and walked away instead.

"Coach Start," Bolger yelled, "Coach, come over here."

"Okay," he called, trotting over. Guilt was written across his face.

"I'm not going to get into a discussion with you as to why the game started early—and why you didn't wait for Mr. Hughes."

"Mr. Cooper said …," he started weakly.

"If this was the first time, Coach, I might listen to you. But this crap with you and Cooper is disgusting. I called him last night and left word that Paxton was to be reinstated, and that Hughes was to referee this game. I also left the same message at your office. I am head of soccer referees for the conference, and Mr. Cooper is done, so you'd better find yourself another boy. I've no jurisdiction over you, or your position here, but there will be a full report filed with the conference. For now, Mr. Hughes will referee the second half. The game is being played under protest. And Mr. Paxton will be allowed to play. Any questions?" He didn't wait for an answer. "Good, then let's play."

Hancock huddled them together. "The first half is gone," said Hancock. "There's nothing we can do except give these guys the game of their lives for forty-five minutes. That's plenty of time if we play all out. Pappy, you can play anywhere on the field you want. Call out the switches. Move to the open spot. And contest *every* ball. Don't assume your teammate is going to do it for you. Let's set a goal this half—twenty-five shots on goal. If we lose this game, it's a long time until next season." He looked at his players' faces, but their minds were already out on the field. "Let's go," he added quietly.

Andrew Paxton jogged to the middle of the field. It had been a long time since he last played. He looked over the opposition but didn't see McNair … There he was. He'd talked his coach into letting him play keeper. He was trotting toward the goal, chattering with some girls next to the goalpost. As Roland Santander walked by to kick off, Andrew said quietly, "Left side." Roland looked up but didn't acknowledge him. The referee asked both goalies if they were ready. McNair waved over his head, still talking to the ladies in an animated fashion while pulling on his goalie shirt.

On the kickoff, Penny passed to Santander, who went around the first defender, and bumped a five-yard pass to Paxton to his left. Andrew was open; he took one step and shot. He caught the ball flush, and it leapt off his foot like a round rocket. It rose no more than fifteen feet off the ground, with topspin, heading left of the goal. It looked as if it would sail high and wide. An instant later, a Kirkwood player screamed "Keeper!" at

McNair, who turned without looking and trotted back out. Wrong move. Pappy had struck the ball with the outside of his right foot, and it was now slicing back to the right, toward the goal, at around fifty miles per hour. The wind made it knuckle and dip, and it sailed under the crossbar. The referee immediately signaled the goal, turned toward the center line, and pointed. Now it was three to one, Kirkwood.

McNair laughed it off, bent over, and hiked the ball between his legs and back toward the center line. The Black Knights kicked off. McNair's attitude wasn't shared by his teammates. The right halfback controlled the ball and passed it into the corner, where the wing made a perfect cross head-high to the left wing about ten yards out on the far goalpost, and he put it in the upper left-hand corner. Just that fast it was four to one.

The Titans kicked off, and the ball went back and forth for a few minutes. Then the Knights' center forward broke past the fullbacks with the ball and was just outside the penalty box when Andrew Paxton took him down. The ensuing free kick sailed high.

That was too close for comfort. Pappy started calling out plays to his teammates. The defense tightened. He pushed the ball up the field, working pass plays with Santander and Penny. At the twenty-minute mark, Paxton intentionally chipped the ball into the arm of one of the fullbacks inside the penalty area for a handball. McNair wouldn't let the Kirkwood coach insert the starting goalie. Santander set the ball on the penalty line, went back three steps, came forward, and swung his hips and leg to the left. McNair took the feint and dove to his right as the ball sailed inside the right goalpost. Four to two, Kirkwood.

Just then, there was a commotion off the field. A bus pulled up to the curb, and sixty-two Bainbridge football players stormed off, banging their helmets and lining the far side, where the Kirkwood fans were sitting. Suddenly, the troublemakers were outnumbered and dwarfed by the bodies around them. The football Titans began crowding and bumping the worst offenders, with several players "accidentally" stepping on the hands of those sitting on the ground.

Andrew ran to Brian Barrett, standing on the sidelines. "How do you feel?" he asked hurriedly.

"Great, man, I want to play." Pappy looked at Dr. Millwood, who came over to examine his patient again.

"Take a deep breath," he said, pressing on the rib bandage. Barrett did, but he winced slightly. By then, Coach Hancock was there.

"That's not too bad. His ribs aren't broken. He'll either be able to breathe or he won't."

Both Chiefs looked at the coach plaintively.

"Coach, put him in," said Pappy. "Nakano and I will protect him."

"Okay, go on. Barrett, you so much as flinch out there …" But Brian was already running full speed onto the field, waving back over his head.

Momentum was now with the Titans. Paxton and Barrett were on fire. The Black Knights were getting bumped on every play. They cut off passing lanes and cleared the ball back into the Kirkwood end. McNair was embarrassed and furious. He charged every ball that came his way, sometimes to the edge of the penalty area and beyond.

Thirty minutes in, Millwood took the ball deep into the corner and lofted a perfect cross twelve yards out front. As Paxton charged forward, he saw McNair racing toward him. Pappy leapt into the air to head the ball, shouting, "Mine!" At the last moment, he stopped dead and ducked. The ball was way over his head, but McNair was so intent on smashing it away and getting a piece of Paxton that he swung and missed, his momentum sending him colliding with the crouched Andrew Paxton, and he somersaulted onto his back. It was the perfect ball for Santander, who headed it into the open net. Four to three.

The Kirkwood coach sent in the first-string goalie. McNair, red with rage, donned his regular jersey and raced back out. He jumped into the middle of the kickoff, taking the ball away from his own teammate. There was no way he was going to pass to anyone, and when he went around Pappy, Nakano barreled through and stole the ball, passing it to Caldwell on the right wing. Andrew Paxton knew what was coming and lagged back. McNair was sneaking up behind Nakano, and just before he got there, Paxton screamed, "Hey, hey, hey!" The referee turned involuntarily, just as McNair punched David on the side of the face. Andrew stepped in front of his teammate before he could retaliate. Hughes blew his whistle rapidly six or seven times, running toward the players. He pulled out his book. McNair cursed and stalked toward the sidelines, but as the referee turned toward the scorekeeper, McNair ran back at Nakano. Bad idea. David was still watching, and he was ready. He blocked the first three wild punches before he threw a left-right-left combination that immediately puffed out both of McNair's eyes and knocked him to the ground. None of his teammates came to his rescue. Hancock was on the field, restraining Barrett and the others from joining the fray. The Bain football team quickly put an end to any thought of fans getting involved. And now Kirkwood was playing a man short.

Pappy gathered the team quickly at the center of the field.

"Listen, losing that jerk is only going to make them play harder. They're still up. There are only about ten minutes left ... or less. We still have to win every ball and shoot. They won't start anything without McNair, and the football team has taken care of the crowd. Barrett, blast the crap out of the ball and we'll run our guts out after it ..."

Direct kick Titans, thirty yards out, near the far sideline. Too far for a shot. The Kirkwood defenders looked as if they were going to pull forward and catch Bain offsides, so Pappy lofted a long pass to Caldwell, who took it to the corner and hooked a cross back to the middle. Kirkwood's middle fullback cleared to the midline, but Barrett intercepted and lofted the ball to the right side of the penalty area. Santander hit a perfect header to Paxton on the left. Two Knights charged him, leaving Penny wide-open eight yards behind. Andrew dropped the ball at his feet and bumped it to Penny. He shot wide, but Santander immediately deflected into the right side. Tie game. Four to four.

The Titans let out a scream and raced back to the midline.

"Pressure, pressure, pressure," said Paxton as they stormed the kickoff. It was all the Knights could do to clear the ball. With only five minutes left, Roland Santander dribbled past one fullback inside the penalty area and then suddenly pivoted and flicked the ball with the outside of his right foot. The goalie never moved, and the ball hugged the inside of the right goalpost. Five to four, Titans.

Barrett stole the ensuing kickoff and took a wild forty-yard shot. On the goal kick, Paxton intercepted the ball near the sidelines. Two Kirkwood players charged forward. He could have passed to Millwood, but he cut left and down the sidelines. Suddenly, he drilled the ball straight left and dead center into the groin of an obnoxious Kirkwood fan, who folded like a lawn chair. Paxton turned and ran back on defense as the Titans' football team and fans laughed and cheered.

The whistle blew, announcing the greatest comeback in the short history of the Bainbridge Titans' soccer team. They tried to hoist Hancock up on their shoulders, but he would have none of it. Everyone congratulated Barrett and Paxton, but Pappy said that without Randy Williams in goal, Al Landon and the other starters hanging together in the first half against the Black Knights, and the referee, it would have been nine to zero. They all thanked Roland Santander, who'd created most of the goals.

As they gathered their equipment, it began to sink in. They had done it. They were in the conference playoffs.

They headed across the field and mingled with the football players, who were boarding the buses for the short ride to the stadium. Pappy looked over at Littlefield, who was with Paula, Barrett, and some of the other girlfriends. She smiled and waved, and then she came running over.

"Unbelievable!" she exclaimed, throwing her arms around him and hugging him tightly. "You were amazing. All of you." Pappy's heart was pounding worse than in the game.

"Everyone was great. Thanks for being here," he said. Suddenly, she kissed him full on the lips.

His teammates and the football players began shouting.

"Whoa!"

"Hey!"

"Whoo!"

"All right, Pappy!"

He pulled away … but not very far. Now he was flushed almost purple. "I-I need to go …," he managed to spit out.

"We're staying for the game," she said, releasing him from the hug but holding his hand. "Pound those guys," she said, still smiling. Andrew turned and ran toward the bus, terrified that he would do or say something horrific that would be remembered forever.

Louis Paxton could barely contain himself. More than once during the game, he had to be gently restrained by Otto Millwood from running onto the field and choking the crap out of the referee. Now they had won, and he was going to see his son play football.

On the bus, the football players cheered, and Pappy thanked each one individually for coming to the game. The stadium was just down the road, but they took the bus anyway. Bolger didn't want his players, now on an adrenaline high, precipitating an incident. He was always amazed at how much trouble college students could get into in just a half a mile.

An exhausted Pappy sat back, his lungs burning. All he could think of was Littlefield. What had he done? What had she done? Wasn't it great? Just like the movies. Winning the big game and getting a kiss from a beautiful girl. Her blonde hair was soft and silky, and her lips were a perfect fit ...

"Hey, Pappy, isn't that Barrett's old girl?" asked someone.

"Yeah, you dog. Looks like she's ready to trade up," said another.

"Let's go, guys," said Coach Jugovic. "We're in the locker room on the left. Straight in, gear on, and sit down. Anyone needing to be taped, get it done early ... Congratulations, Paxton. Great job today."

"Thanks, Coach," said Andrew.

The locker room was a ruckus of activity. Watching the dramatic comeback of the soccer team, Nakano decking McNair, and the behavior of the Kirkwood fans had the squad out for blood. The Knights were an average team and hadn't beaten the Titans in a decade. Despite the abysmal record, or maybe because of it, the fans would be as rude and offensive as those at the soccer game. But not as bold. They would spit, curse, and throw stuff as the Titans came out of the tunnel, but they weren't crazy enough to stand where the players could retaliate. However, it would be a miserable time for the Bain fans. A handful of Kirkwood fans milled around behind the visitors bleachers, hurling obscenities, as well as eggs, mud, and any kind of trash available.

The Titans went through their pregame drills. Pappy took half a dozen kicks from the extra point line and then another ten from various places on the field. Finally, he went to midfield for kickoffs and pounded one ball after another into the end zone.

About a half hour before game time, the team went back into the locker room. The Kirkwood fans were already in fine form, throwing cups of water and soda—until the campus police made their halfhearted attempt at crowd control.

Coach Sam Bolger had had about as bad a week as one could have. And he had had enough of the Black Knights' coaches, fans, and referees. His remarks were brief.

"We came here to do a job. No stupid penalties. No turnovers. Execute on offense. Execute on defense. I expect them to try trick plays, end arounds, halfback passes, fake punts, and kicks. Play your positions. Stay in your lanes." He paused and looked around. "And I want their fans to go home by halftime." The team erupted into hoots, cheers, and hollers. They crowded to the door.

"Wait!" called Joe Tagliarino. "Where is Paxton? Pappy, get up here."

Andrew came to the door. Tagliarino pushed him in front of the mob.

"Let's go!" he shouted, and they stormed onto the field and across to the far sidelines. The Titans lost the coin toss and would kick off. Paxton was warming up when he noticed a commotion in the stands. The Titan fans were standing and screaming at a group behind them. Hancock and some of the parents were holding the soccer players back, and he saw Littlefield bent forward, holding her head. Her blonde hair was streaked with something that looked green.

Paxton's temper flared. He started to go under the bleachers, but someone grabbed his arm.

"Let's get even on the field," said Coach Jugovic. Paxton said nothing but took the tee and ran out with the team.

"Wait. Where are you going?" called Jugovic. Andrew just waved back over his head. In the locker room, he'd asked Bolger if he could take kickoffs as well. He was now by far the longest and most accurate foot they had. Bolger relented, but not before Paxton promised he'd avoid all contact, which the coach assumed Pappy had no intention of keeping.

The Titans lined up as Andrew placed the ball. He looked over the opposition. Number twenty-five was their better return man, but Paxton didn't care. He was going to kick the ball high and relatively short. The hang time would allow his teammates to build a full head of steam before the receiver caught the ball.

He paced back seven yards and then four paces to the left. The referee blew his whistle. Andrew dropped his arm and ran forward, catching the ball in a high, hooking arc that Kirkwood's return man fielded on the eleven. The ten Titan defenders slammed into the blockers. But Pappy didn't run off the field. The ball carrier cut to his right toward the sidelines and the Titan bench. Jugovic went to yell at Paxton, but Bolger took his arm. "Watch," he said.

The Titans had overpursued, and the runner broke through about the thirty-five yard line. He had a blocker out front when Andrew Paxton arrived at full speed. The lead man wasn't concerned. It was only the kicker. Pappy ducked his shoulder and caught the blocker in the sternum under the middle of his pads, lifting him off the ground and slamming him backward into the runner, knocking both on their backsides out of bounds. The Titans' fans gasped at the whump made by the collision and then exploded into cheers.

That collision set the tone for the entire first half. The Knights had to punt all five possessions and got no closer than the Titans' forty-three yard line. Bain scored the first four times they had the ball, and Pappy added a field goal to make it thirty-one to zero at the end of the half.

At one point in the first quarter, Barrett came down to where Pappy was standing. He told him that the Kirkwood fans had used surgical tubing connected to a plastic pail to fire several water balloons into the crowd. Most missed, but one containing green food coloring had caught Littlefield a glancing blow. A group of Bain fans, led by Louie Paxton, berated the campus cops until they called the local police. Pappy's father then flashed his fire police badge, and the local cops joined the Kirkwood security in protecting the stands.

Just before the second-half kickoff, Coach Hancock beckoned to Andrew. He looked solemn.

"Unbelievable," he said. "Clarkson won two to zero. They're in—and we're out."

"What …? How?" asked Pappy in disbelief.

"The pro team called up the two players from Stratton State, and a couple of the others were ineligible, so they fell apart. We're done." He smiled at Paxton. "We'll be back. And you'll be back."

Bolger left his first team in until the beginning of the fourth quarter, and it was then forty-five to nothing. All the starters, including Paxton, had their pads off by the final whistle at fifty-two to zero.

The team showered quickly. Pappy decided to ride back with the football team so the soccer squad could leave early. He said good-bye to his dad, who had to return to Buffalo for inventory at the parts department on Sunday.

The bus was relatively quiet. Despite the blowout, it had still been a grueling four quarters. The second team was grateful for the extra playing time, and everyone was looking forward to the playoffs.

Pappy suddenly felt woozy, and then he realized it was almost five o'clock; he hadn't eaten in eight hours. His legs began cramping, so he found a couple of water bottles and emptied them in seconds.

The bus stopped at a steak house on the way back. Pappy ate by himself while the others gathered to listen to Coach Jugovic's recap of the game. Sam Bolger came over and sat down.

"Andrew, you've done a tremendous job for us in just a few weeks. We appreciate your coming on board on such short notice." He lowered his head and his voice. "And again, I am ashamed of the actions of my coaches and players … and of Dr. Hardwell." He paused. "You're a fine young man. Your efforts on both teams today were outstanding. That was one of the greatest, most exciting comebacks I've ever seen … and I never knew or cared much about soccer until now." He leaned in. "And that hit you put on that Kirkwood blocker will be talked about for years."

"Thanks, Coach." Andrew took a deep breath. "I thought all football players were like Rattigan until I met the rest of this team. Even though they're only Division III, they play as if they were the Boilermakers."

Pappy sat back in his chair. "The guys said Holmes is coming back."

Bolger was surprised and embarrassed. "Yes, he is. The doctor has cleared him to play."

"I've been thinking about it …," started Andrew.

"You're welcome to stay. We want you to stay," interrupted Bolger emphatically.

He shook his head. "No. Holmes is the best. He's one of the great Division III kickers of all time. He's a senior, and this is his team. He deserves to play … and I've had my fun."

Bolger heard the resolve in Paxton's voice.

"You've had your share of *experiences* this fall, that's for sure," said Bolger. "But somehow you need to get past them. This is a good school. Hancock is a fine coach. The players on both teams think the world of you. You're a leader."

"Coach, I think I need to get away from this for a while," said Andrew. "I'll be back. I'm the only one of my family to go to college. My parents saved all their lives for me to come here. I just need to clear my head."

Bolger sighed and stood up. "Words can't undo what has happened. I wish they could. You know how we feel. The guys on this team will miss you, and the coaches will miss you."

"Thanks, Coach."

Bolger turned away. "Okay, let's get back to campus. I'm sure you guys want to put in a big night studying for finals."

Everyone laughed and booed.

They piled on the bus. The temperature had dropped twenty degrees or more, and there was a stiff north wind, so they shivered and yelled at the bus driver to kick up the heat. The forecast was for a dusting of snow.

On the ride back, Andrew handed his football equipment to the manager. Several players saw him, but none said anything.

They arrived at the field house around seven. Andrew left without saying much and went back to the dorm. Barrett was already gone, but he'd left a note saying that they would be at Fitzgerald's celebrating with the team—and that he was to get his butt down there immediately. He sat on the edge of the bed, staring at the note. The outdoor chill had invaded their room, and the bare tile floors felt cold and impersonal. He pulled out his suitcase …

Andrew made the fifteen-minute walk to Fitzgerald's in ten, the wind pushing at his back and frosting his ears. He could hear the jukebox blaring Credence Clearwater's "Born on the Bayou" three blocks away. The place was packed, people were dancing, and cigarette smoke hung heavy in the air. There were a small collection of old townies at the bar, gawking at the college kids (particularly the girls). The booths around the dance floor were ringed by the soccer players, their girlfriends, and their dates. Barrett and Paula waved at him, and he pulled up a chair next to Penny and Millwood. The girls from Paula's floor were there, including Littlefield and Patty.

Barrett lifted an empty glass and a pitcher. "Season's over, goddamn it! Beer?" he asked.

"Beer!" said Pappy, taking the glass and chugging the entire contents. Everyone cheered. He immediately had another. It tasted good, even though it was 3.2.

"Let's dance," said Barrett, getting up and taking Paula's hand. "C'mon, you old goat," he said to Pappy, dragging him up. Soon they were all dancing in a group, Paula slowly, with as much strength as she could muster.

The place was rocking. Pappy tore off his sweater and heaved it into the booth.

When the song was over, he stood in front of Littlefield and took her hand. "Want a beer?" he asked. "Sure," she said, but the music started again.

It was the Rolling Stones' "Play with Fire." The soccer players began singing along with the lyrics, screaming out, *"But don't play with me, 'cause you're playing with fire."* Paxton and Littlefield embraced in an awkward hug, moving back and forth to the music. Beth was almost as tall as Pappy, and she put her head on his shoulder. Her body was hot but smelled like beautiful perfume.

Barrett and Paula were dancing, her feet on his. Halfway through the song, Pappy looked at Beth and they kissed. There were beads of sweat on her upper lip, and she tasted of mint and salt. She hugged him tightly and ran her fingers through the back of his hair. A flood of adrenaline shot down his spine, and his heart pounded against hers. The music was over, but neither noticed.

The song changed to Credence Clearwater's "Rollin' on the River." They stopped kissing and pressed their foreheads together, smiling. Andrew held her close, and she kept her arms around his neck.

"I can't believe I've known you all my life," she said. "But I never really knew you until now … I mean, I never really thought of you … I mean, I…" He kissed her again.

"Oh, wow, too much beer," he said.

"Me too," said Beth, blushing. "Be right back." She went to the ladies' room, which was small and always crowded. As usual, one stall was occupied by a girl tossing her cookies while her two friends took turns flushing and keeping the victim's hair out of the water.

Beth Littlefield's head was spinning. She'd only half believed when the girls had told her about Pappy's long-standing love. A month ago, all was lost. Now her scalp tingled just at the thought of Andrew's embrace. He was strong, smart, kind, liked by everyone. She looked in the mirror and checked her hair and makeup, but she couldn't focus. Her mind kept flashing back to their kiss. It was almost hard to breathe.

Finally, what remained of the girl driving the porcelain bus was removed. Someone had the courtesy to spray a strong burst of perfume to cover the smell of regurgitated beer.

Littlefield went back out onto the dance floor, which was now wall-to-wall people; more football players had arrived.

Beth squeezed through the mass to the booth where the Chiefs were sitting. Barrett looked up and smiled broadly, as did all the others.

"Well, it's about goddamn time," exclaimed Millwood in mock exhaustion, raising a beer. "Now Pappy can stop chewing a hole in his mattress every night. I can't believe that the entire world has known for years, and you girls, who're supposed to have great intuition, didn't have a clue. The guy has taken more cold showers than a damn Eskimo!" Littlefield blushed.

Tim looked around. "Well, where the hell is he? You caught him ... Don't tell me he got away. Oh, crap! He probably drank those beers too fast and is puking his guts out. You may be the one taking the cold shower tonight," he said to Littlefield. "Let's go get him." He pushed Penny and McIlroy out of the booth. "Anybody got a big trash bag?" They went to the men's room.

Littlefield stood there awkwardly. "Well, have a seat," said Barrett. "Don't worry. Pappy is a very calm and nerdy drunk. It's our turn to take care of him. He's done it enough for us."

The Chiefs returned from the lavatory and began looking around. They split up, circled the dance floor, and then ended up back with the others.

"He ain't in here," said Penny. "I bet he dragged his ass outside to barf. Man, the sidewalk is going to be a mess. Maybe he had the decency to go around the corner out of sight ... Chiefs to the rescue," he said, and they all put on their coats.

"I'll come with you," said Littlefield.

Paula whispered something to Barrett. "Yeah, I think we better call it a night," he said. "I'll drop Paula at the dorm. Ol' Pappy might be needin' a dunk in the shower."

They filed out the door and looked both ways up and down the street. No one. It was freezing, and there were a few flakes of snow in the air.

"You guys go left around the corner," said Barrett. "We'll go this way. Holler if you see him or need help." After a few moments, they met back at the door.

"Well, one of two things," said McIlroy with an air of authority. "Either he pissed his pants or barfed on his clothes, or both, and beat it back to the dorm." He looked at Beth. "Sorry, Littlefield—you hooked up with a cheap drunk. The good news is that this will give us enough to rag on him about for months."

Beth smiled, trying not to appear worried or disappointed.

Millwood looked at her with glazed eyes. "Well, there's always me," he said, opening his arms and taking one step toward her. He then turned 180 degrees and vomited down the side of the building.

"Great," said Penny. "Now there are two of them. Enough already."

"You guys go find Pappy," said McIlroy, waving them off. "Don and I will drag this Casanova back to his room."

Barrett, Paula, and Beth walked back to campus. After a few minutes, Brian picked up an obviously exhausted Paula and carried her. By the time they reached the dorm, she was asleep. He couldn't take her to her room, so he lay her down on the sofa in the lobby.

"You go find Pappy," said Beth. "I'll take care of her. Call me when you do. And be gentle," she joked. Then she looked up at him and touched the side of his face. "You are a prince," she said, kissing him lightly on the cheek. "And you have found your princess."

"You take good care of your prince," said Barrett, turning to go out the door. "He's the best, and he deserves the best ... And so do you."

Barrett went up the hill to Roberts Hall. The floor was unusually quiet for a Saturday night, but most were probably celebrating the football victory down at the student union. He opened the door to their room.

"Hey ...," he said, and then he stopped. There was no one there, and Pappy's closet door was open, as were a couple of his drawers. His suitcase, comb, and shaving kit were gone.

There was a piece of white notebook paper sitting on the side of his desk. *This can't be good,* Brian thought, reading the note:

Brian—

Too much has happened in the past few weeks. I need to get away.

You and Paula are great. She's a dream come true, and you are doomed. I always thought Littlefield was your true love. I want you to know I never even looked at her until you started dating Paula.

Beth is the best. Maybe too good for me. My dreams finally came true too. But now that she knows how I feel, I am more afraid of her than ever. So I'm going to take the easy way out. I'm going to see what this California thing is all about. My bus leaves at midnight.

Westward ho. Next stop Disneyland. Or Hollywood. I'll be back by Christmas.

I'll call my parents tomorrow. My mom won't understand, but Dad will cover for me. He always gets stuck cleaning up my messes.

Tell Littlefield I went nuts, and she should find someone who is more than two steps out of the mental ward. If she does, I'll kill myself.

Hail to the Chiefs. We had one hell of a run. Can't wait till next year.

Pappy

Barrett shook his head. The room was silent and empty. He took a deep breath and then exhaled. What more could happen in one semester? He locked the door behind him and headed down the corridor. Littlefield was standing outside, peering through the glass. A blast of cold air hit him as he opened the door. Neither said a word, but she saw by his expression that something was wrong. He handed her the note.

She read it and then pursed her lips.

As he passed, he touched her shoulder. "Don't worry," he said softly, "He'll be back. He's just a *little* nuts. And he didn't wait for you all this time just to walk away."

Brian pulled the collar of his coat up around his neck and walked on down the hill. Beth put the note in her pocket and sat down on the steps.

Andrew Paxton strode quickly down Weatherly Avenue. He avoided Limestone Street so he wouldn't see anyone returning from Fitzgerald's. The sidewalks were deserted, and the lights glowed a lonely white in the swirling snow. Man, he hoped it would be warmer in California. It was now in the twenties, and the wind was relentless. The bus station was empty, save for a driver standing inside the door drinking coffee … and a woman in her fifties behind the ticket counter.

"Well, you're a brave one out on a cold Saturday night," she said with a slight smile.

"I called about the ticket to California," said Pappy, pulling out his checkbook.

"Yes. The bus leaves in about thirty minutes. That will be forty-six fifty, including tax."

She handed him two slips of paper, one pink and one yellow. "You'll change buses in St. Louis. This is your transfer. Have a safe trip."

The driver led him out and then banged on the bus door, forcing it open. Pappy climbed the three steps and went to the back. It was empty. The engine was running, and diesel exhaust was everywhere. But the heat was welcome. Andrew felt sick. He always second-guessed himself about every decision, and this was a big one. He would have to call his faculty advisor and make some sort of provision for finishing his courses. Maybe he should come back for finals. Now he was *really* feeling sick.

Then there was Littlefield. What would she think of him now? He'd led her on and then run away. He didn't want to hurt her of all people. He put his head forward against the seat back.

There were voices and a bang on the door. More passengers. *Please no screaming children or drunks,* pleaded Pappy in his mind. A head appeared and looked around. Barrett. He climbed the steps and came down the aisle, followed by Millwood, Penny, and McIlroy, all carrying duffel bags. They plopped down in the seats around him.

"Hey, look who's here," said Barrett.

"Yeah, a damn football player," added Millwood, who slurred his speech and looked pale.

Pappy was stunned.

"Don't look so surprised," said Barrett. "We're all drunk. Somebody said we should take a bus ride, and we wound up here ... Sit back and relax. California's great."

They were all quiet for a few minutes. Millwood put his head down. Penny was fidgeting.

Now Pappy added feelings of selfishness to his already loaded guilt bag. "Sorry ...," he began.

"Stop!" interrupted Barrett. "I am pissed," he said quietly. "I wouldn't be on this team if it wasn't for you. You've been a brother and a father to me. You've put me, and the rest of us, to bed smashed more times than I can count, and you've kept me from driving drunk. I probably wouldn't be alive except for you.

"You always think of everyone else first. The first to forgive us and the last to forgive yourself. Well, now it's time to—"

Just then, the door opened yet again. There was beautiful blonde hair and then crystal-blue eyes. They belonged to Littlefield.

"Oh, Jesus, thank God," blurted Penny. He jumped up and moving swiftly toward the exit. "Time to go. The cavalry is here." He smiled as he passed Littlefield, who had an anxious and uncertain look on her face.

Andrew looked over at Barrett and the others, but they appeared as surprised as he was. All sat there, their discomfort growing, not really knowing what to do, as she drew closer. Pappy felt as if he were six years old in the doctor's office, about to get a polio shot.

Penny stopped at the door and motioned emphatically for the rest to follow. They all got up and filed out. As they passed, McIlroy took her hand and kissed it. She tried to pull away from Millwood's beer breath, but he grabbed her and planted one on her chin, missing her lips. McIlroy seized Millwood's head and kissed him soundly on the cheek. He wiped it off in disgust, and McIlroy rubbed his lips vigorously on his sleeve. Lastly, Barrett just smiled. Then they were gone.

"Disneyland?" she asked.

The bus driver labored up the steps and collapsed decisively in his seat. He turned up the windshield wipers, checked his mirrors, found first gear, and pulled away.

Big, beautiful white snowflakes were cascading down as Andrew and Beth stood on the platform, watching the bus disappear into the night. He picked up his suitcase and then hers. Damn, it was heavy. She really was packed to go somewhere. As they started back down Weatherly toward campus, she hopped on him piggyback, hugging his neck and kissing his cheek. Suddenly, it wasn't cold anymore.